A Collision with Love

A Gripping Second-Chance Romance

Tricia T. LaRochelle

FLAMING HEART
PRESS

NO AI TRAINING: Without in any way limiting the author's [and publisher's] exclusive rights under copyright, any use of this publication to "train" generative artificial intelligence (AI) technologies to generate text is expressly prohibited. The author reserves all rights to license uses of this work for generative AI training and development of machine learning language models.

No part of this book may be reproduced in any form or by any electronic or mechanical means, including information storage and retrieval systems, without written permission from the author, except for the use of brief quotations in a book review.

This book is a work of fiction. Names, characters, and incidents are either products of the author's imagination or are used fictitiously.

Manufactured in the United States of America

Copyright © 2024 by Tricia T. LaRochelle

ISBN 979-8-9909107-2-0 (paperback)

ISBN 979-8-9909107-1-3 (ebook)

All rights reserved

Published by Flaming Heart Press, United States of America

Distributed by Ingram Book Group

Cover design by Damonza

❦ Created with Vellum

In A Collision with Love, Cassie adores her big sister, Trina. In light of this powerful connection, I dedicate this book to my big sister Mary, who brings such joy to my life (and makes me laugh like no one else), and to all the sisters and brothers out there, who make each other feel valued and understood.

A Collision with Love

Chapter One

"What time do you get off work tonight?" Daniel stood at the kitchen counter fixing his coffee. *A sprinkle of stevia, a dollop of oat milk.* "Big night at the Garden Patch."

My ears picked up the slight lift in his tone while I continued to study my notes. In my periphery, my husband paused to knot up his long, lustrous, dark-brown hair—with just the right amount of wave—into a sloppy bun. It was a style he often relied on to keep it out of his way. Daniel had hair that made both men and women jealous, me included. The scruff that often coated his defined jawline, which lately had grown into a very short beard, was one of those soft beards, and I loved to run my fingers through it.

It was a dark morning in Virginia, an August rain drenching the windows, the sound like tiny pieces of rice pattering the glass. A thick layer of clouds hung low and heavy in the sky, blocking out any chance of sunshine and requiring the use of internal lights to see properly.

Virginia leaned toward drought conditions during the

summer months, so the rain felt cozy to me, a way to replenish the earth and provide a much-needed drink for the grass, which was now so dry it crinkled when you walked across it. It was a good day to snuggle in bed with your hubby doing all sorts of intimate things. But unfortunately, it was also a Tuesday, and my husband and I had obligations. Places to go. People to see. More importantly, *bills to pay*.

If I hadn't been so focused on my work, I would have at least taken a moment to enjoy the sight of this gorgeous man standing in my kitchen who, after eight years, still made my heart flutter. He was dressed in his typical not-so-white T-shirt, one of many he'd splattered with food graffiti from his years spent cooking and concocting in this kitchen or that. Didn't matter, the fabric never had any trouble molding perfectly to his muscular chest. Just like his boxers were equally happy to define his enjoyably rounded butt, so luscious I wanted to squeeze it daily. My husband was a chef, and everything about him was yummy. Head to toe, this man came into the world blessed with good looks.

"I'm assuming you have to work late . . . again?" His expressive eyes, two entrancing pools of chestnut with a splash of honey, found me sitting at the kitchen table going over my briefs.

A junior partner in my law firm, I was hoping to sign this big client I'd been courting for months. Into the Open - Equipment Inc. was a lucrative outdoor recreational franchise that also sold apparel. If I could make this deal happen, it would raise my status within the firm. My goal, senior partner. I'd been with Wilson & Bates for seven-and-a-half years now (three years at another firm), so it was time, according to *my* watch. I wasn't sure what the main partners, Isabella and Gregory, thought about that. I hadn't mustered the nerve to ask. But if I signed a multimillion-dollar client, that would change things.

Considering the last major client I had signed granted me an actual office, I was optimistic.

Daniel cleared his throat. "Uh, Cassie?"

"Huh? Yes, I'm sorry." I pulled my focus away from my notes, meeting my husband's lovely eyes from across the diminutive room. "I'll try to get out on time. Did you just say you have something big going on at the restaurant?" God, I hoped he hadn't told me already. Lately, I'd been a bit distracted by this new client.

It was disgraceful really how much time I devoted to my job. Eight-hour days didn't begin to manage my workload. No, I put in nights and weekends too. And even a few holidays that I could get away with.

At first, Daniel was understanding about it all. *I knew I married a brilliant woman*, he'd often say. *They're lucky to have you, my love. But not as lucky as I am.* He'd follow that compliment with a tender kiss.

But as time wore on and my schedule grew more demanding, I could see him struggle with the loneliness of not having his wife around.

Unfortunately, I had my own issues. With my thirty-sixth birthday arriving in less than six months, a couple of my internal clocks were ringing in my head like Big Ben. My career and where I stood on the corporate ladder was *my* main focus. Starting a family was Daniel's.

We'd discussed parenthood before we were married, and, at the time, I was good with having a couple of kids. But then I got this job with one of the most prestigious law firms in Virginia, and I wasn't quite ready to give that up. I mean, why should I have to? If only men could carry the babies and alter their bodies for the better part of a year. *A year?* My big sister had three kids—ages ranging from six through thirteen—and neither her figure nor her professional life had bounced back yet. And she'd started having children early, in her mid-twenties.

But she was good with that.

I wasn't. Then again, most careers allowed for parenthood. And I hoped mine would as well. *Someday.* I had to get where I wanted to be first. Being a lawyer required a demanding schedule, especially when trying to achieve something as grand as senior partner.

Still, I loved McKenna, Bailey, and Noah, but I also loved that I could send them home whenever I wanted. Now that Bailey was ten and Noah thirteen, they were easier. McKenna was six, which meant hide-and-seek and playing pretend were still some of her favorite pastimes—that and asking a ton of questions until you cried uncle (or aunt in my case). She was a lot like me when I was six.

"Hmm. You forgot, then?" Daniel stared me down, his eyes challenging my brain to remember something it was ill-equipped to do at the moment.

Think.

"You have . . ." I taxed my memory banks until something sparked. "Oh, yeah. The food critic, right?" I said the words as if I were a contestant on a game show, which judging by his furrowed brow and tight jaw, Daniel didn't appreciate.

It wasn't as if he had a lot of time on his hands either. My husband owned a small eatery, which was mainly a sandwich shop at the moment. (He also served a growing number of soups and salads.) Eventually, he planned to offer full-course dinners *and* drinks when he could afford the menu upgrade and a respectable wine and liquor selection.

Daniel's Garden Patch was a name he had come up with when he was in his twenties. Interestingly enough, he was gardening at the time. His menu catered to a very specific crowd of patrons who struggled with food allergies (he served regular food as well, everything locally sourced and organic). Why did he choose something so specific? Daniel told me his mother had battled intestinal problems for as long as he could remember. In fact, Jayne nearly died when her intestines flared up so badly, she'd doubled over in pain and fell to the floor in their home. According to Daniel, it was one of the scariest moments of his life. A trip to the hospital via ambulance revealed she'd nearly burned a hole in her intestinal lining, the result catastrophic if things had gotten any worse, which, thank God, they hadn't. It happened twenty years ago when Daniel was about to graduate high school and when knowledge of gluten intolerance wasn't as common *or* widely understood. After losing his father from a heart attack ten years ago—when the man was in his mid-forties—Daniel grew very protective of his mother and her health. He also exercised and ate well, hoping to stave off any health problems for himself.

My husband shook his head, a slow hiss escaping from his lips. "I guess I should be thankful you actually remembered." He wrapped his palm around his coffee mug and strolled over to the bistro table, where I remained seated.

I rose and approached, taking his one free hand in mine. The scent of sugar and cinnamon wafted off his olive skin and his clothing from the sticky buns he'd made at the crack of dawn this morning when I was still asleep. His customers loved those sticky buns, whether they suffered from food allergies or not. (According to Daniel, it all came down to which gluten-free flour he used for which recipe and, believe me, he had *many* variations.)

"Don't be that way, hon. I can't help my schedule. We've *both* been busy."

Where I was a night owl, often working well past midnight, Daniel was an early riser. We were different, no doubt. But I'd always believed opposite personalities were the perfect combination for a lasting marriage. My mind processed things differently than his, which came in handy when helping him buy the restaurant at a fair price and making sure his business plan was solid. (Even *with* those things, opening a restaurant was risky.)

Daniel was social. I was more of an introvert. As a lawyer, I relied on knowing more than the people around me to get by. Give me a subject I knew; I could talk your ears off. Put me in a social situation where research did little to bolster the conversation; I grew tongue-tied. Not my husband, though, who could talk to anyone about any subject, even topics Daniel knew little about. He had a way of listening to the people around him, making them feel valued and understood. It was a rare gift and a good reason why his customers often returned. His tasty food and delectable looks didn't hurt matters.

When Daniel didn't respond, I tried again. "I'll admit. Work has been particularly crazy lately. I've got this one major client close to signing with me. I know I told you about it." *Had I?*

"When isn't work crazy for you, Cassie?" He exhaled a breath of frustration, making me want to do the same.

I flung a hand up. "Well, your schedule isn't much better." I was grasping at straws here but, at the same time, I had to come up with something.

Daniel tilted his head, his eyes not buying my argument. "You run circles around my schedule, and *I'm* a business owner. We never get to see each other anymore." He quirked his brow. "Need I remind you that you were the one who had talked me into this restaurant? I'm grateful for that, don't get me wrong. But you said we'd be doing this together, remember? Lately, I feel like I need to make an appointment just to see you."

He wasn't wrong. It seemed like a lifetime ago when we could go for romantic walks, cuddle on the couch sharing a bottle of wine, or making love anytime we wanted. I'd become a stranger in my own personal life, my husband suffering from my negligence.

The problem was, we wanted different things right now. I wanted financial security, a nice house, *and then* a family. Daniel wanted those things, too, but he wasn't concerned with their order.

However, sometimes our differences were good. What I lacked in patience or skill for anything food-related, Daniel excelled, which I appreciated when I awoke to the scent of cinnamon and fresh pastry floating through the air, my mouth watering as my eyes fluttered open. It was hard to hide such a thing in our seven-hundred-square-foot apartment that barely fit one small bedroom, a kitchen just forgiving enough to allow a bistro table and two chairs, and a laundry room that required a stacking washer and dryer and little else. The laundry basket had to wait outside the room like an unwanted guest. Oh, and we had one bathroom. The walls came in the same color: brown. As if that was all the landlord could afford at the time. At least we had a unit on the top floor, so we didn't have to endure footfalls back and forth all night long like we'd had to do at our last place. There were times when I'd sworn an elephant had moved into the apartment above us.

We needed a house. An actual house with a yard and possibly a garage. And of course, a nursery. I'd been saving for one since I'd married Daniel, but then two years ago, my priorities shifted.

Daniel was working for a caterer friend of his named Josh, who went to culinary school with him and who had convinced Daniel to work with him here in Virginia. And although Daniel continued to dazzle Josh's customers with his cooking prowess, there was no room for growth at Savory Sensations. Josh wasn't interested in a partnership. Believe me, I had asked. Regardless, if you'd brought up the topic to my husband, he'd say he was happy. The man even hummed as he worked.

I appreciated my husband's positive attitude, but it was clear to me that he still needed a change. Josh wasn't paying Daniel what he deserved (according to Josh, it was because he wasn't making enough), even though Daniel had worked his tail off creating wonders in Josh's commercial kitchen.

And so I did something about it. I convinced Daniel to open his own place. "It's always been your dream. We've got the money. And I can help you find a good location. You married a lawyer, Daniel. It's time you reaped the benefits of it. We'll do this together." I was willing to promise him the moon and the stars.

He was shocked at first. "But you were saving for our house. I can't take that money. You worked hard for it. I see how hard you've worked for it. Christ, a racehorse couldn't keep up with you."

I did work hard, but I could also see him floundering, even if he couldn't see it himself. When we'd first met, Daniel talked about owning his own restaurant all the time. The foods he'd make, the joy he'd take from serving something wholesome to his customers. But that aspiring voice had gone silent.

I loved being a lawyer. It challenged me on so many levels. I wanted that for Daniel, something he could call his own and embrace. He was brilliant in the kitchen. It was time the world got to experience his gifts.

Deep down, a small part of me worried he'd grow tired of waiting for me to work normal hours. Having his own restaurant would satisfy his time until I could join him on our next adventure. I truly believed this could happen. *Then.*

"We'll get the house, too, it just may take a little more time. I want this for you. Please let me do this, Daniel!" I'd pleaded with my eyes and my voice. And I continued to plead until he finally agreed. I was good at convincing people.

By then, he was so touched by my generosity he'd teared up over it. With shiny eyes, he'd smiled at me, touching my cheeks with the back of his fingers. "I will never forget this."

He hadn't forgotten, even when I had arrived late for the restaurant's grand opening. He'd invited the mayor, along with the local TV station. A large ribbon draped across the door just waiting to be cut, a small crowd of family and friends there to support this momentous occasion. Only Daniel *wouldn't* cut the ribbon until I was there to witness it, which happened two hours later than I had planned. My mother had filled me in on the goings-on. "I had a court case that dragged on," I explained. "I had an irate client who was being sued."

Was Daniel upset with me? No, he improvised, offering free drinks and appetizers to the crowd, telling stories about his journey toward becoming an entrepreneur, and asking members of the crowd what they liked to eat most. Food for thought, so to speak.

When I walked in the door, shamefully late, he'd raised his glass of champagne and said, "And here is the woman who made it all happen." He grabbed the ribbon off a nearby table to reapply to the entrance and gathered the crowd out front again. Together, we cut the ceremonial ribbon, celebrating the special event. He wasn't angry, he was grateful, which only made me feel worse about my constant tardiness.

My work at the firm continued to interfere with our lives. Not only had I missed his birthday this year, but I was also obnoxiously late for our anniversary dinner, one Daniel had prepared himself, candles lit, a bottle of wine uncorked and ready for sharing. He'd closed the restaurant early because I had *promised* him that I'd be home at seven.

I dragged my tired feet through the door at eleven o'clock

that night, my apologies filling the air with yet more excuses. "I'm so sorry, hon, I had meetings all day, and then I had to play catch up. I've got to be in court at nine tomorrow morning, and I had to prepare." I droned on, sick of my own drab voice.

Instead of protesting or pointing out what a selfish wife I had become, Daniel sat me down, poured me a glass of wine, and delivered my warmed dinner plate from the oven, the salmon dried out, the roasted potatoes with rosemary, shriveled.

He even rubbed my shoulders as I filled my belly. "So, tell me about your day."

We made love that night, despite my exhaustion and my early morning schedule. That was May. I could count on one hand the number of times we'd made love in the three months since.

And here I was back in that same kitchen, hoping to avoid letting my sweet husband down yet again.

"Leslie comes at eight tonight. And from what I hear, she can be a tough critic. I was hoping you could come by later for moral support. You know, after work." His voice reached out to me, his tone wavering with uncertainty. "This is important, Cass. And in case you forgot, I need this woman to promote the restaurant." He practically huffed.

This woman had a name, and it was Leslie Thompson, a famous food critic and blogger who also ran her own podcast called "Something Chewed." If Leslie liked your morsels, she'd reward you with lots of free publicity and attention, but if she didn't . . . Well, she'd caused more than one aspiring restaurant to go under before it had a chance to get off the ground.

"I want her to sample a few of my new recipes if I can manage it. Kendra's been awesome, but I'd like *you* there for a change."

This was what several years of neglect had done to my

husband, who never used to say things like "in case you forgot" and "for a change."

"I've got recipes for three soups I want your opinion on, and I'm experimenting with that roasted beet salad. The one I had put on special last week. My customers loved it." He moved closer as if hoping to persuade me while I grimaced inwardly at the name *Kendra*, who had moved to the States from South Africa when she was little.

I might have been the yin to Daniel's yang, but our pastry chef, Kendra, was a perfect match if you considered her talent for baking and her flawless looks. And since Kendra was *always* at Daniel's Garden Patch, more than one customer had mistaken her for his wife, probably because of the easy and fun-loving banter they shared. I had witnessed it firsthand. She even called my husband, her *partner in crime*. Argh.

Daniel softened his tone and leaned in. "If I can get enough money coming in, you can *finally* take some time off from work." His lips found mine for a sweet kiss, a hint of sugar lingering on his lips. Honestly, the man was irresistible.

Taking time off from work didn't quite work in my world. Not if I wanted to make senior partner. I hoped Daniel understood that the distance my job was creating between us had nothing to do with a lack of love in my heart. In fact, every time I stared deep within Daniel's chestnut eyes, I fell in love with him all over again.

With the features of an Italian model, Daniel was very unassuming about his appearance. He always had been, which only made him more attractive to me. *That* and his gentle demeanor. Daniel was the type of man I would imagine sitting along a riverbank strumming his guitar and serenading his sweetheart, a blanket providing cushion from the ground and a placemat for a vintage bottle of wine, a cluster of grapes, and a slew of local cheeses, direct from Naples, no less. (I read a lot of romance novels when I was younger, my excuse for such musings.)

What I could never quite figure out was what this Adonis had seen in me, a girl with thick thighs, unruly auburn hair, and a side order of nothing special. We met at my college roommate, Brianna's, wedding, the year before I landed my new job at Wilson & Bates. Daniel was part of Josh's catering crew. His duties included slicing perfect portions of roast beef at a carving station, along with a few hams, everything baked slowly to mouth-watering perfection.

Brianna came from money, and it showed in the designer outfits she wore and the cars she drove. Christ, our dorm room looked like it belonged inside of a mansion by the time Brianna was finished decorating it. The curtains matched her bedding. Her bedding matched the rug, everything compatible and top-of-the-line. Our fridge never sat empty. Our private bath was never low on toiletries. So, when it came time for her wedding, I wasn't the least bit surprised to learn it had cost her parents well into six figures. According to Brianna, that was, who also loved to boast.

I grew up on the other end of the financial spectrum. It took my mother fifteen years to achieve her promotion as bank manager, my father a few less to become a licensed electrician. Don't get me wrong, we weren't poor. My parents worked hard for every penny they had. So when I had told them I wanted to become a lawyer, they fell over themselves with joy, offering to help in any way they could. An eventual LSAT score of 172 set me on the right path. I was on my way.

My higher education was the result of good grades and generous scholarships, not trust funds. Financial aid did its part. I had applied for *everything* I could get, which I had learned from helping my older sister, Trina, do the same. Not that it had done *her* any good. She had dropped out of college her sophomore year to sell real estate and later became a full-time mother instead. It wasn't a bad thing. From what I could see, mothers worked harder than anyone. Her husband, Mike, a handsome financial analyst who worked mostly from home, supported Trina and all of her choices.

They'd been together since high school, and Mike had become like a big brother to me. They were three years older. He was a star player on his high school lacrosse team. Trina was an average player on hers. What she lacked in lacrosse skills back then, she'd made up for with her long, silky brown hair, high cheekbones, and striking hazel eyes. At least Mike thought so.

Why I managed to inherit my mother's thick thighs and unruly hair, and my sister got the perfect proportions was beyond me. I loved my sister, despite our many differences.

"I haven't forgotten. And I would like to be there *for a change*, believe me. It's just that I'm this close." I spaced my forefinger and thumb approximately one inch apart. "If I can just sign this new client—"

"You'll make senior partner." Daniel's deadpan tone rode up the back of my neck like a zing of static electricity. "I'm well aware of this, Cassie. But do you really think they will promote you? You have done so much for that firm already . . . given up so much of your time." His eyes filled with despair. "You'll be thirty-six soon. I'm thirty-seven. How are we gonna find time to be together or even start a family?"

The answer flew from my lips. "When I make senior partner. Then *I* get to call the shots." I was so full of shit on that one. Senior partners worked longer hours than anyone. They just drove nicer cars traveling back and forth from their mansions.

"Yeah, right. They will never let you *call the shots*." Daniel shook his head and wandered out of the room, probably to get dressed for work. His bare feet padded sadly across the cheap linoleum spread across our kitchen floor and over the shag carpeting in our living room that looked like it belonged in the year *The Breakfast Club* had premiered in theaters. (I shuddered to think what lived within those carpet fibers.)

"Look, I've worked hard to get where I am. I can't just up and leave my career. We need more money coming in if we ever hope to get out of this dump *and* afford children."

No response.

I followed him, my defiant side ready to plead my case. When I reached our bedroom Daniel was prying his chef's coat out from our overstuffed closet with the same amount of effort one would need to pull a root from the ground. (Our hangers literally overlapped each other from the squeeze.)

If our apartment was the size of a shoebox, our bedroom closet had the dimensions of a postage stamp. Figuratively speaking. Thank God for the free standing clothing rack Daniel had scored at a yard sale that kept *my* professional attire from crumpling into a wrinkled mess. It was either that or I swear I would have resorted to hanging my clothes from the shower curtain rod in our bathroom.

I complained about this, along with the lack of hot water, the HVAC that managed to blow hot air in the summer and cold air in the winter (or it could be those leaky windows), plus a long list of other grievances often.

Unlike me, Daniel always tried his best to embrace the silver lining. Probably because material things never mattered to him. They were a means to an end. People and relationships, however, ranked high on his list. His mom lived in California along with his two younger brothers, Coulter and Thomas. Daniel called each of them at least once a week, ready for updates about their lives. And he made sure to visit as often as he could afford. My husband didn't do these things out of obligation. He did them because he actually cared. My family got the same preferential treatment, which was why they all adored the man.

As I watched Daniel pull a pair of pants from the upper shelf of our closet (the only space willing to accommodate), I reminded myself how hard this man worked and the passion he had for what he was doing. It came down to one thing: healthy eating. And he wanted to provide that for everyone he could.

My career was important to me too. I loved litigating on behalf of my clients. They say the devil is in the details, and I studied those details to the nth degree. If there was a loophole or a missing detail that could help me win my client's case, I'd find it. And boy did I love winning, knowing that I had done my job well.

The memory of my parents and my sister in the courtroom as I argued my first case, their eyes filled with pride, their smiles supportive and loving, would always soften my heart. I didn't win that one, but I'd won many more since then. In a lot of ways, Daniel's career and mine weren't so very different. We both helped people. Just in different ways. He fortified. I defended.

I released a pent-up breath and lowered my guard. "I'm sorry, hon. I'll be there right after work. I promise." I rubbed a hand across my forehead. "I won't work late." *Just please don't be mad at me.*

There weren't a lot of people in my world who I cared about what they thought. My friends were sparse, my family small. (I hadn't spoken to Brianna in years.) But I did care what Daniel thought. Probably more than anyone, outside of my parents. His heart was selfless. And his feelings were genuine. I knew this as fact, not speculation.

Daniel stopped preparing his outfit and tossed the chef's jacket and pants on a small plastic folding chair in the corner.

He turned and faced me, the hint of a smile inching up the corners of his beautiful mouth. "Thank you. Look, Cass, I know your job is important to you. And I'm so grateful for all it has given us." He approached, his hands embracing my upper arms. "I get it. I do. But I'm afraid that if you . . . that if *we* aren't paying attention, time will pass, and it will be too late to start a family." He ran a hand down the side of my face, his palm warm and soothing. "I love you, Cass. And there is no one I want to start a family with more than you."

Why? You can have anyone.

He blinked, letting his chestnut eyes draw me into his beautiful aura.

My pulse couldn't help but ramp up, loving the attention we'd had little time for lately. All I wanted to do was give back to him all the things he had so willingly given to me: His love and devotion. I was the luckiest woman on the planet, yet I never quite understood my good fortune.

His lips found mine, his hands sliding up and down my back with a firm but gentle rhythm. "What time do you need to be in the office?" he whispered, his breath and his essence so inviting I wanted to capture it in a jar.

I shot my gaze to my nightstand where my clock flashed 6:45 a.m. with its annoying red neon digits. "I've got a little time." I eased my head back, my fingers gliding up the sides of his waist, my grin as wide as I could make it. "Why? What'd ya have in mind?" I kept my tone seductive, trying not to melt into his arms.

The tips of my husband's fingers breached the waistband of my pj shorts. "I have a few ideas, wife of mine."

Wife of mine. That was his nickname for me, one he'd started using the day of our wedding, and one I'd grown to appreciate ever since. Who wouldn't want to be his?

His hand ventured lower, along my hip and closer to an

area of my anatomy that was already moist and ready for fun. He backed me up to the nearest wall, the only wall not covered by a modest-sized dresser (which only fit bras, socks, and our underwear), a chair, or a window.

"I know it's been a while. I think I need to remind you how much I *love* getting my hands all over your gorgeous body."

"Oh, I remember" was all I could muster. I was practically panting, my insides longing for his attention and touch. Honestly, I was jealous of all the people in Daniel's orbit. And that included his family. The way he showered them with kindness. I wanted all of it for myself.

Down his hand ventured. When his fingers slid between my legs, my sexual appetite went into a frenzy.

"I love how wet your pussy feels." He glided his fingers back and forth, in and out, exciting my insides with the prospect of more.

I moaned, my eyes rolling back, my muscles turning to jelly. It was all I could do to stay upright.

"That's what I like to see. You're always in control. Let it all go, Cass. I've got you."

I moaned some more. "Just don't let me fall." I was barely hanging on at this point, his fingers doing all sorts of amazing things to me, inside and out.

"I won't let you fall." His lips hovered near my ear. "I can't promise that I won't make you fly, though."

From outside my T-shirt, he suckled my nipple, throwing a torch on the embers firing inside of me. I was ready to combust. His touch knew me well, wasting no time to give me exactly what I wanted. "That's right, go with it."

Tingling sensations rode a tsunami-sized wave throughout my sexual organs until the intensity reached a crescendo of carnal adrenaline so massive it threatened to swallow me whole. "P-please d-don't stop. Oh, God." I slapped my palms against the wall behind me, not sure I could take much more.

Daniel kept his one free hand braced firmly against my lower back. "Let it happen, Cass." His lips crashed over mine, his tongue hungry, his erection pushing against my hip, eager to join the party.

When the orgasm slammed into me, all I could do was cry out with abandon. My lungs nearly hyperventilated. Daniel didn't stop fingering me until my breathing had tempered. His smile reached all the way to his eyes, filled with delight. "Now *that* was fun to watch. In fact, I could watch that all day long." He kissed the end of my nose.

With legs like rubber, I struggled to come down from this high he'd created. "Wow. That was intense." I kissed my man again, pulling his lower lip out a smidge with my teeth. I knew we weren't done yet, and my heart was grateful for that.

It was difficult to let go of this rush. It was even more difficult to let go of *him*. I craved having Daniel all to myself, witnessing the side of him that he only showed to me. The passionate man with carnal urges, one who would stop at nothing to satisfy his woman and himself.

"I love the way you melt into my arms. And the way you're always wet when I touch you." His gaze traveled downward, the splash of honey in his eyes darker and more intense. "Now, let's get those clothes off. My dick can't wait much longer."

* * *

Forty minutes later, I was up, showered, and getting dressed, the atmosphere in our bedroom creating its own glorifying sunshine despite the rain tapping on the windows.

Daniel had just taken a quick shower, too, and was shouldering his arms through the sleeves of his chef's coat. "That was amazing. I'd like to get back to doing that *a lot* more often. It's been way too long. I missed you. You just say when, wife of mine, and I'll be your sex slave. Day or night. Deal?"

"Sex slave, huh? And what would you like in return, husband of mine?" I was eager to hear more, finding it difficult to concentrate on anything else.

He took a breath. "How about you stop taking those birth control pills?"

Not what I had expected to hear. *How are we back to this?*

Chapter Two

After Daniel's colossal-sized question speared right into the center of my chest, he paused to gaze over at me with timid eyes.

I stepped into my pencil skirt, trying to stay calm. The topic of parenthood wasn't exactly taboo for me, but I'd told him I wasn't ready yet, and I thought he'd understood. How many times did we need to go over this?

"Your cycle comes in a few days, right? How about you take a break from the pill for a while?" He resumed buttoning the front of his coat, his hands brushing down the wrinkles along his abdomen. He then reached for his pants.

I removed a white silk blouse off its hanger to shoulder my arms through the sleeves, trying not to glower. "Now? You want to try *now*?" I buttoned the front with frantic fingers. I hadn't realized how soon he had wanted this to happen. Well, I did, but I figured after our last conversation—at least a year ago—he was willing to wait a bit longer. Apparently not.

Too many thoughts and fears caused a commotion inside of my brain. What if I was one of those pregnant women who got really sick? My sister had a tough first trimester with all of her kids. She took naps. She slept late. I didn't have those luxuries. And if Isabella and Gregory learned I was pregnant, would that hinder my becoming senior partner? *Of course it will.* Anxiousness churned the acids in my belly, my chest building a wall of heartburn.

Daniel shrugged as he stepped into his trousers. "We don't have to call it *trying*. We just won't *not* try anymore. You know, see what happens. You've been on the pill since we met."

I grumbled to myself. This felt like an ambush. *Oh, what a great idea, Daniel. It's not as if I have anything important going on in my life. Let's just throw caution to the wind and say fuck it, right?* My inner voice allowed me to say things that my lips never dared.

I waited until I had my blouse straightened and then I fanned my hand out across the room. "Look where we live, Daniel. Where the hell are we supposed to fit a baby? In the bathtub?" I zipped the side of my skirt tight, reaching for my blazer off the rack.

"We'll get a bigger place, Cass." He continued into the bathroom next door, his stride casual as if he hadn't just thrown a humungous monkey wrench into my plans.

This was one of those differences between us that I *didn't* appreciate. I was a planner. Daniel was a dreamer. If it hadn't been for all of my research, connections, *and* financial assistance, he never would have gotten that restaurant. *Things will work out* wasn't a philosophy I embraced. Things worked out when you worked hard and planned ahead. I had an uncle who was a dreamer and at age sixty-two was still hoping for that big break. My mother said Kenny'd always been that way, waiting for something spectacular to happen but putting little effort into making it a reality. He was a painter, slash poet, slash unemployed loser who left his wife, and now had his kids paying for his tab, every one of them disgusted with the man.

As Daniel brushed his teeth, I approached, placing my hand on the door casing. "I'm not getting pregnant until we have a house. And you and I both know we aren't financially ready for that right now. We need at least a year *or two* to save enough money. Trust me on this. I didn't steer you wrong with the restaurant, and I won't steer you wrong now." I stared at him, hoping to implore his sensible side. This was the first time Daniel had actually come out and asked me to stop taking the pill. I sensed his urgency.

He rinsed his mouth and wiped it dry, the wheels turning behind his eyes.

"Look, Cass, if we wait until everything is perfect, it will never happen. You don't even know how long it will take for you to get pregnant."

I crossed my arms over my chest. "My sister got pregnant right away."

"You're not your sister." He draped the hand towel over a narrow rack by the sink. "I'm just saying. We have to start sometime."

Have to? I was already shaking my head. "Not right now. I'm not ready. I need to prepare." Heat rushed into my cheeks that were just moments ago flushed with sexual bliss.

"You're thirty-five, which is already considered high risk, and about to turn thirty-six. I did some research. We need to get this ball rolling soon. Especially if we want more than one." He stood before me, his face tensing up.

I felt mine doing the same.

"I told you; I'm not ready." I glared at him, wishing he'd understand.

His voice grew deeper. "Look, no one respects you more than I do. You're the smartest person I know. And you have always supported my dreams. You act as though I'm trying to take something away from you, but I'm not. I thought you wanted this as much as I did. We used to talk about it all the time. Why can't you be a lawyer *and* a mother?"

"How? If I had to take time off to have a baby, I'd never make senior partner. You know this."

He scrubbed one hand down his face. "Do you have to be senior partner? You've been working your ass off for them for over seven years. You could just as easily work another seven and find yourself in the same position you are now. Only by then, you'll be over forty."

My chest tightened. "I'm not ready!"

His tone grew sharp. "When *will* you be ready?"

I got all flabbergasted, huffing and puffing, my hands now flailing. "I don't know, Daniel. You're not the one who has to carry the kid."

He released a heavy sigh. "It's not a kid, Cassie, it's a baby. And, no, I don't have to carry it. If I could, we'd have a family by now."

A family by now? He was a lot more eager about this than I had realized. Stupid me for thinking otherwise. Our first year of marriage, Daniel and I had broached the idea of parenthood. The second year, we spoke about it casually. *Wouldn't it be cool if?* And as each year passed, he'd brought it up more, and I'd brought it up less. The last time was about a year ago when the restaurant was still fairly new. I had explained to him that having a new restaurant at the same time as having a new baby was probably not a good idea. He nodded, and didn't mention it again. Until this morning.

I thrust my hands to both hips, my chest filling with outrage. "A family by now?" My inner voice took over, which I rarely allowed. "So what? We'd live in the restaurant, then? Oh, that's sounds just great, Daniel. Maybe we can all live in that cramped storage room. Or how about the walk-in cooler during the summer months. Sound good to you?" I was angry at him. Why did he have to ruin our special morning?

The muscles in his jaw flexed. "Don't be ridiculous. It's not helping."

I pointed with conviction. "You're the one being ridiculous." And he was. What in the hell was he thinking? "Putting aside the fact that we have virtually no room for this child, who's going to raise him or her? You work all the time at the restaurant."

"I'll cut back at the restaurant to support you. You'd only have to take a short time off from work." He lowered his chin, staring up at me from under his brow. "And if they give you a bunch of shit about it, you could quit."

"*I* could quit?" I practically coughed the words out. "Are you crazy? My salary is the only reason your *Garden Patch* hasn't gone bankrupt. After two years, you're only *now* starting to turn a profit. It's not enough, Daniel. And I refuse to give up the only stable income we have right now." And I didn't want to.

This pipe dream of making senior partner wasn't coming out of nowhere. Last year, Isabella and Gregory announced they were looking for an additional partner. *We may go outside, or we may promote from within. This is your opportunity to show us what you can do for this firm*, Isabella had announced in our staff meeting. She'd glanced over at me, and for a moment, it felt purposeful, as if she were hinting that I was being considered. So far, no one had been promoted or hired. The game was still on, and I couldn't for the life of me step out of the ring now. Not after all I had done to prove myself.

Daniel shook his head as he walked slowly past me. "I knew you were going to fight me on this. You always do." He mumbled something else as he walked away, something I managed to hear loud and clear. "I'm not sure how much longer I can do this."

I turned on my heel, blood pumping like a geyser through my veins. "You're not sure how much longer you can do what exactly?"

Daniel stopped and faced me briefly. "This." He motioned with his hand between us. "Play house with a woman who has no intention of ever starting a family with me. Have you ever stopped and considered that having a family would allow me to see more of you? You're like a ghost around here. I've been patient, Cass, you know I have. I've waited years for you to warm up to the idea. I'm thirty-seven. I'm done waiting." In an instant, he was gone, out the door, and on his way to his beloved restaurant, the one *I'd* paid for.

I felt like I'd been punched in the gut. It was obvious. Daniel *had* ambushed me. The love making and then the bomb he decided to drop in my lap a moment later were all part of it. Because it was *my* lap. Regardless of his age or mine, *I* would have to carry the baby. *I* would have to leave my job. *I* would have to care for it. And then *I* would have to figure out how to afford this pipe dream of his.

I grew up with parents who constantly worried about finances. At times, they had to rely on credit cards to get by, which only exacerbated their problems. *That* happened when my father was suddenly out of work for two years when his boss had laid him off due to budget cuts.

Of course, Daniel would be the first to point out that because of Daddy's layoff, he had time to get his license as an electrician, which only helped him in the long run. What *I* remembered were those two years they stressed over expenses and when he couldn't find legitimate work. My mother contemplated selling our house. I remember feeling guilty about every cent they spent on me for my birthday and for Christmas. Even though it was years later when I had applied to law school, I refused to put that financial burden on their shoulders. Hence, the need for scholarships and financial aid. I had worked my ass off to make it happen for me. It was stressful to say the least. And I told myself back then, I'd never want that for my family.

Where was the urgency? I was thirty-five, not forty-five.

Daniel aspired to open his own restaurant, and I never let him forget that dream. Even if my motives were somewhat selfish—giving him somewhere to focus his energy—it was *me* who had made it happen. And I never required anything from him in return, other than his patience. When we met, I was already a lawyer—education behind me—trying to make my way in the corporate world. My being a lawyer only helped him achieve his professional goal.

If only Trina had your drive, my mother would often say. *We are so proud of you, Cassie-boo.*

Cassie-boo. She'd called me that since I was little. (It apparently had stemmed from several years of playing peek-a-boo.)

What would my parents think about me quitting my job and giving up on my dreams? Especially since I was the *only* one who had finished college. They never said they were disappointed in Trina—and they showered my nieces and nephew with love—but I could tell they wanted more for her. It showed in their eyes.

Well, fuck this.

I slammed around our apartment as though I was having a battle with everything from the toaster to the coffee pot. I stubbed my toe not once but twice. I thought I was going to lose my shit. My hands shook so badly, I couldn't even clasp the necklace I wanted to wear to work. Frustrated, I threw it on our tiny, undergarment-holding dresser and stormed off.

By the time I was on the road toward work, I was literally yelling at no one. People driving by me must've either thought I was fighting with someone on speakerphone or insane. "How dare you expect me to drop everything to serve *your* needs?" I patted my chest. "What about my needs? My job is just as important as your restaurant."

Rain continued to fall, dampening my spirits even more.

"You want me to give up my body and my career. Yet you won't even let me have a say as to when all of this is supposed to happen?" I shook my head vehemently. "What kind of marriage is that, *Daniel? Mr. Perfect.* I guess you expect me to fall in line for just being with you, right?" Again, no one answered my rants, and I preferred it that way. "You think marrying me was *your* contribution, *your* charity?" I grabbed the steering wheel hard, causing my knuckles to turn white. "Because let's face it, *sweetheart*, you know you could've done better. That's the real point, isn't it? You think I owe you this?" I was making zero sense, and I didn't even believe the bullshit I was spewing. I just had to get it out when no one could hear me. No one except the Universe that was.

The foul weather, matching the storm inside me, encouraged bad drivers to become worse drivers. It was as if the storm had washed away everyone's common sense, like how slow they could possibly drive. *This isn't snow. It's just rain.*

One car was going *so* slow, I had to pass the idiot, just missing a truck in the oncoming lane. Either that, or I could have walked to work faster. "You got a gas pedal, bonehead, use it." My wipers whipped back and forth with abandon, doing little to help visibility.

"You know what, *Daniel?* You don't get to dictate to me how I treat my body. I'll have kids when I'm good and ready. And you aren't going to push me into something neither one of us is ready for."

The sound of a horn blared, interrupting my rant. It came when I passed through an intersection on a stretch of narrow roadway with no shoulder. The only other vehicle around was a truck with big tires and fog lights on the roof. *Did I just drive right through that stop sign?* I couldn't remember. *Not good, Cassie.*

I took a stabilizing breath. "Okay, calm down. You don't need to kill yourself over an argument with your husband." Daniel would come around. He always had. And he was reasonable. He knew it wasn't fair to push motherhood onto me. *Right?* The knot in my stomach said otherwise. Possibly because he'd never said *I'm not sure how much longer I can do this* before. When a reasonable man said something like that, it spoke volumes.

Honk!

"Jesus Christ!" My hand flew to my chest as I looked in my rearview at that truck from the intersection. His overly loud horn scared the life out of me. "What? Did I cut in front of you, asshole?" The stretch of road I traveled was narrow but only for about five miles, and then I'd find the ramp to Interstate 64 West, which would take me to Richmond, and, in no time, I'd be at work. At least I only had a twenty-minute drive, unlike Daniel, who had to go all the way to Carytown, which took another ten minutes on a good weather day. *Was he ranting in his car like I was?* Knowing him, probably not.

More honks confronted my nervous system from the jerk driving behind me. A Bubba truck, that's what it was, one big enough it could swallow my BMW in one gulp.

I glared through my rearview mirror. "What the hell, dude?" Their persistence told me the driver was obviously pissed that I hadn't stopped at that intersection. It wasn't as if there were a lot of cars waiting. This was a remote area. But that didn't seem to matter to him, *or her.* The headlights grew larger as the driver came up behind me. It was daytime, but it was also somewhat dark. He beamed his floodlights from the top of his roof, his truck inching closer to my back bumper by the second. It had to be a man. And if he didn't watch himself, I'd sue his ass for reckless endangerment.

Still, I was getting nervous. Road rage wasn't something to toy with. Not in these stressful times.

I didn't intentionally rush through that intersection anyway. And thank God a cop wasn't around at the time. Well, maybe *not* thank God, since I could actually use a cop right now. The rain refused to help, dumping water from the sky in sheets as I approached a wide turn up ahead. I placed both hands on the steering wheel to keep my wheels steady.

This was one of those roads where the vegetation from bushes and trees loved nothing more than to encroach upon the pavement creating a seasonal canopy. These places were rarely ever manicured. Picturesque when the sun was out. Dangerous when it was dark, and visibility remained low.

As the asshole-on-wheels edged even closer, I decided I would pull off at the next side road or parking lot and let him pass. I peeled my eyes for anything that could help, trying to focus through the deluge.

Swish, swish, swish. My wipers slapped back and forth across the windshield, my gaze darting between my rearview and the road in front of me, which was now pooling along the edges.

All at once, the headlights along with the obnoxious floodlight vanished, although the spots across my vision remained intact from their intensity. At least it was over, and my vision would recover. *Phew.* For a split second, I enjoyed the reprieve. That was, until I realized where the truck had gone. It was right beside me now, its horn blaring.

"Jesus! What the hell are you doing? Trying to get us both killed?" I couldn't help the outburst. I did my best to navigate the wide turn when he rushed his oversized truck into the lane in front of me, shoving my front bumper out of the way.

The front of my car went one way, the back the other, my tires fishtailing as if I were driving on a skating rink. I struggled to maintain control, not sure where to turn the wheel as the Bubba truck faded into the distance with one final blast of his fuck-you horn.

I didn't have time to be angry. The edge of the road grabbed my tires, and I slipped off the pavement, losing control of my steering. In an instant, it felt as if my trusted vehicle had grown a mind of its own, thrashing around like a bull just released from its pen. My heart was in a race with my mind, trying to problem solve. Everything happened so fast. Yet, each second passed in slow motion. All I could do was close my eyes and prepare myself for impact.

Daniel.

Suddenly, our fight felt small and insignificant. All the ranting I had done was for no other reason than to release pent-up anger. Yes, I wanted a family with him. It was important to me too. Admittedly, I'd even imagined what our children would look like. Our son with Daniel's captivating eyes, our daughter with my auburn hair and logical mind. I'd envisioned it all. And as my world folded into chaos, branches slapping my car, everything whizzing by, that was all that I could think about in that very long moment.

I promised myself I would never leave Daniel angry again. How selfish I'd been. He was way too important in my life. And I'd taken him for granted. I'd taken *us* for granted.

Please, God, grant me the opportunity to fix this.

Chapter Three

I awoke feeling groggy as if I hadn't slept enough. It was something that happened every now and then, mostly during allergy season or when I *literally* hadn't slept at all, which wasn't the case here. My brain longed to doze back off, but the clock flashing 7:30 a.m. in my face told me I didn't have the luxury. I was late already, or I would be if I didn't get myself moving.

As I lay there, I thought about the incident on the road yesterday. What a scary moment *that* was. Luckily, my BMW 2 Series grabbed hold of the gravel, the tires skidding to a stop, and right before I was about to tumble down a very steep ravine.

I had jumped out of my car and took a moment to collect myself, rain pelting my face and shoulders. My hair was soaked. Not a vehicle was in sight, certainly not the asshole in the Bubba truck who had just about killed me to make a point. I looked over the edge and shivered. If my car had fallen victim to that gully, I'd probably be dead by now. The thought of it made me shiver even now, despite the lagging AC in our old-ass apartment.

    The next thing I did was call the police from inside my car and report the incident. With no license plate number or definitive description of the vehicle—other than it was a Bubba truck—the woman I spoke with invited me to come in to fill out a statement, but admitted all they could do was register the complaint for now. If I ever saw him again, I'd be a lot more observant. Even the color of the truck had escaped me.

    Although clumps of mud and dirt had clung to my car's front fender, my beamer had made it through unscathed. The branches hadn't even penetrated the paint. And I *really* looked, knowing how expensive repairs would be. It wasn't something we had the money for these days. Since I wasn't able to get the license plate number of the truck, the driver was responsible for absolutely nothing in this near catastrophe. He probably bragged about the incident to his friends. *Dickhead.*

    I wasn't sure how long I sat in my car after that, trying to accept what had happened and reassure myself that everything was okay. All I knew was that when I finally did snap out of my haze, I realized the time and how late I was for work. Since there was no way I could go into the office looking like a drowned rat, I dashed home to an empty apartment to change, the lingering scent of Daniel's sticky buns infusing the air in the kitchen, our lovemaking telling another story in our bedroom.

    I remembered Daniel's last words to me: *I'm not sure how much longer I can do this.* His jarring confession had only added insult to my already injured day—a day which turned out to be filled with high-maintenance clients and one delayed court case. By the time I had returned home last night, Daniel was already in bed. I didn't bother to wake him. I undressed, brushed my teeth, washed my face, and dropped into bed like an anchor falling to the bottom of the sea.

Now, as I lay here, I glanced over at the vacant pillow next to mine, feeling sad. The only remnants of my husband, a small indention where his gorgeous head used to rest. I often woke up alone, given Daniel's early schedule and my often late one, but somehow, today, it felt significant.

I yawned and then I yawned some more, the cells in my brain struggling to find clarity and energy. I decided the only way to really wake up was to rise. I threw my blankets back, swung my feet over the side of the bed, and sat up to help the waking process along. Was I still in shock? Yesterday *was* pretty traumatic. I didn't crash into anything, thank God, but my muscles ached as though I had collided with a tree. And not just in any one area either. My entire body hurt. A swath across my chest felt especially tight. It had to be from the seat belt. If only I had gotten that jackass's license plate number, I would have had more information to report to the police.

The sound of pans clanking from the kitchen motivated my legs to stand and shuffle my feet toward the source. When I arrived, Daniel stood over the sink washing an oversized muffin pan, a plastic container next to him filled with muffins of some sort. Our counters were always loaded down with baking sheets or pans for the oven or stovetop. We also had a baking rack that hung over the bistro table. It wasn't pretty, but we needed the storage. This was the same rack we'd had at our last place. After removing it, we'd plastered the holes in the ceiling and painted before we had moved out to avoid losing our damage deposit. We planned to do the same here when the time came, which, for me, couldn't come soon enough. Needless to say, our kitchen always remained cluttered, regardless of whether or not the pans were clean or dirty. I found it bothersome as though the kitchen reflected our lives in some way: disorganized and chaotic. And then my gaze rested on my husband, a man so beautiful he took my breath away every time he entered a room.

"Good morning." I approached Daniel, my hands sliding along his waist while I kissed a spot between his shoulder blades, his hair up in a man bun, allowing me full access.

With my cheek pressed against his back, I inhaled, my nose welcoming the lavender scent coating his T-shirt combined with the usual sugary sweetness.

I peered around his shoulder. "Are those blueberry? They smell yummy." I leaned in, admiring the bursts of blue hiding beneath the crumbly top, made with brown sugar and butter, if memory served. My mouth watered at the sight *and* the smell.

Daniel continued to wash his pan before wiping it dry. I was standing right behind him, yet he didn't acknowledge my presence. No, *Good morning* or *How did you sleep*, like he normally said. This was a cheery man who found goodness in everything and everyone. For me, his silence was as loud as a foghorn in my ears *and* in my heart.

"Daniel?" I grew skittish, pulling my hands away and stepping back as though I didn't have the right to touch my husband anymore. My gut clenched at the thought.

He put the pan he'd dried into the drawer beneath the oven (the only *other* place large enough to store it) and approached the coffee maker as if I were invisible. He poured himself a full cup, the scent of hazelnut complementing his fresh muffins. "Just in case you were wondering. Leslie liked my menu."

The food critic? Oh, no!

"According to her, my soups have a unique flavor that she hasn't tasted before. If it hadn't been for Kendra, I would have been stuck. We barely got the menu together in time. The staff was too busy dealing with customers. Kendra made her hummingbird cake, which was also a hit." Daniel's gaze found mine, his eyes lacking anything resembling warmth. "Thanks for showing up." The sarcasm in his voice sliced through the air as he turned to leave the room.

I was dumbfounded, and for more reasons than one. "I'm sorry. I meant to go. I—"

"Don't." He raised a palm as he stopped and faced me, his cheeks heating up uncharacteristically. "I was planning on you being there. You gave me your word. If it hadn't been for—"

"Yeah, I know. *Kendra.*" I said her name with the uttermost contempt because that's what I felt for the woman. I let my hands fall, slapping against my thigh. "Wouldn't we all like to be as perfect as Kendra?" It was childish of me, but something about her connection to Daniel drove me crazy. My husband valued everyone he met. The people who went out of their way for him held added importance. Kendra had helped Daniel *a lot.*

He shook his head, a slow hiss escaping from his lips. "I don't have time for this. I've got a shipment of fresh vegetables coming in at nine. I need to be there for it."

"Daniel, please. Can we just talk for a minute?" My hands reached out to him. "I was in an accident yesterday, and it totally threw my day off."

That stopped him in his tracks. Something sparked in his chestnut eyes as he turned to face me again. "What kind of an accident?" With his brow furrowed, he placed his mug down on our bistro table and closed the gap between us, his hands gripping my upper arms. "Are you okay? When did this happen? And why didn't you call me?" His gaze washed over me in a more discerning way, as though looking for cuts and bruises.

Oh, good. You still care.

"Yes, I'm okay. It happened on my way to work yesterday. I encountered some asshole in a Bubba truck, you know, the kind with the big wheels and the chrome bar across the back?"

He nodded, his attention fixed.

"Well, I guess I went through a stop sign without meaning to. It was raining so hard it was difficult to see. That seemed to piss this guy off. He followed me, and then he went to pass me and bumped the front fender of my car, causing me to skid off the road. He did it on purpose. It happened over on Riverdale, where the road narrows and there are no shoulders. You know where I mean, right?"

He nodded again, his jaw muscles taut.

"Well, that's where it happened."

"Jesus! Are you hurt? Did you go to the hospital? Did the cops come? Why didn't you call me?" he asked again. His eyes narrowed, a list of questions piling up inside of his brain.

Why *didn't* I call him? I shook my head, not sure of the reason. "Since everything was okay, I didn't want to disturb you. I knew you had a full day."

Daniel stood back, his shoulders rising with outrage. "*Cassie.* You know me better than that. If you were in an accident, I'd want to know about it. You didn't call *anyone*, not even the police?" He was being intense, making me nervous and unsure of myself.

"I *did* call the police, but since I didn't have a chance to get his license plate number or a proper description of the vehicle, there wasn't much they could do. It was really hard to see. And I was okay. I didn't see the need for a hospital. I checked the car, and it's fine. No damage."

Daniel's head flinched back as if shocked by my latest revelation. "Wait a minute. You just said that he hit your car. You had no damage? How is that possible?"

Good question. What the hell was wrong with me? How did this make any sense?

He angled his head in a more discriminating way.

A Collision with Love

I grew paranoid about my recollection. But that was how it had happened. I was sure of it.

"I mean, I *think* there wasn't any damage. It just looked like a bunch of gravel around the wheels and mud on the paint." I tried to remember. "It was still raining when I got home last night." I glanced out the kitchen window at more gray sky. At least it wasn't raining anymore. "I guess I better go check now that the rain has stopped."

My husband had already thought of that and was heading for the door. He grabbed my keys off a hook on the wall on his way out. "*I'll* check." He opened the door, alerting us both to a humid August morning.

"Wait. I'll come too." I grabbed a long raincoat from our tiny hall closet to cover my pj's and slipped my feet into a pair of flip-flops, laying haphazardly on the floor as I tried to keep up.

Our apartment unit was rather small compared to others we had toured closer to Richmond. This one had the best price, though. There were two upstairs units and two downstairs. Our unit exited onto a very small deck that descended two flights of wooden stairs. Old stairs coated with thick brown paint. The kind that grew slippery when wet, so I made sure to be careful. I didn't need any more mishaps.

Daniel walked around my BMW 2 Series doing a cursory inspection first. "Yeah, you've got a fair amount of mud covering it."

I stood a few feet behind him admiring the Melbourne metallic red paint that glistened like Dorothy's ruby slippers when the sun allowed, *and* it was clean, which, right now, it wasn't. I was glad it wasn't damaged. This car was my baby on wheels.

I lived in a crap apartment. I bought my designer suits at a discount. I even brought my lunch to work in my briefcase when I didn't have client lunches to attend. But when it came to my car, I *had* to have something that screamed success. And as expensive as this car appeared, it was considered one of the more reasonable models. *And* I leased. Daniel, who drove a used Subaru wagon, didn't quite understand the point. "What difference does it make what you drive?" he'd asked me once when I had leased my first BMW. (This was car three.) "It's only a car. A way to get from A to B."

I had struggled with my answer, mainly because of how pompous it had sounded inside of my head. "If I want my clients and the partners to take me seriously, hon, I need to look successful. Like I know what I'm doing. Driving to work in some beater, doesn't exactly send the right message."

Daniel just shook his head and kissed me on the cheek. "Whatever you say, Cass. It's just a car to me."

I couldn't correct him. This car and the ones before it were material objects. They didn't cure cancer or do anything but burn gas and take your money. But what my husband didn't quite understand was how things worked in my world. To be a successful lawyer, you also had to look the part.

And I'd seen what happened if you didn't play the game by *their* rules. One junior partner came to mind named Andy, who hadn't quite grasped this superficial philosophy. Andy drove a clunker of a car to the office (I once heard it backfire inside the parking garage and thought a bomb had gone off), wore mismatched clothing (often wrinkled), and often ate his homemade lunch during meetings, once with a client there. He didn't hide any of it. Andy was smart too. One of the smartest men I had ever met when it came to the law. A truly gifted mind. He'd found loopholes that none of us had even considered. And he'd helped us settle several cases as a result. Eccentric, yes. Smart, you better believe it. But Isabella didn't like the image he portrayed in front of our clients, and soon, Andy was history, brilliant mind and all.

I leased my first BMW the following week.

"I don't see any damage." Daniel's voice brought me back to the moment as he bent down to examine the driver's side fender more closely, his fingers brushing against clumps of dirt. "Just a bunch of mud. We should run it up to the carwash and make sure." He straightened up, his gaze traveling over my long coat and flip-flops. "Why don't I take it up? You're not dressed for it. I'll be back in a few minutes."

* * *

When he returned, I was sitting on the bottom step of our apartment stairs waiting. I hadn't even changed my clothes.

Then again, he wasn't gone long.

My car approached all shiny and new, and boy, did Daniel look hot driving it. I imagined him as a big-time banker, jetting around the world, making deals, and earning more money than he had time to count. I don't know why I always imagined my husband doing things far more extravagant than what he actually did in real life. In my mind, he exemplified the persona. Or maybe it was because, deep down, I felt he deserved more.

He climbed out of the car and approached, my keys jangling in his hand. "I don't see any damage. Just a few scratches. How could a big truck bump you off the road and not leave more than a few small marks?" He loomed over me, until I stood, unsure of how to answer his question.

"I-I don't know. I just know it happened."

Daniel moved past me to ascend the stairs. "Hmm" slipped from his lips.

I followed, defensive and rattled by what was happening. "I'm not lying, *Daniel*."

We entered our tiny kitchen, where Daniel hung my keys back on the hook. "I'm not saying you are! It's just . . . *strange*. A truck knocks you off the road, but doesn't leave a dent?"

Something about his closed body language and clipped tone indicated that he *did* think I was lying, even if he hadn't come right out and said it.

I hugged my waist, needing support. "Admit it! You think I'm lying."

He didn't reply. All he did was stand there staring at the floor, his cheeks rosy.

I firmed up my courage. "You think I'd lie about being in an accident? Tell me, *loving husband of mine*, what would motivate me to do such a thing?" The disdain in my voice conveyed exactly how I felt: offended. I wasn't the most attentive wife in the world, and I surely wasn't a custom baker like Kendra, but I prided myself on truth. Finding the truth was one of many reasons why I chose to be a lawyer, despite what people thought about our shark reputation. It was a perception I hoped to change.

Daniel rubbed his forehead, his breaths coming out in sighs. "I don't know, Cassie. You told me you'd make it to the restaurant last night. You *promised* me you'd be there. I texted you numerous times, and you never replied back. What I'm guessing is that you got caught up in work, just like you always do. And you conjured up this . . . *story*, so I wouldn't be upset with you."

"Then where did the mud come from, *Sherlock*?"

He ran a hand down his face. "Maybe you were distracted by your cell or with work stuff and accidentally drove onto the shoulder."

We've been married for eight years. How can you think this about me?

The outrage that flew from my lips was loud and angry. "I

would never do any of that! And I don't recall seeing any texts." I wasn't lying about that either. I didn't remember seeing anything of the sort. I'd have to check my phone to be sure.

I dashed out of the kitchen and into our bedroom to grab my phone and redeem myself. As I opened the screen, several texts from Daniel flashed in my face. Five to be precise:

Are you still coming?
Where are you?
Why aren't you texting me back?
I can't believe you're blowing me off.
I really needed you tonight.

I stared in disbelief at my husband who had followed me in. By now, I was tongue-tied. "I don't understand. I-I don't remember seeing them. Maybe they got caught up in the cloud." It had happened that way before, texts taking hours and sometimes days to materialize.

I just wished it hadn't happened in this particular circumstance. All at once, my stomach twisted into knots, my head too light to hold itself up much longer.

As I lowered myself onto the edge of our mattress, something else occurred to me. "I don't feel well. Maybe I did hit my head." I placed my palm against my forehead, the fuzzy feeling I had awoken with returning with gusto. "You could be right. Maybe I *should* see a doctor."

The look on Daniel's face was one I had never witnessed before. Those beautiful eyes that I had come to love and trust grew cold, his face flat and unforgiving. He perched himself on my side of our bed. "I don't know what's happening with you." He pinched the bridge of his nose with his thumb and forefinger, exhaling. "I don't want to spend my life waiting for you to show up. I'm sorry. I know I'm not supposed to say that after all you've done to help me. I just can't help but think that maybe you don't want this anymore."

"What are you saying? You think I don't want *us*?" I struggled to focus on him, tears burning my eyes.

Instead of answering, he rose and wandered out of the room, allowing his comments to poison the air between us.

"Of course I want us! I love you." My lips trembled as I said those words, my heart trying not to break in two. At the same time, I thought I was going to be sick as the room spun around me. I placed my hand over my mouth to stop whatever was happening from gushing out.

Please, Daniel, come back.

Chapter Four

For the first time ever, I called in sick to work. I explained that I'd had a fender bender and was pretty shaken up by it. Our receptionist, Barbara, who we'd adopted at the firm as everyone's mother, was immediately worried.

"My heavens. Are you all right? Do you need to go to the hospital?"

I assured her that everything was fine. I just needed a day to decompress from it all. What I didn't say was that the accident had occurred yesterday and *before* she had seen me all day in the office. It felt deceitful to admit such a thing, so I decided to strike it from the records. The fact that Daniel thought I was a complete liar didn't help me feel okay about this. I didn't lie to Barbara about the accident. That was true. I'd just fudged the timing of it. No harm.

I spent the next couple of hours in the fetal position on our bed, trying to sort out a few things. Mainly, how I had missed those texts from Daniel. Was I *that* busy yesterday? I could barely remember the day. I often got caught up in cases or meetings with clients and lost all sense of what was going on outside my bubble. But I had promised him I'd be there. And then I didn't show. That wasn't cool of me. When I told someone I would do something, I usually followed through.

I hated it when Daniel was upset with me. He was such a reasonable guy. He'd been waiting years to start a family with me. I knew this. But something deep within me wasn't willing to walk away from a career that was about to take off. If I made senior partner, money wouldn't be an issue anymore. We could buy that house. And if I became a mother, we could afford childcare. We'd have options. Right now, we had none of those things. In fact, we were barely scraping by.

I wasn't rich. I wasn't Brianna.

Brianna threw out clothes she'd barely worn and food she'd barely eaten. It was hard for me to relate to my college roommate at first, which was probably why we hadn't kept in touch since. Back then, when it was just the two of us, Brianna was kooky and relatable. But with her snooty friends, she was a carbon copy of them: cold and critical. *Entitled.* Which version was the real Brianna? I'd often wondered.

She and I were never besties, but we enjoyed each other enough that she'd asked me to be in her wedding, and I had accepted. And for that reason alone, I would be forever in her debt.

And what a wedding it was, held at her parents' Tuscan-style estate nestled high on a hill in central Virginia, its features inspired by a famous Italian architect. Several feet below, the James River flowed lazily by without a care in the world. The sky wore a brilliant blue, encouraging pompous clouds full of puff to sail across the abyss like they were floats in a parade.

An enormous tent provided shade for the nearly two hundred guests across their back lawn, its size ample for a full crowd, an impressive buffet, *and* a band who came with their own staging equipment.

I hadn't eaten enough on that day. Still, I *had* enjoyed several glasses of champagne for this toast or that as the wedding party dressed within Brianna's en suite, her mom, sisters, and aunts fluttering around her like butterflies, primping and bestowing heartfelt advice to the bride. Photographers captured moments of twelve bridesmaids dressed in matching silky pajamas, then hairdressers doing our hair and makeup, before they took more photos of us all polished and pretty later on. This happened *before* we'd even walked down the aisle. Brianna's mother, Helen, had food brought in, but I was too wired to eat any of it.

Normally, fancy weddings provided sit-down dinners, but not Brianna's, who couldn't seem to decide what she wanted to serve. Her solution to this dilemma was to offer everything she could think of. She included an authentic meat-carving station and others for barbecue, Italian fare, Mediterranean, Chinese dim sum, Northeastern seafood, Japanese sushi, and seasonal vegetables, in addition to bread and cheese of various types. Dressed in full waitstaff garb, men and women stood at their designated stations, serving each guest with a smile. And with such a vast selection, lines remained short. Another perk.

My stomach wouldn't stop growling at me, so I didn't waste time filling *my* plate. I wasn't into seafood or sushi, but my lagging stamina required protein. Either that, or I was destined for a very early night, which I knew would not go over well with the bride. The flurry of meats that wafted around the tent made it hard to choose. The gorgeous man lingering at the meat station, however, helped my mind decide.

The man was stunning, presenting a bashful smile. His face deserved a starring role in one of those European films, the ones I used to watch when I was lonely or bored. My knees grew feeble, my heart pitter-pattering at the mere sight of him. I'd met handsome men before, but something about Daniel's soft chestnut eyes and unassuming aura drew me right into his trajectory, man bun and all. He was tall, six-foot-one, his shoulders and broad chest filling out the white double-breasted chef coat to perfection. His sleeves, folded up toward his elbows, revealed strong forearms and hands. The black-and-white checkered pants he wore, didn't reveal a lot about his lower half, other than a trim body and a sensationally round ass.

A young couple had just walked away, their plates full, when I stepped up to the counter, one covered in a white tablecloth and loaded with plenty of meat for everyone. Most of the stations had more than one attendant, except for this one, which was fine by me. I wouldn't have wanted someone else carving my meat on that day.

Hopped up on alcohol and the day's nuptials, I stumbled over my words. "Wow, where did *you* come from?" Knowing how ridiculous I sounded, I think I might have slapped my own forehead to snap out of my stupor.

Daniel just smirked, his lips plump and mesmerizing. "Well, I work for Savory Sensations, one of the caterers. Can I get you a slice of beef or baked ham, miss?" He reached for a large knife and a meat-carving fork, an oversized wooden cutting board at the ready to catch his trimmings.

"Ignore that comment." I lifted my champagne flute and shook my head, my cheeks flaring. "Too much champagne. And sure, I'd love a slice of both. Don't be afraid to cut them thick. I'm starving." I handed him my plate from a stack positioned on my right.

"Yes, ma'am."

"What kind of beef is that?"

"That would be London broil."

A waiter came by collecting my now empty flute.

"What's on it?" My nose picked up the rosemary, but I wasn't sure what else coated the beef. *Me and my inquisitive mind.*

"Those are herbs to season the meat: rosemary, thyme, oregano, sage. If you'd like I can cut you a center—"

"Oh, no." I lifted a palm. "That sounds good. It smells yummy. I was just curious. Did you cook all of this yourself?" Making a fool of myself in front of a handsome stranger seemed like perfect fun. Why else would I be blabbering?

"I sure did." He stabbed the fork into the ham and began slicing with slow but purposeful precision.

"That's a lot of meat. I bet *that* took some time." My gaze wandered over several roasts standing by. "Your caterer must have a huge oven. What other stations are you guys in charge of?"

All I could think in that moment was *Shut the hell up, you're talking too much.* Did I stop? Nope. But I *did* try to recover.

"Sorry. I don't mean to grill you."

Daniel placed a slice of ham on my plate and then turned toward the London broil to his right. "Interesting choice of words. And you are not *grilling* me. We are also in charge of the barbecue station. You may want to check it out. We smoke the pork barbecue for eight hours and the brisket for over twenty. It's all homemade rubs and sauces. Trust me, it'll melt in your mouth."

"Yum. I love barbecue." I was practically licking my lips. "I will definitely have to check that one out. Do you know if they have coleslaw?" I waved him off. "Never mind. I'll find out for myself."

"Yes, I believe they do. It's nice to see a woman with a healthy appetite." His eyes shined with amusement as he sliced the London broil for me, the muscles in his forearms flexing in a sexy way. Even his skin glowed as though the sun had spent hours kissing it to just the right shade.

Lucky sun.

"You're my first bridesmaid today."

I knew what he meant. I was the first bridesmaid who had approached the carving station on that day, but I still liked the idea of being *his* anything in that moment. I also knew Brianna's friends well enough to assume none of them would be filling their plates with an abundance of food—meat or otherwise. Brianna's maid of honor was too busy popping pills to keep her appetite down and her size 2 dress fitting like a second skin. If any of them wandered over this way, it was for the hottie, not the cuisine. Luckily, they all had dates.

"That's a beautiful dress. And I love the color of your hair." Daniel's gaze washed over my auburn hair, falling in choppy layers just below the nape of my neck and my off-the-shoulder, size 8 navy gown with wrap-around waist, the columned skirt plunging all the way to the floor.

What he couldn't see were my strappy silver sandals, lifting my height four inches and pinching my toes in the process. The outfit cost over five thousand dollars, a gift from the bride and way too rich for my taste. (I hadn't worn it since.)

Every one of Brianna's bridesmaids looked like they walked a runway, with the exception of her ten-year-old niece and me. I mean, I wasn't ugly by any stretch of the imagination. In fact, *some* men thought my green eyes were quite spectacular. My thighs were a tad thick, my hair often unruly, and my complexion on the pasty side.

"I'm sorry. I didn't mean to—"

"No, it's okay. And thank you. I appreciate the compliment." I hooked a thumb over my shoulder. "Standing next to those bridesmaids, I was starting to wonder if I should just give up and put a bag over my head." I giggled, only half joking.

Daniel tipped his head to one side as though contemplating my words. Then he wagged a finger. "But if you put a bag over your head, we'd miss those exquisite green eyes of yours, and *that* would truly be a shame." He pursed his lips. "I have a feeling nothing gets past *those* eyes. In fact, I bet you're sizing me up right now." Daniel handed me my plate filled with succulent meats. "Plus, why should the bag get to have all the fun?"

Why should the bag get to have all the fun? I remembered thinking. *Is this guy a player or one of the nicest men I'd ever met?*

The wedding party was still strewn about (photos over), grabbing food, and chatting. And I was starving. *How bad would it be for me to take a few bites while I'm here?* I took a chance and set my plate off to the side. I grabbed a fork and knife from a nearby table and cut myself a piece of the tender beef, tucking it into my mouth and savoring the rich juices as they tantalized my tongue. While I chewed, I pictured my stomach waiting like a catcher in a baseball game to collect the sustenance.

"I hope you don't mind if I eat a few bites while I'm here. You made it all sound so good. I couldn't wait."

"As long as *I'm* not eating, I think we're okay." Daniel tipped his chin toward the bar area. "*And* as long as your date doesn't mind."

My date. Ha. Oliver and I had been friends since he'd started at the same firm where I had *used* to work several years prior. Even back then, when he was in his mid-twenties, the man never looked a day over fifteen due to his small frame and baby-boy face. It had frustrated him every time he got carded, which was all the time. But Oliver had Marsali, who also never seemed to outgrow her adolescent appearance. To this day, both of them could pass for high schoolers or siblings to their two children.

Oliver had accompanied me to this wedding as a favor, unlike asshole Seth who had broken up with me the month prior, saying I talked too much. Seth was definitely a jerk, but that didn't stop me from turning inward. Insults were hard to shake.

"Stay as long as you'd like ... miss ... ."

"Cassie."

"Well, Cassie, I'm Daniel, and I'd love the company." Daniel's smile brought warmth to my insides, my chest filling with fuzzy delight. I think it was because I sensed he meant what he said. He wasn't just being polite.

Several more guests approached, Daniel slicing various portions for everyone, a hint of a smile never leaving his alluring mouth. Most of the couples were elderly. The younger crowd seemed to prefer the sushi and the dim sum judging by the length of those lines.

I was amazed at how precise Daniel was with his knife, each slice of meat proportioned just like the last. I'll never forget what I said next: "You sure are good at handling your meat." My comment was meant to be funny, but it came out kinda perverted. Before I could apologize *again*, Daniel chimed in.

He smirked. "Thank you." His voice gathered a more serious tone. "Seasoning, cooking, and even slicing meat is more complicated than most people think. Just like the flowers and the soil affect how a grape will taste in a fine wine, how you cook and cut a good piece of meat does the same." He held up his blade. "But when you get to this stage of preparation, it all hinges on the proper knife ... ." Daniel went on to explain everything there was to know about various cuts of meat, my mind taking a ride on the savory train with him. "See, you have to bear down gently against the grain of the meat." He sliced his next portion slowly and methodically as he spoke, placing the sliced piece on the cutting board. He reminded me of a jeweler placing a necklace on a pad of velvet to put on display.

I imagined most girls would have been bored by this conversation, but I wasn't. Looking back, I appreciated how Daniel seemed to care about what he was doing. "I've never met anyone who cares so much about meat." Yup. I was full of stupid phrases on that day but, at the same time, it was all I could come up with. I also hoped it didn't come out sounding condescending or rude.

"Well, not everything is about meat"—he grabbed his trusty slicing knife and pointed with it haphazardly—"but I get your point." With no one around to accept the slice he'd just cut, Daniel scrapped it off into the trash can at the back of his station. "I make it my business to know a lot about food in general. And I've seen how eating the wrong foods can make a person very sick. Most people don't pay enough attention to what they put into their bodies."

I remember thinking, *how about you put a thing or two in my body*. I'd even chuckled to myself for going there. What I *actually* said was "I'm impressed. I guess I never thought about it before." And I hadn't. I just ate what I felt like eating, which was probably why I wasn't as thin as those bridesmaids.

Daniel shrugged one shoulder, his eyes reflecting something more somber. "My mother had some issues with food allergies. She has celiac. Almost died from eating gluten. That's why I started paying a lot more attention to it. The more I researched food and health, the more interested I became."

"Is that why you work for a caterer?" I wondered what other aspirations, if any, he had for himself back then.

"You could say that. It's a good job . . . for now. I know the owner. I hope to open my own restaurant someday. My goal is to offer food that tastes incredible but doesn't rot your insides."

He straightened his shirt, his gaze washing over his workstation with discerning eyes. He scraped the cutting board clean, the trimmings going into the same small trashcan at the back of the station. He then grabbed a thick, white terry cloth and began wiping down the area around the cutting board. "We've been programmed to believe that healthy food has to taste bad." When he was finished, he placed the cloth on a table behind him, the one next to the trash can. "I hope to change a few minds about that." He leaned into his stance, crossing his arms and glancing up at me with those incredible eyes.

I was enjoying listening to him, to the point where I almost forgot to reply. "Well, if you ever need legal advice for your new restaurant, I'm your girl."

At that point, another couple, middle-aged and dressed formally, looked as if they might approach.

I almost wanted to shoo them away.

"*My girl*, huh?" Daniel looked at me as though trying to figure out what exactly I was offering. His thick stare and slight smile drove goosebumps up my arms. "So, you're a lawyer." He didn't say it as a question, more of a confirmation. He half-nodded. "That suits you. I bet you and those green eyes are a force to be reckoned with in a courtroom." He lifted his index finger. "*That*, I'd like to see."

Bashfulness heated up my chest. "I'm sure I'm not that interesting to watch." With most men, telling them I was a lawyer seemed to set them off. Like I was too smart to consider romantically. It was entirely possible that they simply didn't like meeting a woman who might be smarter than they were. Even the lawyers I dated had some sort of competitive edge to them. Needless to say, I hadn't dated a great deal.

"I hope your companion doesn't mind you spending so much time with me. I also hope it's not serious between you two."

Daniel greeted the middle-aged couple upon their arrival. I used the time to take a few more bites of my food.

"Doesn't this look delicious? I'd like some ham please," the woman said, wearing a light-blue blazer and matching skirt, a large brooch adorning her lapel.

Daniel filled her plate first.

Then her husband stepped up in a light-gray suit, complementing his wife's color scheme (I assumed she was his wife).

Her hair was poufy. *His* hair was mostly gone. "I'm a meat-and-potatoes man. None of the sushi-goosey food. Give me a cut of both." After Daniel had satisfied his order, the man took the plate from Daniel's hands. "Thank you, young man. I trust this will be to my liking." The couple strolled off.

"Where were we?" Daniel asked, wiping his hands on a towel, leaving a few smears of meat juice on the fabric.

"You were asking if my date would mind that I'm chatting with you." I paused for effect. "The answer is no. He's just a friend." I tapped my finger against my lips. "But then you said, you 'hope it's not serious.' May I ask why?" With a good-sized portion of ham and London broil in my belly, I was feeling stronger and more alert.

Daniel met my gaze square on. "Because any man who would leave a woman of your beauty and intelligence alone at a wedding reception *for this long*"—he fanned a hand out over the crowds—"doesn't deserve you."

"Is that so?" I chewed on my lower lip, Daniel's stare zeroed in on my mouth.

He leaned toward me. "*That*, lovely Cassie, the lawyer with the captivating green eyes, is most certainly so." He stared deep, not blinking, his unspoken message coming through loud and clear: *I like you.*

We were married six months later.

I awoke with that blissful memory fading from my mind. I

hadn't realized I had dozed off. This morning was one of the strangest of my life. I needed to do something about this rift between my husband and me. I got up *again* and dragged my sorry ass into the shower. I might not have made it to the restaurant yesterday, but I was sure as shit going to make it there today.

Chapter Five

In what was now a very shiny car, I drove across town toward Daniel's Garden Patch, making sure to take a different route. Every time I thought about that angry truck trying to run me off the road, I shuddered, and I found it hard to swallow. *Or* breathe.

After yesterday's rain, the clouds scattered, allowing patches of blue sky to poke through, the sun hoping to make an appearance. The recent storm also encouraged dried vegetation to bloom, as I would imagine desert rain would do for those hearty plants and flowers that only received a momentary reprieve from their drought conditions. The birds chirped from the trees, the leaves and flowers all too happy for the chance to gulp up some water and replenish. It seemed nature was in a good mood.

I was not.

All I could think about was what would have happened if my car had gone down that ravine. Would I be dead right now, and would Daniel be trying to find me? The road I often took to work was more direct but also narrow and not highly traveled.

Vegetation grew thick in the summer months, challenging visibility on a good day. Would anyone have come for me? Tears stung behind my eyes at the thought, uncertainty forming a lump in my throat.

It wasn't as if I could rely on the driver of the truck to provide any help. He was long gone, happy to return to his day, and probably feeling completely justified for teaching *that rich bitch in a beamer* a lesson. I was projecting, but what other type of person would do such a thing?

As my thoughts spiraled, the entrance ramp for Interstate 64 West appeared, and soon I was on the highway, appreciating the traffic around me for a change and not dreading it, everyone bearing witness to my presence among them. Keeping my eyes peeled for big trucks, I spent the remainder of my journey ruminating over my situation with Daniel. I wanted to be mentally prepared for when I saw him again. My brain wasn't exactly sharp as of late.

I had to believe he wasn't done with me, despite what he'd said. We'd made love yesterday. And he wasn't rude or cruel about his words, either. He never was. What I witnessed was resignation—like people arrived at when they'd tried everything else—and that worried me even more.

Adding to my sorrow was the fact that he hadn't believed me about the near accident. What did that say about us? If the tables were turned, I would *never* consider questioning Daniel's honesty. I was a litigator; I dealt with liars all the time. And I swear I felt that truck bump me. Several questions came to my mind. Could my car be so well built it staved off any damage? He'd hit me hard enough to send me off the road for God's sake. But not hard enough to send me down that ravine. Or had the edge of the road made me *think* he'd hit me when all he had done was come close? I could have compensated for his close proximity and veered *myself* off the road.

The dull headache I'd awoken with was still hammering away, and this line of mental questioning was only making it worse. I couldn't explain the oddities. All I could do was tell the truth. It sickened me to think that Daniel believed I could be so cunning. I might have been wrong about what had happened—under duress I'd seen clients mix up the facts—but I definitely wasn't intentionally lying about it. If only I had seen those text messages. *Stupid cloud.*

The throbbing beneath my skull had strengthened. I placed a hand over my forehead, hoping to soothe the pain. That same tightness across my chest had returned as well, and along with it, a serious case of nausea. It got so bad that I had to pull off the interstate where I found a small convenience store parking lot to collect myself. I contemplated calling Daniel, but given the events of yesterday and from this morning, I chose not to, assuming he wouldn't believe this either. I put my head back and closed my eyes, flashes of the almost accident taunting my tired brain.

How much time passed, I had no idea. When the pain subsided and my stomach settled, I pulled myself together and resumed my trek toward town. This time, I focused on figuring out a way to convince my husband to wait a little bit longer for that family he longed for. I also wanted to make sure he understood that I did *want* this life. And with him. If I could do that, we had a chance. If I couldn't, I'd come up with another strategy. My work-life balance was imbalanced. Career. Husband. Future kids. Financial security. I was a juggler, trying to keep all my priorities in the air. Often, I wasn't sure which way to turn.

All I knew was that this new prospective client, Into the Open - Equipment Inc., could be the key to a new financial future for Daniel and me, especially if it led to me making senior partner. My income would increase substantially.

I suddenly regretted calling in sick to work now. I'd have to make a point to touch base with CEO, Lindsey Coleman, and Owner, Brad Tanner, from Into the Open to make sure all was well in their world. Lindsey and Brad were in their early forties. They were smart. They were honest. And they were determined to make their company well known around the world.

Lindsey's short blond hair, blue eyes, and natural beauty blended well with Brad's wavy medium-length brown hair and fuss-free appearance. They were fit, their smiles healthy and wholesome. Perfect poster children for the company's website and mission statement. I rarely saw them in formal attire, which also supported their outdoorsy message. Nature was their vibe. Clean living. Much like my husband, so I could relate.

Still, new clients required a lot of courting, and I didn't want to drop the ball with them. I knew many more lawyers were vying for their business. Lindsey and Brad were nice people. Professional all the way. We'd met at the office, and I'd taken them out for lunch a few times. They seemed happy with what I had to offer. They also liked the firm and its solid reputation, or so they said.

I was lucky. Most of my clients were fairly easy to deal with. With the exception of Mrs. Dunbar, a woman in her early sixties who had survived three divorces and was working on her fourth. I swear the woman made an art form out of marrying men with lucrative bank accounts, only to do her best to drain those same accounts during their split.

Mrs. Dunbar made sure you knew where you stood with her. And if she was upset, she made no bones about that either. We'd knocked heads a few times over her unreasonable divorce terms.

All those marathon meetings might have given me indigestion, but they also taught me a lot about negotiation. In the seven-and-a-half years I'd been with Wilson & Bates, I'd litigated two of Mrs. Dunbar's divorces, even convincing her to bend on certain issues as a result. "You're not like my last few lawyers," she'd said once. "You're a straight shooter. I like that. And you tell me what I *need* to hear." Then she'd pointed at me with an authoritarian finger, one embellished with a very long red fingernail. "Just don't push it or I *will* replace you. You lawyers are a dime a dozen. Know your place, young lady."

I exhaled at the thought as I approached the Carytown exit which would eventually lead me to the western portion of this small but bustling marketplace curled up in the heart of Richmond.

Nothing along the mile-long stretch of shops, restaurants, and entertainment venues stood over a story or two high, each building uniquely decorated, some painted with murals and all contributing to the bohemian culture. Almost everything was privately owned, which only bolstered its individuality. People came here to shop and to eat, but mostly, they came to experience. It was no wonder Carytown developed a reputation for being one of the coolest places in Richmond.

Restaurants prided themselves on farm-to-table cuisine, something Daniel had embraced years ago. When I had first toyed with the idea of helping him open a restaurant, and not just dreaming about it, I never imagined we'd find a space here. I also knew *I* would have to fund most of it. Working for a caterer didn't exactly pay well. And Daniel had culinary school debt to pay off.

Little did we know, I had an ace up my sleeve. Mrs. Dunbar might have been a pain in my ass most of the time, but having rubbed elbows with the *old money* of Richmond for years, the woman had connections. And it was those connections that had helped us find a location, the home of an old music store whose lease was up and wasn't being renewed. A corner unit, too, with plenty of space for a restaurant. The problem was the owner of the building was selling, not leasing anymore. Rarely taking no for an answer, Mrs. Dunbar wouldn't stop until she had negotiated a workable selling price that we jumped on.

My salary over the last seven-and-a-half years had afforded us a savings ample enough to buy a house with little left to finance. I *had* the money. Well, *we* had the money, and we used it. All of it by the time the remodel was completed. Things were moving along.

Mrs. Dunbar was also a huge flirt. She had to be to attract all those rich men, right? When she met Daniel, she just about stumbled over herself to help this handsome man who *must be a model*, according to her. There were times when I worried the woman might steal Daniel away from me, which we had laughed about. "She may be rich, Cass, and not bad looking, but that woman can be scary as hell. Don't ever leave us alone," Daniel had warned more than once. "I'm afraid she'll steal my soul," he'd added with a smirk.

All of this meant that Mrs. Dunbar wasn't just a client anymore. She was someone who I now owed a favor. A *very* big favor. And her generosity didn't stop there.

We'd hired contractors to transform the music store into a restaurant, found booths, tables, chairs, and other restaurant paraphernalia at auctions and going-out-of-business sales. Everything one might need for a commercial kitchen. Although I didn't have much free time to paint or clean, I could organize, most of which I did from my laptop. I'd even insisted on a few weekends off from work to help. My savings account drained like water from a tub. I'd made the mistake of mentioning this during one of my meetings with Mrs. Dunbar. (Her first name was Ruth, but she'd never allowed us lowly lawyers to call her that.)

Using her connections once again, Mrs. Dunbar found us a commercial grill and our new high-powered dishwasher at a very reasonable price. That was when I put my foot down, even though we needed those things desperately. "You've done more than enough. I don't think I can ever repay your generosity." I did offer free legal advice for her and her friends, though Ruth was rich as were her friends. They didn't need *free* anything. And I had to be careful about that sort of thing and what the senior partners would allow.

Every time Daniel and I had thanked her profusely for her help, she'd just say with a wink, "Anything for my Danny Boy. And when you decide to leave this very capable redhead whom I've entrusted as counsel, I'll be waiting." The lilt in her voice was nothing short of provocative.

The woman has to be kidding, right? I'd often wondered to myself.

The comment always brought an adorable splash of pink to Daniel's cheeks. "How about free meals for as long as you'd like?" my husband had added, which she'd agreed to with a *humph*.

Unlike *my* savings account, which was starting to cough up moths, Ruth's were more than ample for whatever struck her fancy. I also knew she reserved a small portion for philanthropy. She said it was for tax purposes but deep down I got the sense she liked helping people less advantaged than herself. People like Daniel and me. Whatever the reason, I wasn't about to question it.

As I drove along Cary Street, the gridlock halting the traffic to a snail's pace, Daniel's Garden Patch rose up in the distance.

Okay, focus.

I parked in the nearest parking deck, on the opposite side of the road, gathered myself together, and walked along the sidewalk, weaving in and out of people who were either window shopping, chatting with their companions, or darting in or out of restaurants or shops. Pedestrian traffic was as abundant as the vehicles on the street.

Savory scents floated out from various doors or patios, hosting patrons for lunch, a cold blast of air conditioning riding its coattails. My gut suddenly felt hollow, my energy dwindling. I realized it was probably because I hadn't eaten anything all day. I'd wasted the morning in bed. By now, it was just past noon.

Not eating was unusual. I always had *something* for breakfast, even if it was just a cup of coffee and a piece of toast, although Daniel normally offered a better option than that. *Breakfast is the most important meal of the day*, my mother used to drill into mine and Trina's heads. *If you're gonna skip a meal, make sure it's not breakfast.*

Today, lunch would have to do. I was sure Daniel had something ready I could grab and eat. In fact, I was counting on it.

Before I crossed the street, I passed by a small ice-cream shop with half a dozen little girls sitting around a table eating their ice cream and giggling while they chatted with one another, colorful paper party hats crowning their small heads. They couldn't have been more than six years old, my niece McKenna's age, their mouths coated with either chocolate smiles or something in the vanilla or strawberry category. One girl donned red pigtails and bright red cheeks to match (probably from the summer heat).

She stuck her face into the small bowl in front of her—more precisely the mound of chocolate ice cream rising above the rim —coming up with a dollop of sweet goodness stuck to her nose. I could envision myself doing something similar at her age, hoping for a laugh. And that was precisely what the little girl received as her friends cracked up with abandon, a couple of them following suit. It was the cutest thing I had ever seen.

Boxes wrapped in brightly patterned birthday paper, along with several gift bags, stood off to the side while small clusters of balloons tied to each of the children's chairs swayed in the breeze. A few young parents mingled among themselves until a rather handsome man with dark hair and a toned body, descended upon the table to stop the little girls from plastering their faces with stickiness. His lips moved a mile a minute as he wiped mouths furiously, another woman joining his efforts, both *trying* to look disgusted but having a hard time not smiling at the display. An elderly woman (probably a grandmother) took pictures, capturing this moment of pure silliness.

This was our future, Daniel's and mine, playing out right in front of me. And what a pretty picture it painted. Daniel would be the father who would always let our kids get away with everything. I'd be the stickler who had to remind everyone to use their good sense. Daniel and I would smile across the room at each other, knowing that even though we appeared as good cop and bad, we were totally in this crazy adventure together.

"Oops. Sorry. My bad." Breaking through my daydream, a teenage boy with spiky blond hair and multiple piercings on his ears and face bumped into me as he rushed past.

I'd stopped walking and was standing there staring when I suddenly became aware of myself. Before I continued on, the little girl with red hair gazed over at me. I hoped she didn't think I was a threat. *Stranger danger* and all that. I smiled and waved at her, and she returned the gesture.

Yes, I wanted that life. I absolutely did. If I could make senior partner, I would be willing to try as soon as possible. I reasoned that Isabella and Gregory couldn't very well fire me as a senior partner, now could they? Discrimination and lawsuits were there to prevent such things. And I'd be making more money right away. Yes, I'd explain all of this to my husband.

I stepped off the curb and rushed across the street where the nearest intersection allowed and approached our brick building. The mural of a garden, including vegetables, sunflowers, and a few cows, chickens, and goats grazing throughout a set of rolling hills dominated the brick wall facing our side street. A farm. We didn't raise the meat or grow any of the vegetables (although someday Daniel hoped to change that). But we served both and did so with a conscience. My husband had gone to great lengths to source local produce and meat that was raised organic. The farmers in the area knew him well.

Matching the hand-painted mural, large orange awnings hung over the door and the oversized floor-to-ceiling windows out front, shading the sidewalk for any patrons passing by. And arching across the glass, the words Daniel's Garden Patch welcomed customers while window art weaved leaves, vines, and more flowers throughout the letters.

Local artist, Emily Pierce, had offered us a generous discount if we agreed to sell her framed artwork inside, which we did without hesitation. Why wouldn't we want to decorate our walls with local art? Emily was relatively unknown at the moment, which was the real reason we could afford her services, but I didn't expect her to remain that way for long.

I pulled one of the glass doors open, forcing a bell to ring overhead, alerting the owner and the staff that someone new had entered the premises, a cool draft from the AC refreshing my tacky skin.

Before I took another step, I inhaled the scent of baked goods, garlic, and too many other delectable ingredients to identify. Murmurs from various conversations drifted around the room like a gentle breeze, most of the tables occupied for lunch, some with businesspeople, others with families enjoying the last of their summer break. A few chair legs scraped against the wood floors. Utensils clanked against porcelain. An elderly man and woman sat nearby sipping coffee or tea; I couldn't tell which.

As I took a few more steps, the old wood floor squeaked its little squeak, something we decided to leave as is due to money constraints and an appreciation for the building's history. The dark mahogany floors that matched the thick trim framing the walls, as well as the beams spanning a ceiling that reached fifteen feet high, had been here since the beginning. Other than some refinishing, they'd remained unaltered as the structure's observer of the past. We chose to keep it that way.

Daniel's Garden Patch seated six good-sized tables along each wall, a row of booths cutting down the center, providing him with quite an audience today when the place was nearly full. He'd hired a few college students to wait and bus tables, but no one ever stayed long. Haley and Ezra were the latest hires, both attending VCU nearby. Ezra was working on her nursing degree, and Haley specialized in accounting.

We also had a few full-timers assisting in the kitchen, washing dishes, and waiting or busing tables. Ten staff members in total, not including Kendra, who had been with us since the restaurant had opened two years ago. As Daniel's restaurant inched toward turning a profit, he was hoping to offer benefit packages to keep the full-timers around a bit longer. There wasn't a great deal he could do about part-time work. It was what it was. A lot to consider when running a business.

Taking refuge at the back of the restaurant, an L-shaped food counter stood proudly, along with ten retro-style swivel barstools with red cushions and chrome bases, each one bolted to the floor. Daniel had scored the counter at a consignment sale. It came from a diner that had long since closed its doors.

The counter brought a nostalgic atmosphere to the restaurant and a place for singles to sit for a quick meal. Kendra loved working the counter, mainly because it provided a place to display her desserts, most of them stored in glass or on ceramic cake stands of various heights, while a few remained in the fridge out back.

Behind the counter, a swinging door led to the kitchen where all the magic happened. As I made my way there, Kendra offered a middle-aged man a slice of her hummingbird cake, probably the one Daniel had told me she had made for the food critic. Her dark and expressive eyes lifted her gaze toward me as I approached.

The peach-colored floral sundress she wore today allowed a hint of cleavage, the length a chance to show off her long legs, which I'd seen many men notice over the past couple of years. She kept her hair short, tight curls framing her high cheekbones beautifully. Large hoop earrings hung from her lobes, adding to her style. Kendra was a woman who had it goin' on, yet she never stayed with any one man for very long.

"Oh, hi, Cassie. I didn't know you were coming in today." She smiled, but there was something disingenuous about the way it didn't quite reach the rest of her face. "Does Daniel know you're here?" She sliced a piece of cake for her customer and placed it in front of him on a plate. "There you go. I hope you like it. I just baked it yesterday." She topped off his coffee, the nutty aroma swirling through the air, its blend sturdy.

Before I could make any progress toward the kitchen, her gaze found me again. "Do you want me to let Daniel know you're here?"

Why would I want you to tell my husband I'm here, when I can do it myself? I tried not to show my annoyance. Daniel liked this woman and, according to him, he couldn't live without her. *And* she was gorgeous.

I hated myself for feeling this way, but her appearance made everything harder for me. Honestly, the woman could have been posing for covers of magazines if she had chosen such a career path when she was younger. Not that she was old now. She'd turned thirty-two last April. I had to assume her singlehood was by choice. Possibly, she was waiting for Daniel to come to his senses and leave me. I couldn't help but go there. And I did often, which was one of the reasons I didn't care for the woman.

"No, I can tell him I'm here. I'm headed there now." I pointed toward the back. "He's in the kitchen, right?"

As if she had suddenly morphed into a traffic guard, Kendra rushed around the counter to cut me off at the pass, her palms raised.

What is your problem?

"I think he's in his office meeting with that food critic." Kendra beamed. "Did he tell you that she asked him to be on her podcast?" She even clapped her hands with excitement. "She thought I was his wife." She grinned with a shrug, then waved me off. "Don't worry, I set her straight."

Did you now? I grimaced but tried not to show it. "That's great. I'm so glad. He was worried about her liking his food." I ran a hand through my hair, feeling sheepish. "I wish I could have gotten here yesterday. I meant to."

Kendra's face fell, her brows knitted together in an almost somber way. "Yeah, Daniel said you got caught up at work again." Her tone was edgy but subtly so. That was also Kendra. She wanted to make a point without having to be obvious about it. I caught the meaning, though. *You let him down again.*

At that moment, a new customer plunked down on one of the vacant stools at the bar, a man whose fingers appeared to be stained by grease. The name "Tom" was sewn into the fabric's name tag adorning the chest of his short-sleeve, dark-blue work shirt. If I were to guess, I'd say he was a mechanic of some sort. "Excuse me, I've got a customer. You may want to wait until he comes out to tell him you're here." She rushed over to Tom. "Welcome to Daniel's Garden Patch. Let me get you some water and a menu." She practically hummed the words.

"Great. Where's the can? I'd like to wash up." The man stood.

As Kendra instructed Tom about where to find the bathrooms, two things caused my stomach to clench. One, Daniel hadn't told Kendra about my accident, which meant he still didn't believe me. Two, Kendra felt she had the right to tell me when and where I could see my own husband. She was getting bolder, and I didn't like it much.

The last time I came by when I happened to be visiting a client in Carytown and I had a few extra minutes, she said he was gone on a delivery and wouldn't be back for hours. I found out later he hadn't even left yet when I was there. True to form, Daniel passed it off as an easy misunderstanding, but I knew different. *Talk about being honest.*

I ventured into the kitchen, anyway, despite Kendra's rumblings about my interrupting Daniel at an inopportune time. What I didn't do was *actually* interrupt when I saw him speaking with the food critic through his office window. This time Kendra was being honest with me. I hovered around the kitchen, trying to stay out of the way. While I did so, I nibbled on a turkey and cheddar sandwich from a tray that Daniel would often make for the staff. Man, it tasted good, the bread as fresh as the added veggies. The herb aioli a perfect sandwich companion.

"Hey, Cassie, nice to see you, girl." Marcus smiled at me from his usual spot at the grill, his white apron tied tight around his thick waist, grease stains adorning the front.

In order for Daniel to offer things such as paninis and

burgers (both regular, gluten free, and vegan), he needed a grill. And after Ruth had scored said grill, a charismatic man named Marcus came strolling in, professing he was the expert when it came to such things. Marcus had moved to Richmond from NYC and, according to him, he'd seen and done it all. He'd suggested we use grill mats to separate the vegan and gluten-free food and knew how to avoid any additional cross-contamination. His infectious smile and broad shoulders always made me think of a teddy bear. (His hugs only supported that persona.) Marcus was a big man with a tender heart.

"Hey, Marcus. How's it going? I haven't seen you in a while. How have you been?"

Marcus lifted his metal spatula as he spoke, the sizzle in front of him sending tasty aromas into the air. "Well, if you came 'round here more often, you'd know the answer to that, young lady." His smile stretched wider, his teeth bright and beautiful. "Been datin' a fine-lookin' woman. Thinkin' this one might be the one." He turned his attention to a panini and a few burgers on his grill, most of which appeared to be vegan.

I took another bite of my turkey sandwich as I moved closer. "I know, work's been crazy. But I'm excited to hear about your love life, though." I nodded my approval. "Sounds serious."

"Oh, yeah, Jasmine makes me weak in the knees." He giggled, not taking his eyes off his grill. As he often did, Marcus had a way of adding humor to his words, in an almost rhythmic banter. "I call her *Jazzy* because she's so complex and unpredictable." His laugh that followed reached into my heart.

I just adored this man.

I laughed right along with him. "Jazzy, huh? That's too funny, Marcus. I can't wait to meet her."

"Ain't that right, Ant?" Marcus lifted his chin *and* his gaze toward our dishwasher, Anthony, who had short brown hair, a scruffy beard, and a body as skinny as a rail. Unlike Marcus, Anthony was more introverted. His clothing mostly consisted of old T-shirts and jeans that hung loose from his narrow hips. From what I'd seen, Marcus seemed to enjoy drawing him out of his shell from time to time.

"Yup" was all Anthony offered as he sprayed down a new pile of pans before placing them into the dishwasher. "Whatever you say."

"Oh, come on now, son. That's all you got to contribute? I think my Jazzy deserves more attention than *that*!"

I stepped away as Anthony's cheeks flared and the two of them began their comical kitchen back-and-forth.

Sandwich finished, and as Daniel's meeting continued on, I decided to find a comfortable seat to wait for him, which turned out to be a vacant booth toward the back of the restaurant. The cushions were thick, and I was tired. Tired from *what* exactly I wasn't sure. The location also provided a direct view of the swinging door to the kitchen. I didn't want to miss Daniel when he came out. I filled myself a cup of coffee and took a seat. The lunch crowd was thinning, so I reasoned I wasn't taking up any needed space.

The food counter was also right in front of me, but I could ignore Kendra. In fact, I preferred it that way. In my periphery, she conversed with customers at her counter, keeping her attention off me for a change.

Time passed and before long, my eyes grew heavy. Until the ringtone from my phone startled me awake. I lifted my head off the table and wiped the corner of my mouth. Since yesterday, I couldn't seem to rest enough. I considered going to the doctor about my current state of unwell-being, but I didn't even have any bruises. None that I could see, anyway. And I'd checked.

This had to be one of those stressful moments which had

thrown me off my game. I fell down a set of stairs once, producing similar mental fatigue. *Shock.* That's what it was.

"Hello?" I loaded my voice with enthusiasm that my brain struggled to produce, hoping it wasn't obvious that I had been sleeping.

"Cassie? This is Isabella. What's going on?" Her voice was gruff, which I didn't quite understand, given the fact that I'd called in sick due to an accident. "Lindsey Coleman and Brad Tanner have been waiting for you in the conference room for twenty minutes! Gregory is in there with them now." She released a tense breath.

"What?" I tried to swallow with much difficulty. "Didn't Barbara tell you I was—"

"Unless your house is on fire, I expect you to get in here pronto. This is *not* how we treat prospective clients. Frankly, I'm surprised you'd blow off an important meeting like this. Are you sick or something?" She huffed, and I imagined her gray eyes burning with ire.

That nauseous feeling returned. The tightness in my chest, closing in. I wasn't able to process. "Um, I-I."

"If you have any hope of making senior partner, you best get yourself into this office *now!*" *Click,* the phone went dead.

Why didn't you tell her what happened? At the very least, why hadn't Barbara told her? I gazed down at my capri pants and blouse with trepidation. Would this outfit suffice? I closed my eyes and tried to center myself, hoping the awful feelings from my chest and gut would subside.

At that moment, the door to the kitchen swung open, my husband appearing with an attractive woman on his arm. The woman, who I assumed was Leslie Thompson the food critic, had silky black hair pulled back into a braided bun. The black sleeveless jumpsuit she wore with a belt gathered at her tiny waist and a pair of strappy black sandals on her manicured feet enhanced her sleek figure. Another attractive woman in Daniel's world. *Great.*

The two of them strolled over to the entrance, Daniel never once noticing his wife sitting right there as he passed by. If I was hoping for an introduction, it wasn't happening. *Has he already written me out of his life?* I turned in my seat and watched them wander away.

They spoke to each other in a casual manner for another few seconds, Daniel touching Leslie's arm the way he often did with most people, men and women. This was part of his charm, which I was sure Leslie appreciated judging by the gleam in her eyes and the smile on her face.

Once she had disappeared out the door, Daniel rushed over to Kendra to tell her the news, a thumbs-up signaling their meeting was a success.

Kendra smiled with delight. Did she mention to Daniel that I was sitting right there? Nope. It was as if she enjoyed making me feel invisible.

I spoke up instead. "Daniel?"

He stopped and turned to face me, his eyes going wide. "Cassie? What are you doing here?" He rattled his head. "I mean, I'm so glad you came." He softened his tone.

Thank God. For a moment, I worried he was going to kick me out.

As I stood, he approached, placing a light kiss against my cheek. He smelled of rosemary and thyme, remnants from one of his signature soups, I surmised. His hair was still up in a bun, his chef's coat a tad soiled.

For me, he was a sight for sore eyes.

He motioned toward the door. "That was Leslie. If I'd seen you sitting here, I would have introduced you." He stood back, his eyes taking me in, his hands anchored on his hips. "Are you here for the rest of the day?" His voice sounded so hopeful. He placed his hand on my arm, ushering me toward the back. "I can't wait to tell you what she said." His gaze diverted toward the food counter. "Kendra, I'll fill you in in a minute."

"Sounds good." Once again, her smile didn't quite reach the rest of her face. "I'll be waiting."

I'm sure you will be.

Daniel's hand found the small of my back as he leaned closer to my right ear. "Listen, I didn't mean what I said earlier *or* yesterday. I was just upset. I know your job is important." He fanned one hand out. "It's the reason we have this place." He brought me into his tiny office and closed the door before he kissed me properly, my heart soaring. "I love you, Cass. And I'm grateful for everything you've done." His voice lifted even higher. "I'm so glad you're here." He gestured toward the only chair on the opposite side of his desk while I thought about Isabella's threat.

If you have any hope of making senior partner, you best get yourself into this office now!

"Have a seat and I'll tell you all about—"

"I'm sorry, Daniel, but I have to go." *And quick.* I'd already wasted too much time. All I could imagine was Isabella standing near the office elevators watching the clock, her arms crossed, and the toe box of her Manolo Blahnik's *tap-tapping* the marble floor impatiently. I had clients waiting. *Important clients.* My ticket to becoming senior partner.

It took a moment for the smile to melt from Daniel's gorgeous face. I wondered if he thought I was kidding.

"I'm so sorry, hon. Isabella just called me. Apparently, I had a meeting scheduled with that new client I'm trying to sign." I looked down and then up into his disappointed eyes. "This is the client who can help me make senior partner. And Isabella made sure she reminded me of that fact before she hung up on me."

Everything from Daniel's shoulders to his face drooped. "Can you at least stay long enough to hear what happened?"

This was killing me. "I'm so sorry. I should have gotten here sooner. I wasn't feeling well." My head filled with cotton, my stomach tilting nauseously. I clasped the doorknob in my hand. "I-I have to go."

And with that, I rushed out of his office, through the kitchen, and out of the restaurant. I glanced back one last time as Daniel came up to stand beside Kendra, both of them watching me leave.

Jesus Christ, why was this happening to me? I needed this client. I needed this promotion. Once that happened, everything would work out. I had to believe this to be true.

Chapter Six

I tried to call Daniel repeatedly on my way across town, hoping he would tell me his good news over the phone. No such luck. My calls kept going directly to voicemail.

Today, Kendra would receive his wonderful news. Lucky woman. And unfortunately, I didn't have time to stew over it. I was in too much of a hurry.

The elevator doors to the top floor of our office building *whooshed* open to reveal Isabella standing guard, just where I had imagined she'd be. Her gray eyes, the shade of an elephant's skin, dismantled me in my tracks. I took particular notice of her attention to my outfit.

"Is *that* what you're planning on wearing to a meeting with a client that could potentially bring millions to this firm?" The disgust in her voice was razor sharp.

"I-I was in an accident. I'm surprised Barbara didn't tell you. I wouldn't miss an important meeting for no reason." As I said those words, I struggled to organize my schedule in my head. It was as if I had taken stupid pills since yesterday. That Bubba truck had *literally* knocked the sense right out of me.

"I never heard anything about an accident. Barbara had to rush out of here earlier for personal reasons. I requested a temp to cover her desk until she returns." With her arms crossed over her chest, Isabella stared me down, her light-pink designer wrap dress and matching shoes doing nothing but adding to her impeccable facade, her long brown hair gleaming under the office lights. "Are you hurt? You don't look hurt." Her voice was a mixture of concern with a heavy dose of interrogation. The FBI had nothing on my boss.

I shook my head, my confidence waning. I was starting to wish I *was* hurt, so people would take me seriously. "Uh, no, I don't think so. It was just very scary—"

"If you're not hurt, we have clients waiting. *Very important clients.* And you can't wear *that*." She lowered one hand down in front of me, her upper lip, the one coated in thick pink lipstick, curling. "We have a reputation to uphold." She took a step away, beckoning me with her fingernails, also pink. The woman took coordinating her colors to another level. I wouldn't be surprised if she had a manicurist on call to match all her outfits. If that were true, that would make this *pink week*.

"Come. I have something that will work."

I followed along as though I were her minion and had no other choice. *Maybe I should drag one leg behind me and wring my hands like Igor,* I thought to myself.

We entered her opulent office, more specifically, the area beyond, where a small kitchenette, bar, bathroom, and closet awaited. The bathroom alone was larger than my entire office, everything marble and modern.

Within no time, Isabella had me dressed and primped for my meeting. The dark-maroon skirt she chose for me to wear was a tad tight in the hips, but it wasn't anywhere near as uncomfortable as the black pumps she forced onto my feet. (She didn't really *force* them onto my feet, but she wouldn't take no for an answer, either.) The heels were four inch, way too high for my comfort zone. I was a two-inch gal. I hadn't worn heels this height since Brianna's wedding. They were also half a size too large. *Too small would be worse*, I consoled myself. Thankfully, the matching blazer and white silk blouse fit just fine, her flowery perfume permeating the fabric. I was dressed for success.

I wore the outfit and made the meeting, apologizing profusely for my tardiness to my clients and Gregory, who had left quickly. In direct contrast to my stuffy outfit, Lindsey wore a loose-fitting light-blue top and white capris, Brad khaki shorts and a plaid short-sleeve button down. Nothing tailored, just comfortable. The irony wasn't lost on me.

When I told Lindsey and Brad I'd been in an accident, they lowered their guard, their eyes filled with concern.

"Are you all right?" Lindsey asked me. "Should you see a doctor?"

I explained that I was fine, just a little shaken by what had happened, which I also took a moment to tell them about. I played my sympathy card well. I had to. Things weren't exactly working in my favor. I then went on to discuss what I thought we could do for them. I asked questions about where they hoped to be in five years and used that information to bolster my services even more. I had this. We discussed problems of the past and how I would have handled certain situations versus what their previous counsel had done.

For once, I was hitting it out of the park. Our earlier meetings were more about introductions and niceties. It was time for getting down to business.

"I can assure you that I am up to the task of being your lawyer. I'll be ready for anything: compliance, contracts, taxes, intellectual property, dispute resolution—most of my disputes never even see a courtroom—business litigation, mergers and acquisitions, and anything else you need. I carry a hefty number of clients on my books, and I can put you in contact with any one of them for a reference." I had been sitting at the table looking over the company's mission statement and information, which I had seen many times before. In fact, I had it memorized. I sat back in my chair and crossed my legs. "Again, I apologize for my late arrival today."

Before I could say more, Brad waved me off. "Please, you were in an accident. The fact that you showed up at all speaks volumes." He smiled at me, his gaze also finding Isabella sitting right next to me, breathing down my neck. At least that was how it felt to me.

We all stood. "I appreciate your patience and your understanding. And when you make your final decision, I will be ready and eager to have you sign the necessary contracts. I already have them drawn up." I smiled and reached out for a handshake from both of them.

Following my lead, Isabella did the same.

Together, we strolled over to the elevators where the words *Wilson & Bates* embellished the wall, informing everyone within view who *exactly* was in charge.

"I'll schedule a dinner for next week if you're free. I'd love to bring you to one of my favorite steak houses in Richmond. People come from miles around to experience one of their award-winning steaks." I thought for a moment about whom I was speaking with. *Outdoorsy people. Naturalists.* "Unless you're vegan, in which case, I know of another place that specializes in vegan cuisine. Also excellent."

Standing in the elevator, Brad reached for the button that would carry them to the lobby, when Lindsey smiled. "I could go for a good steak. I haven't had beef in the better part of a year. My wife has been trying to lose weight and get off her blood pressure meds, and she's convinced going vegan is the only answer." She rolled her eyes and raised one of her palms. "I'm so sick of kale shakes and salads. I can't even tell you." She shook her head, her upper lip curling.

Brad nudged her with his elbow. "Ooooh, you're gonna cheat on that diet Erika has you on?" He giggled with a comfort only friends would share. "You'll have to pay me for my silence."

Lindsey pointed directly at his face. "You better not tell." Her gaze found me and Isabella next as she wagged that same finger. "You two, either." She half smirked.

Using my forefinger and thumb, I sealed my lips shut with an invisible zipper. "My lips are sealed. And I promise you the steaks they serve will melt in your mouth. You won't even need a knife. That's their specialty. That and seafood."

"I may just have to come along for that one." Isabella inhaled, placing her hands on her abdomen as though she needed to suck in her gut. "We can't diet all the time, now can we?"

Give me a break. The woman had porcelain skin and a perfect body. She even had an exercise bike tucked away in her en suite for those long days when she couldn't get to the gym. She could afford a steak now and then. Or maybe to pull the stick out of her ass!

With that, the doors swung closed, and our meeting had concluded. I followed Isabella into her office, peeling off to use her bathroom to change. When I was back in my regular clothes, I found her waiting for me. She wasn't sitting behind her enormous desk as she normally was. This time, she was seated on her cream-colored sofa, a glass side table positioned on each corner hoisting modern lamps with a swirly design, both turned off to allow the sun beaming through the wall of windows to do its job and brighten the room. Recessed lighting bolstered its efforts. Outside, Richmond, Virginia's skyline painted a perfect portrait of corporate America, and what could be achieved if you struck career gold.

Layered over marble flooring, the same color and style that matched the bathroom, wool area rugs spanned throughout the room offering comfort and style. The interior walls separating Isabella's (and Gregory's) corner offices from the hallway and reception were made of thick glass, frosted to provide privacy and aesthetics. The walls separating the offices themselves were mostly honey maple, a perfect backdrop for their expensive artwork.

In comparison, *my* office looked like a storage closet for filing cabinets and bankers boxes. It didn't even come with a window. I was lucky, though, I *had* an office, unlike my junior-associate counterparts, who had to work in the common areas with cubicles and half walls.

Signing my last client had provided me an upgrade. I was hoping signing Into the Open would do the same.

"I hung your clothes on the hangers in your closet and put the shoes back in the box. They're right under the skirt. You can't miss them. Thank you for loaning me the outfit." I started to head for the door when her words reached out and stopped me.

"Got a sec? I'd like to speak with you for a few minutes." Sitting with her arms spread wide over the back of her sofa in true diva form, her legs crossed, Isabella smiled.

It was hard to tell what her smile meant. Was she about to promote, console, or fire me? It was anyone's guess. I was sure her poker face helped immensely in the courtroom.

On timid feet, I found a seat in one of two cushioned chairs across from her, my legs crossing and then uncrossing. *Stop fidgeting.*

"Would you like a drink?" Isabella sat forward.

"No, I'm good. But thanks."

She sat back again. "I wanted to apologize for my behavior earlier. Barbara must've forgotten to tell anyone about your accident. Her brother had just suffered a stroke, so she was distracted."

Now it was my turn to sit forward, a wave of sadness weighing heavily on my heart. "Oh no. I hope he'll be okay. Does he live nearby?" Where Isabella and Gregory kept a stoic demeanor, never revealing one emotion or another, and if they did, watch out—and where most of the junior associates walked around with their heads down, hoping to avoid reprimand for one reason or another, Barbara was the exception.

Pushing her early-seventies, she'd buried George, the love of her life, three years prior (heart attack), with no intention of replacing him. She'd raised four children (one boy and three girls), had six grandkids, and was settled into her life. Barbara wasn't a lawyer, nor did she aspire to be one. She'd worked all of her life. She'd also saved every penny, adding to George's modest life insurance and pension (he was a lineman for the local power company). I knew this because she'd told me when we'd visited at this holiday party or that, or I'd taken her out to lunch, which I tried to do at least a few times a year.

I don't have the time or the patience to worry like you youngsters do, she'd told me. *I say, 'If you don't like my way, then fire me.'* She made that message perfectly clear years ago. She was also the warmest individual I had ever met, always thinking of others. Barbara worked at the local food bank whenever she could, delivered meals to senior citizens with what little free time she had, and provided a warm shoulder whenever one of us was about to lose their shit from the long hours or daunting demands of the job.

"No, her brother lives in Texas." Isabella distracted me from my thoughts. "I believe she was going try to get the first flight out of here. I told her to take all the time she needs."

And I was sure Isabella meant what she said.

From years of dedicated labor, Barbara had earned her status in the firm, and no one questioned or disrespected her as a result. I'd even seen Isabella lower her shield around Barbara in a way that our senior partners reserved for a select few.

Curly gray hair, a few extra pounds around her midsection, and a winning smile that could melt the frostiest of hearts, Barbara was our bona fide office mother. And we were lucky to have her.

"Of course. If there is anything I can do, please let me know. I can help at the front desk if you need me to."

Isabella waved me off. "We have temps for that, and if we need to hire one for a longer period, Jeffrey will handle it."

Jeffrey was the office manager, whose bright red hair and pale complexion resembled that of a tall leprechaun, although he had no connection to Ireland that I was aware of.

Isabella cleared her throat. "Anyway, I wanted to apologize for my stern behavior when you arrived. I was in a car accident when I was a teenager, and it can shake a person up. I didn't get my driver's license until I was *twenty* for that reason." Her gray eyes softened, something I hadn't seen often in the seven-and-a-half years I'd been working there.

"I appreciate that." I ran my palms over my thighs, wiping the tackiness onto the fabric of my capris. "It was quite jarring."

"Yes, it sounded it."

That's right. She was there when I told Lindsey and Brad about what had happened.

"It's too bad you didn't get the license plate number. We could have pressed charges."

Lindsey had asked me about that as well. "I know. I'm kicking myself over it." I sighed. "If I ever run into him again, I'll be ready."

"Yes, quite." She paused. "The Medical Director at Saint

Mary's is a close personal friend. If you'd like, I can get someone to give you a proper examination."

I shook my head. "That's okay. I'm fine. Just shaken up." I'd had a few moments of discomfort, but I chalked them up to shock, stress, or anxiety, all of which I had experienced before, just not quite this severe.

Isabella exhaled, as though to reset herself. She changed her tone. "Okay, then. I am sure you are well aware how important signing this client is." She didn't wait for a response. "And they seem to like working with *you*. I am also aware that you are hoping to make senior partner."

My left leg jittered as she spoke, my nerves getting the better of me. *Calm down.*

"You know there are several junior partners vying for that spot?" This time she did wait for me to answer.

"Yes, I do know that. And I hope you will consider me. I've been here—"

"Yes, yes." She waved a noncommittal hand in my direction. "You've been here seven-and-a-half years. I know how long *everyone* has been here. And you have done great work. But all our junior partners have done great work, with the exception of a few."

Oh God, who's about to get the axe now, I wondered.

Isabella ran a hand down her silky hair as she inched toward the front of the sofa again. "I just want you to know, you are being seriously considered. You land this client and keep a good standing with your existing clients, and we'll see what we can do." She stood on her four-inch heels as though they were sneakers.

I rose. "Thank you, Isabella. I will do whatever I can to prove my worthiness."

She raised her brow up and then down with a tilt of her head. "We will see. I trust you will make up the work from earlier today? I put a stack of cases on your desk. I'd like you to look them over . . . thoroughly. They include the list of possible pro bono cases that we take on every year. It's that time again. I want you to pick out three that you feel are worthy of the firm's attention. I'd like your recommendations by the close of business tomorrow." She strolled over to her desk. "It's quite a stack. Plan on burning the midnight oil." She took a seat at her impressive black lacquer with brass accent desk and picked up the receiver of her phone. "That will be all for now."

Realizing it was my cue to leave, I headed for the door.

"Oh, and Cassie?"

I stopped and turned my head. "Yes?"

"If you change your mind about having a doctor examine you, please let me know."

"I will. Thank you." I headed out the door, trying not to slouch, but that was exactly what my posture wanted to do. I was hoping that after my meeting, I could dart back over to the restaurant and spend some time with my husband. My wants and needs were in a tug-of-war with each other, and, at times, I felt as if I were being torn in half. The look on Daniel's face when I had told him I had to leave . . . again. He went from disbelief to that same look of resignation I had come to expect. He needed me there. He wanted me there. But for how long? As appreciative as he'd been about all of my financial help, when would that well run dry? I'd done my part from a distance. And I'd supported him in every way I could. But I also knew there was a limit to how much a person would allow themselves to be shoved aside for other priorities.

Chapter Seven

As I made my way down the hallway, I thought about all of the office parties, client dinners (the ones that included spouses), and family obligations Daniel had attended with me, never once showing the least bit of resistance. (Except for that one time when he had the flu, and it couldn't be helped.) That was the problem. Even though I wanted to, I couldn't physically be there as much as he had been there for me. I'd only been able to fly out to California with him *twice* to see his family in eight years.

I dragged my feet into my pocket of an office where a large stack of manila folders confronted me. This would take some time. *Well, might as well get started.* I plunked down in my office chair and went to work. As the sun dipped below the horizon, I had only researched a few of the potential pro bono clients that Isabella and Gregory were considering. This type of research required background checks, financial records, and more. Were there any disputes with these organizations? Had they ever been accused of anything? The last thing Isabella wanted was a pro bono case with negative press attached to it. I had to find worthy causes that also had promise. No sense in backing a sinking ship.

I texted Daniel multiple times.

I'm so sorry I had to rush out. I really want to hear about your good news. Isabella slammed me with work. But she also brought up the possibility of me making senior partner. I'm close, hon. We're close. I love you.

As the hours passed, I tried again: *I know you're upset with me. And I don't blame you. Please let me know that we're okay. I love you. I do want to start a family. I just need a little more time. Please call me so we can talk.*

At midnight, I wrote: *Is this payback for my missing your texts? I didn't see them. I swear I didn't. And I didn't lie about the altercation on the road.*

By two o'clock in the morning, my eyes grew heavy. I texted yet again: *I'm still working. I may have to pull an all-nighter. You're probably in bed. Get some rest for the both of us. I'll plan to spend the weekend at the restaurant.* I paused. *If you still want me there.*

No response came back. Not one. I'd even tried calling a few times but stopped as the hour grew late. Like me, Daniel worked hard. I didn't want to wake him.

Alone in this large and desolate office building, no one around but the cleaning crew, I thought about the spectacle Isabella had made about my outfit earlier. I wondered what Andy would have done, the brilliant lawyer they had let go, citing budget cuts. We all knew the real reason for Andy's dismissal. His old clunker of a car, his informal attire, and his tight budget; none of that fit what Isabella and Gregory wanted to present to the world, more specifically their clients. When Andy took one of his clients out for a rather inexpensive dinner (if memory served, it was a chain) and the senior partners had caught wind of it, I knew his days were numbered. Too bad. He was such a nice man. As friendly and supportive as they came. Barbara loved him.

The distant hum of a vacuum cleaner whined down the hallway. I yawned and then went to grab a cup of coffee from the break room. I recalled the time I had run into Andy two years ago. By then, he'd been gone from the firm for four.

On a chilly October evening, I was walking along the sidewalk toward the nearest parking garage, ready to *finally* call it a day (or a night in my case). Funny the details that came to mind, like how the wind blew the leaves around in circles as though on purpose, just to watch the spectacle. And how the temperature had dropped, requiring a jacket or a sweater, the days growing shorter by the hour. The streetlights glowed, office windows shining from within. It all came back.

Daniel's Garden Patch was just about to open its doors. I was distracted, doing my normal juggling routine between my work and my personal life. In fact, Daniel had been so absorbed in his new business venture, the topic of parenthood had gone on sabbatical for the both of us. He was also extremely grateful for my help, both financially and otherwise. Uncharacteristically, Isabella had cut me a *tiny* bit of slack that fall (sixty-hour work weeks instead of eighty), knowing Daniel's restaurant was taking its toll on me. Nothing ever went unnoticed with her or Gregory, though, and I had to make up the time throughout the winter.

Out of nowhere, a friendly voice nudged my eardrums. "Well, aren't you a sight for sore eyes."

Distracted by my cell phone, I pulled my gaze upward, my eyes welcoming Andy and all of his jocular mannerisms. He'd gained a few pounds, his shirt trying to decide whether it wanted to be tucked in or hanging loose, his necktie slightly askew.

He hugged me immediately and then stood back to engage me in conversation.

"Hey, Andy. It's so nice to see you. How are you?" He might have been a half-made bed of a man, but he was beaming.

"You probably don't know, but Piper and I had a baby girl last year."

That explained the wide smile offset *only slightly* by the dark rings underscoring his blueish gray eyes.

I put a hand over my mouth. "That's amazing." I hugged him again. "Congratulations. I'm so happy for you." I was remiss for not keeping in touch, although Andy hadn't shown any hint that it had bothered him. Then again, he was too nice of a man to comment on such things.

"Yup." He nodded. "Piper Junior is keeping us on our toes for sure. You should see my office."

That brought up a whole new list of questions. "Where are you working now?"

He leaned into his stance, rubbing his chin, something he used to do a lot during thoughtful conversations. "Well, I opened my own firm." His cheeks flushed a tad as though he was feeling bashful about it.

My hand flew back to my gaping mouth. "Wow. That's incredible. Are you located here in the city?"

"Not exactly. I'm down in Chesterfield, but I hope to move up here in the next few years. I partnered with an old friend of mine. His name is Jim Tucker." He made a face, his head teetering back and forth subtly. "I've always called him Jimmy. I met him when we started our own chess club back in college." He reached into the back pocket of his pants and pulled out his brown wallet, the leather worn and pliable. From there, he handed me a business card, the words Livingston & Tucker scrolled across the front. The letters L and T were larger and embossed, the etching of a Greek column centered above the heading at the top of the card. Phone numbers, a website address, and an actual address for the office ran along the bottom, and the paper's stock was heavy. Classy came to mind.

Once he put his wallet away, he showed me several adorable pictures on his phone of Piper Junior. Puffy cheeks, fluffy curls, her hair the color of corn silk—I could see where his smile came from. His wife, Piper, a carbon copy of her daughter *only older*, posed in several, her eyes glowing with motherly joy.

"I'm so happy for you. Wow. A family *and* your own firm." And I *was* happy for him. A tad jealous too. At the time, I was working like a crazy person. When wasn't I?

"Thank you. Yeah, I've only got a few clients so far, some with low budgets. Piper's father owns the building we're leasing. He's allowing us to rent the upper floor to live in for now. Hoping to buy a house soon."

Boy, did that sound familiar. "Daniel and I hope to get a house someday soon as well." It was wishful thinking even then. The restaurant had already gobbled up most of our savings.

"How is Daniel? Still making those delicious sticky buns?"

I was already nodding. "Oh, yeah. He'll always make those. Everyone loves them, including me." I took a breath. "I have some news myself."

Andy quirked a brow. "Don't tell me you have a little one on the way as well? I can just envision our playdates now." He chuckled, his gaze finding my abdomen as though he couldn't help himself.

Is he looking for a bump? I had thought.

"I'll bring the bourbon. I always knew you two would start a family."

I shook my head and forced a smirk to hide my inner

struggle with this issue. "No, no. But we *are* about to open Daniel's new restaurant in Carytown." *Daniel's baby.*

Andy's eyes sparkled, his enthusiasm brightening to a whole new level. "That's tremendous. Daniel's an excellent chef."

Back before Daniel's Garden Patch had become a reality, my husband had concocted all sorts of yummy recipes, which he had sent in with me to work to stock our break room. Even Isabella and Gregory had tried a morsel or two. Mrs. Dunbar was also the recipient of those goodies, which might have had a hand in her willingness to help us. At Christmastime, we gave her baskets full of muffins, sticky buns, wine, and several soups to freeze for later.

"You'll have to bring the family and come by. We'll treat you to lunch or dinner."

"You can count on it." Andy fanned his hands out. "Look at us." He shook his head as if in disbelief. "I've got a baby and my own firm. You've got a new restaurant. I imagine it's not easy carrying your job at the firm *and* the restaurant on your shoulders." Brows arched, he made a face, his eyes going wide. "I know how demanding Isabella and Gregory can be." He stared off for a moment. "You know, my workspace is small and looks more like a daycare than a lawyer's office, but it's ours and we're happy." He gave me a light nudge with his elbow. "Maybe someday you can come work for me. I've always thought you were one of the sharpest litigators at the firm."

That was high praise coming from someone who I had placed in the category of brilliant.

He smiled. "Our casual Friday goes all week long. And you can bring your kids to work if you need to." He pursed his lips and wagged a finger. "When that day comes."

It all sounded great. But I wasn't willing to move or take a major cut in my salary. I just smiled and appreciated the flattering remark for what it was. "That is so nice of you. I'm good, but thanks." I placed my hand on his upper arm. "Give my best to Piper, and kiss that baby from me." I took a step away.

He pointed with a friendly finger. "If you change your mind, don't hesitate to call. You won't even need to interview. The job is yours." Before long, he was gone, down the sidewalk and out of sight.

All these years later, I often wondered if I had made the right decision to stay where I was. What would my life be like if I had made such a drastic change back then? Would Mrs. Dunbar have come with me? Or my other clients? Wilson & Bates had a solid reputation. A new firm in the small town of Chesterfield didn't.

And what would our finances look like? Would Daniel and I be struggling to make ends meet even more than we were now? Our savings account wasn't large, but we had what we needed. I'd made sure of it.

During marathon workweeks or moments of despair I'd looked Andy up on the internet. From what I could ascertain, he and Jimmy were doing just fine. And I wouldn't be surprised if Piper Junior had a sibling by now.

With a hot coffee in hand, I returned to my office, sat at my desk, and sighed, not a soul in sight. Everyone was home sleeping in their beds. Even the senior partners were gone. I was alone, the decisions of my past left behind to torment me.

I was often faced with critical junctures such as this one. And Andy wasn't the only one who had offered me employment. What did I do about it? I let a good education and a reliable paycheck guide me through, ensuring a stable future for both Daniel and me. And I was able to offer him his dream from the fruits of my labor. But what about *my* dream? Didn't that matter anymore? If I surrendered myself, would Daniel's hopes and aspirations consume me? Would I later resent him for making me choose?

I loved Daniel with all of my heart. And I had never asked him to change. I had only asked him to wait. To allow me time before I gave up the only thing I knew how to do well. Surely, I'd still be a lawyer, even after parenthood, but how much of me would be left for that type of thing? Kids required a lot of attention and energy. You weren't just a parent for any given period of time. The job lasted forever. Some would say it was the most important job in the world.

My thoughts returned to the moments we had discussed children over the years. It mostly came up after we'd made love. What better time to discuss babies, right?

There was this one time as we lay in each other's arms, both of us sweaty and satisfied, when Daniel had kissed my forehead before he'd smiled at me, his fingers brushing a few strands of my auburn hair away from my face. "You are so gorgeous. You know that? To this day, I have never seen eyes as green as yours." He kissed the end of my nose. "I'm a prisoner of those eyes. A willing prisoner." A small smile spread across his beautiful face. "They are the eyes that see all."

I had gotten all flustered at the time. I wasn't comfortable receiving compliments, especially ones this big. My go-to had always been to shrug it off. This time, I wanted to hear more about what this hottie of a man saw in me. "What makes you think that?"

"I could tell right away you were a person who paid a lot more attention than people realized." He ran a finger down my cheek, his chestnut eyes causing my heart to beam. "You are extremely observant. Not a lot gets by you. It's one of many things I love about you." He paused, his eyes filled with reflection. "Remember that time you noticed the little boy wandering on the beach? No one around seemed to notice him. *I* didn't even notice him. Mainly because it was crowded and families were everywhere. But *you* noticed that something wasn't right."

The time he was referring to happened several summers ago when we went to Virginia Beach for the day. An adorable little boy had caught my eye, more importantly, how none of the adults around him seemed to pay him any notice. Everyone was basking in the sun, making sandcastles, throwing a Frisbee or a ball, or visiting. Amid the bustle, the boy just kept walking around aimlessly, undetected. He was too young to be alone.

Approaching him in a very non-threatening manner, I had asked him where his parents were. He wasn't even old enough to speak clearly. All he could do was stand there, his eyes filled with confusion, *Momma?* escaping from his young lips.

Daniel continued. "Before long, you'd called the lifeguard over, had the boy in her custody, and had a search underway for his parents, who we found an hour later. I can't imagine how that boy had wandered off without anyone noticing." Daniel shook his head. "Man, if you hadn't intervened, who knows what could have happened to him." He paused again. "And remember when you kept saying you noticed a sulfur smell near our last apartment? Again, no one noticed it, including me. But you wouldn't let it go and got the gas company out there to inspect the area until they located a leak." His eyes grew wide. "If you hadn't noticed or been so diligent about it, the place could have blown up. I've seen it happen on the news many times. And it was you who found the space for the restaurant."

I sat up to face him. "No, that was Mrs. Dunbar, remember? *She* found it."

Daniel was already shaking his head as he also sat up. "You're not remembering it correctly. *You* found the space, and then she helped us get it. You found the location and the potential. You also found a few mistakes in the closing contract and made them correct them before we signed. And in case you forgot this, too, the reason Mrs. Dunbar was so eager to help us was because you had noticed some wording in her divorce decree that didn't look right, the papers her previous lawyer had drawn up. You saved that woman thousands."

My memory might have been a tad askew, but my inquisitive mind never stopped. Sitting idle wasn't in my wheelhouse. Giving me a problem to solve was like giving candy to a baby. My brain just ate it right up. Except for when it came to Daniel. He was a puzzle that I hadn't solved. *Why me?* And I'd been working on that question for eight years. When we met it was as if the Universe was pulling us together. I felt as if I had already known him. And even though I always felt he was out of my league, I couldn't deny the chemistry between us. I had never dated, much less imagined marrying a man like him.

What was the pull for *him?* Why had he always been patient with me, all those times I had stood him up? Did he want my money? Nah. I sensed that if I hadn't pushed the restaurant issue, he'd still be working for Josh and happy to be doing what he loved: creating.

I leaned over and kissed his luscious lips. "Don't be so modest, husband of mine. The reason Mrs. Dunbar was so eager to help us was because she had a major crush on *you*."

His eyes said he wasn't convinced. "Nah, she's just a big flirt. It was you and that sharp mind of yours. It's a steel trap. I sensed that about you from the moment we met."

"How? How could you have known that?"

Daniel wiggled his head subtly. "I'm not sure. I guess the way you watched me work at the wedding reception. You seemed so curious about what I was doing." His eyes twinkled. "You may have been flirting with me, but I also sensed you were interested." He lifted his brow. "And let's face it, most women weren't all that enamored with baked ham or London broil *or* how I sliced it." A smirk played on his lips.

I didn't have the heart to tell him that my curiosity on that day *was* geared more toward him than his food. My low blood sugar might have played a hand in the other stuff, but I chose not to admit anything. Why ruin his image of me?

The conversation turned.

"Given that intelligent mind of yours, I've always wondered what kind of daughter you'd have. You'd be a great mom, you know." His eyes glazed over. "Can't you just see a couple of little ones running around?"

As I sat before him, he took my hand in his. "Our daughter would have your auburn hair, and our son, your commanding green eyes." His voice softened. "They'd be beautiful and smart, just like their mother."

Once again bashful, I had *tsked*. "Let's hope they get both of our smarts but *your* looks." I mean, was he kidding? Even though he always made me feel beautiful and special all at once, did he ever look in the mirror?

It was too late to convince him otherwise. He'd already leapt onto the parent train which had left the station, all of its possibilities packed on board with him. "We'd make kick-ass parents, you and me. And I won't be one of those dead-beat dads, either. You can expect hands-on services from me. Diapers, feedings, and driving them to soccer practice, I'm all in, Cass."

And as I thought about all of this now, I reminded myself once again how much Daniel embraced life. Whether it be his customers at the restaurant or our future children, the man wanted to spread his love as far as his beautiful hands could reach. How lucky his children would be to have a father like him.

I saw my contribution a bit differently. Making enough money to set us up for life was what mattered to me most. Not entirely, though; my husband owned a good portion of my heart, and I couldn't imagine my life without him. If Daniel forced me to make a choice, it would be him. I just hoped it wouldn't come to that.

I'd always known Daniel was a better person than I was. Or I just chose to believe that to be true. I had never been a particularly confident person. I was smart. I was driven. And I was a good daughter. As a wife, I wanted to believe I was good at that too. But was I?

His words from yesterday crashed into me. *I don't know if I can do this much longer.*

A nauseous feeling settled into my gut, not as bad as before, but not good, either. I took a sip of my coffee, nearly gagging. As I set the coffee down, something occurred to me out of the blue: *Could I be pregnant?*

Chapter Eight

As the morning sun crept over the skyline, bringing definition to my office, I awoke. For a moment, I forgot where I was. I lifted my head, a sheet of paper stuck to the side of my face. *Ew.* I ripped it away, my mouth parched with dried coffee and long hours of little hydration. In my desk drawer, I found a compact mirror to examine my face and hair. The Bride of Frankenstein came to mind. I looked at the stack of folders beside me, most of them vetted but not all. My eyes couldn't help but glare at the stack as though the workload itself was trying to ruin my life.

The quiet that loomed sent a message that no one had arrived yet, the hour just past six-thirty. I took advantage of the privacy. I grabbed my toiletry bag from the bottom drawer of my desk, the one stocked with a small container of liquid soap, toothpaste with brush, and a few other essentials that I'd often need when pulling all-nighters. The firm's policy didn't allow us to bring in clothes, unless absolutely necessary, and even then, we had to be discreet. Isabella and Gregory were the exception. They always were.

I headed for the newly cleaned bathroom, where I washed my face and armpits, then brushed my teeth and straightened my hair. By the time I returned to my office, I contemplated whether or not I should forge forward and get this pro bono shit done or go home and change. If Isabella saw me like this, would it be yet another strike against my chances of making senior partner? I decided that it would and made tracks out the door (or the elevator in my case).

Outside, the August temperature was already climbing, the wind still, and the humidity strapping the air with moisture. And that was without a strong sun to influence, which wasn't quite full yet, its distance far away on the horizon. I suspected we were in for another scorcher.

A garbage truck rushed past, a rancid aroma lagging behind it, a few cars on the road, the drivers making an early start to their day. I passed a man outside of a flower shop, its lights still off as he washed down the sidewalk with a hose. "Good morning, miss," he said with a smile.

"Mornin'," I said, returning pleasantries.

I jogged up the concrete steps to my parking deck, my head feeling light from the exertion. On level two, I found my BMW and plunked into the drivers' seat, the smell of fresh leather and *new car* welcoming my senses to familiar quarters. I needed a minute. Not only was my head struggling to stay grounded, but my stomach was both queasy and hollow. It was then that I remembered this same feeling from the night before, more precisely the question that had resulted from my condition: *Am I pregnant?*

Since the almost accident, I couldn't remember if I had taken my birth control pills. How many days had it been? *Two, if memory serves.* Not that long, but also not smart when missing one day of the Pill could encourage unreliable results. I shook my head. What was I thinking? If I were in fact pregnant, it would have happened long before now. The last two days would have had little effect on this moment.

Another option broached my thought process: Could it be PMS? I did suffer from various ailments just before that certain week on the calendar approached. There were too many possibilities.

I started my car and tried not to worry that I was going bonkers. Everything felt surreal lately, as though I was walking through a dream. Isabella had offered to contact her friend at Saint Mary's hospital. I wasn't going to take her up on that offer. The less Isabella knew about my personal life the better. If I was pregnant, that would be a career killer for sure. But as I drove out of the parking garage and made my way east toward our dingy apartment, I did consider going to *my* doctor. I'd have to see how quickly she could schedule me in. With that thought in mind, I made a mental note to call when they opened at eight. I'd tell her about the near accident and everything that had been going on with me since. Hopefully, she'd have some words of wisdom, and a definite answer to my stomach issues. Although, if I were being honest with myself, it wasn't just my gut in turmoil. Every now and then, a strong, pungent odor rose up out of nowhere, bothering my nostrils. Adding to it, a tight feeling across my chest. What was that all about? *Bruises from the seatbelt?* But my skin remained unmarred. At times, the pain nearly took my breath away. I chalked it up to anxiety again, which might very well be the cause.

When I'd first become a lawyer, I'd suffered a few anxiety attacks. Even though I was always prepared when I entered a courtroom or a conference room, for that matter, I'd never been a fan of public speaking. The jitters upsetting my system back then were different from what I was experiencing now. Then again, I was mid-thirties now. My body wasn't as young as it once was. In the spring, I had my annual exam and physical.

Thanks to my husband and his healthy lifestyle, my bloodwork was good, my vital signs right where they should be. That told me whatever I was experiencing was new, which hopefully meant temporary *and* not serious.

Twenty minutes passed before I was exiting Interstate 64 and heading toward home, both eager to see Daniel *and* heedful. I wasn't sure he would be there. Since he hadn't replied to any of my texts, it was anyone's guess. That type of behavior wasn't like him. I realized that I only knew the version of Daniel who was in love with me. The attentive man who was committed to us and our future together. I had no idea what he'd be like as an ex. And I didn't want to find out.

I passed by the shortcut that would bring me home, often ten minutes earlier—depending on traffic and stoplights—but I refused to take it. After what had happened with the Bubba truck, I would probably never take that road again. I drove along, my satellite radio playing soft rock through the car's speakers, my nerves doing their very best to settle.

Should I tell Daniel I could possibly be pregnant? No. It would be better to wait. Why get his hopes up when I had nothing to go by, other than a sour stomach and some strange symptoms. My cycle wasn't even due for a few days yet. I had to ask myself how *I* would feel if a baby were now growing inside of my uterus. The notion conflicted me even more. It came down to stability and finances for me. And that damn apartment, not big enough to change your mind inside of, much less a baby's diaper.

Stained by streaks of black mold, the roof of our apartment building rose up in the distance, two thick oaks standing guard by the entrance to our small parking lot covered in gravel. Soon after, four mailboxes appeared, each one lined up in a row. I took several stabilizing breaths to prepare. Everything would be okay. It had to be.

As I rolled my tires into the modest-sized parking lot, the sound of crushed gravel reached my ears. And there sat Daniel's Subaru wagon waiting vacant. On the other side of Daniel's car, our neighbor, Brandy's pale-yellow Volkswagen Beetle kept his car company. She lived below us. The other side of the parking lot housed the cars for a young couple who lived on the first floor next door and the middle-aged man who occupied the upstairs, a recluse who rarely showed his face.

I shifted the car into park, cut the engine, and climbed out, my gaze zeroing in on the windows peering down at me from our second-floor unit. Who *wasn't* staring down at me was Daniel. By now, it was just past seven, so he might have been sleeping. *But he is always up with the chickens, making his morning treats.* God, I hoped this wasn't going to be ugly.

Trepidation dragged my feet up every step, my mouth running dry and my stomach doing flips again. *Not now.* I inserted my key into the lock and opened the door, my nose picking up the nutty aroma of coffee. No scents of baked goods flourished in the air of our tiny kitchen. *Unusual.* Daniel always started his day with something baked and sweet from the oven. In fact, I asked him once why he did this. *You have a full commercial kitchen, why do you bake stuff here?* He'd smiled at me. *I stop off at the food bank on my way into work. The volunteers there love my morning treats.* And that was when I learned my husband was a saint. Only today, the oven sat cold and vacant. Was my saint out of order?

"Hello?" I entered what felt like the lion's den and looked around.

The coffee pot sat full, and Daniel's chef's coat hung over a chair situated at our bistro set.

All at once, Daniel entered the room. "I was just about to call you. I guess you worked all night?" Dark circles under his eyes told me he hadn't slept well, either.

I hung my car keys on the hook by the door, slipped off my shoes, and crossed the room where I placed my purse on the bistro table. "Yeah, didn't you get my text messages?" I struggled to make eye contact, which was silly. I hadn't done anything wrong. I *had* to work. Isabella hadn't given me much choice.

When Daniel didn't answer, I forced my gaze upward, meeting his beautiful eyes. "Daniel?" My lower lip started to quiver. I bit down to stop the tremor from spreading. Was this it? Would he tell me he was leaving me for good? I braced myself.

He just stood there for what felt like an eternity, staring through me.

I wasn't able to move, my nerves frayed, as a thick layer of silence spread throughout the room.

Finally, my husband shook himself out of whatever thought process was going on inside of his head. "I did. Sorry. I should have responded. I also had to work late. We had a plumbing leak in the kitchen that made a hell of a mess. I had to close the restaurant early." He rubbed his eyes and exhaled, his jawline shadowed by scruff. "I didn't actually get home until after midnight. Luckily, Marcus had some plumbing experience and was able to stop the leak before it flooded the entire restaurant. I called a plumber who is meeting me over there at ten. I'll have to keep the restaurant closed until he can fix it. Do you remember when they installed the sink and dishwasher? They said they had to do some jerry-rigging with the plumbing connections?"

I nodded.

"Well, that's where it's leaking."

I exhaled heavily, relieved that at least there was a legitimate reason why he hadn't gotten back to me. "I'm sorry to hear that. I'm glad Marcus was there to help. Do you want me to . . . ?" My words trailed off.

"What? Do I want you to . . . what? Help?" His mouth hardened. "You can't even spend more than a few minutes there; how are you supposed to help?" He ran a hand over the top of his head. "I'm sorry. I'm just . . . frustrated."

I'm sorry, Daniel. I wanted to say those words, but I couldn't. I was sick and tired of being sorry. I was sick and tired of working my ass off so he could live his dream. Mostly, I was sick and tired of being treated like a lying, unsupportive spouse. My stomach rumbled. My head filled with what felt like helium. Maybe if I ate something. I took a step before everything went black.

"Cassie, wake up! Cassie, *please* wake up!"

I forced my eyelids open, finding Daniel kneeling over me. I regained full consciousness, my gaze darting around our kitchen. I was on the floor, my head cradled in Daniel's hands.

"Jesus, Cassie. Are you all right?" He handed me a small glass of water. "Here, drink this."

With a shaky hand, I lifted the glass to my lips, the cool water refreshing against my mouth and tongue. I sat up, allowing Daniel to release his grip on me. "What happened?"

"You fainted. I've never seen you faint before." His voice was frantic. "When was the last time you ate something? You can't just work all night and not eat, Cass. Your blood sugar must be rock bottom right now." With strong arms, he helped me up, guiding me over to our loveseat in the living room. (The space was too compact for a full-size couch.) Once I was seated with my glass of water clutched close, Daniel darted into the kitchen. He returned a moment later with a bowl of yogurt in his hands, sliced banana piled on top. "Here, have a few bites. It will make you feel better."

I did as he asked, the peach-flavored yogurt mixed with

banana doing a nice job of replenishing my energy, their fruity aromas equally welcoming to my senses. When I was finished, I placed the bowl on the coffee table my parents had given us when we had moved in. It was old and covered in dings, but it sufficed.

I placed a hand over my forehead. "What time is it?"

Daniel looked around, his eyes dumbfounded. "I don't know. Seven . . . ish?"

I moved to the edge of the loveseat. "I need to get back to work."

His long, wavy hair pulled back into a ponytail, Daniel placed both hands against his head in exasperation. "No fucking way are you rushing back to work." He glared at me, his eyes filled with outrage and fear. "Are you trying to kill yourself?"

Tears threatened to spill, my throat thick with anguish. "But Isabella—"

"I don't give a flying fuck what Isabella told you or wants." He grabbed my shoulders as though to jar me. "Look, I love you, but I refuse to watch you kill yourself for that place. You've given them seven-and-a-half years of your life. And what have they done to show their appreciation? Your office is a closet. You're still working around the clock. And all they can do is dangle senior partner in front of your face, so you'll keep busting your ass for them." He tightened his jaw, his eyes glassing over as emotion battled against his anger.

I could see it. He cared so much it hurt.

I dropped my face into my hands. "I don't know what to do. I need to finish this job for her. After that, I can come help you." I felt like a child and about as powerless as one. "Please, Daniel. I need to make senior partner. Then everything will be good again. I can take care of us."

He released his grip on me, his forearms rested on his thighs. "Cassie. It's not your responsibility to take care of us. We can do that together. Why do you put this solely on your shoulders? Don't you see? Life is passing you by. When are you going to wake up? How long are you gonna wait for that promotion that may never come? They announced the partnership a year ago. It's bullshit." He wrapped his arms around my shoulders, pulling me close.

And that was when I lost it. Tears ran down my cheeks as though the dam had broken. And it had. I wept for this trap of an existence I had confined myself to. I wept for the constant struggle that refused to relent. And I wept for the uncertainty of what was to come.

My intentions were pure. I only wanted what was best for both of us.

My mother's voice rang in my ears. "You are the only one of us, Cassie-boo, who finished college. And we never thought we'd have a lawyer for a daughter. Your father and I are so proud of you." Her eyes, a paler shade of green than mine, grew distant. "I wish I had . . ." Pursing her lips, she stopped herself from revealing something that had obviously weighed heavily on her heart. Suddenly, she reset herself, her shoulders back and her resolve strong. "Promise me you will never compromise your principals or your ambition for anyone. You deserve to follow your dreams. All the way to the end of that rainbow." She had pulled me into her embrace, the scent of rose petals lingering on her skin from her perfume. "Just remember. No one can make your dreams come true but you." It was the only time she'd ever said this to me. And it was the only time she had to.

Oh, Mom. Why does everything have to be so hard? I really needed her in that moment. But she and my father were away, out west, visiting my Aunt Alice. A phone call could help, but I longed for her shoulder and her wisdom. I thought about my big sis, Trina.

As though he could sense my vulnerability, Daniel hugged me closer. "Don't cry, Cass." He leaned his head against mine while I sobbed. "It's gonna be okay. I think you should consider looking for another place to work. A firm less demanding. I would never tell you to stop being a lawyer. That would be like you telling me to stop being a chef. It's our passion, but it's also what we do. Not who we are."

I thought about Andy and his offer, which I hadn't told Daniel about, knowing he would have probably tried to force me to take the job. What arguments would that have caused?

"You are the smartest person I know. And I have to believe there are smaller firms out there that would love nothing more than to have someone as sharp as you on their team." He kissed the side of my head. "Let me get you a tissue." He sprang from the loveseat once more, returning with a box of tissues in record time.

I pulled one from the box, then two, wiping my cheeks and eyes. I finally sputtered out what I wanted to say, hoping my husband would hear me. "You don't understand, Daniel, if I started at a new firm, they'd expect more out of me. I'd have to prove myself. It would be like starting over." It was true. Probably not at Andy's firm, but at most. I'd rubbed elbows with enough colleagues to hear their stories. Newbies rode the low end of the totem pole.

"Then leave and start your own firm."

I chuckled through my despair, my voice lacking any humor. "That takes money. A lot of money. And we don't have it."

Daniel seemed to ponder this. "Then we'll sell the restaurant." A shadow passed over his face before his eyes regained focus. "I mean it. We'll sell. We can open another restaurant later on."

I couldn't believe my ears. "You can't do that. You're just starting to make a profit. It's taken you two years to build your regulars and find good help. This is your dream." Guilt and an abundance of love filled my chest.

"*You're* my dream." He touched the area over my heart, before returning his palm to the same spot on *his* chest. "What you and I have is my dream. Having a family with you is my dream. The rest will work itself out."

Wow. A feather could have knocked me over. All this time, I had assumed Daniel was just as driven as I was, chasing his dream and trying to find that pot of gold at the end of his rainbow. But what he'd just proven to me was that he wasn't. His restaurant wasn't his pot of gold—*I was*. For the first time in a very long while, my heart opened like a flower against the sun. I was inspired, flattered, and more in love than ever. I had everything I needed. I didn't need more. *The rest will work itself out* made perfect sense now.

My tears dried, my lungs returning to normal as I sat there admiring this man. As he pointed out, being a lawyer was my job. It wasn't who I was. And what good was being a successful lawyer if I had nothing to show for it? No family. No happiness. Work was supposed to support our lives, not the other way around.

The clouds had cleared inside the caverns of my mind and things were starting to make sense. I rested my head against Daniel's shoulder. "Okay."

It was as if a bolt of electricity had funneled through my husband, his eyes lit up with excitement. "Really? You *finally* agree?" He brushed a few strands of hair away from my face.

I nodded, a smile rising up from the roots of my despair. "I do. I'll start looking right away. And I'll also do research into starting my own firm." That would take years, but a dream had to begin somewhere.

He inched his head back and arched a brow. "You're not just telling me what I want to hear are you?" He waited with what seemed like bated breath.

I cradled his scruffy chin in my hands. And then I kissed him. "No, I'm not just telling you what you want to hear. I'm all in."

This time Daniel kissed me back, his arms coiling around my body. I almost felt trapped. *Not quite.* In truth, I was loving every second of his hug. We'd built a bridge between his world and mine, and I never wanted that connection to crack again.

For the next several minutes we continued our make out session, my husband's hands running through my hair, his tongue roaming inside of my mouth with passion and a sense of relief. We'd taken the gloves off. We'd opened our hearts. And we'd come together, more in love than ever before.

As the minutes passed, I began to wonder, *Are we going to make love?* Daniel's lips waltzed down my neck and over my chin, before returning to my mouth. "I love you so much. We got each other's back. And I never want that to change." He pulled himself away as though it was torture for him to do so. "I hate to stop this. Right now, all I want to do is make love to you." He released a pent-up breath. "But I've got that plumber coming." His gaze roamed the room for the clock on the wall.

Reality set in. "That's okay. I have to go too." I raised a palm before my husband was able to distrust my words or my motives. "I am all in. But this isn't going to happen overnight. I need to get this project done for Isabella and check in with my clients. Mrs. Dunbar is coming in this afternoon to discuss a possible business venture she's looking into." I ran my schedule through my mind. "I need a good reference, right? *And* my clients to come with me, wherever that is."

Daniel nodded.

"And don't sell anything just yet. Let me see what I can do on my end first. If I can find a good firm, it's possible my years of experience will help get me in the door and bolster my status as a new hire. Especially if I bring a respectable roster of clients with me. I know of a few with a good reputation for keeping morale up." Once again, I withheld Andy's offer. Mainly because Andy and I had spoken two years prior. A lot could have changed since then.

Just like with the possibility of me being pregnant, there was no need to get my husband's hopes up unnecessarily.

A warm hand cupped the side of my face, the most loving lips on the planet offering another appetizing kiss. "I trust you. And I agree. We can't be hasty here. If this is going to work, we need to do this right." A delighted grin beamed from my husband's face. "I can't tell you how happy this makes me, Cass. I feel like everything is changed, and we have so much to look forward to now." His eyes were red, dark rings to boot, but I'd never seen this man happier.

I rose from the loveseat and made my way toward the bathroom, forming in my mind a plan for my next course of action. There was a lot for me to think about: a new job and a possible pregnancy.

I turned on the shower, jumped in, and let the water replenish my tired skin.

Before he left, Daniel peered into the bathroom as I stood at the mirror, a fresh towel wrapped around my body, which was now all clean and smelling fresh. "You still feeling better?"

I nodded.

"Okay. Good luck today. I'll keep you posted about the water leak." He blew me a kiss before he went out the door. "Love you, wife of mine."

Tricia T. LaRochelle

The first thing I did after I got dressed was look up my doctor's phone number.

Chapter Nine

Dressed in a black knit three-quarter-length sleeve dress, two-inch heels on my feet, also black, and my hair and makeup as good as it gets, I drove back toward Richmond. It was nine-fifteen, but I was okay with that. *Most* lawyers didn't start work earlier than nine-thirty or ten. Mainly because we often worked so damn late. I normally came in earlier than the general crowd, hoping to get a jump on the day.

Everything felt different in my world. Hopeful. I no longer believed I was being forced to give something precious up, something I had worked fucking hard to achieve. Instead, I realized I wasn't giving up anything. I'd still have a career, but, in addition to that, I'd also have a happy life. And there was nothing more important than that. Or my husband, who changed my world when he married me.

Before I returned to work and became entrenched in the tasks of the day, I called my doctor and had a strange conversation with the receptionist. "I'm afraid, Dr. Hutchinson is out on leave. She left several months ago."

"She did?" Hmm. That was odd. Hadn't I had my checkup just a few months ago? My head got all fuzzy as though a migraine was approaching. I suffered from those every now and then, mostly ocular migraines that cast blurry spots across my vision and made it difficult to concentrate and see. *Is that what is happening to me?* "When will she be back?"

"I'm afraid she's not taking any patients this year. I can get you in to see someone else if you'd like." The sound of fingers typing away on a keyboard implied the receptionist was already checking various schedules. "It says you had a physical with Dr. Hutchinson just before she left. What is it you need the appointment for?"

"Um." How to explain this. I was in an accident, but I wasn't really in an accident? Nothing happened to me, but I'm experiencing some strange symptoms? I also wanted to take a pregnancy test? In my head, I sounded insane. "Uh, let me check into some things, first, and I'll call you back. Have a nice day." I hung up feeling confused and had too many other things to process. Dr. Hutchinson had been gone for six months? The calendar didn't quite jive in my mind. Then again, I'd lost track of time before. The year we opened the restaurant was a complete whirlwind.

I decided I'd just purchase my own pregnancy test to begin with. If my symptoms were stemming from that, I'd need to know *before* I saw a doctor, right? For a woman who prided herself on making decisions, I was struggling lately. *Can pregnancy cause that too?* I remember Trina telling me being pregnant was like donating your body to science for a year. *Everything you've grown to expect physically or rely on to be true, changes. But don't worry, it changes back once the baby is born . . . mostly.* Since I had never been pregnant, I had to assume my strange symptoms could very well be coming from that possibility. But I wasn't late yet.

***

When I arrived on the top floor of the firm, several colleagues mulled about, some of them standing off to the side to discuss one client or another. The phone rang from the reception desk over and over. Barbara hadn't returned yet, but a young woman with short blond hair and a perky attitude kept busy answering the calls and redirecting clients. A copy machine hummed from the admin room around the corner, the faint scent of coffee wafting down the hallway from the break room.

I made a beeline for my office where I spent the morning finishing up my analysis of the candidates for pro bono work. I had three that looked promising, all of them nonprofit, one of them a food bank that had expanded exponentially over the years. In fact, the company had just purchased a whole new facility to expand their kitchen and delivery service, which went to senior citizens, the homeless, and those in need of a break . . . or in this case a free meal. They also provided job counseling and transportation services for those needing medical care. It was my favorite *and* my top choice. But I knew better than to offer just one candidate. Isabella wanted options. She always had. Either way, I felt confident that she and Gregory would be pleased with my findings. I began gathering my notes and typing up my analysis. I was good at researching and making sure I had left no stone unturned, which was probably why she had asked me to do this project. The morning seemed to rush by in an instant.

I grabbed a chicken salad sandwich from the cafeteria, an unsweetened iced tea, and an apple, then returned to my desk to prepare for Mrs. Dunbar's meeting later in the afternoon. My cell rang just after I had taken my first bite. Timing had never been on my side with this type of thing. If I was waiting for an important call, it would most certainly come when I was in the bathroom. If I was expecting a delivery at home, it would arrive when I was either in the shower or right after I had just stepped out the door to run a quick errand. A phone call when my mouth was full—well, that was a regular occurrence. I chewed fast and answered with a muffled voice.

"Hello?"

"Hey, sis. Sorry to bother you," Trina said.

I swallowed my bite of food then took a quick sip of my tea. "No problem. How's it going? You caught me at a good time. I was just having lunch at my desk."

"Oh, good. I was planning on leaving you a message if you were in a meeting." She paused.

"Is everything all right? Are the kids okay? And Mike?" Trina didn't often call me at work. It wasn't totally out of the realm of possibilities, but she knew my schedule was hectic at best. I started to worry.

"Yeah, everybody's fine. Noah has lacrosse starting up soon. He's taking some time to relax before practices begin. Hanging out with his friends. You know, that type of thing. I think he's a little anxious about starting high school, so I'm cutting him some slack, letting him spend a lot more time with his buddies. They're good kids. I've known most of them since they were in diapers. I was planning on taking them to the beach for his fourteenth birthday in a few weeks. It will be a day trip." She took a breath. "Bailey just got back from art camp. She made a few friends there as well." Her voice changed to a more mocking tone. "McKenna and I have had *a lot* of mother-daughter bonding. Let me tell ya. Poor kid. We've taken a couple of day trips to the amusement parks and to DC to see the monuments. And Mike's been busy with work. Same old, same old. Summer's flying by as usual. School will be starting up soon."

Trina took another breath, and all I could think about was

how lame it was that she had to provide me with these details over the phone. I should know these things from personal experience. "Sorry, didn't mean to monopolize the conversation. It's been a while since I've spoken to you. How are things?"

"Great." If she'd asked me that yesterday, I would have said, *Terrible*.

"Glad to hear it. Hey, I have a big favor to ask. Big, big, favor. And I know you're busy with work right now." Trina was being polite; I was *always* busy with work.

"No worries. What's up?"

"Well, as you know, Zach is getting married this weekend."

Zach was Mike's best friend growing up. They'd lived next door to each other all through grade school and until they had graduated from high school. Mike went to college at the University of Richmond in town while Zach decided on the University of South Carolina, where he met his sweetheart, Mandy. And since Mandy's family was from that area, Zach eventually moved there to be closer to her.

"Yes, I did remember that. You guys are flying out tomorrow afternoon, right?" Tomorrow would be Friday, and I was looking forward to the weekend and time away from this place. After the week I'd had, the walls were starting to close in. Plus, Daniel and I had some reconnecting to do, depending on *his* schedule.

"Yeah, well, Mike's sister was supposed to watch the kids, but she's come down with a nasty stomach bug, and I do *not* want my kids catching it. I know this is a lot to ask, but could you come here and stay the weekend? Mom and Dad are out of town. I'd ask Noah, but he's been preoccupied with his friends, and I don't know how well Bailey and McKenna would listen to him. And if there was an emergency, he's not driving age. A night out for dinner is one thing, but an entire weekend would be tough. I want to have a good time. I don't want to have to worry about who's fighting with whom while I'm gone. You know what I mean?" She sighed. "Please, Cass. Noah said he'd stay with the girls until you can get out of work tomorrow." Her voice took on a whine that wasn't necessary. I was happy to help. In truth, I hadn't spent a lot of time with the rug rats lately, and I missed them.

"Yeah, I can do that." I loved my sister's house. It was large and modern, and even came with an in-ground pool. Escaping from my shitty apartment sounded like food for the soul. I hoped Daniel could come, too, but with his recent plumbing issues, I wasn't sure how free he'd be.

"Are you sure? Do you need to check with work first? Or Daniel?"

I thought about that for a millisecond. "Nope. I've worked the last two weekends and pulled an all-nighter this week. Work can deal. And I'm sure Daniel will understand."

She gushed. "Oh, thank you, Cass. I really appreciate it. I'll stock the fridge and cupboards with your favorites, even though I know Daniel makes much better meals, and I'll get plenty of wine and drinks for you two to hang. The kids will be so excited to spend some time with their Auntie Cassie." I could hear the smile in her voice.

"Sounds good, Trina. I'm not sure what time I'm gonna get out tomorrow, but I'll find out and let you know later on tonight."

"You are the best, Cass. I owe you big time." She made several loud kisses over the phone. "Love you." She ended the call.

I finished my lunch, and soon, it was time for my meeting with Mrs. Dunbar. Her sand-colored blazer and matching skirt were thick for this time of year yet held a certain style that came with experience and lucrative taste. Her blond bob stopped short of her shoulders, her nails colorful and shiny, and her makeup doing an adequate job of enhancing her pale skin and blue eyes. If I were to compare her to an actress it would be Helen Mirren, nearly twenty years ago, but with a snootier aura about her. She was a knockout for sure, but a handful. Regardless, I grew to adore the woman.

At first, Mrs. Dunbar went over her new business venture, a small chain of boutiques that carried designer clothing for women, along with soaps, lotions, and other gifts. The kind of thing rich women would enjoy.

I skimmed the mission statement and the financials as I listened to her tell me about it. "Everything looks good, but I'd need more time to give this a thorough analysis. We can set up a meeting for next week to go over everything in more detail. How does that sound?"

As we sat across from each other in one of the firm's two conference rooms, she stared down her nose at me. "I'm not asking for your permission, young lady. I'm asking you to make sure my investment won't go belly up." She reached into her purse and pulled out a compact mirror to examine her face. This was something she often did, almost like a nervous tick or a habit to pass the time. After she gave her reflection a decent appraisal, she'd either add lipstick to her already coated lips or put the compact away and lightly primp her bob.

I paid way too much attention to these things. Detail-oriented people often did.

"Yes, I understand that. But I still need to look it over. Unfortunately, I have plans this weekend, or I'd go over it sooner." I was stepping onto thin ice with this declaration. It was a no-no to tell clients these things. But after my talk with Daniel, I felt more brazen about *my* needs for a change. "I'd like to take at least one day early next week to do some research and make sure you're investing in something that will *make* you money, not lose it."

My client flipped her manicured fingers at me. "I have a financial adviser for that."

I knew her financial adviser, his name was Trent, and he was good at his job. "Yes, but let me check all the wording and make sure you know what you are getting yourself into. You know me, I can't help but check *everything*, Mrs. Dunbar." I gazed into her blue eyes and smiled, trying not to shrink in her presence.

This time, she smiled back. "Suit yourself. And I am well aware of your talents."

I held the folder up. "Why don't I have our office manager make a copy while you're here?"

"No need, Cassie. That copy is for you to keep."

"Excellent. Thank you." I closed the folder and rested my forearms on the conference table, its walnut surface cool against my skin. At our end of the enormous table stood a glass pitcher containing filtered water surrounded by a ring of glasses, all crystal. "Would you like a drink of water?" I leaned over, ready to grab the pitcher.

"No, I'm fine, thanks."

I settled back into my seat. "Okay, then. If that's all, I will have our receptionist set up a meeting for next week. I'll have more answers for you by then."

My wealthy client appraised her nails this time, her hand extended out in front of her. "That will be fine. How is my Danny Boy? Is he ready to leave you yet and run away with me?" A smile fought against years of plastic surgery, trying its best to provide Mrs. Dunbar with an expression of amusement.

"Oh, ha-ha." I wagged a playful finger at my client. "Now, Mrs. Dunbar. Don't start. I'm gonna have to keep my husband under lock and key when you're around."

Her returned laughter came out sounding like she was channeling Cruella de Vil, which was more of a cackle than a laugh. "You needn't worry. He's got all he can handle with his spitfire of a wife, I'm sure." She blinked, her eyes filled with warmth.

Yes, the woman was entitled and, yes, she was rough around the edges but, deep down, a warm heart shined through, especially with *some* of her actions. Helping people like Daniel and me was a good example. She'd also sent an anonymous donation to a family in Richmond last winter who had lost their entire house to an electrical fire. No one knew who had sent the generous donation to their Go Fund Me account, but I knew. In fact, I was the one who had arranged it, not Trent her financial adviser, which had surprised me at the time.

As the years passed, Mrs. Dunbar seemed to rely on me for more than just legal work. She even took me shopping once to pick out a gown for a fundraiser she had planned on attending. "I need another woman's opinion, and my friends are all too busy," she'd said. "We can discuss the terms of my divorce while we shop." She was referring to her second divorce at the time.

She also never had kids of her own, just stepkids from all of her previous marriages, none of which she ever spoke of fondly.

Maybe that was it. Me being the age that I was and her being the age that she was allowed her to have a maternal relationship with me. Not always. In fact, not often. But every now and then, I sensed something caregiving from her heart when she offered advice or tried to help in some way. That rare instance when her walls came down and Mrs. Dunbar stepped aside for Ruth to emerge.

We shared one of those tender moments as we sat across from each other in this space dedicated to everything professional and nothing personal. What I felt from her didn't come from words but from a lightness of spirit as she smiled at me.

And with that, she rose on her Manolos. "Thank you, my dear. I trust you'll be in touch."

I got to my feet and followed her out to the elevators. "Yes. I'll text you the meeting time before I leave for the day." I waited as she loaded onto the elevator and pushed the button for the lobby. "Tell Danny Boy I'll be thinking of him." The glimmer in her eyes told me she wasn't being serious. Just having fun with me. Although, I'd have to share her message with my husband and *definitely* have some fun with it. Watch him squirm a little. His flustered reactions were adorable. I was glad we were back at a place where we could laugh a little again. I was worried that day would never return.

"Oh, I will. Have a nice weekend." I returned to my office to finish up my pro bono recommendations. As time flew by, I recruited a newbie associate to help me type up my notes. *I was a newbie once and had paid my dues, so I felt it was okay to utilize this source.* I made sure Lily (that was her name) knew how much I appreciated her assistance, offering her a free dinner out with her boyfriend for helping me.

Once I was finished with that, I contacted Lindsey and Brad from Into the Open to check with them about which night next week they would be free for dinner, and then I asked one of our administrative assistants to make the reservation. I also had her schedule the next appointment with Mrs. Dunbar.

Before I forgot, I sent a text to Barbara filled with well wishes. *Let me know if there is anything I can do. I'd be happy to check on your place, water plants, or contact family members if you need me to. We are all thinking of you, Barbara.*

An hour later she replied: *Thank you, Cassie. You are a dear. I am all set for now. My brother seems to be improving. I'll keep you posted on his progress.* The three dots continued to flash onto my screen. *I just realized I forgot to tell Isabella and*

A Collision with Love

Jeffrey you planned to be out yesterday. I'd lose my head if it wasn't attached. I hope I didn't cause you any strife.

My response was quick. *No worries, Barbara. You had a lot on your mind. Everything is fine here. Just focus on you and your family. Sending our love and support.*

And then, it was back to work.

I touched base with a few other clients, filed some paperwork with the court, and then organized my thoughts for the final draft of my pro bono project. It was six-thirty by the time I made it to Isabella's office, the sun still keeping the city warm but heading toward bedtime soon.

Isabella had set her deadline for this project by the end of business day, which in my mind, meant before I left for the night. And after my conversation with Daniel, I was less inclined to worry about it. I agreed with him. I'd spent seven years busting my ass for this firm.

When I arrived at Isabella's office, Gregory was there, decked out in a tux, his cologne filling the air around him with a hint of jasmine supported by subtle woody notes. I suspected his cologne cost a few pennies, knowing Gregory's penchant for expensive things. His mansion was nothing short of spectacular and the theme of several home and interior designer magazines, both local and from across the country. That was how I knew. (Our office manager, Jeffrey, had bragged about it in the break room one day.) I'd never stepped foot inside his house and probably never would. His cars and his clothing were beyond anything I could afford, nor would I want to. Daniel had taught me that *things* in life weren't the most important. People and relationships were what mattered most.

I'd never seen Gregory out of a suit, but a tux was a step above, even for him. *Is he pursuing a new client? Going to the opera?*

Wearing a light-gray pantsuit and white silk top, Isabella sat on the couch, Gregory in the easy chair across from her, both with a crystal glass of something amber colored in their grasp. I suspected scotch or bourbon, which they both enjoyed often after a long day . . . or week.

They were chatting with each other, their voices low, as they sipped on their drinks, until Isabella's gaze found me first. She uncrossed her legs and sat closer to the edge of the couch's cushion. "Cassie. I didn't see you there." Her jocular expression hardened, but only slightly, just enough to indicate she had switched from speaking with a partner to someone lower in rank. Her attentive eyes zeroed in on the folder in my hands. "Is that your recommendations for the pro bono work I had assigned you?"

Gregory placed his glass on the side table next to him and turned in his seat. "Oh, hello, Cassie." Age had forced Gregory's reddish-blond hair to transform into a light brown with gray highlights, accentuating his pale blue eyes. His face always donned a slight tan, only now that face was lined with a few more wrinkles around his eyes since I had first started working here. For a man in his late fifties, he was fit and sharp, not missing a step when addressing the board or *anyone* for that matter. He wore confidence like a second suit, never showing weakness for any reason. It took me two years to be able to speak to the man without breaking out in a sweat.

"Yes, Isabella, this is the information you had requested." I slid my gaze over to Gregory, who rose from his seat. "Nice to see you again, Gregory." He hadn't been around much, so I meant what I said. I waved a hand down in front of me. "Don't you look nice. Special occasion?"

Gregory smiled, his fingers straightening the collar of his dinner jacket. "Thank you. Yes, it's my wedding anniversary. And I'm taking Adrianna to the theater in New York."

His wife, Adrianna, was one of those dark-haired beauties

who drew attention everywhere she went. I suspected she was a model, although, I had never asked. She was young. Younger than some of Gregory's children, and I often wondered how well that went over within the confines of his family. Gregory's ex-wife, Joanna—another dark-haired beauty but with a decade or two on Adrianna—had long since remarried.

On his own, Gregory was impenetrable and reserved. But anytime I'd seen him with Adrianna, at the office or at a holiday party, Gregory showed his attentiveness, his arm always wrapped around his new wife's tiny waist. It was such a cliché, the rich older man with the hot younger wife, but it was also none of my business, so I kept my opinions to myself.

"Happy anniversary. Give my best to Adrianna as well."

Gregory gazed down at his Rolex. "I will, and it appears I need to run, Isabella. I've got a plane waiting."

A plane waiting? He couldn't possibly own one. If he'd hired one, this was an expensive date. Daniel and I would often settle for a romantic dinner at home. *To each his own.*

She stood. "Certainly. Enjoy the theater. Give my best to Adrianna as well."

Gregory rushed past me on his way out, his cologne spicing up his tailwind.

After collecting Gregory's nearly empty drink, along with her own, Isabella disappeared into her en suite, the sound of running water and glasses clanking a moment later. She returned promptly, finding a new seat at the head of her desk. She reached her hand out. "Okay, let me see what you've got."

I crossed the room and handed her the folder, hoping she would be satisfied with my results. "I chose the food bank organization as my number one choice because they show great potential for growth and rank very low on the risk factor. Right now, they are in a dispute with the county over some land that I think we could help them with. It would be great PR."

Isabella opened the folder and perused the data as I spoke.

I cleared my throat. "The nonprofit for families with disabilities is also a good one, but they just won a major dispute with the city over wheelchair access to some community buildings. I don't see any areas that look like they need legal help right now. The nonprofit for helping female minorities start their own businesses had some sketchy stuff. I read something about one of the administrators pocketing money. It didn't sound good to me." I mentioned a few others and why I did or didn't give them my vote. I took a seat on the opposite side of her desk and let her read without interruption. She was a fast reader. This wouldn't take long.

She closed the folder.

I sat forward. "I included financials, mission statements, and all the background checks I could get done within the timeframe you had requested. If you like my choices, I can do a deep dive into the top contenders." I peered over her desk at the folder. "As I said, I liked the food bank the most."

Isabella offered a small nod. "Yes, I see that. Why don't you do that deep dive into your top three, and I will leave the final decision up to you." She lifted the folder up a few inches before setting it back down. "I'd like your final decision by Monday morning. Gregory and I meet with the board on Monday afternoon. I trust you can work on it over the weekend? I need your decision to be ironclad. No surprises down the road. Nothing that will upset the board. Double-check everything and then triple-check."

Here we go again. My schedule flashed before me. I was stuck in meetings for most of tomorrow morning. And I had also agreed to mentor one of the new hires coming in tomorrow afternoon to get a tour of the place and to see where his desk would be in the common area before his first official day on Monday morning. In fact, I was supposed to take him out to lunch beforehand to welcome him to the firm and go over the office's code of conduct. Lisa from Human Resources was also planning to attend.

I had to analyze a few legal issues, write two briefs, check on some court proceedings, and begin researching Mrs. Dunbar's new business venture. I was sure there was more, I just had to check my calendar. Regardless, there wasn't enough time for me to get the pro bono project completed before the close of business on Friday, and I wasn't about to sacrifice the weekend when I'd committed my time to helping my sister, which I hadn't even told Daniel about yet.

"Um." I scratched my neck nervously. *Am I breaking out in hives?* "I actually . . . My sister."

Isabella leveled her gray eyes with mine. "Is there a problem?"

This was it. Do or die. I thought about Daniel's words. *Don't you see? Life is passing you by. When are you going to wake up? How long are you gonna wait for that promotion that may never come?* His words caused me to stand, pulling my shoulders back and preparing myself for resistance.

"I'm sorry, Isabella, I can't work this weekend."

"Oh?" Her brow lowered.

"My sister asked if I could babysit my nieces and nephew this weekend. She's going out of town for a wedding with her husband." I pivoted toward the door. "She just called me a little while ago. And I already told her I could do it. I'm sorry. I'd try to get the pro bono work done tomorrow, but I have a full day. I actually need to leave by four." I was pushing it. I couldn't work the weekend, *and* I wanted to leave early? *Sacrilege.* Surely, I was dead meat by now.

"I see. Can you bring your laptop and work while you babysit?"

I started to say yes, relieved that she wasn't angry with me, but then I stopped myself. "No, I can't. I'm sorry. I can work on it Monday, or I can give my research to one of the other junior associates to finish." This wasn't protocol. Once I started a project, I *always* finished it.

"Hmm." Isabella leaned forward, her elbows propped on her enormous desk, her chin rested above her hands now clasped together. If she was trying to intimidate me, it was working. "This doesn't sound like you. I don't just give anybody these assignments." She paused, the wheels turning in her bear trap of a mind. "If you want to make senior partner—"

"I don't anymore." Was she really going there? Daniel was right. She was just going to continue to dangle that carrot for as long as I would allow her. They say you teach people how to treat you, and I was teaching her to treat me like a doormat.

"You don't what, anymore? Don't want to make senior partner? Want to triple your salary? Don't want job security?"

It was as if I had floated out of my body, and Daniel was taking over my brain . . . and my mouth. "I have been working here for seven—"

"Yes, yes, I know."

"Let me finish, please."

That prompted Isabella's eyes to widen like saucers.

"I have been working here for seven-and-a-half years. And in that time, I have rarely put in less than eighty hours. And when I have worked less than eighty hours, I have made up for it."

"What about the other day when you came in late and dressed for the grocery store? You kept two *very important* prospective clients waiting. We could have lost them."

Man, she was pouring it on, not letting *anything* pass. This time it was okay. I was ready for her. "I told you why. I was in an accident. And I was pretty shaken up by it. I just worked the entire night to get this pro bono business done for you on time. I haven't even had a good night's sleep since the accident. But that isn't the point. My personal life is suffering from all the hours I'm putting in. If seven-plus years and countless late nights and weekends doesn't prove my worth, nothing will." I took a breath, trying to stave off emotion. This wasn't the place to fall apart. "I can't keep this pace up. My sister asked me for help, and I told her I would do it. I barely see her or my nieces and nephew anymore. If that takes me out of the running for senior partner, so be it. You can expect my letter of resignation right after you give the promotion to someone else." My heart was beating at such a rate that I struggled to breathe. I half expected it to beat right out of my chest and flop onto Isabella's desk. *Splat.*

With all the self-control I could muster, I turned to leave, not able to face this woman for another moment. If she pressed me on this, I feared I'd lose my temper, which I *really* didn't want to do. I was a professional, and I wanted to remain as such. Instead, silence followed me out the door, the only sound from my heels moving across her wool rug as fast as they could without appearing as though I was running scared.

What started off as a slow-and-measured stroll, resorted to nearly jogging when I was out of sight, all the way down to the ladies' room, where I splashed water onto my face and held a wet paper towel to my mouth, trying to quiet my nerves. While part of me was in a tailspin about what I had just done—drawing a line in the sand with no turning back—another part of me felt liberated and free, as though I had finally grabbed back some semblance of control of my life.

What happened now was anyone's guess.

Chapter Ten

The restaurant was still closed when I arrived, the sun going down to brighten another part of the earth's day, the moon starting to climb its way into the sky. A few stars had poked through the darkening canvas, not quite bright yet, but ramping up for something spectacular.

A large sign stuck to the inside of the glass door confronted me, informing patrons about the plumbing leak. Daniel had pulled the blinds, limiting visibility, which was probably a good idea. We didn't need people peering in at all hours.

I unlocked the door, prompting the bell above my head to jingle. Daniel came rushing out soon after. He leaned in for a kiss, his manly scent, a combination of hard work and perspiration, reaching my nose. "I'm so glad you came. I've been thinking about you all day. How did it go at the office?" He was holding a sodden towel in his hands, his gray T-shirt spotted with wet grime, his black gym shorts equally so. Wisps of hair had escaped from his man bun, a slight sheen coating his forehead.

Wearing a colorful head wrap, Kendra came bursting

through the swinging door from the kitchen a moment later. Her peach-colored tank, the one that fell short of covering her toned abs, was also soiled by dirty water, in addition to her skimpy jean shorts with a fringed edge. She rocked that look, her ample breasts revealing a hint of cleavage, her long legs drawing attention. *My* attention since Daniel was focused on me. At least he was for the moment.

What is he thinking when he peers across the room and sees her bent over in that outfit, her slim body glistening with sweat? He was loyal, but he was also human.

"Oh, hi, Cassie." Kendra cut through my unpleasant thoughts, her tone less than enthused. She could have just been tired. But something told me it was a little more than that.

"Hey, Kendra. It was nice of you to stay and help." I smiled, but it didn't quite come off as genuine either. The two of us seemed to dance around polite banter, both of us threatened by the other. I might have been mistaken, but a woman knows these things. I was sure she wanted my husband. "It's late. You should go home and rest. I'll take over from here."

Kendra's dark and expressive eyes shot Daniel a look who had turned to face her. "Daniel, Barry needs to see you." There was a sense of urgency in her voice as if Daniel needed to come at once.

"I've only been out here for like thirty seconds. And I haven't seen my wife all day. Can you tell Barry I'll be in in a minute? And Cassie's right. You should go home and get some rest. If you want to take tomorrow and the weekend off, I've got things covered here. I'm sure we won't be open."

That didn't sound good. Not the her leaving part, but the *not opening*.

He smiled, despite his dire prediction. "I'll make sure you're compensated for all of this extra time."

"Oh, I couldn't leave my partner in crime." She

approached, giving Daniel a high five that made my stomach clench. "We got this. Right, boss?"

We, huh? My gut roiled, but I tried not to show it.

My husband's cheeks took on a pink hue that did nothing to quell my uneasiness.

"Plus, aren't you working again all weekend, Cassie?" Kendra's discerning gaze found me again. She knew my schedule as well as Daniel did.

I hated that.

"Nope. I've got the weekend off!" I said those words with conviction, adding in a hint of *screw you,* which I was sure she noticed. The tension between us was as thick as molasses.

Daniel's head snapped in my direction. "Wow! The whole weekend?"

I nodded. "Yup. The whole weekend."

My husband seemed a tad rattled for a moment. He returned his attention to Kendra. "You've been great, Kendra. Partner in crime for sure." He kept his tone jocular as though they were pals, not a man attracted to his workmate. Daniel even playfully shooed her away with his hand. "Now go home. Get some rest. Spend a couple of days having fun. You're not missing anything here. That's an order." He gazed over at me and winked.

Okay, *that* helped set my mind at ease.

Kendra's brow rose. "Ooookay. If you're sure." With a little less spring in her step, she sauntered across the restaurant, disappearing through the kitchen doors.

My husband ran a hand down his face as if to reset himself. "So, tell me about your day. Sounds like a lot happened."

"We can talk about that in a minute. How are things going *here?*" I slid my purse from my shoulder and stepped out of my shoes, my toes thanking me with a little wiggle. "I'm pretty sure I have a change of clothes in your office, so I can help out now."

Man, did it feel good to say those words. I always wanted to help. It was just that my schedule refused to allow it.

"Well." Daniel used his free hand to rub what was probably a knot in the back of his neck. He let out a breath. "Not great, to be honest." He pointed a thumb over his shoulder. "Barry, he's the plumber, thinks this may be a bigger problem than just one pipe springing a leak as we had hoped." He stifled a yawn. "If it's what he thinks it is, we may need to replace several pipes. He said the system is old in that area of the building and in need of upgrading. Apparently, what we have wouldn't pass an inspection. It's *that* old."

"Oh shit. I guess we should have paid more attention when they installed the sinks and the dishwasher, as you said."

We were hemorrhaging money back then, looking for ways to cut corners. In fact, we had remodeled as little as possible at the time, trying to avoid the cost of gutting the entire place, which would have been a fortune. Other than small holes left behind by whatever the previous music store had displayed—everything easy to patch—the restaurant side already had walls trimmed in beautiful mahogany. Daniel and his workers sponge painted the rest in earth tones of gold and coffee to create a textured surface, and even *that* was mostly hidden behind artwork. And since the stainless-steel appliances and shelving—some freestanding, others anchored—obstructed the kitchen walls, we did what little we had to do to function properly.

I placed a hand on Daniel's upper arm, letting him know I was here for him while trying not to get lost in the feel of his firm bicep. "It sounds expensive." I thought about our meager bank account.

Daniel was starting to make a profit—albeit a modest one—and we'd actually been able to put a few bucks away. It seemed every time we came to this place, though, something like this would happen and bring us right back to where we had been before: broke. This was an old building, and old buildings came with a lot of aches and pains. Old HVACs, old roofs, leaky windows. We'd seen it all. Leasing would have been a better option for us, but it was too late to cry over that one. We had wanted this space. It was available. So, we jumped on it.

"Yeah, I hope not, but we'll have to wait and see what Barry says. Either way, I don't see us reopening *this* weekend, which means no money coming in." His brow tensed as though realizing the impact of the situation.

I rubbed my hand up and down his arm. "Well, I haven't quit my job just yet, so we still have *my* income. I did, however, say a few things to Isabella."

That caught Daniel's interest. "Oh?" His eyes fixed on me.

I spent the next several minutes bringing Daniel up to speed with my rant in my boss's office.

When I was finished, his mouth hinged open. "Holy shit. You said all of that?" My husband rubbed his jaw, his gaze dancing around the large room as though trying to imagine the scenario I had described. "Way to go, Cass." His hand jostled my shoulder. "What did Isabella say?"

I let my brow rise and fall, a sigh escaping from my lips. "Well, she didn't say anything actually. She could be writing a request for my letter of resignation right now, for all I know." I couldn't even remember whether she looked shocked or not. I was too busy rushing out of there. It was also the reason I was late getting to the restaurant. I finished up my work, and then I waited until she had left, not sure what I'd do if she cornered me. My bravery only went so far. When I was sure she had gone, I made my escape to the elevators.

Daniel shook his head, his lips defiantly pursed. "Nah, she wouldn't do that. You're one of the best lawyers in that firm, and she knows it." He tossed his wet towel onto a nearby table and took me into his arms. "I'm proud of you, wife of mine."

His voice landed on my ears as soft as cashmere. "I know that wasn't easy for you to do."

He couldn't have been more right, it wasn't easy, but I reveled in this attention and the way he kept me close, his hands roaming my back, making it all worthwhile.

"Thanks." As difficult as it was, I managed to detach myself from his embrace. "If I still have a job, I do have to work tomorrow, but I've got the whole weekend off."

Every inch of Daniel's face lit up. "I still can't believe it. That's awesome. Shit, I feel like I should plan something fun for us to do. You're never off. If it were a regular weekend, I'm sure I could take a day. I just hope we don't have to spend it here working all weekend cleaning up shit."

"Well, that brings up another subject I need to tell you about." I informed him about my sister's plight and how I had promised to watch the kids. "I checked my weather app. It's supposed to be in the low nineties. If you can get away, we can hang at the pool and have some fun with the kids." I had another thought. "And if you get stuck here, I'll bring the kids over, and we can pay them to help. They love that crap, especially Noah who is always saving up for Steam cards or something for his gaming system. The girls just like helping." I altered my voice to a sillier tone. "It makes them feel like grownups, you know." I thought about the time when ten-year-old Bailey had helped me make dinner, chatting away as though we were girlfriends and not auntie and niece, her six-year-old sister, McKenna, trying her best to act mature but failing miserably. That was eight months ago, when Trina and Mike had gone on a date night. Those girls were adorable. Shame on me for not seeing them sooner or more often.

Daniel nodded contemplatively as I spoke. He took my hand. "Let's go see what Barry has to say. Then we'll know what we're up against. A dip in your sister's pool sounds fucking great to me right now."

I slung my purse over my shoulder, grabbed my shoes, and together, we strolled across the restaurant, the feel of the old wood, smooth under my feet. I'd left my briefcase containing my laptop in the car. Another first for me. Actually, I stored it in the trunk, hoping it wouldn't get stolen. I tried to push the thought from my mind. In a lot of ways, my laptop was like Linus's security blanket. All those files were my professional lifeline.

"Kendra's been here all day? That was quite a skimpy outfit she was wearing." I made every attempt to keep jealousy out of my tone, but it was difficult when that was exactly how I felt.

"It can get hot when you're mopping up shit all day. She's been great. With no running water, she had to run next door to fill some buckets for washing and using the bathroom." With his hand around my waist, he leaned his head over to tap against mine. "And I didn't notice her outfit as much as you think I did." He raised a definitive finger. "Now had *you* been wearing an outfit like that"—he smirked—"I would have definitely noticed."

I bumped my body into his. "Yeah, right. Like I have anything on *her* perfect looks." For a moment, I considered adding that *I should just give up and put a bag over my head* but then remembered I'd said those same exact words at Brianna's wedding. My reel had gone full circle. *Why do I let people make me feel so diminished?*

Before we reached the swinging door that would allow us entry into the kitchen, Daniel stopped and lifted my chin with his index finger and thumb, his chestnut eyes filling my heart with warmth. "What is it going to take, wife of mine, for you to understand how in love with you I am? And after what you did today, I am over the moon." His voice grew all husky. "Just wait until I get you home." He placed a tender kiss on my lips. "But first, let's go see what the damage is."

Wet towels, forming clumps, cluttered the gray ceramic tile floor of our commercial kitchen, several buckets and mops standing by to soak up and distribute more water to its rightful place. A drain sat in the center of the room, catching tiny bits of debris, which blocked some of the water's passage. I suspected they'd cleaned that drain multiple times. To me, the kitchen looked as though it had suffered a flood, a musty scent hanging in the air to support that theory. On a far wall, a large hole revealed piping running in various directions; two men bent over the area discussing something. One of the men I recognized as Marcus. And thank God for Marcus, too, since he was the hero who had temporarily stopped the torrent.

"Wow." I didn't realize it had gotten so bad. I gazed around in wonderment.

"Yup" was all Daniel had to say.

I followed him over to the two men, tossing my shoes and my purse on a vacant chair in his office, its door open, along the way. To my delight, Kendra had gone out the back entrance.

"Kendra said you needed to see me?" Daniel stood behind the men, who both straightened up upon his approach and turned to face him.

"This is my wife, Cassie, by the way." My husband turned his body a smidge in my direction and then back to face Barry.

"Wife?" A man with thinning brown hair, streaked with gray, stepped forward, his bluish-green eyes filled with confusion. This was Barry, according to the monogrammed patch on his dark-blue work shirt, the one sewn into the fabric just above his left breast pocket. The scent of hard work and old water rippled off him as he removed an old rag from his back pocket and began wiping his hands. "Huh. I thought *partner in crime* meant—" He paused, an awkward silence filling the space between us.

Yeah, yeah, yeah. You thought Kendra was his wife. I wanted to mock but didn't. It was hard to blame someone for making an honest mistake, even if it *was* annoying. And incorrect.

Then he seemed to shake off whatever thought he'd entertained. "Nice meetin' ya." He continued to wipe his rugged hands, the buttons of his shirt straining to hold in an ample belly.

If I were to guess, I'd say Barry was in his mid-fifties, judging by the lines etched around his eyes and mouth, a neck starting to sag. Even his clothes had an aged feel, his shoes scuffed with wear.

"Hey, girl." Marcus offered a light punch to my shoulder, barely strong enough to feel. "What's crackin'?" He smiled, his face welcoming and kind.

"Nice to meet you, Barry. And not much, Marcus." I flashed both men a warm smile. "So, what's the damage?" I set my eyes on the hole in the wall, hoping to cast the attention off me.

As it turned out, there was quite a lot of damage. Barry explained that a good section of piping was corroded, which had resulted in the leaks we were experiencing. "If you don't replace this piping now, I suspect you're gonna be dealing with some bursts that will be far worse down the road." Barry scratched at his short brown-and-gray-colored beard, which matched his hair perfectly. The way the streaks of brown flowed so evenly, it almost looked dyed, but I suspected it wasn't. Barry didn't strike me as a man who would go to such lengths. "Frankly, I'm surprised you were able to buy the place with these pipes in this condition. I would have thought a building inspector would have caught it. But I guess it wasn't a kitchen back then, was it?"

We both shook our heads before Daniel spoke. "No, it was a music store. They had a bathroom back here and a break room with a sink. We put the larger sinks in and the dishwasher. The dudes who installed the appliances did mention that the plumbing needed some tweaks to hook them up." He rubbed the back of his neck again, the strain drawing his eyebrows together. "I should have dealt with it then. *Fuck.*" He placed his hands on his hips, his face not happy.

As I often did, I ran my hand along his lower back, hoping to ease his worries. "We didn't have the extra money, hon, it wasn't your fault."

As Barry listened, he scratched at his beard some more. "The pipes in the basement seem fine. I think the previous owners must've redone the basement pipes and the ones in the front of the building, but they hadn't gotten around to the back area yet. It happens all the time, doing it piecemeal. Who did your inspection? Was it Davey Driscoll?"

"It's been so long, I can't remember. Do you remember, hon?" I gazed over at my husband.

"I can't remember either. Davey sounds kind of familiar, but I don't recall." Daniel stared off as people do when searching the airspace for an answer.

Barry's cell phone rang from his back pocket. He took it out, examined the screen, and then silenced it, returning it to his pocket a moment later. He leveled his hand out in front of him, reaching chin level. "Was he a short guy with a thick mustache?" He moved his hand around his mouth. "You know, one of those horseshoe mustaches? Funny looking, dude?"

With all the people we'd met over the past two years, along with the remodel since then, I had no idea who anyone was, and I suspected Daniel didn't either, until he wagged a finger in the air. "You know, that does sound familiar."

Barry made a *pfft* sound. "Well, it doesn't matter. Davey

has a tendency to get distracted is all. Human error. He may have checked the basement pipes and most of this floor and missed a few in the back." His expression took on a more positive light. "The good news is it seems to be just in your kitchen, but it's gonna take me a couple of days to get it all changed out. Week tops." He scratched his head. "I can move a couple of jobs around and get to it this weekend, or I can work on it next week."

"I can't open with it like this, right?" I knew what Daniel was contemplating: how to get some money coming in.

Suddenly, I regretted speaking to Isabella. I needed my job right now, and this recent situation only proved it. Even though Daniel wanted me to quit and start a family, I was reminded of how impractical that plan was. Unless we sold the restaurant, but I didn't want to do that, not unless we had to.

Barry made a face. "I wouldn't open. You don't want customers in here if those pipes burst. In fact, I'd keep the water line off until I can get to it."

Daniel took a deeper breath, the stress of the situation pulling the corners of his mouth downward. "If you work over the weekend, won't that cost more?" He raised a palm. "Sorry, we don't have a lot of extra money coming in right now."

With his arms crossed, Barry seemed to size up my husband. "I do charge extra for weekend work, but I could cut ya a break and offer my regular fee. I need to make a few calls before I can commit. Either way, I can git 'er done by next week."

For the next half hour, Barry sat in Daniel's office making calls. I changed into a pair of shorts and a T-shirt, grabbing my sneakers out from a small locker in our break room, the same break room that served the music store before us.

As it turned out, Barry couldn't free up his Friday or Saturday schedule. In addition, he had a piano recital to attend

A Collision with Love

for his grandson that he told us about as he rolled his eyes. "If you ask me, nine years old is too young for recitals. Christ, the kid's still wet behind the ears. But if I don't go, my wife will *not* be happy. And you don't want to see Flo when she's not happy. That woman scares most *men*." He outwardly shivered. "Scares the shit out of me, too, always has."

Daniel and I smiled at his rant, which might have been Barry's intent. He seemed sensitive to our situation.

"Nice to see a young couple makin' a go like this. I'll do what I can to get ya back up and run'n. And I'll be here right after church on Sunday. We go to eight o'clock mass. After we have breakfast at the Waffle Barn, I can be here by ten. I'll make a good start on Sunday. And finish up next week. That's the best I can do."

"I appreciate that, man. And thanks." Daniel reached his hand out for Barry to shake, which he did promptly.

After Barry left, and we shooed Marcus out the door in the same manner we had Kendra—to get some rest and take the next couple of days off—I helped my husband clean up the kitchen as best we could. We were down to one bucket of clean water, not enough to do a lot. Also, the mess was only going to get worse, we decided in unison.

While Daniel went into the bathroom to clean up with our last bucket of water, I brought the two buckets of *dirty* water over to the sink to dump before I squeezed the mops as best I could using the bucket wringer. Not paying attention to where I was pointing the handle of one of my mops, I knocked over a stack of stainless-steel pans, making a horrendous racket that echoed off the tile floors and the appliances. The crash was deafening.

"Oops, just pans. Nothing broken. My bad. Sorry." I bent over and collected what I could, then lowered onto my hands and knees to reach the lid of one pot that had sailed under a stainless-steel stationary table the staff often used for meal prep. As I was pulling out what I needed, a pair of hands gripped hold of my butt—warm, determined hands.

"Circling back to your earlier comment, you're about to see what happens when I have to watch *you* work in that skimpy outfit." He bent his body over the back of mine, his erection pushing against my butt. His warm hand slid up my waist. "Yeah, I'll take this over hard work any day. This is a much better way to spend my time." He massaged my nipples, rendering me both aroused and helpless. I didn't want to move, enjoying the sensations revving up my insides. If I were an engine, my motor was intent on high throttle. He slid my shorts down and with them, my panties. His erection brushed up against my overexcited lady parts.

"Are you up for this? Right now?" I sure hoped so because I was already gushing.

His breath heated my back. "Oh, yeah. I need to let off a little steam. The question is, wife of mine, are *you* up for this?"

I backed up into him and started to move.

Chapter Eleven

I arrived at the office at 6:55 a.m. on Friday morning, discovering Isabella's lights were off. On a normal day, she'd beat everyone here, regardless of the time, probably to send a message: *No matter how hard you work, I work harder.* I swore the woman slept here on occasion. It was the reason I had rushed out of here yesterday morning after my all-nighter when I had looked like the Bride of Frankenstein. Frankly, I was surprised we hadn't crossed paths.

Most lawyers started their day later, but not our fearless leader.

Next door, Gregory's office was also cast in darkness, the sun hours away from scaling the edges of the skyscrapers outside his wall of windows. I hadn't seen Gregory a lot and wondered if he was contemplating retirement or maybe taking a less demanding role in his firm. Hence, the need for a new senior partner. *We may look outside the firm* was the caveat. *Always* a caveat.

But both offices were dark at this moment, which was unusual. Had I beaten them here? Or were they traveling?

I continued down the hallway, yawning as I flipped the switch for the light in *my* cramped office, a note sitting on my desk waiting for me. Even from a distance, Isabella's signature at the bottom of the page drew my attention.

This is it. She's firing me. And with the restaurant in peril, its doors closed, what an awful time for this to happen. I chastised myself for speaking out to her. I should have waited. I *wanted* to wait. But Daniel had put a mirror up to my life, and I hadn't liked what reflected back.

Upon closer inspection, I discovered the note didn't say anything specific.

> Cassie,
> I'm out of the office today. I need to speak with you on Monday.
> Enjoy your weekend off.
> —Isabella

I started to obsess. Did *Enjoy your weekend off* have a similar connotation to *Enjoy your last meal before we yank the rug right out from under your feet?* Isabella was a master of keeping her cards close to the vest. She would never reveal anything until you were sitting right in front of her. And then she'd lower the boom. I'd seen it play out this way many times before. Ex-employee Andy had thought he was receiving a raise.

I put the note in my desk drawer and plunked down in my chair. As the hours passed, the firm remained relatively quiet, only a few early risers inhabiting the halls like me.

Daniel didn't even question my need to get in early. He understood that I . . . that *we* needed this job right now. We had bills and now contractors to pay. Who knew what other problems lurked behind those old walls or underneath those warped floorboards, just waiting to erupt and throw our lives into yet another tailspin? I couldn't help but wonder if this restaurant was a mistake. Should we have waited or at least found a place to lease and not own? The die was cast. Nothing we could do about it now. Except sell, and that tugged at my heartstrings. I didn't want Daniel to have to give up on his dream. Life never offered a guarantee that it would ever happen again.

A sigh escaped from my lungs, a tired sigh.

At least Isabella would be out today. I could roam the halls without worry of running into her. With that thought in mind, I ventured over to the break room to get some coffee, another yawn threatening to crack my jaw open from the intensity. Man, was I tired. And I couldn't afford to be. If I was taking the weekend off, I had to stay productive today.

I blamed my horny husband for my fatigue, but in a good way. Once he surprised me with a romantic rendezvous at the restaurant, he was ready for more adult fun by the time we had returned home. To be fair, he *had* made me a quick dinner first (pasta with pesto sauce and garlic).

After we had hand washed the dishes, my sweet husband stood leaning against the kitchen counter. "I don't think I'm gonna have you awake for much longer, wife of mine, by the looks of you." He'd tossed one of our hand towels off to the side. "I was hoping we could pick up where we left off at the restaurant." With a twinkle in his eyes, he raised a palm. "I promise to wash up properly this time."

A bucket of water and a bar of soap weren't ideal, but it got the job done at the restaurant.

"Think you can stay awake that long?"

I wanted to say yes. Making love to Daniel wasn't something I ever took for granted. The trouble was, fatigue was crawling up my neck like a vine, pulling my eyes closed and dragging my feet around the apartment like they were loaded with sand.

He took my hand, kissed my knuckles, and then led me into our bathroom. "How about a very satisfying shower before I lose you for the night?"

A shower before bed was always a great way to ensure a good night's sleep, which I desperately needed, so I agreed. He lathered me up, he rinsed me off, his fingers exciting my nipples and between my legs as he worked.

Okay, so *that* brought a burst of energy to my tired brain. I washed my own hair before I decided to lather *him* up next. With gusto. Slippery hands were great for getting my man off. But I didn't stop there. When the water turned tepid, quickly heading toward cold, I shut it off and sat on the edge of the tub, taking all of him into my mouth, my hands massaging where my mouth couldn't. With his hunky body clean, dripping with water, I enjoyed the manly taste of him, my insides growing more aroused by the second. I was so into it—my tongue enjoying every inch of him—I almost came right there, just from my own actions.

Daniel braced his hands against the shower wall. "Man, you're good at this." His voice grew intense. "Fucking great." He moaned, his breaths quick and shallow, until he lost it all together.

For a few seconds, he stood there dazed, and I loved that I was the one who had put him in that condition. I stepped out of the shower, brushed my teeth, and was ready to make a beeline for our bed, when he took hold of my wrist.

"Meet you in there, beautiful. Don't put anything on. Now it's *your* turn." His eyes grew dark and lusty.

My inner thighs quivering with anticipation, I managed to push my legs over to our bed, where I fell onto my back and waited.

Not long after, my husband sauntered into the room, naked and gorgeous. He kneeled over me. "Let's get you taken care of, wife of mine." His eyes glowed, his mouth practically salivating. "I can't wait to lick that luscious pussy. Are you nice and wet for me?"

I had to assume his question was rhetorical. Who wouldn't be wet with an Adonis like him standing before them with a chiseled body and a desire to satisfy? He'd pulled his wet locks into a ponytail, providing me a full view of his handsome face. Those chestnut eyes, the defined jawline coated with just enough scruff to add to his manly appearance, and those lips, plump and soft, he was handsome in overload. They made movies about men like Daniel, love stories where he either broke hearts or repaired them.

He moved my legs apart and sampled my goods with his gentle fingers. "Oh, yeah. Just right." He placed a soft kiss on my lips. "You know, of all the food I make, nothing tastes as good as you do." With that, he lowered himself, kissing along my inner thigh, before he buried his face between my legs and stimulated my most sensitive regions with absolutely no lack of restraint. What that man did with his tongue was a mystery to me. I was sure fingers were also involved, allowing me to enjoy the ride to its fullest.

I was still turned on after that blow job, and therefore, it took all of two minutes to coax a fresh round of orgasmic screams from my lungs. I thought I was going to lose my mind, every cell in my lower half exploding with such ferocity that I grabbed hold his head and pushed him closer, needing every ounce of this sensation to last. And when the screams subsided and my mind returned to reality, I lay there as though I had no bones, my energy completely spent.

Daniel fell onto his side facing me, his hand grazing my stomach. "I was hoping that would take a little bit longer."

Did you say something? On the other side of that mind-blowing orgasm, fatigue refused to wait another second for rest.

My husband lay next to me. He chuckled. "It's all good. I know you're tired." He yawned through his next words. "I'm right there with you, hon." He covered us both up with our sheet and blanket, snuggling in close. Or I think he did. He might have gotten up to brush his teeth first.

My brain dove into sleep so quickly that I experienced several hypnic jerks. It was bothersome, but I was too exhausted to do much about it.

And now as I took my first sip of coffee for the day, the break room mostly to myself, the only thought that came to mind was *what a night*. What a glorious night.

I returned to my office, ready to resume the rat race. I had a lot of small details to chase down, more paperwork to file with the court, and a few customers to touch base with. Normal routine. I wasn't sure what to do about the pro bono stuff, so I worked on that as well. I figured I'd just leave what I was able to get done on Isabella's desk, and she could decide what she wanted to do with the rest. I wouldn't finish it, even if I could. That would send the wrong message. I had told her I couldn't do it in time, and I wanted her to know that I meant what I said.

It was after lunch, which I had eaten at a new bistro with the firm's new hire and the head of HR, when I realized that I had forgotten to get that pregnancy test I had been considering. Had I even taken my pills lately? I had to be several days behind by now. Did I take one last night? What was the matter with my brain? I searched my purse for my pill container—a place I normally kept it—coming up short. Where else did I store it? Trying to sort these details was yet another moment when I couldn't focus. This wasn't me. I prided myself on remembering specifics. It was what made me a good lawyer. My axis was off kilter for sure.

And then those symptoms returned. Everything around me began to sway as though I'd been thrust into a johnboat in the ocean. My stomach experienced a moment of turbulence just as a strong, pungent odor assaulted my nostrils. *What is that?* I dropped my head between my legs to prevent the contents of my stomach from pouring out of me. My chest got all tight as though someone had pulled an invisible strap across my ribs and was yanking it with abandon. I had to sit up, despite my stomach's warning. Mainly because I had to breathe. What I wanted to do was lay down or curl up into the fetal position until the physical storm passed.

I should have gotten that damn test. Were these typical symptoms of pregnancy? My sister had battled morning sickness with all three of her kids. Why they called it morning sickness when the symptoms chose to afflict a woman anytime they felt like was beyond me.

If not pregnancy, what else? Anxiety? A brain tumor?

I closed the door to my office and plunked a few banker's boxes at the edge of my desk, forming a short wall. It wasn't easy, but desperation called for action. I didn't need passersby seeing me in this state. They'd probably assume I was hungover or something worse. I even contemplated going to my car to rest. The problem was, I worried I wouldn't get there in one piece. Five feet away was too far for my legs right now *and* for my stomach. Thank God Isabella wasn't here. If she showed up at my door right now . . .

I rested my head on my desk and waited, hoping this *whatever it was* would pass. Were the symptoms lasting longer? I closed my eyes and tried to center myself. *Don't throw up . . . Don't throw up.*

I awoke fifteen minutes later, according to the clock on my phone, my body feeling . . . *normal?* I rose and rushed to the break room to grab a bottle of water, anxious to cleanse my palate and hydrate. A couple of sips, and I was back in business. I even carried on a conversation with a junior associate about his upcoming litigation.

Not wanting to waste any more time, I returned to my office and resumed working. I also touched base with Trina at three o'clock to make sure everything was in order on her end. "I should be out of here by five at the latest. I'll go straight to your house." I recalled a conversation I'd had with Daniel the night before. "Daniel's coming too. He has some office work to do today at the restaurant and more cleaning on Saturday morning, and he also wants to do inventory of the food in the cooler—things that may go bad like veggies—but he'll spend the rest of Saturday afternoon and evening with us. He's got that plumber coming back on Sunday to start the job." I had kept Trina updated on the restaurant's status through text messages. I wanted to make sure she knew what was going on in case I had to take the kids over there. "I may take the crew over there later in the day on Saturday, but for the most part, we'll just be hanging out at your place. Is there anything I need to know? Places the kids need to be? School starts soon, right?"

"Yes, school is coming up fast. McKenna is so excited to start first grade. Her best friend Brittany is in her homeroom. She was so happy. She'll probably tell you all about it. Other than that, we've done our school shopping. You may see a couple of packages arriving for school clothes and more supplies, but other than that, we're good. The kids are looking forward to spending time with their Aunt Cassie." Her voice lightened in a pampering sort of way.

"I'm looking forward to that too. I need some time to relax."

Trina scoffed playfully over the line. "Well, I'm not sure how much time you'll get to relax. I could barely get the girls to sleep last night. They were so excited to see you. And when I tell them Daniel's coming, they'll probably lose their young minds."

It felt nice to be wanted. Not that I deserved their admiration, given how neglectful I'd been lately. "Cool. I thought about taking them to Piazza, that Italian place just up the road from you." I figured Daniel would be too tired to cook after a long day.

"Yeah, Cass, I know where Piazza is." Her tone mocked. "I'm sure they'd love that. I did buy stuff to make homemade mac and cheese, burgers to grill, and there's a large bowl of potato and pasta salad in the fridge. The girls like yogurt and granola for breakfast, and Noah, whenever he decides to get out of bed, usually makes himself a bagel. Everything is there for them."

"Okay, Daniel mentioned making his sticky buns and possibly one of his egg casseroles. If the girls or Noah don't want it, I'll just eat it." The thought made my mouth water.

"Now you're just being cruel. I know how good Daniel's sticky buns are. Leave me at least one sticky bun in the fridge or I'll never forgive you. Make it two. Don't forget Mike."

"Humph. I'm giving up my weekend for you and *that's* the thanks I get." I loved these teasing matches with my big sis.

"You know me. When it comes to Daniel's cooking, all bets are off." Trina's tone carried the kind of edge that only worked with fun-loving banter. "Would it help that I bought you both several bottles of red blend from that winery you like out in Charlottesville and some ciders for around the pool?"

"Yes, it does. Listen, have a safe flight, and don't worry about anything here. Just go and have a good time with Mike. You two deserve this. I'll keep you posted on our whereabouts all weekend. Oh, and you forgot to text me your itinerary. When do you leave and come home again? And do you guys need a ride to or from the airport?"

"Thanks, Cass. Shit. My bad. I'll do that as soon as I get off the phone. We leave in about an hour. Mike got an Uber. Noah agreed to stick around until you guys come. He may even opt to go to dinner with you all. He adores Daniel. In fact, Noah has been mentioning culinary school lately. I've never heard him say anything like that before. He may have some questions for his Uncle Daniel." She took a breath. "We fly back on Sunday night, and we'll be taking an Uber home as well. Mike's got some credits that he wants to use up. We should be home by six, so you and Daniel can get back to your place at a decent hour. Weather looks good for air travel."

Interference on the line told me she was on the move. "Oh, I wanted to tell you, I spoke with Mom last night. They're having a great time with Aunt Alice. They may stay an extra week. She said, 'Why not?' 'We're retired.' She sends her love. Listen, I gotta finish packing and get Mike off his computer to do the same. Thanks again, Sis. I owe you. Love ya." She spoke rapidly as if trying to fit everything in. "And don't forget to save me some sticky buns." The phone call ended before I had a chance to say love you back. Oh well, I understood what busy felt like and that was *without* three kids.

According to our temporary receptionist, Isabella and Gregory were away on business. Having both of them gone was like playing hooky while at work, not that the firm was filled with children who needed our guardians around to keep us in line. We were lawyers for God's sake.

On this unsupervised August afternoon, the sun and the light breeze outside my window—the one I had enjoyed while having lunch—encouraged me and a few other lawyers in the firm to cut out a tad early—4:45 p.m. to be precise. Several were heading to a local pub for happy hour, which they had invited me to join.

"Summer isn't going to last forever, Cassie. Come grab a

drink with us. Weather's perfect. We'll grab a table at Zoloft's on the patio." That came from Jeffrey, otherwise known as the leprechaun who wasn't Irish. (I was pretty sure he was German, if memory served.)

"Normally, I would love to, Jeffrey. But I promised my sister that I would watch my nieces and nephew. Raincheck? I'm headed there now." I didn't even slow my pace on my route toward the elevators.

As I hustled down the sidewalk toward the parking deck, I called Daniel. "Hey, hon. Are you at home or are you still at the restaurant? I'm headed to Trina's now."

A woman's voice broke through, stopping my feet and my heart. "Oh, this isn't Daniel. This is Leslie Thompson. I'm the food critic. You just missed Daniel. He ran to the restroom. Is this Kendra? Daniel said he was running late. I believe he's going to meet you just as soon as he leaves here. Did you want me to give him a message?"

First of all, why was this woman answering my husband's phone? My blood boiled. *Meeting Kendra?* Second, why was Daniel meeting Kendra? Wasn't working side by side *and* day in and day out enough time spent together? Whenever I asked him about Kendra, he'd shrug it off as though she was no big deal in his life. *Partners in crime*, she'd said. The crime of what, infidelity?

"No, this isn't Kendra. It's Cassie."

A pause. "I'm sorry, who?"

"*His wife*, Cassie." I scoffed. What was her deal? She must've known who I was. She had to.

Another pause. "I'm sorry. I didn't know Daniel was married. I asked him to be part of my podcast next week, so he came by to look over my notes.... I wanted to give him a list of topics to prepare for.... We're at my house.... Well, my office-house.... He just got here about fifteen minutes ago.... He's planning on leaving very soon. . . . Do you want me to tell him to call you?"

Her rambling only heightened my sensitivity to the prospect that they were doing something else. *Other* than work. That was ridiculous I knew, but why was she rambling like that? I also realized that in all the confusion of our lives, Daniel still hadn't told me what his good news had been regarding this woman and her podcast. But Leslie had just answered that: she was hosting him next week.

"You don't need to explain. It's all good. I was leaving work and wanted to touch base with him. Where did you say he was?" I kept hoping Daniel would walk into the room and take his phone back. It seemed rather odd this woman would answer his phone for him. Who did she think she was, anyway? I would *never* do that.

"Oh, I, uh." She cleared her throat. "The restroom, down the hall. You see, my office is attached to my house but with a separate entrance. . . . When I said we were at my house, I meant my office. . . . Do you want me to have him call you . . . ? Does he have your number?" She made a funny sound as though flabbergasted. "I mean, of course he has your number. I'll tell him you called." *Click*, the call disconnected.

What was that all about? As I approached my BMW on the second floor of the parking deck, I literally pulled the phone away from my ear and stared at it in disbelief. Was I expecting my cell phone to conjure up a viable excuse for why this woman would have behaved this way? Did my cell phone know the reason Daniel would be meeting with Kendra for whatever reason? Especially when I had distinctly heard him tell her to take the time off because she wasn't missing anything at the restaurant? Nope. But I had to stare at something, and my cell phone was all I had at the moment.

I slid into the driver's seat, hoping my phone would ring

any moment. But as I closed in on my sister's house, half an hour later, those hopes flew out the window with the afternoon breeze. I thought about calling him again from the driveway, but the minute I cut the engine, my nieces were knocking at my driver's side window. McKenna was literally jumping up and down with six-year-old delight.

"Aunt Cassie, open your door." *Knock, knock, knock.* "Hurry up. Why are you taking so long?"

"Okay, okay." I thrust my door open as McKenna landed in my lap for a big hug, the impact forcing an *"Umph"* from my lips.

Her flaxen shoulder-length hair was pulled to one side of her face by a big pink barrette in the shape of a butterfly, and her button nose and hazel eyes were as adorable as they came.

Whereas Bailey at ten years of age—approaching eleven this year—had long since outgrown the coordinated outfits her mother had always loved dressing her girls in, McKenna hadn't reached that stage of maturity quite yet. Her lilac-colored top with a large butterfly donning the front came with plenty of bling, proving my point, as did the knit shorts that matched to perfection. On her feet she wore sandals with a big daisy on top, like a cherry on a sundae.

A few *short* steps down the generational ladder, Bailey embraced jean shorts today (probably from the Gap or Old Navy) and a black sleeveless top. More fashionable and more adult. Soon, Bailey would be a teenager and probably rejecting everything her mother or any adult had to say. But she wasn't there yet.

I kissed McKenna's fair skin and hair, sending love into those young and energetic hazel eyes that were a combination of Mike's brown and Trina's blue.

Standing back with her arms crossed, Bailey wore a darker complexion, enhanced by her long black hair, the silky kind you wanted to run your fingers through. Honestly, the girl could pose for a shampoo commercial. What delighted me most about my niece, however, were her eyes, the color of moss growing on a rock somewhere like Scotland. My best feature. And hers. And even though she wasn't my daughter, I took pride in the bloodline contribution to her beautiful face. *We have the same eyes*, she used to say when she was littler. In reality her eyes were a shade lighter than mine, something Daniel had pointed out repeatedly, professing *no one had eyes quite like mine.*

That's right. That makes us kindred spirits, I'd said on more than one occasion, which always brought a smile to her face. Somehow, this bonded us, and I reveled in that fact.

I'd be the aunt Bailey would turn to when she couldn't relate to her mother or when the drama in her life was going nuclear. And there *would* be drama. This girl was a knockout at ten. I couldn't imagine what sixteen would look like. *Get ready for some sleepless nights, Sis.*

Interrupting my thoughts, McKenna yanked on my arm. "Want to play hide-and-seek? We can use my walkie-talkies. We can pretend we're in a dungeon or a castle. Come on, please? Wanna play?" McKenna continued to pull at my arm as though I were a piece of rope and she was in a tug-of-war.

"Let me get inside first, sweet girl. Yes, I would love to play, but we also need to plan what to do for dinner, and I need to get settled." I knew I was talking to deaf ears. Kids like McKenna, full of fun and spirit, didn't know the meaning of the word *wait*. From what Trina had told me, McKenna had just about driven Mike and the rest of the family crazy last Christmas, impatient for that doggone holiday (more importantly Santa) to *arrive already*. I was working per usual and had missed out on most of her preholiday impatience. Trina had broken down and let McKenna open an extra present on Christmas Eve, only to get some peace. Unfortunately, that peace didn't last long since McKenna was up at five in the morning. By the time I had arrived at six that evening, she was asleep on the couch, a brand-new Barbie clutched in her little hand.

"Come on. Just one game. We can play one now and then more later." She actually stomped her foot.

"Yes, we can play. But I have to get inside first." Somehow, I managed to get myself out of the car as a slightly more mature Bailey stood back and rolled her eyes at her younger sister. "Come on, McKenna. Don't be such a brat. Leave Aunt Cassie alone."

McKenna thrust her tiny little hands on her hips, her face twisted with rage, a couple of rubber bracelets dangling from her narrow wrists. "Don't call me a brat. I'm not a brat."

My God was she cute, her cheeks turning pink with defiance. I touched her nose with the tip of my finger. "No, you're not a brat. You're my helper, right?" A little flattery never hurt anyone. "Wanna carry my purse? I might have some candy in there for you." McKenna loved Sour Patch Kids, so I always had a supply on hand whenever I knew I'd see her. Bailey liked Skittles, and Noah, peanut M&Ms. There wasn't time for small gifts, so this would have to do, courtesy of a convenience store on the way over.

Needless to say, I brought my big purse today to accommodate.

"Yes!" She clapped her hands together. "What did you bring me?"

"You'll see." My gaze found her big sis. "I got a little treat for you, too, Bailey, and even something for Noah."

"No peeking." I gave McKenna my purse, handed Bailey my briefcase, and then grabbed my suitcase—which I had packed that morning—along with a small bag of shoes before all three of us descended upon the covered porch out front.

My sister's two-story colonial-style house rested on a half-acre of land with a swing to enjoy from the front porch and even a flag with the word *Welcome* and displaying flowers coming out of a watering can, billowing in the breeze. Light-blue shutters offset the natural stone exterior of the front, which also hugged the square pillars stabilizing the porch roof. Respecting the color scheme, tan vinyl siding wrapped around the remaining parts of the house. The bushes out front were always trimmed professionally—a few clusters of flowers adding color within the mulch—the lawn freshly clipped. It was a nice house, really, one I'd envisioned for Daniel and me, and I loved coming here, pretending for a short while what my life would be like with a nice home and children.

I let that thought carry my feet to the door, where six-foot-tall Noah stood waiting. "Hi, Aunt Cassie." He looked around me. "Isn't Uncle Daniel with you?" His voice cracked a bit. Hormones in play.

No, Uncle Daniel is off having secret meetings with two other women. What I actually said was, "Not yet, bud. But he should be right along. I'll call him when I get inside."

Seeming satisfied with that answer, handsome Noah, with his dark wavy hair and big brown eyes, much like his father's, stood back for us to enter before he closed the door behind us. "Cool. Is he coming for dinner? I thought I could help him cook."

Wow. Daniel had missed out on a pretty amazing compliment. I'd have to tell him about it later. Most thirteen-almost-fourteen-year-olds wanted nothing to do with a kitchen unless it was time to eat.

Today, Noah was rocking an old, pale-yellow T-shirt with a sailboat across the front, a pair of navy gym shorts falling just below his knees. He stood there smiling in his bare feet before he leaned in for a hug.

My sister had the nicest kids.

"Nice to see you, bud." I removed my shoes.

"Yeah, you too." He took the suitcase from my hands while I grabbed my shoes to carry with me. "Mom has you and Uncle Daniel in their room instead of the guest room." He led me through the formal dining room, flaunting a tray ceiling and where a cherry dining room set with matching china cabinet offered a great place for family meals.

We approached the mudroom where various jackets, backpacks, and bags hung from hooks on the wall and shoes cluttered up the floor. I stored my shoes near the door leading to the two-car garage.

In the far left-hand corner of the house, the downstairs primary suite awaited, the white carpet thick and soft under my feet, the bedding with the vibrant floral print, plush and pristine, it was hard to imagine messing with it, much less sleeping underneath all that pouf.

I'd envisioned Daniel and me sampling either the large-tiled shower or the oversized tub with jets in the en suite bath next door. That was if I could reach the man, *and* he wasn't having an affair. Even if things were on the up-and-up, something wasn't right here. Should it bother me that he hadn't told Leslie Thompson he was married or anything about me, for that matter? I'd have to have my head examined if it didn't. And what was the deal with him and Kendra?

"Do you guys mind if I make a quick call to Uncle Daniel? And then, I'm all yours."

"Of course," Bailey said as she leaned against the door casing with her arms crossed.

In my sister's bedroom, Noah placed my suitcase on the upholstered bench at the foot of the king-sized bed. "Okay, come on. Let's give Aunt Cassie a minute to call Uncle Daniel."

Just as McKenna was about to protest, her older brother whisked her up in his arms and carried her out of the room, Bailey trailing behind.

"Want me to close the doors?" she asked.

"Sure, sweetie. I just need a minute, and then I thought we could either make dinner here or I can take you all to Piazza. Would you like that?"

Her eyes seemed to agree. "Sure." She closed the double doors.

I made the call. This time, Daniel answered on the first ring. "Hey, hon. Where ya been?"

"What do you mean, where have *I* been? I was at work, and now I'm at Trina's. Where are *you*?"

"Oh. Okay. I'm on my way there. I wasn't sure what time you wanted me. I hadn't heard from you, and I knew today would be busy, so I didn't want to disturb you at work."

A moment of silence sat thick between us as I tried to decide what to say *or ask* next.

"Is everything okay?" My husband's voice wavered a tad, enough that I suspected he knew *something* was wrong.

"You could say that. I called you about forty-five minutes ago. Didn't *Leslie* tell you?"

"Leslie? Why would Leslie tell me? And no, she didn't." Road noise filled in the background.

"Because, as I said, I called you about forty-five minutes ago." I checked the clock on Trina's nightstand. "Maybe sooner. She answered your phone. She said you were in the bathroom." I held back more of what I wanted to say, waiting for his response.

"Huh. No, she didn't mention it. Hmm. That's weird. I wonder why she didn't say anything."

I already had my hand on my hip, my shoulders rising with annoyance.

Daniel didn't reply right away. *Is he checking his phone?* "I don't see any calls on my phone. Are you sure you called today?"

What a stupid question. "Yeah, I'm sure. She thought I was Kendra. Everyone seems to think you and Kendra are together."

Daniel hissed a little. "Cassie, let's not go down that road again. Kendra and I are just friends—"

"Then why didn't you tell me you were meeting her today?"

"What's the big deal? We work together. And I don't appreciate what you're insinuating." His voice grew louder against the road noise. That wasn't the reason, though. He was getting annoyed.

Well, how dare he!

"That's what Leslie said. And you know what else she said?" I didn't wait for him to answer. "She said she didn't know you were even married. In fact, she had no idea who I was." I unzipped my suitcase and grabbed my shower bag, bringing it with me into the bathroom, the one with beautiful ceramic tile floors, granite sinks, and the scent of flowers floating through the air. A curved top window cast warm rays of sunshine onto the shiny surfaces and jet tub. A far cry from *our* tiny bathroom that struggled to keep us clean every day.

Two months ago, we didn't have hot water for an entire week because the hot water heater's temperature gauge had died. The thing was only large enough for one good shower, anyway, leaving the poor sucker who took the second one with a cold blast halfway through. We learned to space washing dishes and showers to avoid the unpleasantness. That was my world. I was a goddamn lawyer living in squalor.

"Cassie, I've only met with Leslie once before, other than on the phone. And that was at the restaurant. You weren't there." He corrected himself. "Well, I didn't know you were there. Anyway, you know that I don't wear my ring when I'm working because it will get ruined. My hands are always in food or water. And it was *you* who had suggested that I not wear it when I was working, remember?"

I did remember. I had noticed one day how dingy his wedding band looked compared to mine. I suggested he get it cleaned and then keep it out of the kitchen. And when Daniel wasn't working, he almost always had it on. Unless, he had gone somewhere *from* work and couldn't get home to retrieve it. At home, he always wore it.

I was contemplating a silicone ring when he huffed.

"I'll start wearing it again. Personally, I don't like not having it on my hand. And I wouldn't like it if you weren't wearing yours. The topic of my marriage hasn't come up yet. I was trying to get Leslie's notes and outline some topics we plan to discuss for the podcast next week, and I was in a hurry. I wasn't trying to hide the fact that I'm married. That's ridiculous."

Daniel had a way of making sense when a situation didn't appear that way. Something else occurred to me.

"Why didn't you tell me you were meeting with Kendra today?"

He released another heavy breath, the sound of his car blinker ticking off in the background.

Where are you going now?

"Kendra called me earlier and asked if we could have coffee. She said she wanted to discuss some work issues." He paused. "To be honest, Cassie, she's concerned about how you feel about her."

"What?" I was outraged.

"It's obvious that you don't like her. Even I can see that. And you seem to be threatened by her, too, even when I tell you repeatedly that I don't have feelings for her. Just yesterday you were making comments about her outfit. I'm not gonna lie.

She's an attractive woman, but I'm married, and she knows I have no intention of breaking my vows."

"What if you weren't married? Would you want to be with her then?" I didn't mean to say that. My mind was pushing garbage out of my mouth, which often happened when I felt threatened in some way.

Daniel didn't respond. He let my insecure comment linger, amplifying its negative connotation.

"What are you trying to say?"

Standing in my sister's bathroom, I bowed my head. "I don't know what I'm trying to say."

"Are you saying you don't want to be married to me anymore? Cause I gotta tell you, keep this behavior up, and you may just get your wish."

Click, the call ended.

Chapter Twelve

I spent the next several minutes pacing Trina's bathroom, processing. I'd overacted. That was apparent, and he was growing tired of me. I understood that, too, since I was growing tired of myself. When had I become this insecure mess? *Forever*, it seemed.

I almost got married once before, right out of college. It was to a man who was also studying to be a lawyer. His name was Bryce Tanner, and he was everything I had *thought* I wanted in a spouse. His light-brown hair grew streaks of caramel in the summer months, enhancing his tanned skin and blue eyes. He was fit, but not crazy about it. And he was nice. We met during one of our prelaw courses and hit it off right away. What I loved about Bryce was his sense of humor. He'd crack jokes about eccentric professors or classmates that always brought a giggle to my lips. We studied together, and we grew close. I helped him pass several classes, which now, as I looked back, was probably the thing he liked most about me.

Before I knew what was happening, we were dating, and in no time, we were engaged, a big rock on my finger that could blind you if cast in direct sunlight. My parents loved Bryce and his fun-loving attitude. My sister wasn't quite as enamored, which seemed odd considering she had been worried about me finding the right guy. During high school, I had developed a Cassie trait, vying for guys who weren't that into me. Deep down, I wondered if my need to win over boys who showed little interest would fix me in some way. If they approved of me, I had to be okay, right?

Why did I need their approval? Even with parents who were kind, a girl's self-image could be crushed by a few popular girls who liked to pick on me for being smart. Whenever I raised my inquisitive hand in class, some of them would actually groan. Miss Know-it-all wasn't a moniker I enjoyed when the girls who said it added a sneer or a mocking smirk. I also struggled with acne and my weight, which didn't help matters. In fact, all through grade school I was quite chubby.

By college, my skin was clear, my weight much healthier, but that didn't stop those inner demons from reminding me I was still nothing special. My intelligence was *not* something I prided myself on. Not back then. Until I met Bryce, who picked my brain practically clean on a regular basis. And he seemed to be as into me as I was with him.

Aside from my sister's nonconformance about liking my fiancé, another warning flag came from his family, who never warmed up to me. They were rich; my family wasn't, so I'd decided back then that that could have been the crux. Later, I realized they knew about Bryce's other women, and never figured I'd stick around long enough to bother with, even though the ring on my finger said otherwise.

Bryce was *the guy*. He made people laugh. He was driven. He was handsome. And he had a bright future.

In the bedroom, he was just *okay*, meaning he didn't work all that hard to please me. If I didn't orgasm in a timely fashion, he'd act bothered as though it was my fault our lovemaking was taking so long. For me, his impatience just made matters worse. Not a lot of foreplay either. So, I faked it. I could have gotten an Oscar for my performances. But back then, I had decided I could live with that too. Everywhere else, this man rocked.

Until I came home early one day to find him sleeping with the receptionist at his law firm. A very sexy receptionist with big breasts and long brown hair. I could hear them from the foyer of our new house. And when I entered our bedroom to find my fiancé's face buried deep between the woman's legs, I'd lost it. He'd never given *me* oral sex. Not once. I guessed he'd saved that perk for his affairs, which I also found ran in his family like water through a river.

He tried to explain that it meant nothing, and when that didn't work, he took another tack. "Look. You and I work on paper. We make a good team. And I'd be willing to have kids *if that's what you want*. But let's face it, Cassie, we don't have that kind of chemistry."

The girl had long since fled out the door, grabbing her clothes along the way, while my fiancé tried to explain his fucked-up logic to me.

Bryce sat on the edge of our king-sized bed while I stood by the door, trying to decide whether I wanted to get the hell out of there or stay and listen.

What did I do? That insecure girl, who could never quite measure up in a man's eyes, stood there and listened, Bryce's words shooting poisonous darts into my heart.

"If you want to have sex with someone else *on the side*, I'm okay with it. All I ask is for your discretion."

I was blown away. In one moment, we'd gone from a happy couple to this? I realized we were never happy. Not only was I not able to let go sexually with him, but I also found myself shrinking in his presence. He talked less to me and more to the people around me. In college, he wanted *my* opinion. Not anymore. I was losing myself.

"Don't you love me?" I had asked for some unknown reason. Looking back, the answer was obvious.

With his pants on and his white dress shirt hanging loose and unbuttoned from his shoulders, Bryce rose. He fanned a hand out. "What is love, anyway, Cassie? What we have is better than love. We have a partnership." He took a step closer, his voice more serious than I had ever heard from him. "My father had loved a woman once, and she broke his heart. Nearly broke *him* too. He told me to never give my heart to anyone. 'Once you do that, son, you've lost control of your life.'"

That was the worst day of *my* life. It was also the best day of my life because I realized I wasn't going to settle for anyone who was *good on paper* and lousy at love. Trina had later told me she had suspected he was cheating when she'd run into Bryce accompanying an attractive blond in the lobby of a fancy hotel in the city. She was meeting a friend of hers there for lunch. Bryce had passed it off as a meeting with one of his clients, but something about his mannerisms told my big sis he was lying. She just didn't have any concrete evidence to prove it. So, she kept quiet for the time being.

My heart was broken, obliterating an already wobbly self-esteem. My dating life became a series of going through the motions, enjoying a few tolerable rolls in the sheets every now and then.

But then I met Daniel. He was so refreshingly different. He didn't come from money, and even if he had, I suspected it wouldn't have made a difference. It took me several weeks to believe this gorgeous man was interested in me. And to this day, I never understood why.

And there sat the weak link in the chain of our marriage—my belief that I didn't deserve someone like Daniel. There had to be something wrong with him. *He wants the benefit of my intelligence. He needs my help. He is still waiting for the right woman to come along. He is just being kind.* And then there was the worst excuse of all—*He doesn't really love you.*

Knock, knock, knock.

From the en suite bath, I entered the bedroom and approached the set of double doors, ready to apologize to my nieces and nephew for taking too long. I had just gotten here. And I was being rude.

Only it wasn't any of them standing on the other side of the doors, it was Daniel, his cell phone clutched in his hand.

"Daniel!" I was almost startled by his appearance.

He stepped around me and into the room, then slowly closed the doors, calling out, "We'll be out in a minute, kids."

He stood before me, my heart aching to fall into his arms. "What's going on with you lately?" His eyes tensed. "You are one of the most caring people I know. Why the sudden anger toward Kendra? And now you're worried about Leslie? This isn't like you." He took my hands in his. "You were the one who hired Kendra. You said you loved her enthusiasm. What's changed?"

I *had* hired Kendra. And I had even felt at one point we could be friends. But then my job pulled me in one direction while the restaurant pulled Daniel in another. I guess I resented that she could go along with him on his adventure, and I couldn't.

How could I possibly explain what I truly felt? My mind swirled, thoughts struggling to manifest in any tangible way. I couldn't answer my husband even if I wanted to, not without sounding like a selfish bitch. Daniel believed I was kind. How could I break the news to him that I wasn't? Not when it came to him.

I grew tired of people thinking Kendra was his wife. I grew tired of her always looking spectacular. Mostly, I grew tired of her always being there when I wasn't. That was it. In some ways, it felt as though Kendra was replacing me. It was silly. And it was totally on me to think this way. But it was *also* standing right there in front of me every time I laid eyes on the woman.

"I'm sorry." I *could* say that and actually mean it. "I feel like I'm coming apart lately, trying to keep up." That was also true. "I'm such a mess."

He took me in his arms and held me close, his heart beating in my ear. "You are always so in control. You take care of everyone. But yourself. You work your ass off. It's time you lived for Cassie." He lightened his tone. "And your husband, of course." He pulled back and stared deep into my eyes. "Don't you see it? You can't go on like this. You are the smartest person I know. You can do anything you want. There is no need for you to have to be this miserable."

Daniel appreciated my intelligence, but he never took advantage of it. It was me who had forced our savings onto him for the restaurant. He respected my opinion. He listened to me. And he did his best to show me how much he cared, sexually and otherwise.

I nodded, hoping to show him I was listening.

"You want to know what *I* want? I want my wife back. The woman who takes the world by storm." He grabbed my upper arms, holding them firmly. "And the one who doesn't worry about stupid shit that only stresses us both out."

A round of persistent knocking interrupted our intense moment.

I snapped out of my pity party. "Okay. I'm sorry, I . . . " My words faded away as I shook my head, my gaze falling to the floor. "I don't know what's happening to me."

My husband firmed his voice. "Nothing is happening to you. We've just had a bad week. Things will work out."

I gazed up at him, my heart trying its best to reopen. "Promise?"

"Absolutely!" He smiled down at me, waving one hand out. "Look on the bright side. We've got a nice place to spend our weekend. I even brought my swim trunks." A cunning smile washed over his face as he wiggled his eyebrows. "Unless you want to wait until later and we can go without." He touched his forehead against mine.

Knock, knock, knock. "Come on, Aunt Cassie, when are you coming out? I'm sick of waiting." My poor niece was losing patience, and I couldn't blame her. Not one bit.

On the other side of the double doors, Bailey took up verbal arms. "Stop bothering them, *McKenna Dilemma.*"

McKenna Dilemma, huh? Was that Bailey's new nickname for her little sister? Trina used to call me Cassie Assie when she was angry with me, and boy, did *that* make me mad.

"Don't call me that, *Bailey . . . Bailey.*" Poor McKenna's six-year-old mind couldn't seem to muster up a nickname to combat her big sister's snappy wit.

"What's the matter? Can't think of anything to say back, *McKenna Dilemma?*"

"I said, don't call me that!"

"How about Bailey Ukulele" came from Noah's voice, followed by his chuckle.

McKenna jumped all over that one. "Yeah, Bailey Uki . . . malee."

"You can't use it if you can't say it, shrimp. And shut up, *Noah Boa Constrictor.*"

Daniel smirked, his gaze and mine focused on the closed doors.

"Ooooh. Aren't you talented, *Bailey Ukulele,* you can think up nicknames. Ooooh, you're as smart as a fart." Sarcasm dripped from Noah's voice. He had a tendency to stick up for his littlest sister whenever the two of them went at it.

Daniel quirked a brow as he scratched at his temple. "We better get out there before the names get worse."

"Yup." I approached the doors and flung them open.

Having abandoned the knocking, all the kids stood facing each other in a circle ready for battle, McKenna's face red, Bailey's and Noah's eyes filled with mischief.

"Well, since your last name is Franks, I think you're all *cranks*." I outwardly cracked myself up.

My husband smirked and the rest of the younger generation just stared with disgust, Noah's eyes a tad more forgiving than the others. I grabbed McKenna and started tickling her, making her squeal. "Hey. What do you want from me? I don't have your talent for rhyming."

I followed up my tickling with a firm hug for my niece. "Okay, let's get dinner planned. Do you guys want to go to Piazza, order pizza, or make dinner? Your mom said she made some salads. Uncle Daniel and I just need to check out the fridge and the cupboards." Still holding onto McKenna, I buried my head in her neck and gave her a big wet kiss. Her hair smelled like strawberries and cream. "But first, I think we have a game of hide-and-seek in our immediate future." I released my niece from my clutches.

McKenna clapped her hands together, her bad mood long gone. "Yay."

"You guys go play hide-and-seek, and *I'll* check out the cupboards and the fridge. I brought plenty to work with from the restaurant as well. I need to use up some of the produce." Daniel took a step away.

"Can I help?" Noah caught up with his uncle.

"Sure, man. I'd love the help."

"I'm taking a class at school about cooking . . ." And soon, the men were out of sight.

"So, it's the three of us, then?" I gazed over at Bailey, hoping she'd comply.

A slow smile spread across her face. "Fine! But I get to count first."

* * *

After three games of hide-and-seek, followed by a pretend tea party in McKenna's room (she had the table and chairs already arranged), the women of the house plopped ourselves down on the recliner sofa in the living room and started primping. I painted McKenna's fingernails light pink while Bailey did her own in teal. Thankfully, Bailey had the nail polish since I hadn't brought any.

A beam of sunlight reached across the room, draping over Bailey's hair and making it shine like a hardwood floor just after a good polish, encouraging notes of caramel and dark chocolate browns. Aside from her eye color, she was a carbon copy of my big sis, who was much prettier than I ever was. I used to love brushing her long locks. "You have such beautiful hair, Bailey. Why don't you let me brush it out and do a French braid? I promise I'll be gentle. It will look great."

Memories of Trina and me sitting on the lid of our guest bathroom toilet, styling our hair, or doing each other's makeup brought an affectionate tug to my heart. I hoped that once these two put their sibling rivalry to rest, McKenna and Bailey would learn the benefits of sisterhood. Who did I turn to whenever I felt down? Trina. Who did I jump up and down with whenever life had handed me an unexpected moment of joy? My big sis. And vice versa. She was the first person I had told about Daniel. *He's hot as hell, Trina, but he must have a screw loose somewhere to be so into me.* Her reaction was immediate. *No, he just has taste, unlike the dickheads you normally meet. And don't talk about my little sis that way, or I'll knock you silly!*

I felt bad for anyone who didn't have someone like that in their lives. Someone who loved you through and through. Someone who had been there since the beginning. Trina accepted me, blemishes and all. Daniel had accepted me, too, but there were times when I suspected he wished for a more accommodating wife, or one who wasn't as driven by her career.

I finished McKenna's nails and screwed the cap on, placing the bottle of nail polish on a side table. The chemical smell hung heavy in the room. I was tempted to open a window, but with the AC running, I chose not to. I'd gotten sensitive to smells lately, especially whenever I wasn't feeling well. Not wanting one of those physical oddities to return, I shook the thought from my mind and picked up a brush from the same side table that held our manicure essentials. "What do you say, Bailey? I used to do a pretty good job on your mom's hair." I held the brush up.

She shrugged, which I had come to assume was her way of saying yes since she hadn't outwardly objected. "I have to let my fingers dry anyway" was her excuse as she plopped down on the area rug in front of me and fluttered her hands to create a drying breeze.

"You braided Mommy's hair?" With her little body perched next to mine, McKenna stared over at me in wonder.

"Oh, yeah. Many times. Your mommy had the softest hair. I used to love brushing it out and braiding it."

"Do you think *my* hair is pretty too?"

"Yes, I do, McKenna. Women pay good money for hair that color, believe me." Flaxen locks with just the right amount of wave, the girl was as striking as her sister.

Her brow lowered. "Huh? Pay for hair?"

"Never mind. I was just joking. Your hair is beautiful. Tell you what, I'll braid yours next, okay?"

"Yay." She clapped her hands together and sunk back on the couch, her little feet dangling over the edge of the cushion.

I put on the TV to give us something to watch, landing on the Disney Channel and a show McKenna loved called *Bluey*.

I went to work, brushing Bailey's lustrous locks. "Did I ever tell you about the time when your mother's first boyfriend, Kenny, had broken up with her?"

That got their attention.

"Really?" McKenna said. "Mommy had a boyfriend that wasn't Daddy?"

I had to laugh. Funny how young ones only saw their parents with each other. They weren't people to them. They were Mommy and Daddy, a.k.a. superheroes, fairy godmothers (or fathers), and larger-than-life individuals. And when those same kids morphed into teenagers, parents were nothing short of lame or a pain in the ass. "Yup. Let me tell ya, she was a mess on that day . . ." I went on to regale them with a short story about how a broken heart was mended by fresh makeup and curlers. While I'd played hairdresser back then, Trina unloaded about how thirteen-year-old Kenny, with peach fuzz on his chin and a voice that would often crack whenever he got excited, had asked Bethany Chambers to the eighth-grade dance instead of Trina. Trina professed *she* was his girlfriend since they had kissed once and held hands twice. It was the end of the world for her . . . until some kid named Adam had smiled at her the next day during lunch. The Universe had aligned again.

From the kitchen, pans clanked, feet shuffled, and conversations remained light and airy as the men prepared dinner, cabinets and drawers opening and closing.

While Bailey sat on the floor in front of me, her little sis remained cozied up right next to me watching TV, playing with her newest Barbie. Bailey had never been into dolls. Her mind enjoyed Legos or anything that involved problem solving. Girl after my own heart. *Kindred spirits,* and she had the green eyes to prove it. I could never boast about something like that in front of her little sister. That would be cruel. And I wasn't one to play favorites.

Before long, garlic, something nutty, and other savory scents found their way around the corner and into the living room where we all remained. When I was finished with her hair and had started on her sister, Bailey got up to see what was cookin', telling me she was enjoying the aromas as much as I was.

McKenna described it as "Yummy smells."

It was 6:45, and we were all ready to eat. Or I was, anyway, my stomach rumbling.

Bailey set the table in the formal dining room beforehand while I arranged drink glasses and opened a bottle of red blend for Daniel and me to enjoy. Soon, we were all seated around the table. I even put a soft rock station on the stereo in the living room to provide a welcoming vibe to the evening.

Daniel had brought several large tomatoes from the restaurant, which he parboiled and peeled, some pine nuts, which he toasted in a pan, and fresh basil, also from Daniel's Garden Patch. He food processed those ingredients, adding fresh garlic and newly shredded parmesan. Adding in a few more ingredients, the man made us a pasta dish that was so delicious, I had to go back for thirds. Even the kids loved it, who were normally big fans of mac and cheese, pizza, or french fries, exclusively.

With the guidance of his uncle, Noah had assembled a spectacular tossed salad with chopped orange and yellow peppers, fresh cucumber, scallions, and basil, along with butter lettuce and mixed greens. Daniel had already made a tasty

Italian dressing with fresh herbs earlier that day, which we drizzled over our salads and enjoyed. He also brought a large baguette that we munched on after adding plenty of butter. The kids were literally licking their lips. He told me later he had used a few of my sister's spices to show his appreciation for her supplies. The butter also came from her kitchen.

"Are you all excited for school to start?" I asked as we ate.

Noah nodded but didn't offer anything beyond that.

"My best friend, Brittany, is in my homeroom," McKenna said with a ring of pasta sauce around her mouth. "We're gonna sit together."

"That's great." I took a sip of my wine.

"How about you, Bailey?"

She let one shoulder rise before releasing it. "It's fine. Not looking forward to homework from Mr. Anderson, who is a total butthead." She smirked, clearly amused with herself.

"You can't swear. I'll tell Mom." McKenna had taken on the role of house monitor, something six-year-olds loved to do, but would definitely outgrow.

Since McKenna was sitting right next to me, I patted her arm. "It's okay, sweetie. We'll let it go this one time."

Daniel grinned at her. "Yeah, I had a few teachers who were butts too."

I thought McKenna's jaw was going to hit the floor, which made Noah laugh.

"Tell you what, McKenna. Don't tattle on me to Mom and Dad, and I'll let you know what I brought for dessert. Deal?" Daniel beamed a smile at her.

"Deal!" She nodded once with distinction. "What'd you bring?"

Sticky buns.

I suddenly regretted my third helping.

Once we cleared the table, we enjoyed my husband's sticky

buns from the Alaskan white granite breakfast bar, all of us chatting away about how good they were. Daniel just stood back and watched us, his eyes shining with delight, his glass of wine clutched in his hand. I caught his gaze and smiled back at him. *This could be us*, reflected in his eyes, a message I received loud and clear, even without actual words attached to it.

After dinner, we all jumped into our swimsuits (I helped McKenna with hers) and enjoyed some pool time. Daniel did backflips from the diving board, prompting Noah to join him. Before long, we had a little competition going on that lasted for quite some time, *woo-hoos* and applause bouncing off the waves.

As the sun dipped lower in the sky, spreading ribbons of red, orange, and yellow across the horizon, we all dried off and got ready for showers and fresh clothes. I helped McKenna untangle her braid, wash the chlorine from her hair and body, and dress her in a fresh pair of Barbie pj's.

Bailey and Noah took turns in their Jack-and-Jill bathroom doing the same thing. McKenna had the hall bath all to herself.

I sat on the couch with my sweet niece, brushing out her hair and waiting for Daniel to take *his* shower, so I could take mine after him. *SpongeBob SquarePants* played on the TV for the moment since we planned to watch *Inside Out 2* when everyone was ready. I'd loved the original movie, so I was excited about the sequel.

"Why don't *you* have kids?" McKenna asked as she sat on a pillow on the floor in front of me. (She needed a little more height than her sister had.)

Wow, even the younger generation was hounding me about this issue. "Well, we don't have kids *yet*, sweetie. That doesn't mean we *won't* have them." I brushed the ends of her hair, first, hoping to work my way inward to avoid pain and too many tangles, her fruity shampoo strong and pleasant.

She gazed up at me with her adorable hazel eyes. "How come it's taking so long?"

Although I wasn't thrilled with having this conversation, I was relieved she hadn't asked me where babies came from. That was a topic saved for Mom and Dad, and *not* me.

"I'm not sure." I touched her button nose again, which I couldn't help but do. "That's a good question." I had to think about my answer. "I guess your uncle and I have been busy. Uncle Daniel has the restaurant, you know, and I have my job at the firm."

McKenna faced the large TV positioned just over the mantel. "Daisy is *my* baby." Daisy was McKenna's fluffy white unicorn with a rainbow-colored horn. Daisy slept with my niece every night and cuddled with her whenever she was tired, which was right now.

"Yes, Daisy is a great baby." I peered down at the stuffed toy in my niece's lap.

She gazed back at the TV, her short attention span moving onto SpongeBob and his signature laugh.

I finished her hair, the color of corn silk, in no time. That was when I thought about the candy I had brought. I was quite shocked that McKenna hadn't hounded me about the treats. Since we had launched right into hide-and-seek, and then our tea party immediately afterward—then dinner and pool time—I guessed she had forgotten about it. So had I.

"Okay, missy. I brought you and your brother *and* sister a little treat, which will be perfect for when we watch the movie."

She sprang from the floor, her eyes bright with curiosity. "What is it? Can I have it now? Please, Aunt Cassie, can I have it now?"

I giggled. "Yes, go grab my purse on the kitchen counter, and I'll show you what I brought."

A Collision with Love

"Here, hold Daisy for me." She handed over the stuffed toy.

Not two minutes passed before she was back in the room. I let her fish out the candy, which she seemed rather thrilled about. My sister had them on a strict sugar diet, making this extra special. Mike was borderline diabetic, a good portion of his family members suffering from the disease, so Trina didn't want the kids to grow up depending on sugar for sustenance. Living with Daniel, I grew to appreciate the benefits *and* the dangers of food, so I got it. Which was the reason I had texted my big sis, asking if this would be okay. *Sure, once in a while is fine.*

"Can I have it now?" My niece held up the Sour Patch Kids like a trophy or a pom-pom since she stood waving it in the air. She didn't say anything about the Skittles or the peanut M&M's. She knew who wanted those.

"Let's save it for the movie." I slapped my hands down on my thighs, ready to rise from the couch. "You wanna help me make the popcorn?" I set Daisy on the cushion beside me.

McKenna's face lit up once again. "Uh-huh. I'm a great helper, you know."

"I *do* know that. That's why I asked you, sweet girl." We ventured toward the kitchen when Daniel appeared, his wet hair pulled up into a man bun and the scent of musk riding alongside him. "You go take your shower, hon, and I'll help make the popcorn. McKenna can tell me what to do, right? You're the boss." His gaze found the candy, waiting anxiously on the side table to ramp up someone's energy. "Ooh, I see Aunt Cassie brought you a treat."

My niece nodded enthusiastically. "Aunt Cassie said I have to wait for the movie to eat my candy." If McKenna was hoping her Uncle Daniel would circumvent my authority, she was wrong.

"That's probably a good idea. Plus, I can't make all this

popcorn without you." Daniel knew which buttons to push, just like I did.

Before I left the room, I took a moment to enjoy these two as I walked away.

"I'm a better cook than Noah, you know." Her indigence was also quite cute.

A smile blossomed in my heart as Daniel rested his hand on the top of his niece's dampened head. "I have no doubt you are a great cook. What do you think? Should we use smaller bowls for each person?"

Aw.

By the time the movie was over, McKenna was so tired, Daniel had to carry her upstairs. He made sure to include Daisy. Neither Bailey nor Noah argued about bedtime, either. I suspected Noah planned to play or surf on his phone, but as long as he didn't stay up too late, I was okay with it.

Bailey yawned, her feet dragging toward the stairs. "Want some help cleaning up?" She yawned again.

"Nah, Noah will help. Right, bud?"

"Yup." Wearing a pair of gray cotton shorts and a white T-shirt that substituted well for pj's, he rose from the couch, his bare feet padding across the room.

"Get some rest. Sleep tight. Don't forget to brush your teeth," I called after Bailey before she was out of sight.

Bailey waved her hand haphazardly as she lugged her tired feet to the second floor. "Night."

I brought our empty popcorn bowls into the kitchen to stick into the dishwasher. Noah brought the cups and the used napkins, along with the candy wrappers. (The candy was gone within ten minutes of the movie's premiere.)

Kitchen relatively clean, I checked the front and back door to make sure they were locked. Noah followed me.

"I don't mind you playing on your phone for a bit, Noah,

but just don't go on any sketchy websites." Even though he was mature for his age and looked older, the boy was still only thirteen. I'd seen many court cases where predators had taken advantage of people just like him.

"My parents put controls on my phone, so no chance of that." He said it with a tad of disgust in his tone, but I could tell he wasn't actually *all* that bothered.

In my mind, kids (some kids) appreciated parents who looked out for them, setting up guardrails so they didn't drive themselves into a ditch. I planned to be one of those parents.

It was eleven o'clock when I met Daniel in the primary bathroom, brushing his teeth. "McKenna go down okay?"

He nodded, then spit, before rinsing his mouth clean of toothpaste. He rinsed down the sink. "Yup. I had to brush her teeth for her, and then she went right down."

"Thank you. I poked my head into her room and saw that she was out already. Sorry I didn't get there in time. I wanted to get the house in order and check the doors before bed."

My husband wiped his mouth. "No worries, wife of mine, I had it covered." He kissed the side of my head, his breath all minty and fresh.

While I took out my toothpaste and brush, something occurred to me. I checked my shower bag first before I followed Daniel into the bedroom with my toothbrush clutched in my hand. "Hey, I can't seem to find my birth control pills. I usually keep them in my purse, but they're not there, and I didn't see them when I packed my shower bag earlier." I gave him a funny look, hoping he hadn't hidden them from me. If we planned to start a family, it wasn't a good idea to start out sabotaging.

Daniel pulled the decorative pillows off the bed, placing them in an oversized wicker basket off to the side, one precisely large enough to fit them all. My sister had thought of everything. "No idea, hon. And why are you looking at me like that?

I didn't take them if that's what you're wondering." He almost scoffed at me.

"I wasn't wondering *that*, Daniel," I said, even though I kinda was. "I just find it odd that I can't find them is all."

Once Daniel had cleared the bed of all the extra pillows, he pulled the comforter and top sheet down. "So, you haven't been taking them?" His voice carried a smidge of excitement that left me feeling conflicted.

"I know. It's been a couple of days . . . I think." I shook my head, that foggy sensation returning to my brain. *Please don't do this to me now.*

"You start your cycle soon, right?"

"Yeah."

"Then don't worry about it. Let's just see how this plays out. If you're pregnant, we'll know soon enough."

"Daniel, I'm not ready—"

"Look." He raised a palm as he approached me. "If you've missed a few days already, then there isn't much you can do about it now. If you're not pregnant, you will know in a couple of days." His voice lowered. "And then, you can resume taking them again . . . *if you want*." He was so transparent in that moment, his desire for a family written all over his excited face. "I'm not sure how long you can go without taking them before it would make any difference to double or triple up on them, anyway." He placed his hands on my waist. "What's done is done. Let's just see what happens."

Once again, *Let's just see what happens* had never been a mantra I'd embraced. I took a stabilizing breath. Maybe it was the fact that we were at my sister's house with all of this luxury around us, playing house and mimicking what our future *could* look like. Or possibly it was due to the fact that Daniel and I had spent one of the best evenings together in months. Noah looked up to Daniel, just like I envisioned our son would. The girls were equally enamored with me. That kind of admiration was hard to find.

Even at bedtime, when I went to check on Bailey earlier, she'd said, "Night, KS."

Confused, I paused at her doorway. "KS?" I'd hoped it wasn't some lamo name for her lamo aunt. *The girl was ten going on eleven after all. And* she'd proven earlier she was the master at nicknames.

She lifted her head off the pillow and said matter-of-factly, "Yeah, Kindred Spirit." It was as if what she just said was no big deal at all as she turned over and snuggled into her pillow, leaving me teary-eyed as I closed the door. "Kindred Spirits for sure, sweetie," I'd said as the door clicked shut.

Whatever the reason, I couldn't come up with an argument for Daniel's logic. Instead, I looked him square in the face. "Are we really doing this?" The hint of a smile played at the corners of my mouth, my heart racing, but not in a bad way this time. In fact, my head couldn't have been clearer.

My husband's face illuminated with joy. "Yeah, I think we are. Now, hurry up and brush your teeth, I've got some fun planned for us in bed." He patted my butt and winked.

If there was even a *chance* my husband could put a baby inside of me, he was determined to give it his best shot.

Chapter Thirteen

The next morning, Daniel made his special sausage-and-egg casserole, his sticky buns a nice complement to the meal. The kids were not only up early, but they also jumped into action, Bailey setting the table in the breakfast nook, Noah pouring the orange juice, and McKenna helping Uncle Daniel flip the blueberry buttermilk pancakes he *decided* to make at the last minute when McKenna had begged him to do so. She also wanted to help, and according to her, she was an *espert* at flipping. (To her credit, she only flipped one pancake onto the floor.) I made the coffee.

The kids seemed to enjoy having us around, which warmed my heart and made me all the more comfortable with not taking the last of this month's birth control pills. That's what my strange symptoms had to be: I was pregnant, and as soon as I could take a test and confirm it, I'd let my husband know the good news. It gave me goosebumps just thinking about how he would react, the elation he would feel. Would he pick me up and twirl me around? Or would he fall to his knees in gratitude?

We wolfed down our breakfast feast, and before long, Daniel was heading off to take care of some paperwork at the restaurant and to make sure everything was in order for the plumber to arrive the next day. "I want to move some shelving away from the walls, so Barry has full access."

I hated to see him go. Last night was magical, all of us together—not to mention the fun Daniel and I had afterward—but I took comfort in knowing he'd be back soon, and we could resume our joyous weekend.

"Want to tag along, bud?" Daniel asked Noah, whose eyes widened at the prospect as he shoved his last bite of pancakes into his mouth.

He rose from the table immediately. "I'd be down. Give me a minute to change." He hesitated. "Do you mind, Aunt Cassie?"

I waved him off. "Not a problem. Go ahead. I'll enjoy more girl time with these two. Right ladies?" I fluffed McKenna's hair as I spoke, who now had maple syrup all over her lips. The bees would love her. The girl couldn't seem to eat without wearing the evidence all over her mouth and face. Soon enough, she'd be self-conscious about that sort of thing too. Conditioned to worry about what other people thought. I preferred *this* version.

I rose from the table and began stacking plates to bring to the sink to rinse first and then place into the dishwasher. I couldn't wait for the day when *we* had a dishwasher. Hand washing *every* dish, pan, utensil, or cup got old and when you didn't have a lot of counter space. The sink in our apartment was about half the depth of my sister's and smaller in diameter. Two mugs would take up enough space that they needed to be washed and put out of the way.

The girls helped me clean up. After that, I left the plans for the rest of the day up to them. Did they want to hang by the pool, go out to lunch, or shop in town? "We can do whatever you two decide." While I awaited their answer, I contemplated running out to the pharmacy to purchase a pregnancy test, but I couldn't leave the girls alone, and I didn't want them knowing about what I was up to. *You're not even late yet.* If I didn't start my period on Monday, as scheduled, I'd get the test and find out.

Both girls glanced at each other.

"I'm sick of shopping." Bailey gazed over at her sister, who seemed to agree. "Let's just hang here."

And that was how we spent the next couple of hours, lounging by the pool, listening to music, chatting about superficial things such as who was cute in Bailey's world or how excited McKenna was about sharing her first-grade classroom with her BFF, Brittany. I made lemonade, and by lunchtime, we were all hungry again, so I had the girls help me put together ham and cheese sandwiches. I also pulled those salads my big sis had told me about from the fridge. Trina might not match Daniel's expertise for cooking, but she had culinary skills in her own right. The dill in the potato salad was a nice touch. I'd have to remember to tell Daniel to try it.

Speaking of which, I was about to suggest we bring some lunch over to the guys at the restaurant, when Daniel's Subaru wagon pulled into the driveway. For a moment, I got a sense of what it would feel like to have my family return home. No, they weren't *my* kids, but I enjoyed having the band back together. This weekend was just what I had needed to make a decision about children. It sure seemed like the Universe was trying to tell me something.

Unfortunately, all good things had to come to an end. Saturday came and went, Sunday's duties forcing Daniel out the door once again. Bailey's friend Kaitlyn called to hang out, and since she'd been so great about spending time with us this weekend, I allowed it. Kaitlyn came to our house, and the girls hung in Bailey's room for the rest of the day. After checking with his mother first, Noah took off to practice lacrosse with a buddy of his. Now that Uncle Daniel was gone, his need to be close had dwindled.

That was also something parents had to deal with, I surmised: their kids wanting time to themselves. I'd remembered how Trina had said that poor McKenna had gotten lots of mother-daughter time this summer, and it all made sense now. I spent the afternoon getting in touch with my six-year-old self, the one who loved to play Barbies and experiment with makeup. We even had a small fashion show for her dollies.

My sister and Mike's Uber rolled into the driveway just past six o'clock, both of them tired and ready for bed already. Their bloodshot eyes and pale complexions told a story. Apparently, the wedding was a blast, the reception a blowout. They danced, they partied, and they reminded themselves who they were outside of their jobs and their roles as parents. Trina didn't say those words, specifically, but I understood what this weekend had meant to them, just as I understood what this weekend had meant to Daniel and me.

I didn't want to go home to that rundown apartment, so I went to the restaurant instead. And I was also starting to fret over that note from Isabella. Would tomorrow be my last day at the firm? A part of me—a very small part—hoped that it was. I was ready for a new adventure now, and it was hard to go back to the status quo, even if I loved my job *and* my clients. *You work to live, not the other way around.*

As I unlocked the door and entered the restaurant—and the bell rang above my head—no one came out to greet me this time. As soon as I reached the kitchen, I was faced with a room in total disarray. Shelves were pulled away from the walls, along with our dishwasher and fridge. Everything moved to the center of the room—or as far as the power cord would allow—and out of the way. Gaping holes revealed old pipes, old wiring, and insulation that all needed an upgrade. For now, it was the plumbing's turn to get the facelift.

Daniel was hunched over next to Barry, both of them examining something at close range.

"Wow. You guys have been busy."

Daniel straightened up and came over to place a kiss on my cheek, his eyes somber. "Yeah, this is a total cluster fuck. When Barry's done, we're gonna need someone to come in and repair these walls." Blood rushed to Daniel's cheeks. "I don't think we're gonna be open for at least a week."

My eyes bugged. "A week?" I felt bad about my outburst. Not that Daniel would be angry with me. Clearly, he wasn't any happier about this development than I was. *Say something positive.* "It's okay. We'll be fine. It's just one week, right?"

Daniel forced a slight nod.

"We've got all the time in the world to make it up."

"Maybe this was a bad idea . . . opening a restaurant." Daniel rubbed the back of his neck again.

"Nope. Don't go there." Just like he had done for me in my sister's bedroom when I was floundering about my insecure feelings regarding Kendra and Leslie, I placed my hands firmly on his upper arms, his biceps like rocks under my grip. "Shit happens. Who said achieving your dreams was ever going to be easy? No one. But this restaurant is worth the gamble." I tightened my grip. "We've got this!"

He repeated my words with slightly less vigor. "Yeah, we've got this."

* * *

A Collision with Love

Daniel and I climbed our tired bodies into bed around midnight. And even though I was dog-tired, I struggled to sleep. All I could think about was what I'd face in the morning. I kept reminding myself that the worst they could do was fire me. I had to believe that to be true. They wouldn't ruin my reputation over this, *would they*? Had I watched too many dramas on TV?

I could tell by his uneven breathing that Daniel wasn't sleeping either. Any hope that this recent dilemma could be fixed quickly had vanished. And we had to hire more people to get the kitchen back to where it was before this catastrophe struck.

Please don't let the wiring be the next issue. I never said the words, only thought them.

Neither Daniel nor I had enough energy for small talk over breakfast, which consisted of coffee and a bowl of cereal for us both, stale Cheerios that had been in the cupboard so long the expiration date had faded. I took a very quick shower, dressed, and met Daniel by the door on my way out. "Good luck today." I forced a smile from my wearied lips.

"You, too, hon."

Just like on Friday, I made it to the office bright and early, hoping to beat Isabella there. No such luck. The lights were on in her office, although she wasn't in view. *Bathroom?*

I hustled to my office, trying to keep my thoughts straight and what I was going to say when she confronted me. My mouth ran dry, but thus far, I hadn't had another attack since last Friday. That was a good sign, although my heart was pitter-pattering to beat the band thinking about what was coming down the road (or down the hall in my case).

As was her typical strategy, my boss waited until mid-morning, when I was just starting to relax and get into a rhythm with work, to show up at my door. She knocked on the casing, scaring the life out of me.

"Got a minute?" she asked.

"Of course." I gulped inwardly, my pulse ramping up like I was about to jump off a building. In some ways, this felt like I was doing just that, my career about to take a tumble, only to go splat on the street below.

"Meet you in my office in five?"

"Sure. I'll be right there."

"Great." Isabella disappeared as quickly as she had come.

With shaky hands, I rose from my desk and made my way there. Considering the stress I knew I'd be under, I made sure to wear flat shoes today, my softer-than-soft gray skirt, and my loose-fitting white blouse to provide comfort to my day. Even *with* those things, a tension sweat brewed across my forehead and under my armpits, though I had doubled up on the deodorant.

"Come on in." Wearing a sleeveless, light-blue sheath dress and a pair of four-inch silver Manolo Blahniks, Isabella was as cool as a cucumber, strolling across her office as though she didn't have a care in the world. *Ice queen* came to mind as she ran her hand down her long brown hair. She closed the heavy glass door behind me.

I thought about Daniel and steeled myself. I could do this.

"Did you have a nice weekend?" Isabella rounded the corner of her enormous desk and sat, her gaze skimming over a flurry of papers in front of her, ones she shuffled through with her hands. When I didn't answer right away, she stopped what she was doing and gave me her full focus. That was when I realized I hadn't answered her.

My words came out in an almost coughing reflex. "Uh, sorry. Yes, I had a very nice weekend."

My boss's gaze returned to other things. "I see you got some sun." She was like a viper, this woman, who didn't have to look at you to make her strike.

I took the seat across from her. "Yes, I watched my nieces and nephew at my sister's house." I fanned one nervous hand out as I spoke. "She has a pool, so I guess I got a little sun." *For a change*, I felt like adding. Most of the time, I was as pale as a ghost, which was a direct contrast to Daniel's olive skin. The man could don a tan just thinking about it.

"It looks nice."

Did she just pay me a compliment, or did I imagine that?

She placed her forearms on her desk and stared right at me. "I thought a lot about what you said to me on Friday. And thank you for the pro bono files."

I had placed them on her desk on Friday before I had left. It wasn't finished, but I had at least outlined what needed to be done.

"No problem. I'm sorry I couldn't finish it."

Isabella made a noncommittal gesture with her long fingers, her nails white now to coordinate with her outfit. "It's fine. I've got someone who will wrap it up for us. You had already given me your recommendations, so he will just double-check your work." She straightened the folder in question. "I'm sure everything will be in order." She sat back in her expensive chair with lumbar support and made of soft Italian leather.

I sat in that chair once and almost melted.

"As I said, I thought a lot about what you said to me on Friday."

I was too nervous to speak, so I didn't. I sat there and let her tell me what she wanted to say. Only then would I know how to return fire.

"You were right."

I almost fell out of my chair. Or was this her way of complimenting me before she gave me the ax? Once again, I prepared myself. "Oh?"

"Yes, you were in an accident last week, and I wasn't very supportive of what you went through. Even though you weren't physically hurt, accidents can be traumatic. As I told you, I was in an accident once when I was younger. And on top of that, you spent two days in a row here, working through the night. It was unfair of me to ask that of you. And to answer your question, seven-and-a-half years of dedicated service *does* prove your worth. You've also brought us some great clients."

I was glad she had clarified that since I had no idea what question I had asked, and she hadn't answered.

"Thank you for saying that." I forced some needed oxygen into my stifled lungs. I wanted to ask yet another question: *Can I go now?*

"I am going to recommend to the board that you be promoted to senior partner. I've already consulted with Gregory about this on Friday, and he is in full agreement."

Was my mouth hanging open? Were my eyes bulging out of my head? I pictured a cartoon character's brain falling out onto the floor. *Mind blown.*

"W-what?" That was all I could muster. This was not even close to what I had envisioned would happen. My God, I was finally making senior partner? No more pinching pennies. No more crappy apartments. I'd have enough money so Daniel and I could live comfortably. *Daniel.* What would *he* say? This was the best news of my career. Would he be happy for me . . . for us?

The corners of Isabella's mouth twitched upward. "I had a feeling you would be shocked. However, that's not all."

Oh, no. Here it comes.

"When someone makes senior partner, they are required to

also make a generous investment into the firm, to show they are fully committed."

Here it was, the stipulation. Last time I checked, we had five thousand dollars in our business account. I expected most of it to go to Barry and the plumbing job.

"What kind of investment?" I almost didn't dare to ask.

"Five-hundred thousand dollars." She stared across the desk at me as if this were a real possibility in my world. "Both Gregory and I had to make this donation when we started the firm. And we agreed that any new senior partners would have to do the same. You would be part owner."

What was this? A trap? She had to know I didn't have that kind of cash sitting around. And even if I did, I wouldn't throw it away on *this* place. Did she expect me to work for another seven years to save enough money for something like that? Daniel was right. This was just another carrot they chose to dangle in front of my face.

I stood, about to tell her fuck off for the last time, when she rose and lifted her palm. "I realize that is a tall order for you with the restaurant. And I have a way that you can still make senior partner and won't have to contribute a penny."

Jesus, this was torture. "And that is?" I hoped she caught the annoyance in my tone. *Stop wasting my time already.*

"We are opening a new office in London. Gregory has been traveling there many times over the past six months, scoping out possible sites." She paused. "Anyway, we need someone we can trust to help get the firm up and running over there. And you were our first choice."

"But—"

"Hold on." She had both palms raised now. "Let me finish. This isn't permanent. You'd go over there for six months tops. Gregory would be right there with you. And after that, we will waive the investment fee. We will consider your time there as your contribution. You *will* make senior partner. I will draw up the necessary paperwork to assure you we cannot back out of this agreement and that this project will not exceed six months' time. I queried a few board members over the weekend, and the ones I spoke with approved." She flicked her wrist, making her gold bracelets jangle. "The other board members are easier to convince. You are one of our best, Cassie, and we trust your instincts. Your showing me on Friday how you truly felt, only proved you're an honest person who will do what's right when the chips are down. That's what we need over there to get the ball rolling. All you have to do is give us six months, and senior partner is yours."

Chapter Fourteen

I left Isabella's office in a complete daze, my feet moving of their own volition.

I passed by Jeffrey on my way down the hall.

"Hey, Cassie."

I lifted my hand, but no words escaped from my mouth, causing him to give me a double take. He must've been wondering *What the hell is the matter with her?* What was the matter with *her* was that she'd just been given the keys to the kingdom. But, as with anything, it came with a price. Six months. How would Daniel feel about me being gone for six months?

An uncomfortable feeling tugged at my uterus, a cramp that I wanted badly to ignore. When I got to the ladies' room, I discovered I'd started my period. I wasn't pregnant after all. In some ways, the realization was a major letdown. I was so looking forward to breaking the good news to my husband, seeing his face light up, knowing I was giving him the one thing he wanted more than anything else in this world.

On the other hand, it was a relief. Having a baby right now

felt irresponsible and reckless. We didn't have enough savings for a house. And that apartment was sure to burst at the seams if we added another human to the mix. Not only that, but the restaurant also wasn't cooperating, finding new ways to spend our hard-earned money. And then came this offer for senior partner. My salary would triple, not including bonuses. We'd have everything we both ever wanted. We could start our family. Just not right away.

If Isabella had asked me for a year or more, I would have turned her down on the spot. But she didn't. She asked for six months.

"I'll give you a couple of days to discuss this with Daniel. I will need your answer soon, Cassie. Please give this offer some serious consideration. It won't come around again."

"I will" was all I could manage.

I didn't text Daniel or call him. I needed to think this through first. And I wanted to *see* his reaction, not hear it over the phone.

The morning rushed by in a flash.

Until . . .

"Are you sick or something?" Mrs. Dunbar asked me during our once-a-month lunch meeting. This wasn't the same meeting I had scheduled to discuss her new business venture. In fact, I had forgotten about our monthly lunch until she'd sent me a last-minute text. She sat across the table from me at one of Richmond's hottest restaurants, picking at her Cobb salad.

I shook my head, trying to arrange my thoughts. "I'm sorry, Mrs. Dunbar, did you say something?"

Staring down her nose at me, she huffed. "I don't appreciate being ignored, young lady. If you didn't want this meeting, you should have said so."

I reached across the table and covered her hand with mine, the one part of Mrs. Dunbar that hadn't been altered by

A Collision with Love

plastic surgery. "No, that's not it. I've just got a lot on my mind. I apologize. I look forward to our lunch meeting every month." I hadn't touched my caramelized sea scallops and probably wouldn't since the sight of them made my stomach turn. That was a *period* thing for me. My appetite dwindled for a day or two, which I never minded since I was often bloated and happy to shed a few pounds during this part of my cycle. I was also late to lunch, so this was what Mrs. Dunbar had ordered for me. Something told me she knew I wouldn't like her choice but did it anyway to *show me* for being late.

She touched the corners of her mouth with her cloth napkin, tossed it onto her salad, which she also hadn't eaten, and then sat back in her chair. "Okay. Let's have it. What's got you in such a tizzy?" She took a sip of her Old Fashioned, a staple at our lunches.

I couldn't reveal my secret. That would be a major no-no at the firm. Until I was deemed senior partner *in writing*, I had to keep a lid on this. One wrong move, and I could ruin my chances. Isabella said she trusted me. That meant I had to be *trustworthy*.

Crazy how my life had a plethora of problems right now. There were plenty of topics to choose from. "Oh, it's just that we're having problems at the restaurant. The plumbing in the kitchen is shot. Of course, it wasn't a kitchen when we bought it."

"Problems? How bad are we talking?"

"Not nuclear, but we have to get it fixed before we can reopen." I touched my scallop with the tip of my fork, moving it around the plate, a dark yellow sauce leaving a trail behind it.

"Reopen? You're closed?" Her brow creased a smidge toward worry. Hard to show emotion on a face as expensive as hers. As far as I was concerned, she had every right to put her money wherever she chose. And the woman looked at least fifteen years younger than the calendar revealed.

"Yeah. We're hoping to be back open by the end of the week. But you know how it goes. We don't want to lose our regulars, and Daniel has farmers and vendors relying on him for orders. He's trying to field all of that." I thought about my husband across town, working his tail off to keep the restaurant afloat.

"If you need help, my dear, all you have to do is ask." She practically glared, her tone a tad indignant.

I raised my palm with a slight wave to it. "Oh, no. We've got this. But thank you for offering. You've done way more for us than we deserve."

My words prompted a *humph* from her lips, which at the moment, were coated with plum-colored lipstick.

I reset myself, realizing this conversation was unproductive. "Are there any new issues you'd like to discuss? I'm almost finished with my research regarding the boutique you'd like to invest in. I wasn't able to work over the weekend, so I'm not as far along on it as I had hoped, but I did look it over this morning. From what I've seen, I think it's viable, but there are a few details that I need to give a little more attention. I'm curious why those previous investors pulled out. If you don't mind, I'd like to check into that."

She sat forward, opened her small purse, and pulled out a compact to examine her face. "I showed it to my financial guy, and he said he didn't see anything unsavory." She snapped her compact closed as a twenty-something waiter approached our table.

"Can I get you a box to take—"

"That won't be necessary. Just the check, please, young man."

The handsome young waiter with short dark hair and timid

brown eyes bowed slightly. "Very well. Will this be one check or two?"

Mrs. Dunbar sized me up for a moment. "Better give me the check."

I raised a palm again. "Oh, no. I wouldn't hear of it. Please give *me* the check. Thank you." This was a business lunch, and as such, it was my responsibility to pay, even if Mrs. Dunbar could buy and sell me by dinnertime.

We said our goodbyes, and I promised to have all of my research done by Thursday when we planned to meet again.

As the day wore on, the lower half of my body grew more unpleasant. I wished I were home with a heating pad on my stomach. This month's cycle was producing some serious cramps. Somehow, I managed. I always did.

When the sun lowered below the horizon and the firm thinned out of lawyers, I made my way to the parking deck, not at all excited to see my husband soon. I ran into Isabella on my way out, who smiled—she actually smiled—from a few feet away in the hallway.

No stars tonight. The clouds forbade it. A slow mist filled the air, just enough to make your skin feel damp, but not enough to require an umbrella. Driving across town, I ran and then reran my conversation with Daniel through my mind, my wipers intermittently swiping back and forth, the wet roads offering an annoying glare against my eyes. We'd see where this new opportunity would take us. Whatever our course of action, we'd tackle it together.

When I arrived, Barry had gone home for the night, and my husband sat in his office, his head in his hands. He hadn't heard me come in. Just the way his shoulders rose and fell with every breath, told me he was stressed, trying to find a way out of this nightmare while not losing his shirt in the process. *Our shirts*, really.

I knocked lightly on the opened door. "Hey, husband of mine, how was your day?"

He looked up, his face drawn and pale. In fact, he appeared positively frightening, his expression nothing short of anguished. Even his hair appeared frayed, loose ends having escaped from his ponytail.

"What happened? You don't look so good. Is everything okay?"

He rose and expelled a very lengthy breath. "Well, if you consider I have a walk-in that is stocked to the roof with fruits, vegetables, and meat that I can't serve this week. Or the fact that when Barry was working on the plumbing, he found an area of black mold, which probably means there was a small leak somewhere that we never knew about. *And* I can't open until we have it removed." His posture bent, his hands flung this way and that. "And *I* can't remove it because from what I researched, I could actually make it worse, which means we need to hire a professional to do it." He rubbed his distressed eyes before letting his arms fall loose by his side. "Take your pick, and that is how my day's been." For a moment, his eyes showed clarity. "How was your day? I hope better than this."

I rounded his desk and leaned my butt against it, taking his hand in mine. "I'm so sorry, hon." I kissed his knuckles. "We'll get through this. I promise."

With sagging shoulders, he chuckled, not an ounce of humor involved. "Since when did you become my cheerleader? I'm supposed to be that for you."

"I'm always your cheerleader, hon." I knew he was trying to lighten the mood because that was what Daniel did. He always tried his best to either see the better side of things or a silver lining somewhere, even if he had to dig as far as China to find one.

I lifted his gorgeous chin, his scruff tickling the pads of my fingers. "Well, I had an interesting day . . ."

* * *

By the time I was finished with my diatribe about Isabella's offer, Daniel just sat there and stared through me. At one point, I worried he hadn't heard a word I'd said, too consumed with his own plight.

"If you can handle me being away for six short months, we have a way to pull ourselves out of this mess and get back on track." I felt good saying that. We actually had a solution. I sighed, hoping Daniel saw this opportunity the same way I had.

"How the hell are you going to jaunt off to London when you could very well be pregnant?" He shook his head vehemently and rose from his chair. "Absolutely not! I will not have my pregnant wife—"

"I started my period, Daniel. I'm sorry."

I didn't think it was possible for his spine to bend any more, but it did, his eyes void of any joy whatsoever. I'd never seen him sadder.

He circled around me as he flung one hand up and headed out of his office. "Great! Let's just add one more thing to the shit pile that is my day."

I followed him out. I knew he wouldn't be thrilled by my absence or anything keeping me at the firm, but what perplexed me now was how resistant he was, considering our situation. I spoke to his back. "If we can't pay our bills, we could very well lose the restaurant with nothing to show for it or the time, money, and colossal amounts of energy we've expended already. It would all be wasted. The restaurant would sell at auction. I've seen it happen, Daniel." I'd been withholding this knowledge, hoping I never had to go there.

When he didn't respond, I continued to follow him around the kitchen. Old water and perspiration hung *unripe* in the air. A few tools laid off to the side that I assumed belonged to Barry or some of his workers if he'd brought any. I made my way over to a large fan mounted high on the wall and turned it on, hoping to clear the stale aroma.

On one generously sized stainless-steel table sat a crate of fresh greens that Daniel grabbed and carried into his walk-in cooler. I took hold of a smaller crate crowded with onions, scallions, and tomatoes and shadowed his efforts, enjoying the weak note of onion that floated upward. A much better aroma for my sensitive nose. The air in the cooler was refreshing compared to the messy kitchen, but we didn't stay in there long enough to enjoy it.

Daniel was on the move.

I caught up to him as he was sweeping debris that had fallen from a large hole in one wall. I stood in front of him. "Can we talk about this? I don't have to go to London. But don't you think this would be a huge help for us? I'd be tripling my salary." I gestured around me. "We can pay for these repairs. We can get that house." I touched his broom handle and widened my eyes. "We can start a family."

He didn't quite yank the broom handle out of my grasp, but he came pretty close. "How?"

I could feel my forehead tensing up, the chords in my neck following suit. "How what? How can we afford—"

"No! How are we gonna start a family if you're close to four thousand miles away?" With his face pinched with anger, he leaned closer. "Want me to ship my sperm to you? Cause in case you know of some other way to get pregnant without me, I don't follow your logic."

My head flinched back. "Who are you?" This was very unlike my husband. Irritation hardened his voice, causing his cheeks to burn red. I wasn't used to seeing him this way. "*No*, we wait six months, and then, I make senior—"

He scoffed and walked away, the handle of his broom clutched in his hands. "That's what I thought." He pushed through the swinging door to the restaurant.

This was getting out of hand. And I was growing tired of chasing my husband around. But I did it anyway, all the way to the food counter. "Listen to me! This is our way out." I grabbed his arm. "It's only six months. I won't go until I have it in writing. This is an ironclad deal. You said yourself that you don't know what to do. Well, the Universe has given us a leg up."

Having abandoned the broom, Daniel reached into a small fridge under the food counter and pulled out a beer. He popped it open and drank half the bottle down while I stood there watching him. He said one word that sent my insides into a frenzy. "No!"

I stared at him in disbelief. "No? No, what?"

His face impassive, he cut his gaze over to me. "No! You're not going. You'll have to turn down their offer. You can always find another job."

I couldn't believe my ears. "Since when do *you* dictate the rules here?" I tried to calm myself as I patted the air. "Okay, I know you've had a tough day, so I will forgive the fact that you are acting like a chauvinistic asshole."

There went the rest of his beer before he slammed the bottle down on the counter so hard I feared he'd shatter it. "I'm sick of this." He bowed his head as though speaking to himself and *not* me. His tone changed. "I can't do this any longer." He started to walk past me, but I stood in his way.

"What is happening here? I haven't even said I'd go."

He almost laughed with exasperation. "Who are you trying to fool, Cassie? You and I both know you're going." He leaned in again, his eyes intense.

I gulped as I stared into his angry face.

"They got you again." He made a strange motion with his thumb and forefinger as though he were ringing an invisible bell in front of my face. "They dangled that carrot, and you bit it. You don't seriously think work will ever let up enough for you to have a baby, do you? You've told me the hours those senior partner *assholes* put in. This is only going to make starting a family more difficult." He tapped his finger against my forehead. "You know it, and I know it." My husband stood back and stared at me. "Go to London. This is what you've always wanted, right? It's all you've talked about for years. Well, your wish is about to come true, Cass."

When he tried to walk away again, I grabbed him by the arms. "No! That isn't all I've ever wanted. You are. Why can't you see that?"

"Because you know how much starting a family means to me . . . I *thought* to us . . . and if you go, you'll be taking that possibility with you."

"Oh, I get it." I nodded, my mind sizing this situation up for what it actually was. "It's all about *your* dreams, right, Daniel?" I let go of him and crossed my arms over my chest, feeling defensive and equally defiant. "This shithole of a restaurant was *your* dream." I released my arms and patted my chest. "*I* made that happen for you. You want a family, and I was willing to make that happen, too, but not by turning down the one solution that could give us what we need to bring a child into this world." I lost it. I released anger I didn't even know I had in me. For years, I'd be skirting around my husband, hoping he'd give me enough time to achieve my professional goals before I took a step back and worked on our family. All that angst. It had sat in my gut, brewing. As he'd pointed out, years of it. I pointed at the floor. "I don't need your permission to take this opportunity. What I needed was your understanding."

Daniel was already shaking his head. "Bullshit! You weren't looking for my understanding. You were looking for my approval. And if we're being *honest*." He made air quotes with his fingers. "You never wanted a family. Admit it. You just figured you could keep putting me off until eventually nature would make the decision for us."

"That's not true!"

"Really? Why don't you be honest for once about how you really feel? Why not? You've said *everything* else. You don't want kids, admit it."

My hand went to my forehead as I released a very tense breath.

"I've waited, and I've been patient. But that's over with. Right here. Right now. I want you to make a choice. Turn down the job. Find another one, and let's start this family already. Or take the job, and I'll move out."

"An ultimatum? You're seriously going to stand there and give me an ultimatum? I have never asked you to choose between your restaurant and me. I've supported you every step of the way."

"I never asked for the restaurant. That was *your* idea. And I told you I would sell."

"The restaurant wasn't my idea. I just helped you get it." I struggled to understand his reasoning. "And you can't sell this place like this. We will lose everything we've put into it. And we can't start a family with no money. Do you want our son or daughter to grow up with parents who are constantly struggling to make ends meet? *'Quit your job. Sell the restaurant.'* You sound like an impulsive child with no concept about how to build a family." I stood back, staring at him with a whole new perspective. "I won't do it. This is too important a decision to handle irresponsibly."

Daniel watched me, his face turning to stone. "I guess

you've made your decision, then." He moved away from me, his hands on his hips as though in deep thought.

"Let's make one thing perfectly clear, *husband of mine*." I pointed at his back. "It is you who has made the decision. I never said I didn't want a family. But I will not have one forced upon me. And if you wanted a woman who would throw caution to the wind at her own peril, you should have married someone else. That is not and will never be me." It was my turn to walk away, which I did, right out the door.

Daniel never came home that night or the next several nights after that.

Chapter Fifteen

With a heavy heart, I accepted the job. And for the remainder of that week, I came home to an empty apartment that grew emptier by the day. Daniel was moving out. And he was removing his things when I was at work. I hated this apartment before all of this had happened. Now, I despised it. It was agony being there without my husband.

Twice, I drove over to the restaurant and stalked him. I never went in. I just monitored from the outdoors. Kendra came and went, looking great, as well as a few other people like Barry and two of his workers. A small team of men dressed in manual workwear showed up one day, whom I assumed were either there to clear the mold or repair the walls. Maybe both. Marcus made an appearance every now and then.

By Sunday of that week, it appeared the restaurant was open for business again. Our bank account, both personally and professionally, ran dry. I never complained, knowing this had to be done. Not once did Daniel update me on any of this. I had to find out on my own. It was *our* money, yet he'd taken complete ownership of our finances.

This was the version of Daniel who couldn't get everything he wanted. All these years, I never thought I'd witness his selfish side, but here it was, right in front of me.

Isabella offered me a month to get my affairs in order before I had to leave for London, but I asked her if I could go right away. The way her eyes widened at the prospect told me she wasn't expecting my eagerness. "Want to get your six months started early, I see." She rose from behind her desk and came around to my side, where I stood, my resolve doing its best *not* to crumble like a sandcastle on the floor in front of her. She flipped her wrist, causing her bracelets to make that familiar jangle. "Whatever you wish. I can make that happen. I'll get the paperwork drawn up as soon as possible." Her sage-colored pantsuit hugged her body as though tailored specifically for her as the scent of her flowery perfume permeated the air around us. She leaned back against her desk, her tone softening. "The board approved your promotion, by the way. I want to make sure you are 100 percent certain about this." She arched one brow, her gray eyes assessing. Isabella had a way of observing people as though she knew what they were thinking. It was impossible. No one could read minds, although, if they could, she would certainly be the one to pull it off.

I braced myself and spoke. "I am. And as I said, I'm ready to go now." I even had a passport from when I had traveled to Canada three years prior to meet with a potential client in Montreal. Unfortunately, that prospective client had signed with another firm, but since I had dragged Daniel with me, we were able to enjoy a couple of days in the enchanted city, filled with historical architecture and charm. (Those were pre-restaurant days.) A couple of passersby assumed Daniel was a native due to his European features, asking him for directions, which he was unable to provide, of course. We had laughed about it many times. If only he were coming with me now.

"Is everything okay, Cassie? Between you and Daniel." This wasn't like my boss. Isabella never wanted to know about our personal lives. That was *baggage* she chose not to burden herself with. But I *was* becoming a senior partner, so our roles were changing, right along with my life. However, I wasn't ready to open Pandora's Box just yet.

"Everything is fine. It's just as you said. I'd like to get started right away, so I can get back." I left her office before more questions made me any more uncomfortable than I already was.

What I *didn't* divulge was that I wanted to get the hell out of this fucking city, and as soon as possible. The only person who knew what was legitimately going on in my life was Trina, who let me cry on her shoulder for hours about it. She'd told Mike and the kids that I was going to London and about the promotion but nothing regarding the turmoil in my marriage. Her excuse for seeing me several nights during that week was so she could help me pack and get ready. Luckily, the kids were too busy with pre-school stuff, sports, and visiting with friends to want to tag along.

I spoke with my mother about it over the phone. "Oh, Cassie-boo, we are so proud of you. Wow. Senior partner. You've been wanting this forever." My mother's voice filled the speakerphone with joy. "I just can't believe my daughter will be a senior partner in her law firm." I envisioned her shoulders rising with pride, a smile stretched from ear to ear.

"Nice job, Cassie. I guess you'll be the one taking care of us all. I'll start picking out my new sports car." My father had chuckled in the background until my mother fussed at him.

"Now, stop interrupting, Vinny. I'm trying to talk to our daughter." I imagined my mom swatting at him like she did when he got a bit overzealous. "How does Daniel feel about being married to a senior partner?" Her voice carried a hoity-toity flair to it.

"Oh, you know. He's happy. Not thrilled that we have to be apart, but it's all good." I hated lying, but what I hated even more than lying was digging up the grave of my marriage in that moment.

"He's not going with you?" She blew out a breath as if realizing the situation. "Of course he's not going with you. I forgot about the restaurant. My mind sometimes." Her quick breaths told me she was flustered with herself. "I'm assuming they plan to pay you significantly more?"

I assured her that they were. "Oh, yeah. They're paying me *a lot* more, Mom." Considering what I was giving up, I wouldn't be doing this for any other reason. Well, that wasn't entirely true. I basked in knowing I'd be one of the senior partners. It *was* a professional dream come true.

"That's fantastic. You can get that house you both want. Oh, I'm just so happy. I can't wait to tell your Aunt Alice."

I wished I could have shared in my mom's giddiness. It was nice to hear *someone* get excited for a change. Since Daniel had made me feel like this was the worst thing in the world, I'd sort of forgotten about the perks.

I was also glad my mother wasn't back home from her trip yet. Being newly retired, they often took long trips to visit this relative or that. They had sold my childhood home a few years back and bought a condo, making it easier for them to travel unencumbered. If she were here, she'd see my bloodshot eyes and blotchy skin tone and know something was amiss. It was easier to pretend when all I had to focus on was the tone of my voice.

"Listen, Mom. I've got a ton of things to take care of. I'll call you when I get there and settled. Tell Aunt Alice hello. Love you." I ended the call.

I spent the remainder of my week contacting my clients with the news, tying up loose ends, training a newbie lawyer to handle some of the workload in my absence, and sobbing on Trina's shoulder at night. I knew what I was possibly losing—Daniel. The man who I had always felt was above me in some way. I loved him more than anyone I had ever known. But I also knew that if I let him bully me into making decisions that would affect the rest of my life, I'd only resent him for it later on. I *did* want a family. But there was no convincing him otherwise. And I didn't have the energy to fight this battle anymore, especially when he wasn't even talking to me. I'd sent several texts asking if we could meet, a few from right outside of his restaurant. No response, although he *was* making a statement, if not a verbal one. Our apartment grew emptier by the day to prove it.

The following Tuesday was my day of departure. Trina spent that Monday night sleeping right next to me like she used to do when we were kids, and I had been upset for one silly reason or another. She'd asked me to stay at her house for that final night, assuming I must've cried myself dry by now, offering a delicious dinner and a comfortable bed. I couldn't do it. And I didn't want my nieces and nephew seeing me like this. My eyes were puffy and red on a daily basis. People at work must've noticed, but no one said a word. These were my workmates not my friends. I didn't have any close friends, not since college, and even those connections had drifted. I'd put too much time and energy into my career and my husband. They were my priority. They always had been.

"Want me to talk to him?" Trina had asked as she brushed a few strands of my sweaty hair away from my temples. We were lying on my bed, our bodies facing each other. It brought back memories of when we'd discuss boys in school or what was happening with our social lives. I cherished all those times with my big sis. She had always been there for me.

I wiped my nose with my tissue. "No. I've tried to contact him plenty already. He's not interested in communicating with me. It's possible after some time has passed, he'll be better about it, but not right now." I sat up in bed and threw my sodden tissues away in the overflowing trash can next to my nightstand, most of them tumbling to the floor like thick snowflakes. I'd gone through five boxes of tissues over the course of the week. "Even though I won't officially become senior partner until I return in six months, I did stipulate that I wanted my pay to increase now. I'll make sure Daniel knows he can use whatever he needs to keep *his* restaurant running smoothly." I rested my body back down onto the mattress. I felt so tired these days, like I'd aged ten years.

With her head positioned sideways on her pillow, she said, "It's so strange to have you two apart. You've always been like the perfect couple in my mind." Trina smoothed more of my hair away from my face, something our mother liked to do when we were upset. "Did you tell Mom?"

"Not about Daniel. I told her about the promotion and the stay in London, and she was beyond excited for me. I want to see if Daniel comes around before I have to alarm them. You know what I mean?"

She nodded. "Makes sense. I know she's very proud of you." Trina offered a sisterly smile. "We all are."

I took her hand in mine. "I'm just as proud of you, big sis."

She scoffed, but I didn't let her brush me off.

"You and Mike have done a great job raising those kids. And they are actually nice young humans, unlike most kids I see today. That's no easy task. You gave up your career to be there for them. And Mike is a great dad." A tear ran unbidden down my nose and onto my pillow. "Who knows, I may never have kids now. You may be the only one giving Mom and Dad grandchildren."

Trina pursed her lips, her eyes filled with sorrow. "Don't say that, Cassie-boo. You'll have a family someday. You're still young. And I'm betting on Daniel, so he better not let me down." She pointed with purpose.

I sniffled and grabbed for another tissue from the box, sitting between our two bodies like a third member of my pity party. "I'm hoping that once Daniel gets the restaurant in better shape, he'll be more open to talking. He's been extremely stressed about it."

I recalled that day when I had walked into his office to discover him sitting at his desk with his head in his hands. The day we broke up. The worst day of my life.

"He worries about losing money, which isn't like him. But he feels bad about it, *I think*, because the restaurant took all of our savings." I released a shuddering breath, the kind you experienced when you'd cried so much that the rhythm of your lungs was out of whack. I made an attempt at laughter. "I was hoping that he'd fly out for Christmas." I peered into my sister's sympathetic eyes. "It would be incredible to spend Christmas in London with him. He could try out the restaurants there, which would also be good research for him." Who was I trying to convince?

Trina nodded, her smile trying to convey her support and hopefulness. "Yeah, that does sound pretty cool." She patted my arm. "He'll come around. Give him time."

Time. That was the crux of it. If we were in our twenties or even early thirties, parenthood wouldn't be an issue. We'd have that buffer. We *had* that buffer. But the years flew past, and as such, it changed the rules for us.

Before I left for the airport the next morning, I found myself outside of the restaurant once again, its doors not yet open for the day, the lights still off, except for a faint glow coming from the window in the swinging door to the kitchen. It was 6:30 a.m. I knew Daniel was here. In fact, I was pretty sure he was sleeping here. And *man*, did I want to see him in that moment. My heart ached for his touch, my stomach in a flurry over it.

I was about to slip my key into the lock, but my hand froze midair. I played out several scenarios in my mind. If Daniel begged me to stay, what would I do? I knew the answer: I'd stay. I was barely hanging on at this point. One nudge from the love of my life would send me over the edge. But what if he rejected me again? How would I handle *that* situation? My emotions were already fragile.

I took several stabilizing breaths. "It's only six months, husband of mine." I whispered the words, letting the air carry them wherever it saw fit. I slowly put my key away and made my way to the airport, my Uber driver waiting with my suitcases in his truck just down the street. It was early. Carytown was just waking up to begin the day, and the parking spaces were plenty. Not something you'd find in a few short hours.

There would be no goodbye. Except for the note I had left for Daniel as I locked up the apartment for the last time.

> Dear Daniel,
> First and foremost, I love you. I want you to know that. And I am far from done with us. The firm has already increased my salary, so expect our bank account to show the difference. Use whatever money

you need for the restaurant. You don't even have to ask. It's yours. I've left for the airport, so there is no need for you to stay away any longer. Whenever you are ready, I will only be a phone call away to talk. I can even send you airfare. (Christmas in London?) It's just six months, not a life sentence. Before we know it, I'll be back, and we can get started on that family. I do want that. I always have.

Anyway, don't give up on us. We have too much love between us to let it waste away.

Love you,
Wife of YOURS!

I had hoped I'd hear from him, and even as I approached the security check at the airport, I anticipated someone calling out, "Cassie!" and it would be him, wishing me a good trip and reassuring me that he wasn't going anywhere. Only, no one had yelled my name or texted me or even called. Daniel's silence felt ominous, foretelling rough waters ahead. And so, I boarded the plane, my future uncertain and very scary.

My first-class ticket (provided by the firm) offered me my own little nook on the plane to set down my things, watch TV, read, or rest without interruption. The space was tight, but surprisingly private. The flight was rather smooth, and I tried to nap, but every time I closed my eyes, Daniel's face would appear before me, wearing that same impassive expression I had left in Virginia.

When I arrived at Heathrow, I texted: *I arrived. Thought you'd want to know. Love you.*

I waited for my husband to offer something, *anything*.

No response. *Sigh.*

I sent a group text to Trina and Mom with the same

message. Both replied immediately like normal people did. *Thanks for letting us know* came from Mom. *We are so proud of you, Cassie-boo.*

Get some rest and keep in touch, Sis came from Trina. *Love you.*

I missed them both at once.

During the flight, I must've changed my mind a thousand times about whether or not this was even a good idea. At one point, I was convinced I would land at Heathrow, buy a ticket home, and put this whole mess behind me. What stopped me? Daniel. He was the reason I wanted to go home, just as he was the reason I didn't. No matter how angry I was at him, I would never cut off all communication like he had. Never. He was my husband. I was committed to him for life. But when I counted the days, he'd been ghosting me for well over a week now. Not one word came from his side of the wall that he had skillfully built between us.

Feeling a little less sympathetic *and* slightly angrier, I followed the signs to baggage claim and customs, a nighttime sky looming outside the airport's humungous windows. The baggage claim in Terminal 2 of Heathrow was huge, royal blue lighting riding up several metal pillars or along the ceiling, giving the illusion of a nightclub setting, if not for the plethora of baggage carts and hordes of travelers lugging their suitcases in one direction or another. Several areas included large metal sculptures hanging from the ceiling, reminding me of the dinosaur displays at the Museum of Natural History in DC, a place my parents took Trina and me when we were young.

Several billboard-type displays included vacationers staring down at the crowds passing beneath them, the models posing within the advertisements living the perfect life in London. It all just made me feel sad again. Well, sadder. I was already sad and now angry, and tired, and way too many other emotions to deal with right now.

I wished Daniel were here with me, enjoying this once-in-a-lifetime experience. Even if he was still talking to me, he couldn't leave the restaurant. I knew this. But it still made me wish for a different outcome.

I thought about that moment in my sister's bedroom—the night we were watching the kids—and I had lowered my guard and said, *Are we doing this?* after realizing I had missed taking my birth control pills for days. In that moment, I was ready to throw caution to the wind and start a family just to make my husband happy. He knew I wasn't ready. He knew we weren't prepared financially. And he knew I was still willing to let go of all of that *just for him*. Nature had other plans. And a small part of me wondered if this new promotional opportunity was fate's way of telling me to follow *my* dreams. Like my mother had said to me all those years ago. *Promise me you will never compromise your principles or your ambition for anyone. You deserve to follow your dreams. All the way to the end of that rainbow.*

Daniel had professed he was trying to help me de-stress and embrace life again, but was he? Or was he disguising his concern with selfish feelings about his own wants and needs. This was my internal seesaw. One minute, I was ready to dash home and beg for Daniel's forgiveness. The other, refusing to give up my power like that and even feeling angry that he'd want me to.

All of these crazy thoughts shuffled around in my mind as I cleared customs. I followed the signs to the exit. Isabella had said Gregory would be here to greet me, but I wasn't sure where that would happen. Outside of security, I assumed, which was where I had just arrived. This was a busy place, people everywhere, most in a hurry to arrive, depart, or accompany. Several people stood leaning over a metal fence-like partition as though waiting for their companions to appear, every one of them with a searching look in their eyes. No Gregory, though. Not yet. I contemplated the Express Train to London but thought I should get outside, first, and see if my boss was actually here. All at once, my phone vibrated, making my heart leap. *Is it Daniel?*

As quickly as they had risen, my spirits fell when I realized it was Gregory: *Welcome to England. How was your flight?*

Good. Uneventful. Where are you?

Go to Short Term Parking. You should see the signs. It's a two-minute walk. I'll meet you there. I'm in a black town car out front.

Okay. I see the signs. I'll be right there.

When I stepped through the automatic doors, a refreshing sixty-two-degree temperature (according to the digital display) greeted me. I wasn't sure what I had expected to see, a view of Big Ben or Kensington Palace lit up like Disney World? From my research, I knew London was a good hour away, *and* it was dark out. Several cabs, limos, and fancy cars lined up along the curb, the scent of exhaust strong and unpleasant.

The cabs didn't look like cabs at all. They were black with rounded edges, a design one might see in the '60s back home or in a *Pink Panther* movie. But they *were* cabs, according to the lighted sign that sat atop the vehicle like a third eye.

There, leaning against a black town car, stood Gregory, his arms casually crossed over his chest. A male driver in a black suit waited by the trunk, which I was pretty sure they called a boot here.

Dressed in a tailored navy suit, his shoes shiny, his reddish-blond hair with gray highlights fluffing in the breeze, Gregory stepped forward and fanned his hands out, a wide smile spreading across his clean-shaven face. "Once again, Welcome to the UK." He took my carry-on from my shoulder, the driver rushing over to grab both of my wheeled suitcases from my grip. It felt nice to unburden myself, my crossbody purse light in comparison. I had brought designer purses for the office or dinners out, but this one was perfect for travel. I'd also had several more formal outfits shipped directly to where I'd be staying, which happened to be at Gregory's place in Kensington. Not ideal, but it was only for six months.

You'll find Gregory rarely around, and Adrianna won't be there much at all. You'll have the run of the place, and it's quite spectacular as you'll see. More than enough room for you both, and a full staff for whatever you need. I've stayed there a few times. When you get back, we will have your new office all ready for you. Isabella had become my travel agent and coach. She had also gotten a lot nicer to me since I had accepted this post. I thanked her for the information with a gracious smile.

I was curious about Gregory's place as I slid into the back seat of the town car, the scent of fresh leather welcoming to my senses. Was it some sort of estate or more of a city place? I'd done a little research about homes in the Kensington area but not a deep dive. Considering I had left only one week after Isabella had presented this offer to me, I was surprised I was even able to get *myself* ready, much less conduct a lot of research.

From the traffic side of the car, my boss slid in next to me, his expensive cologne touching the air with its subtle woody notes.

"Tired? Jet lagged?"

"A little. I've never traveled outside of the US before, well, other than to Montreal, but that wasn't anything like *this*." My flight had left Richmond at 5:30 a.m., arrived in Newark at 7:00 a.m., and then departed Newark at 8:30 a.m., arriving at Heathrow at 8:40 p.m. with the time change. I stared out the car window at the airport and yawned, the whale of what must've been a flight closing in above us, obscured by the darkness.

"You'll get used to the time change. It's good that you were able to get a day flight and not a red-eye, which is what I often take. Losing sleep like that always messes me up. I think you'll find London quite satisfactory. Strap in, and we'll get ourselves underway."

We left Heathrow Airport in our rearview, allowing my new adventure to begin, my path forward filled with possibilities and, hopefully, not more heartache.

The first leg of the hour-long drive didn't look a whole lot different from Virginia in the late summer—trees and vegetation lush and almost blurry as they whizzed past—other than the signs and the license plates. And the fact that they drove on the opposite side of the road, which didn't bother me since I didn't plan on driving a car here anyway. Most of the journey into London was more of an interstate, where traffic all flowed in one direction.

"I don't know if Isabella has told you, but we are very appreciative that you're taking this position." Gregory glanced over at me. His cell phone had been distracting him for several minutes prior.

"She did, and I'm happy to do it. I'm honored that you trust me with such an important task. I'll do the very best job I can do for you."

Gregory seemed to relax into my response, sitting back and exhaling. "You've been an exemplary member of the firm for many years. And Isabella has always spoken very highly of you. Did she tell you you'll be staying at my place here in town?"

This was strange for me, chatting with Gregory, the elusive senior partner whom I'd been intimidated by for years. But hell, I was in the Twilight Zone, why not just roll with it. I opened my purse to grab a mint for my parched mouth. I'd had breakfast before I'd left Richmond and lunch on the plane, but I had skipped dinner, even though it had been offered. My stomach was having trouble with the travel day, and I didn't want to push it. A mint felt like a workable solution for the moment, which I popped into my mouth before I put the tin away and stashed my purse next to me on the seat. "I'm sorry. Would you like a mint?"

Gregory waved me off. "No, but kind of you to offer."

"Getting back to your question. Yes, Isabella did tell me I'd be staying with you. Are you sure I'm not going to be an imposition? I could get an apartment or a hotel suite." What was I saying? I had no idea where anything was.

"Nonsense. I have plenty of room. And I'm not there a great deal, so you can look after the place for me." Gregory was like an eccentric uncle that no one knew well, but we all respected.

"Well, thank you. I'll be very respectful of your home." Did that sound okay? Jesus, it was going to be tough getting used to this new role.

Gregory waved me off again. "You make yourself at home. There is plenty of room for you to kick back when you need to. And I have a full kitchen and cleaning staff. My chef, Kate, made a late dinner for you, unless you already ate on the plane? I think it's a chicken marsala dish. They asked what you liked, but I had no idea, so I told them anything *somewhat* American would suit." He offered a polished smile.

My stomach rumbled at the thought. "I love chicken marsala. My husband is a chef, and he's made it many times."

Gregory turned in his seat and wagged a finger, his voice filled with enthusiasm. "That's right. I forgot." He snapped his fingers before pointing with his index finger. "Daniel, right?"

I nodded, my heart bruised by the sound of my husband's name.

"If I'm not mistaken, I've tried some of the food you've brought in. I don't recall exactly what I tried, but I remember it being quite delicious." He lifted his eyebrows, his eyes shining with amusement. "Well, I'll have to tell the staff you're a woman with a sophisticated palate who enjoys good quality food." He smirked.

I shrugged him off, trying my best to not break down into tears. "Oh, we don't eat fancy very often. But Daniel does make great meals. You are correct about that. I'm sure what your staff has made will be delicious."

"Yes, well, you're very kind, Cassie. Will Daniel be joining you here over the holidays? I'll be back in Richmond with Adrianna." He lowered his voice a tad. "She's not a fan of spending the holidays away from home. She's very close with her family, you see." His voice returned to normal. "You'll meet Eddie, who is in charge of the cleaning, event planning—if there is any—and anything pertaining to house issues. If you need something cleaned or pressed, or a reservation made, Eddie will take care of it." He looked out the window as he spoke. "Over the holidays, you will have the place to yourselves, so you and your husband should enjoy it. The staff does a beautiful job decorating for the season, and you'll have full use of the car and driver to take you both anywhere you wish to go."

Anywhere? Like home to Richmond, Virginia?

His comment brought to mind a subject that I had wondered about on the flight over. With this trip coming up so quickly, I hadn't had time to get my mind around the details.

"Am I here for the entire six months?"

Gregory glanced over at me. He lowered his brow, his eyes filled with confusion. In fact, the car got uncomfortably quiet, making me realize how my question must've sounded.

I lifted a palm, sliding my purse onto my lap for comfort. "I didn't say that correctly. I'm a little tired from the flight. What I meant was, will I be able to travel home for say a weekend or the holidays that land within the six months."

Clarity rested comfortably within Gregory's eyes. "Ah, yes, I understand what you are asking now." He reached out and tapped my arm, his tone jocular. "You had me worried there for a minute." He straightened his posture. "Yes, I realize we are asking a lot for you to be away from your husband. And you are helping us out immensely. For that reason, we will pay for Daniel to fly out here *anytime* he wants. First class. And he can stay for as long as he wishes. I will be going back and forth a lot, so I need someone here who can field questions and monitor the staff in my absence. We will be hiring your replacement before you go. Not a senior partner, but someone who will be considered for one down the road. I'd like you to be directly involved with that and all the other hiring for the firm. I've already interviewed a few candidates that I will be sending your way for an office manager who will supervise setting the offices up and the furnishings, and any other day-to-day issues." He paused. "Not to get off-track but, yes, we would need you to be here the entire six months." His expression lightened. "I'm a little jealous. I've spent a few Christmases here, and it is something that shouldn't be missed. I trust you and Daniel will enjoy it."

Gregory made it all sound so easy, lovely even. And it would be if my husband were on board with this plan, which he wasn't. I held out hope that I could convince Daniel to come see this place. And me. He could close the restaurant for a few days. Especially around the holidays. People did it all the time. And money wasn't an issue for us anymore.

But would he? If I couldn't get him to speak to me, how was I going to get my husband to travel across the ocean? I'd never seen Daniel more resigned to his principles. In a lot of ways, he felt like a stranger, shutting me out like this. Emotions clumped in my throat, making it difficult to respond, my words struggling to form, but I did my best.

"Yes, that sounds nice."

I said this, knowing I wasn't even sure Daniel would cross a mud puddle for me, much less an ocean.

Chapter Sixteen

The London skyline was quite spectacular at night. An emerald city of sorts. Most cities were rather striking when the sun went down and the lights offered a soft glow, inviting shadows to stretch their arms over the blemishes of wear and tear. With London, I'd always thought the ridiculously tall, iconic buildings such as The Shard along with The Gherkin, famous for its bullet shape—the one I'd always recognized in movies—offered a contemporary glimpse into the future. At the same time, Big Ben, Saint Paul's Cathedral, and even Parliament encouraged London to embrace its past, a perfect juxtaposition of time and the remnants left behind. *Markers. Time capsules.*

In the US, our cities were still rather young and impetuous. But not in Europe where structures had stood tall for hundreds of years.

Putting aside my mental woes, I looked forward to getting to know the very place where royalty still lived. In fact, excitement shot through my veins when I spotted my first double-decker bus, which Gregory must've noticed when my breath hitched. *Rookie move.*

"How about we take a little detour by Buckingham Palace. It's only about fifteen minutes from my place, so it won't take us more than half an hour *tops* out of our way. If you're up for it."

"Wow, you live that close to it?" I smiled, trying to temper my short-lived enthusiasm. "That would be great." I felt like a schoolgirl on her first field trip, not a lawyer who was about to make senior partner. I glanced down at my cell phone, a quarter past ten flashing from the screen. My stomach growled, but I was pretty sure Gregory didn't notice since he was still discussing the area.

"You'll be seeing all of this during your stay, but there's nothing like admiring the palace at night for the first time."

Fifteen minutes later, the majesty of Buckingham Palace stood before us, its size so enormous it could fill an entire city block, the architecture old and regal. Out front, the statue of Queen Victoria stood guard, her golden presence a reminder of the strong women who had ruled with vigor and style behind the palace's gilded gates.

"It's huge. I've seen this place a hundred times on TV or in movies, but it doesn't do it justice, does it?"

"No, it doesn't." Gregory chuckled. "That starry-eyed look in your eyes is the same one I had during my first trip." His gaze reached beyond my window as he spoke. "That was too many years ago to admit." As we circled past, Gregory took on the role of tour guide. "You mentioned size. The building covers over eight hundred thousand square feet. Seven hundred and seventy-five rooms. Can you imagine the cleaning crew for that place?" His smirk encouraged one from my own lips.

"No, I can't. They must have several hundred staff members on the payroll. I've watched *The Crown* on Netflix, so I know something about the history and all the people who have worked for the royal family." I shook my head in amazement. "It's a world unto itself, isn't it?"

"Indeed, it is." Gregory went on to list a few other notable points that were mostly lost on my now tired ears, although I did my best to appear attentive. "You don't find many structures in the US that have been around since the 1600s. Although, I believe St. Augustine and Jamestown are two of our oldest settlements. And both go back that far." He gazed over at me. "You ever been?"

I nodded. "Yes, I went to Jamestown with my middle school class one year. It was cool." Okay, *cool* sounded *way* too juvenile, but my tongue was ready for a nice dinner and my brain, a soft pillow, not more conversation. Nervous about this trip and what it would mean for my career *and* my marriage, I'd hardly slept for days. I was basically running on fumes at this point. My eyes felt sunken, my vision slightly blurring around the edges. Not a lot, but just enough to let me know I needed rest. The excitement of seeing Buckingham Palace provided a short-lived thrill that was now fading fast.

At least on the ride over from the airport, the conversation was mostly one-sided. I nodded where appropriate as Gregory touched on our schedules a bit more and some of the issues we needed to address first and foremost. And there were a lot.

"I've selected three possible sites for the firm that I'd like to show you as soon as possible." As he rambled on, I continued to behave as though I was listening, whether I was or not. What little brain cells I had working at this juncture were now centered on what Daniel was doing back home. God, I missed my husband.

Gregory tapped the headrest in front of him. "Okay, Tobias, let's get this young woman home and settled in for the night."

From the front seat, Tobias tipped his chin upward, his gaze finding us in the rearview mirror. "Very good, sir." Outfitted in a black suit, a crisp white shirt underneath, and a jacquard silk tie in shades of muted pink, Tobias kept his hair nice and short, his chin freshly shaved (had to be given the hour), and his voice kind. He wasn't dreamy handsome, but more of a man who put himself together well. From my perspective, Tobias was paid to serve but his friendly demeanor presented someone who was okay with that. Having him driving us around gave me comfort somehow, as though we had someone in charge of our transportation who cared about his job.

Soon the palace shrank as distance forced it to step back into the city it cherished. And without the spectacle of our tourist attraction, Gregory relaxed into the cushion of his seat. For the next fifteen minutes, silence governed the car, making me wonder if Gregory was as tired as I was. It was getting closer to ten-thirty by now, but my internal clock was still running on Eastern Standard Time. So, for me, it was a good deal later. Or earlier, depending on how you looked at the situation. I even considered skipping dinner and going right to bed, but if the chef had purposely made me a meal, I didn't want to be rude about it. I was married to a chef, so I understood the effort a good meal required.

As we drew closer, I found myself wondering once again whether Gregory's house was in fact *a house* or a townhouse. Or possibly the top floor of a building? I discovered it was all three. Sort of. Our car approached a tall brick building that contained four floors. I had to assume each floor came with ample amounts of square footage, considering the building's wide dimensions.

"I own the top two floors. Two men named John and Chris, who I believe are financial wizards, own the bottom two. Nice fellows. I've only met them a few times when they were out walking their tiny little dog. I have no idea the breed. Adrianna is a cat person."

As the town car pulled up to the curb and came to a stop, two men in navy hotel-type uniforms with gold accents came rushing out to greet us as if we were celebrities or part of the royal family itself. One of the men with short blond hair opened my car door.

"Thank you," I said as I slid out from the back seat.

He even offered his hand, which I took to climb out. I wasn't used to town cars, much less handsome men, who were probably close to ten years younger than myself, treating me with such care.

"Thank you," I said again, not sure what else to add. *Do I tip?* I'd have to ask Gregory about that.

Gregory exited the opposite side of the vehicle and circled around the back. "Cassie, this is George." He gestured toward the blond-haired man who had just let go of my hand.

George gave me a subtle bow. "Delighted to meet you, Cassie."

"And the man standing by the boot is Timothy." Once again, Gregory gestured, but this time to the other twenty-something donning curly black hair and wearing the same outfit as George.

"Good evening, miss."

"Good evening. Nice to meet you both."

A moment later, the trunk *or the boot* popped open and both George and Timothy began collecting my bags. I only had the two large suitcases, plus one over-the-shoulder carry-on. "I shipped some boxes before I came, do you know if they've arrived yet? They contain the rest of my wardrobe."

"Yes, I believe they have, miss." George tugged my suitcase along, its wheels riding up onto the curb. "The boxes are already in your quarters. If you'd like we can unpack your things for you."

"Oh, no. That won't be necessary. I can do that but thank you." *I can get used to this.* And for the millionth time that day, I thought about my husband and realized I couldn't.

White marble floors spread throughout the foyer, embellished with swirls of jet black, presented the building in a posh manner. The walls remained white, a nice canvas for the few pieces of artwork displayed beneath their own lighting source. Above my head, an enormous crystal chandelier cast soft illumination around the room, the floor picking up its reflection with dazzling accuracy. A high counter made of dark wood and capped with a marble countertop, anchored the right corner of the room, providing a station for the doormen on duty, according to the sign on the wall behind it. And off to my left, two thick wooden doors remained closed, flanked by a pair of topiaries that reached waist-high, large brass knockers meeting a visitor's eye level. It had to be John and Chris's place.

I stepped onto a thick tan rug decorated with waves of maroon, olive, and gray, which led a path toward a single elevator with gold doors. Large vases holding impressive floral arrangements stood in the corners of the room, filling the transitional space with color and a sense of nature. I felt like I was at a five-star hotel, not someone's home. If this was what the foyer looked like, I could only imagine what Gregory's home held. It was all too outlandish to fathom.

In what seemed like no time, we were stepping off the elevator and into Gregory's palace of a home. The living room greeted me first. Everything was impeccably decorated, from shiny hardwood floors to the collection of large plush sofas and easy chairs to the artwork and trimmings. Just as the thick rug in the foyer had led us to the elevator, a large beige and cream damask rug spanned across the living room, drawing my eye to a wall of windows displaying nighttime London at its finest. An expansive patio reached beyond the glass, presenting comfortable seating and a fireplace, not lit at the moment, but large enough to warm anyone sitting nearby. Several generous planters provided a stable home for decorative trees, each one covered in twinkling lights, complemented well by the multitudes of step lights, floodlights, and garden lights intermixed throughout the greenery. I pictured a glass of wine out there after a long day. I pictured my husband snuggled next to me rubbing my feet. *Please let that day come.*

Just as I had expected, Gregory's home was right out of *Better Homes and Gardens* or *Architectural Digest*. In short order, I learned that the top floor was devoted to bedrooms, a game room—equipped with a pool table and a bar—and a small spa with a sauna. If that weren't enough, each bedroom came with its own private bath as well as a patio, Gregory's patio with a sunken hot tub. Why not, right? How had I landed into this life of the rich and famous? Well, not famous, but certainly the rich.

Following a trail of sweet and nutty aromas, Gregory gave me a tour of the expansive kitchen, which came with clean and natural surfaces, a large marble island centering the room, and every appliance a person could possibly need, including its own ice maker. We'd relied on ice cube trays back home.

A tall woman with blond hair cut into a pixie style, stood near the six-burner gas stove, preparing what appeared to be my meal, the smell of butter and marsala wine infusing the air. And if my nose was correct, a hint of mushroom and lemon. My mouth watered. The attractive woman wore the same chef's coat that Daniel often wore, a pair of black pants to finish off the outfit, and athletic shoes on her feet. Smart. *Save the feet.*

"Kate, this is Cassie, in from the States."

Kate turned immediately, her smile as welcoming as her light-blue eyes. "Nice to meet you, Cassie. I'm from the States, too, South Carolina. Looking forward to cooking for you." Her accent edged toward southern.

"Nice to meet you. And I'm from Virginia, so I've been to South Carolina many times. I love Charleston."

Kate nodded, her eyes reflective of something familiar. "Oh, yeah, I grew up just outside of Charleston. Great place to sample good food." She gestured toward the stove. "I've got some baby potatoes, asparagus with hollandaise, and chicken marsala just about ready for you. And Gregory has an impressive wine selection if that strikes your fancy." She gestured toward the left side of the kitchen where a tall wall ended, the shadow of open space hiding behind it. "He's got a small wine room just around the corner. I'm sure he'll show you."

"That is correct. And you are welcome to sample any bottle in there, Cassie. I've locked up a few for special occasions, but you'll still have plenty to choose from."

"Do you like red or white . . . or champagne? I can uncork a bottle if you'd like." Kate was so accommodating. "Are we celebrating?"

Not really. I wished I was. I should have been. This was all a huge boost in my career. But how could I possibly take joy in it without Daniel supporting me?

"That all sounds amazing. I think for tonight I'll just have dinner. I'd love to try the wine another time, though." I rubbed the back of my neck, kneading my tired muscles with my fingertips. "I'm a bit tired from the trip. But thank you for offering." The yawn that followed supported my claim. "Normally, I tend to like reds, but I'd love to try whatever."

"Of course." Then Kate gazed over at Gregory. "Gregory showed me your itinerary, so I planned to have your dinner ready for you when you arrived." She turned back to the stove.

"I took the liberty of setting your place here at the island, but if you'd prefer, I can move you into the formal dining room."

A round placemat made of what appeared to be thick burlap provided a landing pad for a gold-rimmed dinner plate, with a smaller plate of the same design stacked on top of it. The cherry on this elegant ceramic sundae, a linen napkin harnessed by a thick gold ring. Heavy and sophisticated silverware and an empty wine goblet, paired with a tall but slender crystal glass—filled with water—supported the ensemble. It was almost too pretty to mess with. Four cushioned bar stools lined up along the island, one of them intended for me. And with only one place setting, I realized I'd be eating alone tonight, which was fine by me given my fatigued brain.

"The island is perfect for me." I smiled. "Thank you again."

Gregory reached his hand out in an ushering sort of way. "Let me finish showing you around."

With her back to me, Kate said, "See you in a few minutes."

And the tour resumed. We ventured past a dining room rich in dark woods and a gleaming table with clawed wooden feet that could easily seat twenty before we reached an office area equipped with a long counter and several office chairs, allowing anyone to work during non-office hours. "This is where I've been working when I'm here. Once we get the space for the firm either bought or leased, we won't need to rely on this room as much. I've got several laptops you can use, but I suspect you have your own."

"I do have my own, but thanks." It was in my carry-on, which I expected to find in my room when I arrived.

A power strip ran along the wall, providing ample places to hook up a laptop or phone, and there was plenty of lighting to read those very long documents that we lawyers pored over.

A few more steps away, Gregory showcased another impressive room. "Here is my conservatory."

Conservatory? Had I suddenly landed in a game of Clue? *Colonel Mustard with the wrench in the conservatory.*

I had to laugh to myself as we entered a small two-story room dominated by glass. The tiled-and-glass roof invited the nighttime sky to flaunt a speckle of stars above us, a few potted trees rising up from planters around the room. Wicker furniture with thick cushions, similar to the ones on the terrace, offered a comfy place to relax when the temperatures outside dipped below freezing or the sky opened up with rain. There was even a small bar off to the side for drinks.

"Wow" was all I had to offer, my head rolling around and my eyes starstruck.

Like before, Gregory reached his hand out in front of him, indicating we were on the move. "Onto the second floor, which in this case is actually the building's fourth." The jocular tone of Gregory's voice made me wonder if he thought he was being funny. A bit stiff when it came to that type of thing, my boss seemed to be doing his best to soften his manner.

I smiled and even giggled a little to show him I was being supportive too. It was hard to be *on* for this long. I craved a moment to myself to relax. My hollow stomach wanted to eat.

He guided me out past the living room, where a curved staircase ascended to another floor, a long glass balcony gazing down from above.

Each step up caused my feet to cry out.

Do I have a blister?

With little time to prepare for this trip, I had bought *sensible* shoes that were also stylish, which meant I hadn't had enough time to break them into their *sensible* comfort yet, and my toes were angry with me about it. I also wore a business suit, knowing Gregory would be the one receiving me at the airport. Not the best outfit for travel, but I was a rookie, trying to play the part of a total professional—a dynamo lawyer who Isabella and Gregory couldn't live without.

Who do you think you're kidding? I mentally brushed off my inner critic, another voice I was too tired to listen to.

When we reached *my* room, I wanted to flop myself onto the four-poster king-sized bed with abandon. The plush bedding in muted gold and natural shades of sand presented a soft and textured luxury as I ran my fingers across it. Layers of pillow shams in various sizes and styles—all coordinated with the natural earth tones of the room—reminded me of Trina's bedroom back home. The recollection made me miss my big sister.

The windows stood tall, each one delicately dressed in cream-colored linen, a shade lighter than the walls. A set of French doors centered the far wall, covered in the same linen drapery and suggesting a clear pathway to the balcony, where two loungers hung out, bolstered by cushions and separated by a small glass table between them. A great place to sip coffee and watch London wake up for the day.

In the corner of the room, a cream wingback chair in paisley print sat ready for an occupant. A lamp rose from the floor, its matching cream shade drooping over the chair like a large sunflower. There was even a small antique-looking table ready to hold a book or a beverage.

As if that weren't enough, Gregory led me into a walk-in closet where a small team of luggage racks held both the wardrobe boxes I had shipped and my suitcases, all stationed for unpacking and organizing. "I trust everything is in order?"

"Yes, it looks like it's all here. Thank you."

That was when Timothy and George appeared in the doorway, their hands clasped behind their backs as if waiting for something. "Will there be anything else, Mr. Bates?" George asked.

Gregory waved them off. "Go home, lads. I'll take care of things from here."

With a "Very well, sir," both men bowed slightly and made their quick exit.

I followed Gregory back into the bedroom area. "Should I be tipping them?" I placed my crossbody purse on an upholstered beige bench, sitting at the foot of the bed.

Gregory made a face. "Given the amount I pay them, there is no need for tipping. And I also give bonuses every Christmas." His shoulders ratcheted back a smidge as he spoke. He took a few steps toward the attached bathroom and flicked the light on. "You have your own en suite bathroom over here, so make yourself right at home." He stood back for me to peer in, which I did a moment later. Everything was marble and shiny, the shower large enough for two, or three, or five. The bathroom could actually put my sister's to shame back home. I'd never stayed at a hotel this nice, say nothing about a home.

"Now, let's get you fed. And then rest. I'll give you tomorrow to unpack and get your bearings. We'll dive in on Thursday. Six months will fly by in an instant with the amount of work we have ahead of us." I followed him down the stairs as he spoke. "Before you know it, you'll be back home." He peered over his shoulder to gaze up at me, his brows arched. "*And senior partner.*"

And there it was. The reason for all of this: a means to an end. A way to secure my future. And Daniel's. I had to remind myself of that fact. I was about to burst through the ceiling of my career goals *with gusto*. I'd never imagined this could happen to me. Yes, I'd wished for it, but not with the assurance of actually knowing it could happen.

How could Daniel turn his back on me during this exciting time? When he opened the restaurant, I was all in, albeit from a distance. I did what I could *when* I could. I had always thought he'd do the same for me. He didn't have to come here to be supportive. All he had to do was let me know he'd be there waiting for me when I returned. The man I married would have. And for this reason, I clung to the notion that he would come around. He was a kind person and reasonable, yet the wall he'd built between us didn't feel like either of those things.

Chapter Seventeen

After a delicious meal, the yawns came nonstop. I hoped I wasn't being rude. Not that there was much I could do about it. Gregory had long since excused himself to call Adrianna and go over some of his briefs.

Kate took my plate and my now empty glass of water (refilled three times) from my place setting at the breakfast bar. "You look like you're about to fall over in your seat. Go get some rest. I've got this."

I rubbed my eyes. "Are you sure I can't help you clean up? And the meal was delicious." I wiped the corners of my mouth, the remnants of the marsala wine still sweet and tangy on my tongue.

She brought the dish to the counter where a stainless-steel dishwasher awaited. "Nah, go rest."

I slid off my bar stool. "Thanks, Kate. I hope you didn't have to work late for my sake." In another hour, it would be Wednesday.

She used the pull-down faucet to rinse the dish before

placing it in the dishwasher while I grabbed my utensils and brought them over to her.

Kate smiled at me. "Thanks. And I didn't mind staying late. I kinda wanted to meet you. It can get pretty lonely around here, even when Gregory is here. I cook for a few other homes, but Gregory paid me a premium to be here full-time over the next six months." She nudged my arm. "Looks like you and I will be seeing a lot of each other. Unless you work like Gregory does, in which case I won't be seeing either one of you."

I totally blanked on what she had just said and stood there trying to remember.

That was when she patted my arm. "Go. To. Bed. Before you collapse onto the floor." She gazed downward and lifted her brow. "And that marble tile does *not* look forgiving."

I didn't have the energy to argue. Instead, I headed for the staircase, the words *thank you* in my tailwind.

Back in my suite, which gave the illusion of my own private hotel, I enjoyed a quick shower, dried my hair, brushed my teeth, and searched for my silk pajamas from one of my suitcases, the ones I loved to wear when I needed a little extra comfort. I looked forward to having my things organized, so I could find what I needed without ransacking everything into a pile. Built-in dressers, shelves, and racks to store clothing (wooden hangers, no less), with additional shelving to keep shoes, gave me everything I needed to get the job done. Going from a single standing rack that Daniel had scored for me secondhand to this . . . *extravagance* had my head spinning.

I clicked the lamp off before I nestled into bed, the silky sheets providing relief, the mattress more than ample to cradle my tired body into dreamland. And as tired as I was, I should have been right out. Like immediately. I wasn't. Flames of unease clawed up my chest, making me hot and anxious. I threw the blankets back.

Damn it!

I clicked the lamp back on. I sat up, pulled my cell phone from my nightstand, and called Daniel. It was midnight here, which meant it was seven o'clock in the morning there. *Not too early.* When my call went right to voicemail, I left a lengthy message. "I wanted to let you know I'm here and all settled in. Gregory offered to pay to fly you out here anytime you wish . . . first class." I spoke through a yawn. "I'd love to spend Christmas here with you. And by then, I'll be almost finished here. Please consider it. I love you so very much, husband of mine. And I hope you can eventually understand why I had to do this. Sweet dreams."

This time he texted: *I'm sorry, Cassie. I don't know. I need time.*

* * *

When Gregory said we had a lot of work to do, he wasn't kidding. I'd gotten used to twelve-to-fourteen-hour workdays back home. Here, I was working even longer hours. A few times, I'd often lost track of the time *and* the day of the week. Thank God for my assistant, Maddie (short for Madison), a young girl in her early twenties with long ashen hair and a petite body. If not for her, I'd have gotten lost within the maze of my own schedule. Maddie told me where to go, when to eat, and when it was time to go home. She was my savior, which I told her on many occasions. I also took her out for nice meals, bought her theater tickets, and even backstage passes to see one of her favorite pop bands to show my appreciation. Showing my gratitude was important to me, no matter the job and no matter the reason.

Just like the vegetation on the side of the road, blurring past

A Collision with Love

our town car, the days flew by in the same fashion. It often felt as if I were functioning in a time-warp video.

Once we secured the location for the firm, I conducted interviews, met with potential clients, formulated and triple-checked all the necessary documents one needed to open a firm, such as indemnity insurance, a strong business plan, financial projections with key outgoings for the year, SRA financial forms, and too many other details to list. We hired lawyers, financial advisers, registered a practicing address, and met with building inspectors for the remodel. Plus, I had my own clients to care for, some of which, like Mrs. Dunbar, refused to work with anyone else back home, even temporarily. "We can conduct our business just fine either over the phone or on a Zoom call," she'd said with indignation. I was flattered, and yet I was exhausted at the same time.

Gregory flew back and forth across the pond, leaving me alone in his expansive home, a luxurious respite to resuscitate my tired bones.

Adrianna visited a few times, and when she did, I made myself scarce. *I don't want to be their third wheel*, I'd told myself, but that wasn't it. I was jealous beyond belief that Gregory had a spouse who supported him.

As the days and weeks passed, I never played one game of billiards or sat in that inviting sauna. I did get to know Kate, who would make me anything I asked for to eat, even a stiff drink when the end of the day (or night) called for one. She was also a good listener when I had no one else to talk to, which, outside of work, was most of the time. We sat around the fireplace on the patio a few times, sampling some of Gregory's wines before she headed home to her wife, Jessica. I was grateful for those late-night moments of kinship, another comfort lacking in my desolate life.

"I see you're married." She glanced at my wedding ring one

night, the flames from the fireplace glistening against the stones. "Will your husband or wife be joining you here?"

Considering I'd only heard from Daniel once, I wasn't optimistic about our marriage. *I'm sorry, Cassie. I don't know. I need time.* What he didn't say in that text was *I love you.* My heart ached, my stomach following right behind it. I rubbed my chest, trying to loosen the tightness that I had grown to expect.

"Husband, and I don't think so," I said to Kate. "He's not happy with me for being here." I took a sip of my wine, my feet stretched out across the lounger.

"Why not? You're not here permanently, right? I thought I heard Gregory say six months? Is your husband a lawyer too?"

"No, he's a chef like you are."

Her brow furrowed. "Oh. Does he have a job where he can't get away?"

I could tell Kate was trying her best to understand my situation.

Good luck with that one. I didn't understand it myself.

"Well, sort of. He owns a small restaurant, so it would be hard for him to get away for any lengthy period of time."

Kate sat forward on her lounger and glanced over at me. "Listen, Gregory's got deep pockets. I'm sure if you ask him, he'll fly . . ."

"Daniel."

"Right, Daniel out here for a day or two. Can he get someone to cover him for that short a period of time?"

I shook my head. "Daniel getting someone to cover for him isn't the problem. He objected to me taking this position." I sighed and took another sip of wine, my tongue sensing dried blackberry and vanilla within the red blend. "It's a long story . . . for another time."

Kate settled back in her seat, taking her own glass of wine in her hands. "Got it. I'll butt out."

A Collision with Love

I swirled the red wine in the goblet, my eyes mesmerized by the viscosity. "I didn't mean it that way. I'll tell you all about it soon. I'm just not ready. I hope you understand." Work had my mind taxed enough.

She made a gesture with her hand. "No worries. I get it."

As I got to know Kate, I wanted to share with her the whole sorted mess of my life. It was difficult to keep it all locked up inside of me, festering like an open wound. The next time we gathered on the patio, I finished my story, as depressing as it was. I made sure to include Daniel's broken restaurant and his obsessive desire to start a family . . . *right now*. The longer I stayed in London *and* the longer I went not hearing from him, the less forgiving my heart had grown.

"Jessica wants a family at some point, but she's never pressured me to give up my job for one."

Jessica worked at a health food store in the city. She was studying to be a nutritionist.

"Well, it helps that you live in the same city. But you're still lucky" was all I could offer.

This *thing* with Daniel wasn't a whim or a moment of weakness. He was downright angry, which I didn't have time to think about since I was working around the clock these days, including weekends. If it hadn't been for a few fancy dinners orchestrated to impress potential clients—or a lunch here and there with my assistant—I swear I would never have seen the social side of London.

One client named Billie Watson turned out to be a bit of a party animal. Billie owned a small chain of supermarkets in the UK and Switzerland. Her short blond hair, high cheekbones, and cheeky demeanor reminded me of Emma Thompson. And man, could the woman party. She took Gregory and me out dancing one night until my toes throbbed, and I was seeing double. I vaguely remembered coming home and crawling into bed. Apparently, we'd done shots. It paid off. Our willingness to party with her until the sun came up must've worked because Billie signed with our firm two days later when I was finally coming out of my hangover.

I'd tried to call Daniel several times, and I suspected I had probably left him a voicemail on the night I had drank the pub dry with Billie and Gregory. No surprise that he never replied. Deep within the recesses of my mind, I recalled shouting at him for ghosting me and throwing what we had away. I think I might have even called him a bastard. Did he listen to my rant? Who the hell knows?

By the end of October, the leaves were falling with Halloween in full swing. The British celebrated Halloween a tad more flamboyantly than we did back home. They even had a parade that passed by on the street below my office window, where I lived most of the time. Halloween wasn't my thing, but I tried to show my *spirit* by wearing a pair of devil horns on the holiday. The firm wasn't open yet, making it acceptable.

I called or texted my family whenever I had the strength, assuring them I was doing just fine. Mostly, I'd text since it didn't require any time commitment. (The *actual* time difference didn't help.) It also allowed me to communicate without hearing their voices, which only made me miss them more and feel miserable in the process.

Even though Halloween hadn't been a big deal for me, the Christmas holiday that loomed ahead was. I hadn't spent Christmas away from Daniel since we'd met, and I struggled with the idea of doing so now. One Saturday night, as snow started to fall outside my gorgeous window in my gorgeous bedroom suite, I made an executive decision and sent Daniel a first-class ticket to come and see me. I paid the extra money to have it couriered to the restaurant, so he couldn't miss it. He'd have to close the restaurant for a few days, or he could ask

Kendra to manage. That was if they weren't sleeping together by now. She knew I was gone. What opportunity did that present for her? I'd shoved the thought from my mind on multiple occasions. And then there was the food critic, Leslie Thompson, who liked to answer his phone. *Grumble, grumble.*

I made sure the envelope containing the first-class ticket required a signature for receipt. I could track it now. Only Daniel never signed for it, nor did anyone else. I could almost see him shaking his head at the courier as he walked away. Once again, Daniel wasn't coming. Once again, Daniel was ignoring me. Even if we patched things up, I wasn't entirely sure I could forgive him for this.

The short snowfall was followed by three miserable days of rain as cold as my heart had become.

I sat in my opulent office watching the rain drizzle down the glass and thought about this latest *nondevelopment* in my marriage. I pondered what to do next. Isabella and Gregory (when he was here) continued to regale me with compliments about what an *exceptional job I was doing*. It helped.

I should have felt alone, and I did marital-wise, but something new was happening in my world, something I hadn't expected: I was making friends. I hadn't had friends since college. Kate and Maddie were fast becoming my circle, even Kate's wife, Jessica, had joined us on the patio for a late-night drink more than once. And now a new friendship was blossoming.

Of all the lawyers we'd hired, one stood out. Her name was Brenda Adamson. Our first official hire. Her résumé was beyond impressive. She'd worked at the top firms and had a long list of clients to share. She was changing jobs because the senior partner at her last firm was closing up shop, and she wasn't quite ready to go it alone. That same senior partner provided a letter of reference, supporting everything she'd claimed. *We'd be lucky to have her.* The only reason she'd applied with us versus other firms in London? *She liked the idea of starting something new, from the ground up. And I find you Americans great fun!*

Brenda was smart, she was educated, and she had a way with people that would set them at ease. In her early forties, the woman with curtain bangs and shoulder-length black hair that enhanced her soft brown eyes, seemed to have the energy of ten lawyers. And she was all of five-foot-two. Where cracks were starting to form in my wall of resilience, Brenda seemed to regenerate, the business of the day only ramping up her enthusiasm.

And she liked me. I knew this because she told me . . . often. "You're my kind of woman," she'd say with a raised index finger. "But don't get any ideas, I still like men." She'd follow that declaration with a wink.

Back when we had secured a building, furnished it, and decorated the new firm with the help of our new office manager, Kieran, who Brenda had recommended, the woman roamed around the ten thousand square foot space just shy of twirling with delight. For a moment, she became Julie Andrews in the movie *The Sound of Music*. What I liked most about Brenda was her positive attitude, which I was lacking as of late. She was also quite the joker, who poked fun at people in a way that often prompted a smile or a round of fun-loving banter.

Despite the positive improvement, my strange symptoms returned. The headaches and the stomach upset were bad enough, and the invisible vice around my chest often made it difficult to breathe. The strange smell had me baffled and nauseated all at once.

It was time to take care of this once and for all.

I booked an appointment with Kate's GP, Dr. Anand, for a physical. He was in a private practice, not NHS, which meant he was more expensive, but I could get in to see him right away. And I definitely had the money.

I left my unsupportive husband a voicemail as I walked into the doctor's office. I told him with contempt in my voice about my symptoms. I finished my update with "Not that you care" and pushed end.

"I see nothing out of the ordinary," said the man from Indian descent, donning a thick crop of black hair, a fit body, and wearing a long white doctor's coat, a stethoscope draped around his neck. Staring through dark-rimmed spectacles, he conducted a few basic tests, asked me a ton of questions, and checked my vitals, his nurse sitting at a small desk nearby to record the results onto her laptop. With that accomplished, he determined my condition was probably due to fatigue and stress.

The sound of my phone vibrating brought my gaze over to my purse, resting in the chair next to my examination table. *Is it Daniel?* I chose not to answer.

"Your color is a tad pale. Could be due to dehydration. Your weight is on the low side of normal (I was barely a size 6 these days), but your blood pressure is good. Make sure you get proper rest, stay hydrated, and keep your diet filled with lots of fruits and vegetables. And try meditating. That always helps my wife," he added with a smirk.

Although I was relieved to hear that nothing was standing out as unhealthy or bad, I was still frustrated by the lack of answers. "I keep smelling this horrible odor. But it only happens when I get the headaches, the stomach upset, and the tightness in my chest. Is that normal?" Nothing made sense about my symptoms, but the pungent odor was the strangest. It was also getting stronger with each episode.

"What type of odor?"

"I don't know exactly. Strong, pungent. It never lasts long."

That opened a whole new series of questions. "Have you received a bump on the head recently?"

"No."

"Have you had your thyroid checked this year?"

"Yes, I had a full physical last spring in the States. My thyroid was normal."

"Did they do a full blood test where you fasted?"

"Yes, they did. They checked everything."

The nurse *tap, tap, tapped* on her keyboard as I spoke.

"I see from your questionnaire that you are not on any medications. Have you taken any medications over the past year?"

"No, other than some Tylenol for premenstrual cramps and my birth control pills."

"Do you get migraines?"

"Yes!" *Is that it?* "I sometimes get ocular migraines. But only when I've been on the computer for too long or the barometric pressure suddenly drops. I've had two this year."

"Tell me about your symptoms."

"Well, fuzzy bright spots cloud my vision so I can't see well. Sometimes I get a headache attached, but not always. It lasts for about twenty minutes. I have to step away from the computer, close my eyes, and wait for it to pass. I actually found these earplugs that come with an app on my phone. The app alerts me when the barometric pressure is about to drop. I put the earplugs in, and they do help. But I haven't had any ocular migraines in over six months, and the earplugs took care of the last one. And when I do get them, I don't have any nausea or tightness in my chest. And I don't smell anything funny either." I guess I just answered my own question. It wasn't the migraines. I knew what *those* were about.

Dr. Anand confirmed my assessment. "It *could* be related. Migraines can cause sensitivity to light, sound, and smell." He pondered some more, scratching at his ear. "How old is the ventilation system where you work?"

"It can't be that. I'm in a new building, but these symptoms began long before I moved to London."

"Hmm." The way his brow furrowed, his eyes contemplating my symptoms, I decided I had perplexed the man. "If you'd like we can take some blood today and run some tests, but I don't see anything obvious that looks wrong with you." He leaned against a counter attached to the wall, which included a small sink, his arms crossed over his chest. "Is it possible you're pregnant? I should have asked you that first. We can do a quick blood test to find out."

I shook my head. "There is no chance of that. I haven't had intercourse since my last period." *Not even phone sex*. I hated how lonely that sounded. Was I really a single woman again?

Dr. Anand pushed away from the counter and fanned his hands out waist high before lowering them in an I-don't-know sort of manner. "Well, there are conditions where a person can smell a substance that isn't there. It's called Phantosmia, but I would have to do more research about it. It could also be a symptom of allergies. There's just so many possibilities. I'll have my nurse draw a bit of blood, and we'll see what that indicates."

I left soon afterward with a small prick in my arm and a Band-Aid, which the nurse called a plaster, covering my tiny wound.

I checked my phone to find a missed call from Daniel. I should have jumped for joy, but I had grown too angry for such frivolousness. In fact, I waited until late that night to call him back, fully expecting to leave him yet another voicemail. Only he *actually* answered the phone this time. On the first ring.

"Hello? . . . Cassie?"

Chapter Eighteen

I was so shocked by the sound of my husband's voice that it took me a moment to answer. "Yeah?" That was all I said. As much as I loved Daniel, I was disillusioned by his behavior. For three months, he'd been ghosting me. Did he concern himself with my wellbeing? I was in another country by myself, with no family around. I was alone.

"I got your voicemail. What did the doctor say?" Daniel's voice sounded different, less tender. Or maybe that was how I chose to hear it.

I kept my own voice monotone. "He said everything looks fine. They took some blood to run a few tests. It will take about a week for the results. Is there anything else you want to know?" I sat on my bed at Gregory's house, fiddling with the frayed edge from one of the decorative pillows, which I held close, much like my niece McKenna would do with Daisy, her stuffed unicorn.

I could hear him breathing. "Are you still there?" I was about to end the call when he finally spoke.

"Yes, I'm here. You said in your voicemail that you'd been

having these symptoms since before you left for London. Is that true?"

Funny how I could barely remember what I had told him. I rambled on, which I often did when I was stressed. "Do you think I'm lying?" My eyes threatened tears. Were we going there *again*?

He exhaled. "No, I don't think you're lying. I just don't understand why you didn't tell me about this before."

My internal filters were off, and so I spoke from whatever my gut advised. "I didn't tell you before because I thought I might be pregnant, *Daniel*. And I wanted to make sure, first, before I got your hopes up. But then I started my period the day I went to see you in the restaurant. I guess after the argument we had, it just slipped my mind." I'd never used this tone with Daniel before. I was both sarcastic and abrupt.

Another moment of silence. "I'm sorry about that." His voice was barely a whisper.

Tears rushed down my cheeks. My heart was in so much pain, I feared it would break apart. This was not one of my episodes. This was what a broken heart felt like. I couldn't even speak.

"I know I've been distant. And I know we don't see eye to eye on things, but I *do* miss you."

All those hurt feelings I had bottled up inside of me came flooding out. And I cried, my whimpers louder than I could control. My throat ached with emotion.

"*Cassie.* Don't cry. I never meant to hurt you. Believe it or not, I'm worried about you. You fainted in our kitchen not too long ago, and now I find out you're having these episodes. This job is killing you. I wish I could make you see that." He kept his voice soft as though trying to comfort and convince. And then he said three words that dismantled every fiber of my being. "I love you."

I had to end the call. I couldn't continue. My sorrow crashed over me, suffocating my lungs. I hugged my pillow and let it all come gushing out. My defenses were not only down, but they were also buried so deep that one false move and I'd crumble into a million pieces. I'd never felt more vulnerable in all of my life.

On my comfortable bed with designer linens doing their very best to soften my grief-stricken body, I remained there crying like a baby without its mother, until fatigue took over and I fell into a fitful slumber.

* * *

I startled awake to a dark room. My gaze shot over to my clock, it's time 3:30 a.m. And then I heard it. My cell phone vibrating from my nightstand.

I knew who it was. I didn't have to look. "Hello?" My voice was scratchy and weak.

"Are you okay? I've been trying to reach you."

I didn't have to see myself in the mirror to know how puffy my eyes were. Or how dry they felt. I'd drained them of moisture. "You hurt me." There, I said it. "I've been trying to reach you for months. I thought you didn't care anymore. I thought we were over." I inhaled, allowing my lungs a short intake of oxygen. "I still wonder if we're over."

"I don't want us to be over, Cassie. I do love you. But how can I share my life with someone who I never see?" I could hear the distress in his tone. "You think I've been distant these past few months? Well, try living like that for eight years. I know it's not the same thing, but you know what I'm getting at. I don't feel like we're partners anymore."

"Daniel. I've already been here for three months. I only have three to go. Nothing has changed. I want the same things you want." And then I waited. His response would tell me everything I needed to know.

"If that's true, then we will find a way."

Ribbons of hope lifted off the horizon.

* * *

The following week, a woman from Dr. Anand's office called to tell me I was fine. Everything tested normal in my blood. Everything they looked for, at least. *It could be the migraines.*

And *that*, as they say, was that. Dr. Anand never followed up, and I never asked him to. He probably didn't take my question all that seriously since it was rather bizarre. One thing I learned about doctors was they didn't like the bizarre. I had a rash once when I was a kid, a line that ran from the back of my heel all the way up to my butt. Two different doctors couldn't seem to diagnose it, one doing extensive research (or so she said). The result: it was a rash. It will go away . . . eventually. And hopefully, so would my symptoms this time. It had been three months.

Daniel and I reopened communication. We talked every day about his day and mine. We made a pact. No matter how late or early the hour, we would touch base, even if it was just to say, "Good morning or good night, and I love you."

It took me a couple of weeks to trust that when I called, he'd answer, but as time wore on, I grew to rely on those phone calls for emotional sustenance. I told my husband how I was kicking butt in London. And how everyone came to me for guidance and leadership. "I've always said you are the smartest person I know, wife of mine. It's time they realized it too."

By the time December 15th rolled around, I was growing antsy for home. I didn't just miss my husband, I missed *everyone*. I even missed that crappy apartment of ours and the way Daniel would hang garland over the cupboards and find a nook for a small tree. He'd moved back in after I had left.

The more Brenda proved herself to be a worthy *future* senior partner for this firm in London, the more I entertained the idea of sprinting home for just a weekend to see everyone. I'd go see Daniel first, wrapping my arms around him and kissing him until my lips grew numb.

I'd visit my parents, Trina, and the kids right afterward. Mom and Dad always stayed with my big sis for Christmas to get the full effect of their grandkid's exuberance over the holidays. I was pretty sure both Noah *and* Bailey didn't believe in Santa anymore, but McKenna was still a wild card.

Two days before Christmas arrived, a new plan formed in my mind, one that I planned to speak with Gregory about on our way home at the end of the day. Somehow, the holiday gave me the gumption to give myself a present. Soon, Christmas would be over, not to return for yet another year. It was do or die. I told Daniel all about my idea.

"You think they'll let you come? I'd love to have you home, Cass." His voice lifted with the possibilities of this plan.

"I'm gonna give it my best shot."

I gazed out my office window at London's festive flair. We had the Tacky Light Tour back home in Richmond, but it did nothing to compare to the explosion of illumination in London this time of year. In fact, being outdoors in the city gave the illusion of stepping into a snow globe, every lamppost, door, window, and tree dressed for the occasion. Glowing orbs with thousands of brilliant stars swayed in the winter breeze while larger-than-life angels spread their enormous wings above the streets with glittery splendor. Everything was over the top.

It was magnificent, but it wasn't for me. I wanted home.

When Gregory and I were riding back from another very

long day, Christmas lights reflecting off our eyes, I dug down deep for courage.

As I took in the streets of London, I inhaled, relieved I was sitting next to my boss in the back of a darkened car and not in front of him. "I know I agreed to stay here nonstop for the entire six months, but Brenda has a good handle on things here, don't you think? We don't officially open for two months yet, and—"

"Whatever you are about to ask me, the answer is yes."

Just like with Daniel, I was so surprised by his response that it took me a few seconds to pivot my argument. "I was going to ask if I could fly home and see my family for Christmas. I can return the following day."

Wearing a full-length black wool coat over his tailored gray suit, a dark Burberry cashmere scarf bubbled up around his neck, Gregory's face drooped in an almost sympathetic manner. This was not something I had seen in the seven-and-a-half years (going on eight) I'd been working for the man.

He turned in his seat. "It's fine, Cassie. We can manage for the holiday. Go home." He blinked, the sadness in his eyes hard to miss, even with the dim lighting of the fancy vehicle. "I'd have to be blind not to notice that Daniel hasn't made one trip over here these past four months. I suspect your marriage is having trouble with this move. And I do feel responsible for it." He stared down at his gloved hands. "I have two loves of my life, Cassie. My family and this firm. How ironic that one of my loves caused me to lose the other . . . the other being my first wife, Joanna. And I'd hate to see that happen to you."

My soon-to-be partner showed me a side of him I never knew existed, placing his hand on the arm of my coat. "Go home. Take a *few* days. Get things on track. I'll stay here."

"Are you certain? What about Adrianna or your family?" My throat thickened, this tender moment moving me more than I could have ever imagined. It was as if my personal hopes and aspirations had been shackled and were now set free.

Gregory sighed. "Adrianna will be spending the holiday with her mother and sister. Your marriage isn't the only one on the rocks. Chandler and Beatrice have kids of their own. They're used to my absence." He exhaled, his gaze unfocused. "That is something you don't want, Cassie, people getting used to you not being around. Isabella and I built this firm from the ground up. We started off with just the two of us, and now we are one of the most sought-after firms on the East Coast. *We* did that. As a father, I wasn't quite as successful." He peered over at me. "Go home. Get your house in order. And then come back. You only have two months left, and then you can focus more on your marriage. If you need more time at home, I will speak to Isabella about that. I will make sure we honor your promotion. I don't want you losing your family over this." With the hint of a smile, he lifted his index finger. "If you two can survive these past four months, you will be okay." Gregory transformed from being an eccentric, elusive uncle to a man with profound wisdom. I wanted to hug the man but figured that was probably a step too far.

When we arrived back at Gregory's place, I didn't walk, I ran up to my bedroom to make the necessary arrangements. I called Daniel once I had my itinerary. I flung the details out of my mouth in rapid fire.

"I can't believe it" was all Daniel kept repeating.

"Believe it, husband of mine, I'm coming home!"

* * *

The next day, I worked like a crazy woman to get all my work in order.

"Who wound your clock?" Brenda asked as I flitted around

the office like Sonic the Hedgehog, a character Noah used to love when he was younger.

"I'm going home, Brenda. Just for a couple of days, but I'm so excited, I can barely stand it."

She giggled. "Well, anyone with eyes can see that. Good for you. Now what can I do to help?"

My flight was scheduled to leave Heathrow at 7:30 p.m. I'd be taking that red-eye Gregory had warned me about. Didn't matter. I would have taken a carrier pigeon to see my husband and family.

Soon, I was saying my goodbyes to Gregory.

* * *

"Got it. Is that all I need to know?"

I had just brought him up to speed with all the office's goings-on. "Yes. I'll be back in three days and can jump right back in. Given the holiday, I don't expect a lot will be happening here." Europeans took fun and relaxation much more seriously than we did in the States. Brenda mentioned on multiple occasions American's workaholic mentality. She wasn't wrong.

I paused to catch my breath. My heart was racing. "Are you sure this is still okay?"

Gregory rose from his leather chair and met me in the middle of his office. He placed a warm hand on my arm. "More than okay. You've gotten us right where we need to be. I worried we'd be behind to open in late February, but not anymore. Go home, enjoy your family, and we'll be here when you return."

"Thank you, Gregory." I hugged him this time, not caring about office etiquette. "Merry Christmas." And then I dashed out to grab my things. I had just enough time to get through security and make my plane. Tobias was a master at navigating the roads, so I wouldn't even have to stress over the trip to Heathrow. He sat in the driver's seat of the town car on the street below, its engine idling. I'd checked twice now.

One last text to my husband: *Getting ready to leave for the airport. See you soon!!!! Love you.*

And then I heard it. "Aah! Somebody help! Come quick!"

Chapter Nineteen

I sprinted out of my office and right into Gregory's toward the source of the screaming. There, I found Brenda on her knees, bent over Gregory's limp body, which was lying unconscious across the floor.

Kieran was already calling for an ambulance. "I don't know! He just collapsed..."

With cheeks the color of a tomato, Brenda stared up at me. "I was walking by and saw him fall. He just went down." She was panting. "Gregory! Can you hear me? This is Brenda. Gregory! Can you hear me?" A small cut bled from his temple, the only color on his pasty complexion.

I fell to my knees and checked his pulse, or I tried to. My own pulse was pounding in my ears. "Do you think he had a heart attack?" The man wasn't moving.

Brenda gave me a frantic stare, her eyes failing to come up with an answer.

I loosened Gregory's collar and undid the top buttons of his shirt. I checked his pulse again, my ear pressed against his chest. I thought I felt a pulse, but I wasn't sure. I started CPR as best as I could remember. Trina had taken a class in CPR right before Noah was born, trying to prepare herself for any emergency as a mom. She'd begged me to tag along. Thank God she had.

Kieran moved closer, anxiety sending blood into his cheeks. "Ambulance will be here in five."

* * *

That happy homecoming I had yearned for never happened. Instead, I spent the next two days in the hospital. I wasn't able to text Daniel about what had happened until hours later. I had never dreaded sending a text more.

Gregory had suffered a heart attack. And not just a regular heart attack, either. *Not that there was such a thing.* This was what we called back in the States the widow-maker, which in the UK was referred to as ST-segment elevation myocardial infarction or STEM. Bottom line, Gregory's left anterior artery, the one that supplies blood to the heart, was completely blocked. If it hadn't been for the fast response from emergency services and my CPR (according to the doctor in charge), he wouldn't have made it.

I shivered every time I thought about it.

Gregory's family arrived the following day, even Adrianna, who didn't stay long. She barely spoke to me. *Bitch.* Couldn't she find it in herself to care about her husband's health, regardless of the status of their marriage? Nope, not from my standpoint.

Without me here in London and Gregory's health in peril, there would be no one in charge of the firm. Brenda made no bones about confessing that she *wasn't ready to take the reins yet.* Isabella insisted she had to remain in Virginia to take care of the firm there. Of course she did.

It was up to me.

Daniel did his best to understand. I could feel him trying when we made our Zoom call on Christmas Day.

"You look tired," he'd said, his voice void of anything merry.

"I am. Exhausted. No way you can fly here?" My heart reached out to him, hoping he'd pull off a miracle.

Daniel shook his head. "No, Cass, I can't. Not on such short notice. I've already given too many of my staff the time off." His jaw moved as though working on a problem.

"Is there something else?" I almost didn't dare ask.

"What happened to Gregory . . . that could be you in ten years. You realize that don't you?"

Ugh! I was not in the mood for this. "Daniel. Can we not do this right now?" I rubbed my eyes as I sat on the couch in Gregory's living room.

My husband and I faced each other on a tiny screen—thousands of miles between us—yet our eyes couldn't seem to connect. "I sent you some gifts. One of them is a cashmere sweater from Harrods. It's so soft I was tempted to keep it for myself." My attempt at cheering up the situation was futile. "You'll have to let me know when they arrive."

Daniel blinked, the screen doing little to hide his disappointment. "When *can* you come home?"

I didn't have an answer for him.

As the weeks stretched on, I began to wonder if I was ever going to make it. It wasn't as if I had been here any longer than I had originally planned. But coming so close to going home and reconnecting with my husband, not to mention, lifting his spirits over my return, made the timeline *feel* longer. Like forever.

Gregory was starting to show signs of recovery until he suffered a setback. Well, several setbacks if you counted the arrhythmias and the scar tissue that put him at greater risk for a stroke. It wasn't as if work at the firm had slowed down a millisecond to accommodate his condition. Oh no, I was working almost around the clock to keep our opening date on schedule, which happened to be on February 24th. It was my gift to Gregory, who continued to stress about it since he'd made the announcement to the board back in December. Stress wasn't good for his health.

My daily phone or Zoom calls with Daniel had fallen off. It didn't help matters when I had fallen asleep one night when he was talking to me or when I had gotten the day of the week wrong on more than one occasion. None of it did anything to assuage his worries that I was next in line for a heart emergency.

The last time we spoke, he said something rather disturbing, and we hadn't spoken since: *I refuse to watch you kill yourself for them.*

That was four weeks ago.

On a lighter note, Gregory was doing much better. He was able to work most days, enough that he could keep an eye on the goings-on. The added time also allowed Brenda to feel more comfortable about taking on leadership responsibilities. I was impressed with how well she handled being thrown into the deep end. Sink or swim? Luckily for us, Brenda swam.

Through some of our casual conversations, Gregory admitted he would be willing to offer her senior partner at the London firm, but not for a few years yet. *Even good lawyers had to pay their dues*, he'd admitted to me one night as we sat at his dining room table enjoying a late-night dinner. (Heart-healthy chicken breasts with lots of greens.)

In my mind I couldn't help but realize the dues *I* had paid. They were the casualties of my profession.

* * *

Opening day at London's hot new firm Wilson, Bates & Griffin was a huge success, making the local paper. We'd brought food and drink in from the finest restaurants, enough for our staff, our clients, and all of their friends and family to enjoy with plenty of leftovers to share. Cases of champagne kept everyone in a bubbly mood.

Every couple that exchanged a quick glance or a smile yanked at my heart in a most unpleasant way. I was miserable.

I waited just over a month to make sure all was well with Gregory, who was healing beautifully according to his team of doctors, before I booked my ticket home. I had to make sure *this time* there would be ... No. More. Surprises.

I packed up my two suitcases on wheels, plus my carry-on, leaving the rest of my things to ship home later, when I was settled. Trepidation churned in my belly like a storm out at sea.

I texted Daniel with my new itinerary. He never replied. We were back there. This time, I understood his cold shoulder. I had once again told him with absolute certainty that I would be home for Christmas. And I had been wrong. In his eyes, I had chosen the firm over him. *Again.* He didn't say those words, but he didn't have to.

Gregory's condition only supported his claim that I was running on borrowed time with my health and my marriage. But I was returning home anyway. Maybe he'd see this was for real, and I was fully committed to our future family now. Hard to convince someone when the argument didn't quite work inside of my own head. I had moved past assurances. And this job was *not* getting easier.

I also called Trina and told her the news.

"For real? Are you sure? I can't believe it. We can't wait to see you. Does Daniel know you're coming?"

"Yes! Well, I texted him my itinerary and also left him a

voicemail. I'm going right to the restaurant from the airport when I arrive."

In the background, voices carried, familiar voices. "Are Mom and Dad there?"

"Yup. They came for McKenna's birthday."

Shit. I had missed that one too.

Trina put my mother on the phone, who practically squealed out of happiness to hear from me. We chatted for several minutes afterward.

I think part of me refused to believe I was actually going home until the plane's wheels lifted off the runway. Even then, I half expected the pilot's voice to come over the loudspeaker. *Sorry, folks, we're experiencing trouble with our right engine. . . . We have an unruly passenger onboard and have to land. . . . The weather across the Atlantic is too volatile for us to cross. . . . We can't let Cassie get home to her husband, so we will be making a detour to Timbuktu.*

The flight home was agony. I wanted to pace the aisles but held myself in check. I was so anxious to see Daniel that I could barely contain myself.

The rest of the trip was a blur, until I was standing outside of Daniel's Garden Patch ready to beg my husband to forgive me. The early April Virginia air was sodden with rain, the buds on the trees ready to burst with leaves, the grass now green and ready to carpet the earth with lushness.

Since I'd taken the red-eye, it was early still, Carytown quiet just like the morning when I had left last August. My six months away had morphed into just over seven, but in my mind, it could have been a lot longer given the circumstances. That would be one of many arguments I had planned to make when addressing my husband.

For a moment, I pondered things and whether or not this was actually a good idea anymore. Daniel and I had been through so many ups and downs already. Would his heart open to me again?

I'd texted him as soon as I had landed in Richmond. I told him where I was and that I'd be seeing him soon. Given the hour, I asked: *Should I go to the apartment or the restaurant?*

I don't live in the apartment anymore. Come to the restaurant was his stark reply, which didn't exactly set my mind at ease. He'd moved out? Finances were better for sure. Did that mean he'd found a better place for us? The knot in my chest wanted to believe it.

I rented a car this time, a place to store my things until I could figure out where I lived these days.

At least my key still worked as I opened the door to the restaurant, stepped inside, and relocked it. The bell rang above my head as it always had, the large room crowded with tables, chairs, and our trusty food counter waiting at the back, all of it cast in muted darkness, the ghosts of conversations long gone as the sun rose, bringing new definition to the room.

My legs suddenly heavy, my heart racing, I baby stepped my way across the expansive room, the swinging door to the kitchen looming, a light spilling out from its window.

All at once, he appeared, my husband, the love of my life. His hair was pulled back into a ponytail, his clothes the same old T-shirt and jeans I had grown to know and adore. It was his eyes that set me off at first. Those chestnut eyes, normally filled with warmth and love. Only this morning, I wasn't sure what they were filled with, so I stepped forward, trying not to run into his arms and hug him, never letting go.

"It's so nice to see you," I said, inhaling his scent. "I missed you so much." While my arms wrapped around this handsome man, Daniel's remained by his sides.

You can't even hug me? This was worse than I had thought. I stepped back. "Can we talk?"

"Yes." He gestured toward the nearest booth, and we walked there, taking a seat across from each other. He hadn't turned on the lights, and that was probably a good thing. I hoped the subtle darkness would hide my distress and allow me the gumption to open up the way I wanted to.

I rested my forearms on the table and leaned into them, needing stability. "I'm sorry, Daniel. I wish there had been another solution for us. And I wish I didn't have to be gone for so long. I want you to know that." I lifted my voice. "But things have changed. I've given the firm over seven months, but now I am home to stay. We can start that family you want so much. I know it's been a hard seven months. But it's over now. We can get back to being in love. And I do love you, Daniel, more than you know. This whole experience has only taught me how much." I took a breath, watching my husband for a reaction . . . for *anything* to reassure me that things would be okay. *We'd* be okay.

Instead, he exhaled as though he'd been holding his breath. "You see, Cassie, that's the problem right there. That's been the problem from the beginning. As you just said, 'that family *I* want so much.'"

I shook my head. "I didn't mean it that way. I'm exhausted, Daniel." Anxiety heated my cheeks, my chest filling with unpleasant emotions. "Are you still upset about this? I told you I wanted a family—"

"Stop." He didn't yell the word. He simply raised his palm, making my mouth run dry. "It was my mistake to force this on you. I see that now."

I shook my head again, tears threatening. "No!"

"Let me finish!" This time he did raise his voice. "It's too late for us, Cassie. I've watched you put your job in front of your health *and me* for too long. You're killing yourself for what? A paycheck? Status in the firm? I *won't* do it anymore.

There will always be an emergency at work. For years, you've missed so much of our time together. And I've been waiting. This trip helped me realize what I've had to endure, worrying about your health and our future. I can't wait anymore. My feelings have changed. I'm sorry."

I sat back in the booth, struggling to absorb his ugly words, my heart burning up like a piece of flash paper. "Your feelings have changed in *seven months?*" My jaw clenched. "In seven fucking months? You have got to be kidding me. I have supported you from the beginning, Daniel. I never asked *you* to choose between your dreams and me, and I never would."

"You're right. And that was unfair of me."

I was flabbergasted, tears streaming down my tired cheeks. "I can't believe this. You're walking away from me? After eight years of marriage? How can you say that you love me and do this? I gave you everything." A tremor of the worst anxiety I had ever experienced rode like an earthquake up my spine, rattling the cage of my soul. The nauseous stomach, the headache, the pungent smell, it all came rushing back.

I had to stay in control.

"I know. You've been very generous. And I have good news." He paused. "I found a partner for the restaurant, so you will get every penny that you put into this place back starting next month. I am so grateful to you for—"

"Fuck you! How dare you say that to me! How dare you treat me this way!" My anger seesawed right into sorrow. "Please, Daniel, don't do this. I love you." My head pounded harder, my stomach doing its normal yet not-so-normal upheaval, the mysterious pungent odor making it hard not to gag.

From his back pocket, my husband pulled out a rather thick wad of paper. "I'm asking you for a divorce, Cassie. I'm sorry, but it's what I want. This will allow you to work as you wish and become the professional that you have always wanted to be. I've just been standing in your way. You know it, and I know it. Let's not fight over this. We've been separated for seven months already. If you don't contest it, we can be divorced quickly."

Quickly? What an awful word. I whimpered. "But I don't want to divorce you, Daniel. I love you. I have always loved you. I'll quit my job today if that's what it takes." With tears dripping off my chin, I pulled out my cell phone, prepared to prove myself. I was devastated, my insides twisting, my chest caving in on itself.

Only Daniel took the phone from my trembling hands. He shook his head slowly, his eyes a mixture of pity and impatience. "No, Cassie. It's over. I don't want to stay married. Don't make this harder than it needs to be. You have what you want. You're senior partner. You'll have all the money you worked so hard for. And once I pay you back, you will have even more. You can get a house or whatever your heart desires. I'm setting you free. Can't you see that?" He stared at me as if hoping that I'd suddenly snap out of my emotional hurricane and realize what a great thing he was doing for me.

"That house was meant for us and our children." I sounded so defeated, which was precisely how I felt. Mentally, I was trying to climb a waterfall. An impossible task.

Daniel didn't have a response for that one.

How could he change his feelings so quickly? That last time we spoke, right before I had left for London, I saw the resolve in his eyes and heard it in his voice. *I guess you've made your decision.* Had he decided back then it was over? But we'd come to an understanding. I *thought* we had anyway. And then Gregory's heart attack. Was that the final nail in the coffin for us? I was angry at Gregory. I was angry at Daniel. I was angry at the world.

My mind sifted through my memories like files in a filing cabinet. Before the almost accident with the Bubba truck, he'd made another proclamation: *I'm not sure how much longer I can do this.* That was the first time he had tried to tell me what he was feeling. Suddenly, it dawned on me. He'd been trying to tell me for years. Waiting patiently for me to come around. Only, I never did. I let my job dictate our lives. I'd brushed his feelings off, knowing, *hoping* he'd wait until the time was right.

I finally got it. And if I could convince him, I'd never take this marriage for granted again. My soul had experienced the best kind of epiphany. My priorities were finally in order. I'd call Andy, the unkempt but brilliant lawyer Isabella had let go and who had started his own firm. *If you ever change your mind, don't hesitate to call. You won't even need to interview. The job is yours,* he'd said. I could do this. I *would* do this.

But was I too late? Another question rose up from my constricted throat, something that I wasn't hearing, but I sensed he was trying to tell me. "Is there someone else? Is it Kendra? Are you two together now?" I had to know if something *else* was adding to his need to be free of me. And as I waited for his answer, I pushed my fingers against my breastbone, hoping to loosen the vice that was determined to steal my every breath.

At first, Daniel hesitated before he spoke. "No, it's not Kendra. And, yes, I have met someone. You don't know her." He lifted both palms this time. "I haven't acted on my feelings, and I won't until you agree to sign these papers." He held up the divorce papers.

Who had drawn them up? What asshole lawyer would I hate for eternity?

"If you don't contest the divorce, we can be done with this. If you do contest, it won't make any difference. You will only be prolonging the inevitable."

You will only be prolonging the inevitable. The words rang through my nervous system like a gong.

More anger came rushing in like the front of a storm. "Don't tell me about the law, *Daniel*." I slammed my hands down on the table, my palms stinging from the impact. "I know the goddamn law!" It was as if someone had sucked all the oxygen out of the room, and I couldn't breathe. "But . . ." I shook my head in disbelief.

He'd found someone else. And that changed things.

"But I love you. Don't you love *me* anymore? What happened to that man who said he'd be there for me? How could things have changed so drastically in seven short months? I don't understand."

For the first time in a long while, Daniel actually touched me. He reached out and put his hand over mine on the table, the warmth of his skin teasing my heart savagely. "I'm sorry, Cassie. I truly am. But this wasn't meant to be. Please, don't fight me on this. I don't want us to become enemies. Help me preserve what is left of us before things turn ugly. I won't change my mind, so there is no sense in fighting me. I'm sorry. I don't like hurting you, but I want a divorce."

Chapter Twenty

I grabbed the napkin holder from our booth and flung it across the room, creating a clatter. Without looking *or caring* what I had hit, I didn't walk, I ran out of there and returned to the airport. A perky attendant tapped away on her keyboard, trying to locate a flight back to London.

"I'll take whatever you've got, but I'd prefer first class if you have it."

Luckily, she did, an 11:30 a.m. flight. I practically threw my credit card at the woman.

I texted my family with my apologies, telling them something had come up and it couldn't be helped. I turned my phone off and ordered the first of many vodka martinis, enough to make my mind numb and encourage a long slumber. Anything to avoid thinking about what had just happened with my soon-to-be ex-husband. I signed his goddamn paperwork, and then I left with my tail between my legs and my heart in my hands.

The breakup with Bryce—the man who was good-on-paper-and-lousy-at-love—was nothing compared to this. I never loved Bryce. I'd given my heart and soul to Daniel. What would become of me now? Who was I without him? Could I survive without his love?

By the time I landed in London, groggy and feeling as bad as a person could possibly feel—and after hours of alcohol-induced reasoning—I decided to embrace the one thing in my world that embraced me back: my job. I couldn't get Daniel to love me again, but I *could* be the best damn lawyer anyone had ever seen. They wanted me at the firm, and I refused to reject them for it. I'd make enough money to set myself up for life. I'd decide what *I* wanted to do. *That's right, Daniel, I'll be happy despite you.*

Since I was committed to staying in London, Gregory expressed his relief. "I wasn't sure I could do this on my own," he'd said. "Will Daniel be joining you?"

"No!"

I didn't elaborate, but something in Gregory's eyes told me he knew. Maybe that was why he convinced me to stay at his place for the remainder of the year.

"Give yourself time to tour London before you decide where you want to live. I can help with that. It's the least I can do for all the dedication you've shown me and the firm." He arched his brow. "Not to mention, saving my life."

The year passed in a blink of an eye. I tried to stay in touch with my family, but obligations kept me from giving them the time they deserved. I could tell my sister, *and mother* for that matter, had grown impatient when their voicemails grew sparse and their texts short. I assured them I would be returning home, but I needed time to mend my broken heart first. How long that would take remained a mystery.

I also reminded my mother that I was following my dreams as she had instructed me to do and trying to make her proud.

The holidays returned the following winter, exacerbating

the aches of my still wounded love life. I had lost the ability to feel any sort of attraction to a man, regardless of his looks or his charm. That meant zero dating.

Living in Gregory's luxury home with a full staff and Kate helped a great deal. My unfortunate chef slash friend had lent me her ear so often I was surprised the appendage hadn't fallen right off her head, especially when I was drinking. Of which, over the year, I had done a fair amount of.

I wasn't the only one suffering from divorce woes. Gregory and Adrianna were also history, not that it seemed to bother Gregory all that much. He was back to dating in no time.

Between Christmas and New Year's Eve, and when I wasn't working, Kate made me the best comfort food I had ever tasted. Cottage pie, fish and chips with malt vinegar mayonnaise, marmalade glazed ham with mashed potatoes, Yorkshire pudding, and trifle were just a few of the delicacies she bestowed upon my palate.

Every time I allowed myself to remember that moment in the restaurant with Daniel when he had flashed his divorce papers in my face, my strange symptoms returned to join the unpleasantness. In some ways, I welcomed the physical pain for it allowed me to focus on something other than my tattered heart.

By New Year's Eve, Kate kept busy preparing several meals, including a Cornish pastry, dumplings with mince, plus a few other breakfast items like toad in a hole—which she assured me didn't include a toad at all—to store in the fridge since she was *finally* taking a week off to be with her wife, a break she well deserved judging by the amount of time she'd spent here over the past year.

"We don't celebrate Christmas," she'd assured me when I tried to shoo her out the door repeatedly over the holiday.

As she finished prepping for her overdue vacation, I sat at

Gregory's impressive island watching her work. (Gregory was out with friends for the evening.) A glass of red wine sat in front of me, waiting to be consumed.

Kate wiped down the counter, her body wiggling back and forth from the effort. "You haven't gotten out once all year, other than with workmates. And you've spent the entire holiday season cooped up here. Why didn't you join Gregory and go to that party?"

That party was held at the mansion of one of Gregory's affluent friends. He'd asked me to join, and I had declined, citing I was planning to binge on my favorite streaming series. But when I couldn't produce the name of one show, he seemed less than convinced.

"Here is the address." Wearing his signature full-length black wool coat over his tailored black suit, and before putting on his customary black leather gloves, he had handed me a business card, the woody notes from his cologne reaching my nose. "I'll send Tobias back here in case you change your mind and decide to come. It's mostly all lawyers, so you'll fit right in. You can wear one of those dresses you bought for our client dinners." He snapped his fingers, which he did often when trying to spark his memory. "Or that green dress you wore for the firm's opening last February. That one was quite nice."

The green dress he was referring to was a detailed Armani gown with V'd straps and a flowing skirt that cascaded all the way to the floor. It was expensive, but it was also magnificent, complementing my green eyes, or so people had told me.

Tonight, however, I was decked out in a very comfortable pair of loose brushed cotton pants, the kind with an elastic waist, and a matching cashmere tunic, some fluffy slippers offering comfort for my feet.

I had taken the card from my partner's hands as I sunk onto his cushy sofa. "Thank you, but I think I'll stay in for the evening." I held the card up. "I appreciate the offer, though." I smiled, even though my heart was anything but happy. "I may even see some fireworks from your incredible view." I fanned one hand out toward the wall of windows and the rooftop patio, providing a remarkable view of London. I planned to start a fire, drink a bottle of wine, and just be. I could have just as easily hung out in the conservatory, but the need for open air made my spirit feel less confined. The vice around my chest was doing a good job of that on its own.

Gregory had stood over me, wrapping his Burberry scarf around the collar of his coat. "I'm sorry things didn't work out with Daniel, I truly am. But you are young, Cassie, and a very successful woman in her own right. There is a time to mourn your loss, but there will come a day when you will need to get back out there and live your life." He seemed to reset himself as though ready to clarify his meaning. "I don't mean professionally. I mean personally. And if you don't mind me saying." He smirked. "And don't sue me, I feel I need to point out that you are a young and very attractive woman in the prime of her life." He pushed his hands into each glove, his eyes focused on the job at hand (pardon the pun). "I am not saying when, but eventually, I hope you get out and start meeting people, other than the ones you work with *or for*. You're great with our staff and our clients. You have a friendly manner about you. Don't store yourself away for too long." He'd turned toward the door. "And I'll still send Tobias back with the car just in case. The party will go well into the night."

Back in the kitchen with Kate, I felt I needed to answer her question regarding why I had chosen to stay home.

I ran my hands over the marble counter, the cool stone smooth under my palms. "I was married for eight fucking years, Kate. And to be honest, it scares the shit out of me to meet someone new." I pursed my lips. "And that's just the beginning of my whole pathetic story. Not very sexy, is it? And sorry about the cuss words."

She waved me off. "*Please,* girl. Shit, fuck, and wanker roll off my tongue daily." She motioned with her hands. "Go on."

"As I said, it scares the shit out of me to be in social settings. I was never very good at it. I relied on Daniel for those things. And the thought of meeting men makes me want to throw up right here." I looked down at the counter.

Kate untied her apron and folded it. "Ever heard the term, nothing lost, nothing gained?" She tossed her apron onto the counter.

I nodded. "Who hasn't?"

"Go to the party. Dress up. You've spent a year mourning your marriage." She came around the counter and touched my auburn hair, which I still kept at shoulder length. "Knock 'em dead with that pretty face. Drink too much and get yourself properly shagged before you close up shop for good." She smiled. "It's New Years' Eve, Cassie, go have fun."

I thought about Daniel and what he was probably doing. He loved New Years' Eve, concocting fancy appetizers, buying champagne for us to sip as the ball dropped. This year, he'd be doing those things with his new love, who I didn't even know the name of. I shook my head, and then I slapped my hands down on the marble.

"You're right, Kate. I'll do it."

* * *

After an hour of showering and primping, I stood decked out in my green Armani dress, a thick stole hugging my shoulders, ready to climb the steps of a mansion in Hyde Park that was something out of a movie, every manicured bush and tree decorated with showy lights, every window donning impressive wreaths, and a door so ornate and impressive it gave the illusion of one entering a portal more than a home. And it did feel like a portal, into another realm of society I had never encountered before.

I stepped over the threshold.

Within seconds, a tray weighed down with champagne flutes appeared held by a young male waitperson, who was dressed in what appeared to be a coat with tails. "For you, miss."

I took the flute and consumed half the glass, my nerves frayed. Tall stone pillars, a wide staircase, statues, floral arrangements, and one of the largest Christmas trees I had ever seen indoors filled the boundless room with festive ambiance. And people were everywhere, the women decked out in gowns, the men in tuxes or tails, or whatever English men wore. I was both terrified of not knowing anyone and comforted. It was almost like being anonymous. That was until Gregory emerged from the crowd with a crystal glass of something amber clutched in his hand.

He kissed both of my cheeks. "I'm so glad you came." He ushered me into the sea of people as a small orchestra played holiday music from a landing halfway up the wide staircase, the one that centered the room.

"Let's check your wrap and then I want to introduce you to Harry." He placed his hand on my arm and gently urged me to keep pace with him.

At first, I wondered if Harry might in fact be Prince Harry, but then I remembered that he didn't live here anymore, so my heart could just calm down already.

The night was filled with introductions, champagne, and small talk. As the alcohol seeped into my bloodstream, the muscles in my shoulders relaxed, allowing me to present myself with a smile and a few entertaining words to say.

The countdown began.

Gregory had excused himself to go call one of his kids, and I was left on my own private island, feeling loose and rather lonely, until a voice rang out.

"As I live and breathe, Cassie Griffin, is that really you?"

Chapter Twenty-One

Shocked that anyone aside from Gregory knew me here, I turned to find Bryce, my ex-fiancé a.k.a. Mr. Good-on-paper-and-lousy-at-love, standing before me. He was older, giving him a more distinguished look, his light-brown hair clipped short, and his blue eyes shining with delight. In fact, his mouth was gaping open.

"I can't believe my eyes." He rushed in for a hug, his spicy cologne latching onto my clothing and skin. "I had heard that you were heading up the new firm for Wilson, Bates & *Griffin* as I understand it." Dressed in a three-piece black tuxedo with matching bowtie and a crisp white dress shirt, his smile stretched wide.

Mine didn't, mostly because I knew I had to correct him. "Hello, Bryce. Nice to see you. Yes, that's true, but it's not Griffin anymore. I'm back to Dunne." I rattled my head slightly. "I got divorced earlier this year."

Gregory had been gracious about the cost of changing the signage, but I wasn't so sure about Isabella. Though I felt like Gregory had smoothed things over with her, I wished I had just kept my maiden name all along, which most of my female counterparts had done. *Spilled milk.*

My heart shrunk having to admit this. I had planned to stay married to Daniel forever. *Till death do us part.* Destiny had other plans.

Bryce's face fell, his expression somber. I wasn't used to seeing this from him. "Oh, I'm so sorry." He placed his hand on my upper arm. "I went through a divorce over two years ago." He rolled his eyes and shook his head. "Not fun." He stood back and gazed at my dress. "You look,"—he rubbed his chin as though searching for the right word—"stunning."

For a moment, the orchestra and the chatter around the room filled the void between us as Bryce stared off, and my thoughts wandered. He seemed to snap out of whatever was controlling his mind.

He opened his mouth to speak when the room erupted with glee, ushering in the New Year. Horns blew, confetti burst, and the orchestra played "Auld Lang Syne."

I couldn't have felt worse if I had tried. Daniel and I had often made love when the clock struck midnight. *What better way to ring in the New Year*, he'd said as he took me in his arms and kissed me with passion. Was he making love to someone else right now? *I haven't acted on my feelings, and I won't until you agree to sign this.* I'd signed those fucking papers eight months ago. He was a free man.

Fireworks exploded from the sky, enticing everyone out back, including Bryce and me. On our way there, Bryce handed his drink over to a waiter holding a tray, freeing his hands up. I followed his lead with my now fourth empty glass of champagne.

Beyond a spacious patio and swimming pool—more statues around its perimeter—an expansive lawn unfurled before me. Spread out among extensive gardens and rows of greenery, some of it sculpted into various shapes, was something I would imagine from a Jane Austen novel. *Where is Mr. Darcy?* I almost expected him to appear. This was hands down the most extravagant home I had ever been to.

Caught up in the moment, I oohed and aahed a few times before Bryce gazed over at me, his eyes filled with sentimental *something*.

Was he thinking about our engagement? Was he regretful? The Bryce I knew all those years ago wouldn't have had the capacity for either.

"I can't believe you're here. Happy New Year." He planted his lips on mine, the taste of scotch lacing his breath. He pulled back and stared intensely into my eyes. "You know, I always regretted letting you go, Cassie. It was one of the biggest fuck-ups of my life. I want you to know that I'm not that spoiled asshole I was back then." His eyes gleamed with sincerity. "Fuck, you look good." He touched my cheek with the back of his fingers. "I feel like this was meant to be."

In my periphery, from just inside the patio doors, Gregory lifted his glass at me as if to say, *Good for you, Cassie, you found yourself a man* before the crowd consumed him in fast order.

Running into Bryce *did* feel like it was meant to be. Pumped up on champagne and the night's nostalgia I leaned in and kissed *him* this time, one that lingered with a little tongue involved. "It does feel meant to be. Let me ask you a question, Bryce Tanner."

He kept his lips close. "Ask me anything you want, beautiful. If it's what I hope it is, I can guarantee the answer will be *yes!*"

I was standing at one of those crossroads in my life, and for a moment, I wasn't sure what to do or say. I had lost Daniel, and I knew I could never win him back. He hadn't only moved on; he'd found someone else. And while that pulled at my heart like a fishing hook—and probably always would—I didn't miss the lifestyle. The penny pinching. The constant worrying about money. The crappy apartment. And the feeling that it could all fall apart if I didn't work my ass off to keep it together. Ironically, working my ass off had been our downfall in Daniel's eyes. He pushed me into a corner, leaving me with few choices to fulfill my dreams. All while he pursued his to the fullest—handed over to him on a silver platter *by me*.

I still busted my butt, but from now on, I was doing it for *myself*. Living in Daniel's shadow, I often felt inferior. Somehow, I always knew he would leave me.

As both Gregory and Kate had pointed out, I was still young, I was unencumbered, and maybe it was time to start living again. Daniel certainly was.

There was also the possibility that Bryce *had* changed. At one time, I had wanted to marry the man. He was immature back then. Most men were. But people change. Daniel was a perfect example. At one time, Daniel was committed to me forever, until he wasn't.

With a flurry of fireworks, noisemakers, and cheer dancing around our heads, I gazed into Bryce's blue eyes. I didn't need a commitment from him. In fact, I didn't want one. This wasn't about that. It was just sex, which would actually tell me all I needed to know. If he hadn't changed in the bedroom, he probably hadn't changed elsewhere.

Here goes.

"My question is, Mr. Tanner, your place or mine?"

Not only did I sleep with Bryce that night (and orgasmed three times), but I also slept with him every night after that—until he had to fly back to New York for business. The man who had refused to go down on me ten years ago, wanted nothing more than to satisfy me now. He would never be Daniel in my eyes or in my heart, but I was willing to take what

I could get. Bryce was fun. He was understanding. And he was full of compliments every time we were together. Perhaps he *had* changed.

Bryce also chose to stay here in London to be with me. He wasn't caught up in the snarl of his dream or mine. How refreshing. Three months later, he proposed, and the following year we were married. Eloped. I'd already done the full wedding with Daniel—Bryce, the same with his ex.

We found a place to live in the city, a nice place with a beautiful view. Bryce worked for a firm nearby that specialized in corporate disputes while I continued to kick ass as a senior partner at Wilson, Bates & Dunne.

It seemed Daniel was right all along. Maybe the two of us weren't meant to be. I had more money than I knew what to do with. As far as kids, Bryce didn't want any, so I decided that neither did I. Life was good. And I was finally living the dream. *My dream.*

I had only one problem. Then why, when the world slowed its pace, and I was left alone with my thoughts, did I still feel so empty inside?

* * *

Two and a half years later . . .

"What time is this *thing* anyway?"

I grumbled to myself before answering. "For the tenth time, it's not a thing, it's my nephew's high school graduation." Bryce and I had just collected my husband's suitcase at RIC's baggage claim. Why he needed to bring a large suitcase was beyond me. I had brought a carry-on, but not my entitled husband, who claimed he *had* to check his bag. We were only here for two days.

Bryce wasn't happy about coming here, but then again, Bryce wasn't happy about anything that didn't provide him with a direct benefit, which was probably the reason he didn't come home last night *again* and why he almost didn't make it to the airport on time. The faint scent of flowery perfume on his collar told me he was probably with one of several fuck buddies he kept on speed dial.

Yup, my husband was having an affair, and not just one. Oh no, that wouldn't be enough for this self-centered prick. Bryce had many.

I stopped caring a year ago when I had caught him once again when the bitch was dropping him off outside of our home, the brunette with a perfect body and fuck-me brown eyes. I initially thought he was doing these things to get my attention. I'd been consumed with my work, forging new avenues for the firm, receiving awards for my benefit work, and winning the respect of my peers. I was on top of my game. Isabella and Gregory came to me for advice now, not the other way around. They looked up to me, and I basked in their admiration.

Don't get me wrong. I enjoyed being married to Bryce . . . for about six months, before I realized he hadn't changed at all. He'd just gotten older and richer. I'd already been divorced once, so I wasn't thrilled about doing it again. To be honest, I didn't care enough to divorce Bryce. He could have his affairs. He could do whatever he wanted. I was happy on my own.

I was living my dream.

Once we slid into the backseat of our hired town car with a driver, we raced across town to my nephew, Noah's, high school graduation. Several schools in the area had conducted their ceremonies at the convention center in the heart of downtown Richmond, but Noah's school wasn't large enough to warrant such expense. It was a beautiful, partly sunny day in Virginia, promising the festivities would most likely be held outdoors, something I looked forward to. Plus, I couldn't wait to see my family. I missed them terribly.

The air was fresh, the sky a powder blue. A perfect day with the exception of the yellow film covering most of the surfaces like confectioners' sugar. Only Virginia pollen wasn't as sweet, and my nose was feeling the effects of its mischievous nature.

"Why can't we stop at the hotel to drop off our things? I could use a drink beforehand." Bryce sat next me, gazing out the window as the houses, trees, and vegetation whizzed by.

"We don't have time for that." I stared at my cell phone for the millionth time, worried we'd be late. "It starts at two, and we'll barely make it there on time as it is."

Bryce didn't respond to that. He just rolled his eyes and huffed, something he did so often, I barely registered it.

As our car pulled up to the high school, the parking lot sat at full capacity, vehicles filling every parking space and along the side of the road. Thankfully, we didn't need to park.

"Pull up here." I pointed to an area where we could make a beeline around the main building with a straight shot to the back area where I had hoped the ceremony would be held. I handed our driver several hundred dollars. "We're staying at The Jefferson Hotel. They will be expecting you there to drop off our bags. I've already checked in over the phone. Will that be a problem?" Our driver took my money and smiled. "No, ma'am. My boss already filled me in." He held the money up. "Thank you for the generous tip. I will make sure your bags are checked into your room. Would you like me to come back and pick you up after the graduation?"

I opened the door. "That won't be necessary. We can get a ride with my family. Thank you . . ."

"Dan," he said as though knowing I was struggling to

remember his name. He'd introduced himself when we had met, but I was distracted and rushed at the time.

"Thank you, Dan." I hopped out, Bryce right behind me, and together we dashed across the school lawn as a loudspeaker filled the air with a woman's voice. "Welcome parents, students, and faculty..."

"Hurry. It's starting."

"Jesus Christ. Why did I even have to come for this shit? I wouldn't know your family if I ran into them on the street. Why do *I* need to be here?"

"Because for the time being, you're my husband, asshole. Now, get moving."

Around the corner of the building, a crowd appeared. Most of the people sat in chairs that ran in rows, taking up one large section of lawn, another filled with empty chairs for the prospective graduates to use once the procession aspect of the ceremony had concluded.

Lifting up on my tiptoes and with my eyes peeled, I couldn't seem to find my family as much as I tried. We grabbed a couple of empty seats toward the back. That ghastly smell I had accepted as part of my life returned, my gut unhappy, and my chest restricted. Even the headache had made an appearance for the occasion. I figured it was nerves and seeing my family again, something I hadn't done for a very long time. I just hoped my generous gifts over the years and my endless apologies had appeased my rudeness for my absence.

While the ceremony took place, Bryce fidgeted in his molded plastic chair. "Couldn't they at least spring for decent seats? Christ, we might as well be sitting on blocks of wood."

I blew out my lips. "It's a high school, Bryce, not a country club. Now shush." I put my index finger against my mouth to reinforce my message.

Close to an hour passed before the graduates threw their caps in the air and everyone hooted, hollered, or applauded. When Noah had walked across the stage earlier, my family had screamed and clapped for joy. I did, too, telling them I was here and where I was sitting. I hoped they had heard me. Just hearing their cheers made my heart smile. I truly missed them all. Noah was close to eighteen now, Bailey fourteen, and McKenna ten. I'd sent them all extravagant gifts for the holidays and for their birthdays, apologizing for my absence but promising I would one day return. That day had finally arrived, and I had goosebumps at the thought of wrapping my arms around each and every one of them and never letting go. Especially Mom and Dad.

As the crowds gathered in one area to congratulate their son or daughter or dispersed to take their party to another location, I located my family and rushed over to them.

I flung my arms around my big sister and squeezed. "Hey, Sis. I missed you guys so much!" When I was finished with that hug, I gave one to my nieces and then to Mike, with one special hug reserved for the graduate. "I'm so proud of you, Noah. Congratulations." I suddenly realized that the enthusiasm and love I was projecting out to my family was met with blank stares.

"Nice to see you" came from Noah, his tone flatter than a tire.

"Wow. Formal much, bud?" I giggled while giving his shoulder a friendly nudge.

I expected his bashful smile in response, not a face cooled by apathy. He wandered off to high-five some friends nearby and chat. He never even excused himself. Noah had always been so polite.

What is going on here?

Even my nieces seemed oddly reserved, allowing my hug

but nothing more. They kept their gaze fixated on their brother, standing fifteen feet away.

"Is everything okay?" I zoned in on my sister.

Trina didn't answer right off. She stepped away as though she wanted me to follow, which I did. When we were mostly out of earshot of anyone we knew, she finally spoke. "No, everything is not okay. You couldn't come home when Mom suffered her stroke. You missed her funeral. Dad was devastated, and you weren't here to comfort him."

Stroke? Funeral? "What are you talking about, Trina? When did Mom have a stroke? Why didn't you call me?" I touched her arm, but she yanked it away as though my hand had scorched her skin. This was so unlike my big sis who had always been there for me.

"You're a piece of work. You know that? What are you even doing here? Don't you have *important* business back in London?"

"No, I came to support Noah . . . and you. And I didn't know about Mom. Did you say funeral? Mom died?" Despair froze my heart, my eyes spilling with tears. I looked around, realizing the crowd was missing another familiar face. "Where is Dad?" I wiped my tears, my chest encased in dread.

"*Humph.*" Trina crossed her arms and stared me down, her mouth crimping into a defiant frown. "Like you care! And don't act stupid, Cassie. You may be a cold-hearted bitch, but you're no dummy. You know Mom died. I left you a ton of messages. Just like you know that Dad fell into a depression and is rehabilitating. He couldn't even come here today, he's so bad off. And when Mom died, he kept asking for you, but you were too busy making money to respond." She twisted her face up, her tone snarky. "We appreciated the flowers, though." Anger filled her eyes, so intense, I feared she'd extinguish me on the spot.

A Collision with Love

I rattled my head. *What the fuck is happening?* Nothing made sense. I hadn't received any voicemails *or* texts. Did she call Bryce, and the bastard didn't bother to tell me? Did he send the flowers?

I was about to grill him when Trina's expression suddenly softened.

She peered around me. "Daniel, so nice of you to come. Noah will be thrilled. And good to see you, too, Olivia."

I turned as Daniel came sauntering over with a small boy in his arms, a woman with long auburn hair pushing a stroller keeping pace with him.

The earth shifted beneath my feet. As my insides went into a frenzy, Trina approached my ex, offering him a side hug around his son. She touched his son's nose with a *boop*, who lay draped over Daniel's shoulder as if half awake.

Seeing Daniel shoved me off my axis. For years, I had been killing it as a litigator and senior partner. I was the woman in charge. But in this moment, I felt more like a kite without a tether, flying into a thunderstorm. I struggled to find my bearings. And man, did he look good. Daniel's hair was shorter, allowing loose curls to frame his beautiful face, his chestnut eyes warm and . . . happy. He hadn't gained any weight nor lost any, his muscular stature just as I had remembered it. This man rocked my world, and as I stood there watching him, I realized he still did. All the love I had pushed down so I wouldn't feel anything came gushing up into my chest, a chest that could barely breathe.

Next to him, the woman with a wedding band on her finger, who I assumed was Olivia, rolled her stroller back and forth as if to keep the baby inside comforted, cooing enough to tell us they were there. Olivia's hair was auburn like mine, but not the color of her eyes, which were as soft and creamy as milk chocolate, a perfect pairing to her husband's chestnut.

The vice around my chest pulled tighter. *I have met someone*, he'd told me all those years ago. Was it Olivia?

"I'm sorry we're late. We couldn't seem to get these munchkins to wake up from their naps." He bounced a little as he spoke, another comforting technique I'd seen my sister do when Noah or the girls were little.

His gaze found me.

My skin prickled, my heart pounding with abandon as I stood there frozen in place. That horrid smell intensified, leaving my stomach twisting like a towel being wrung of water. At the same time, my chest caved, choking off oxygen to my lungs. I was going to be sick. I was sure of it.

"Nice to see you, Cassie. It was kind of you to make the trip." His chin lowered, his gaze staring up at me from under his brow. "I'm sorry about your mom." He blinked.

What are you doing to me? Those compassionate eyes of his drew me in. I was desperate for his touch. I was desperate for his love. And without those things, I wasn't sure I wanted to live another second longer.

Standing next to me, Bryce cleared his throat. "I don't believe we've met. I'm Bryce, Cassie's husband. And you are?" The arrogance in my husband's voice heightened my nausea.

I put my hand to my mouth, hoping to calm my internal aches.

"Daniel." Keeping his son secure on his shoulder, he reached his free hand out to shake.

Bryce abided, his smile more of a sneer. "Right. Daniel. I remember hearing about *you*." Using his typical smart-ass tone, an ugly grin spread wider across Bryce's face.

The contrast between these two men glared at me, reinforcing the loss my heart struggled to comprehend.

If it weren't for Bryce's cell phone ringing and causing him to step away—probably to speak with one of his girlfriends—I might have punched him right in the face or disavowed him for being the loser he always was.

What difference did it make? In my condition, I was too weak to do much of anything.

"Uncle Daniel." Noah came bounding over. "I was hoping you'd make it." He wrapped his arms around my ex-husband and then rubbed Daniel's son on the back. "Hey, bud." He then hugged Olivia right before leaning over the stroller in front of her. "How's my sweet angel doing today?"

His sweet angel? Noah knew Daniel's entire family? So did my sister.

My nieces and Mike appeared next, all delighted to see Daniel with hugs and handshakes for his lot.

The only person they weren't thrilled to see was me . . . and Bryce, who was still chatting on his phone.

I'd never felt more alone and rejected in all of my life. This was my family, my blood. Only they didn't want me anymore. Just like with Daniel, I'd been cast out. But that wasn't true. I'd cast *myself* out. There was no one to blame but me. My body knew it, too, every cell rebelling.

As though a movie was playing out in front of me, I stood back and observed as everyone visited with Daniel and his family, who must've planted at least twenty kisses on his son's forehead as the boy lay groggy in Daniel's arms. What was the boy's name?

That was supposed to be our son. That was supposed to be our baby in the stroller. My gaze remained glued to Daniel's tender hands as they rubbed his son's back or touched his wife's shoulder. I watched his eyes taking in all the love and returning it tenfold.

Daniel was everything, and the people around him knew it. Once more, *I* knew it.

My family had forgotten I was there. I glanced over at

Bryce again, who was still having a conversation with someone who made him smile and laugh, something he never did with me anymore. Even the assholes had turned away from me.

Mom and Dad wanted me. But I'd let them down too. How could I do such a thing? Who had I become?

I thought about my life and my accomplishments. I had enough money to do anything I ever wanted, travel anywhere I wanted to go, and live the life most people dreamed of. But what was the point if I had no one there to share it with?

I didn't love Bryce, and I never should have married him. It took me all of five minutes to realize that. My life had become all about what I *did* for a living and not who I was. I didn't even know who Cassie Dunne was anymore. I produced. I served. I did things that made *other* people happy. And I'd sacrificed my own joyfulness to do so.

My family and Daniel's spoke about a party back at my sister's place. Daniel took his wife's hand and asked her in a light tone if she wanted to attend. He touched her hair. He gazed into her eyes. And she gazed right back, the love between them palpable.

I *had* that kind of love. I *had* Daniel. But I gave him up so I could offer him more, and then *he* gave up on me. He'd waited over eight years for a wife who was present, both physically and emotionally. And I had let him down, even if that wasn't my intention. I was ashamed. *No* job was worth the price I had paid. Regret swallowed me up in one gulp. I couldn't even move. I was riveted in place as all the people I loved, Daniel included, walked away, leaving me in the quicksand of my life.

Regret set into my bones like cancer. I hated my choices as much as I hated the results of them. I wanted a new life. But no matter how hard I tried, and no matter how far I searched, I would never find another Daniel. A love like that couldn't possibly come around more than once in a lifetime. Olivia had Daniel's heart now, the man who would always be a loving husband and father and who would see life for its beauty and not for its uses.

"Let's blow this popsicle stand. I need a drink."

I turned my head as Bryce watched two young female graduates saunter past, one with long blond hair, the other with black, their robes unzipped and flowing, their sundresses allowing ample amounts of cleavage to bounce with each step. My husband couldn't keep his eyes off their breasts. *This* was who I had married? I gave up something remarkable, and this is what I settled for? The stark contrast between my past life and my present was sobering.

Something slugged me in the gut, and I doubled over. That ghastly odor engulfed the air, suffocating my lungs. My chest convulsed, and I worried this time my ribs might actually crack or crush, all my organs mashed together. Pain reverberated through my head as my stomach knotted. All the symptoms I'd been experiencing intensified with the strength of a tidal wave, and I sunk to the ground.

"Help me!" I reached my hand out as Daniel, my sister, and my loved ones wandered off, the image of them going blurry. "Please, someone help me!"

No one came. No one noticed. Everyone around me oblivious to my plight. Even Bryce had disappeared, leaving me there to die alone.

Just when the pain rose off the scales of what a person could possibly take, convincing me it was over, my eyes fluttered open. My world descended into chaos. I wasn't at the graduation anymore. I was inside what appeared to be my car. But something wasn't right. The roof was below me. The windshield shattered, the sunroof also gone, branches and debris bursting through newly created openings, shards of glass scattered around like sand on a beach. Airbags sat deflated; their power spent.

Where am I?

And then I heard it: rain falling fast and heavy, the sound of steam hissing like a snake, and an overwhelming odor snuffing out the good air—the air I needed to breathe.

"W-what's h-happening?" Had I fallen through a wormhole in time? Was this the gates of hell? I couldn't fathom one thing from another.

My car had me pinned, my seat belt cutting across my chest, my head left hanging there, my limbs draping down like clothes on a clothesline. A rumble of thunder sounded off in the distance as rain pelted the car and the flora around me.

Somewhere out there, the voice of an old man reached my ears, his voice gravely. "Over here! Come quick! I'm the one who called it in. A truck forced that car off the road. It's down there at the bottom of the ravine."

I imagined him pointing, but at whom?

"There's a lady inside. She's unconscious. You better hurry cause I'm pretty sure that car is in danger of catching fire. *I smell gas.*"

That ghastly smell I'd been suffering with wasn't ghastly at all. It was actual gas!

As branches crunched and feet slid, a younger man's voice responded. "We see it, sir. Thank you for calling it in. Please return to the road. We don't want you getting injured. We will take care of it." The man had a commanding timbre as more branches crushed outside my car. It sounded like a stampede.

My eyes fluttered open again, my mind returning to the horrible scene before me. The sound of steam and the smell of gasoline grew stronger, forming a toxic cloud. The situation grappled my mind. The seat belt across my chest was tearing me in two. Each breath was a fight.

A Collision with Love

The man's powerful voice returned just as a fireman's helmet breached my broken driver's side window. "Miss, are you okay?" On his knees, he gazed up at me, his eyes filled with concern.

I started to cry. "What's g-going on? W-where am I?"

"You were in a car accident, miss. Your car is upside down right now. Can you tell me your name?" His voice was gentle but strong, the kind of voice that could talk people off ledges or through fires or floods.

"C-cassie."

"Nice to meet you, Cassie. My name is Rob. Do you have a last name to go with Cassie?" While he spoke, his gaze wandered over the car or what was left of it.

"Griffin. C-cassie G-Griffin." I was still married . . . *wasn't I?* I couldn't remember. A moment ago, I was in another place and time. Everything was different. Daniel was gone, remarried to Olivia, my doppelgänger. He was a father. Logic wrestled with that imaginary world from a moment ago.

"You're doing great, Cassie. Do you have family here in the area? I see you're married. Do you have a husband we can call?"

Did I have a husband he could call? Was it Bryce? No, that wasn't real. My perception was playing tricks. "D-Daniel."

"Good job, Cassie. Now I know this is a lot to ask of you, but do you have a phone number or an address where you live? This will help us get in touch with your husband quicker." His voice changed direction. "Sheila, when you get to the passenger side, check the glove box for her registration." Noises from the opposite side of the car reached my ears, but I couldn't turn my head.

"Got it."

Rob returned his attention to me. "Can you remember your husband's phone number or one of your closest relatives?"

With much difficulty, I recited the numbers to Daniel's cell phone. The address was too hard to pull from my memory banks, and I grew frustrated. Tears ran down my cheeks, already soaked from either blood or rain, I couldn't tell which. All I knew was that something metallic was coating my mouth, making me feel sick, and my head pounded like a marching band was stomping through it. "I feel s-sick."

"That's okay, Cassie. You're doing great." Rob's voice changed to a more professional tone as he pulled a two-way radio from his side. "The victim's name is Cassie Griffin. Her husband's name is Daniel Griffin." He recited the phone number I had just given him. Rob waited for a moment, keeping his two-way near his ear.

"Copy that," a man's voice said, followed by a pulse of static. "We'll contact the husband."

"I've got her registration. She doesn't live far from here."

"Copy that, Sheila. Now get back over here." Rob snapped his two-way radio onto a strap beneath his thick fireman's coat. "Okay. Let's get you out of here. I'm going to use a hydraulic device called the Jaws of Life to cut your door away. It's going to be a little loud, but only for a few minutes." He rose to his feet.

What started off sounding like a lawn mower morphed into a very loud saw as Rob cut my door away. It was jarring to have a saw so close, but I trusted that he knew what he was doing. And I really wanted to get out of there.

Within a short time, the weight of the door fell away, Rob and someone else (*Sheila?*) throwing it off to the side.

"W-what happened?" I couldn't remember if he'd told me already. In fact, the only memory that stayed strong in my mind was the graduation. Was it real?

"Cassie, a truck forced you off the road, and your car rolled down a ravine. But don't worry. We're going to get you out."

A Collision with Love

Now lying on his back, Rob shimmied into the car, which, with his thick coat, made him appear larger than life. *A giant squeezing through a mouse hole.* He felt around to where the latch for my seat belt was. The way I was hanging there, I feared what would happen if he released me. Would I plummet right into him? Would I hit something sharp? I was at his mercy.

Only nothing happened other than a few grunts of exertion escaping from Rob's lips.

"That's just what I thought. The latch for your seat belt appears to be embedded between your seat and the console. It's got you trapped for the moment, but we'll get you out. We can cut the seat belt away."

Trapped? Panicking, I tried to move, making the car teeter slightly. I had to get out of here! I was coming unglued. I didn't want to die in this car. *Please, someone get me out of here!*

Staying on his back, Rob raised his palm. "Cassie, I need you to listen to me *very carefully*. I'm here to help you. But you have to do exactly what I tell you to do. Please do not panic. I know you're scared. It's going to be okay. We will free you from the seat belt, but we have to cut it away. And I'll grab you and get you right out. It won't take us long. Just a minute or two." He reached into his coat and pulled out a strange-looking knife, before he shimmied out of the car and got onto his knees.

A minute or two? I couldn't wait that long. I couldn't breathe. White spots floated across my vision. I was panting, yet my lungs strained for more air. Each breath burned as though I'd inhaled hot coals. *My God!* This was it. I died at Noah's graduation, and I was about to die here. No one loved me anymore. I was alone. *No, that can't be true. That wasn't real.*

"You're doing great, Cassie." He cut at the seat belt, each tug driving it deeper into my chest.

295

I cried out, the pain unbearable. "Aah. It hurts."

"Yes, I know it hurts, but we're almost there. Hang on, Cassie." Sweat or rain drizzled down Rob's face and neck. He eased his hulky body beneath me again. "Okay, one more cut, and you are going to fall. But I'm right here to catch you."

"I c-can't breathe."

"Yes, your seat belt is pushing up against your lungs. Believe it or not, your car did well. And so did you. You're gonna be okay."

The person behind Rob spoke again. The woman. "The gas smell is getting worse, Rob. We don't have much time."

"Copy that, Sheila. We do this quickly." By now, Rob had sandwiched himself right below me. "Make sure EMS is standing by."

My ears picked up Sheila using her two-way radio, following Rob's instructions. Crackles and voices were lost on me, my mind losing focus.

The radio spoke, the same male voice from before who said he'd contact Daniel. "EMS is here. They're bringing the stretcher down now. Can you tell us more about the woman's condition? Can she be moved?"

Sheila answered the call. "Yes, she's conscious. She has a pretty deep laceration on her forehead, cuts on her neck, and may have some broken limbs. She also may have a collapsed lung. We're about to extract her from the vehicle now. Over and out."

Rob braced his feet wherever he could find and raised his arms up. By now, Sheila was right next to him. "You cut, I catch, got it?" He handed her the strange-looking knife.

"You got it, boss," Sheila said.

"Okay, Cassie," Rob said. "When Sheila cuts you free, you are going to fall right into my arms. I will catch you. I've done this a thousand times. And then we are going to get you out of here. EMS is right outside your car, ready to take you to the hospital."

Another voice carried through the air. "Rob, the gas tank is leaking."

"Well aware, Rudy. Tell me something I don't fucking know!"

"You better hurry."

"Not now, Rudy."

His cheeks turning rosy and his forehead getting sweatier by the second, Rob kept his arms in position to catch me. "It's okay, Cassie. She's almost got it."

More tugs on the seat belt.

"Rob, if you can't free her in the next thirty seconds, you and Sheila best get your asses out of there. This thing is gonna blow."

Rob took several deep breaths. "Okay, Cassie, she's just about there. Get ready to fall." He nodded to Sheila before his eyes shifted back over to me. "Three, two, one . . ."

Chapter Twenty-Two

The sound of continuous beeping, to the rhythm of a heartbeat, roused my mind. I fought to open my eyes. In the distance, voices carried, commotion muffled. A far-off voice instructed someone to dial an extension number that escaped me.

Once again, I tried to pry my eyes open without success. My left arm felt tight, and the inside of my elbow pinched. The gasoline smell had gone, replaced by a thick coat of antiseptic in the air. I realized someone was holding my right hand.

Giving it all the effort I had left inside of me, I forced my lids open, the light in the room making me squint as though I had turned vampire. I lifted my left hand to shield my face, something hindering my efforts. It was an IV.

"Cassie?" The person holding my right hand was Daniel, who rose and bent over me, bringing his gorgeous face into view. His familiar scent was as welcoming as a summer breeze.

I have never seen anything more perfect.

"You gave us quite a scare, hon. How are you feeling?" His gaze scoured my face.

When I tried to speak, a dry throat forbade it, the sound more like a croak rather than anything legible.

"Here, let me get you something to drink." Daniel reached over and took a cup with a straw off a small table and brought it up to my lips. "Don't drink too much. Just a sip."

I did as he asked, the water flooding my throat with refreshing moisture. I wanted to suck the cup dry, but Daniel pulled it away. "That's good for now. I'll ask the nurse if you can have more." He placed the cup down and then kissed my forehead several times, his tears falling onto my face like a gentle rain. He quickly wiped them away. "Sorry, hon, I don't mean to cry all over you."

I was just glad he still cared enough to cry.

With the back of his hand, he dried his own eyes, a few sniffles persisting. "How are you feeling?"

I tried to sit up.

Daniel jumped into action, fluffing my pillows and helping me find a more comfortable position. He moved so carefully and gently as though I was made of glass and could shatter at any moment.

"I'm okay" came out of my mouth somehow, although I wasn't sure how. My voice was alien and strained. "What happened?"

Leaning into me, Daniel sat on the edge of my bed, brushing my hair back and caressing my cheek. "You left to go to work and some asshole in a big truck forced your car off the road. Several witnesses saw the whole thing happen and called the police. Don't worry, they found the guy, and he's facing charges. I guess this isn't the only time he's been arrested for road rage. Fucking lunatic."

The memories came rushing back. "I-I remember. I was upset. It was raining. And I drove through a stop sign. The driver of the truck was angry. He harassed me on the road."

The scene of my car fishtailing returned vividly as well as the tumbling I did down the hill afterward. "The next thing I remember is someone yelling to the fireman that I was down there. Could I have another sip of water?"

"Of course!" Daniel had the straw up to my lips in no time. "Just drink a little, though." After he put the cup down again, he stayed bent over me like a mother hen.

I stared at my husband's rosy cheeks and bloodshot eyes with a whole new sense of appreciation. "You said you didn't think you could do this much longer, and I was upset."

Daniel let his head drop before those warm chestnut eyes found me again. "I'm so sorry, Cass." He exhaled. "I didn't mean that. I never should have said that to you."

"It's okay." I touched his arm, something I never thought I'd have the chance to do again. "I'm so sorry, Daniel."

His brow bore down. *"You're* sorry?" He shook his head vehemently. "No, *I'm* sorry. You have nothing to be sorry for. This was on me." He stared down at the bed, shaking his head. He lifted his gaze once more. "You've done nothing but support me our entire marriage, Cass. And I had no right to pressure you into starting a family." He cupped my cheek in his hands, tears glistening in his eyes. "This horrible ordeal has shown me that I can live without kids. I always thought having kids would make us a family. But I've realized that we already are a family. The only thing I can't live without is you, Cass. I love you and that is enough for me." He planted a tender kiss on my lips. "I support your dreams as you have always supported mine. If kids are in our future, great, but if they aren't, that's okay too. As long as I have you in my life, I've got everything I need." His voice shook as a tear ran down his cheek, which he quickly wiped away. "I almost lost you, hon. That was the scariest moment of my life. If you can forgive me for being so selfish, I will make this up to you. I promise."

My heart burst open with joy. I had never been so sore and so elated in all of my life. That nightmare was finally over. The true Daniel that I had grown to adore was still here all along. He'd never left. He'd never divorced me. And he'd never remarried someone named Olivia. Whatever that alternate world was —a dream or a hallucination—it wasn't real. As much as this experience had tortured me, it had *finally* answered the *what ifs* of my future. Did I want to be successful in my career at the cost of my personal life? No fucking way! I would always be a lawyer. But I would never again be a slave to it, living the life of someone who I didn't recognize. A person who lost touch with her family. A person who wouldn't even come to her own mother's funeral. That was not and *would never be* who I aspired to become.

Daniel kissed me again, snapping me out of my thoughts. "Can you forgive me?"

I blinked back tears. "Of course, I forgive you." All at once another thought slammed into my heart. "Is my mom and dad okay?" My breath hitched. "And Trina and the kids?" Panic started to rise.

A soothing voice came from my husband's gorgeous lips. He cradled my cheeks. "Yes, they are all fine. Trina already called your parents about the accident. They are flying home now. And Trina's been here since you were admitted. When you stabilized, she ran home to check on the kids. She'll be back soon."

I wept. I wasn't sad, though. I was moved. More importantly, I was grateful. "While I was trapped at the bottom of that ravine, I had a horrible dream."

"Oh? Do you want to talk about it? Did it have to do with your parents? Is that why you were worried about them?" What tears he didn't kiss away from my face, my husband wiped away with his loving hands.

"Yes, and no. It was mostly about you and me." I paused to gather my thoughts. "Do you remember when the plumbing in the restaurant sprung a leak?"

He nodded. "Uh-huh."

"And when we babysat Noah, Bailey, and McKenna at my sister's place last summer?"

He nodded again, his eyes filled with confusion. "Yeah."

"That was all part of the dream, only everything happened differently. I was so focused on finances and stability and taking care of everyone, I let things get out of control." I went on to explain it all, from when I thought I had dodged the almost accident to when I showed up for my nephew's graduation with Bryce, and Daniel arrived with his new wife and kids. "Is this real, Daniel? Am I really here? Are you?" I stared deep within his eyes, trying to find clarity. I knew this was real, and yet I still feared it could all be stolen away.

He hugged me, and then he stayed close, constantly touching my face, holding my hand, or caressing my arm. "First of all, that would never happen. I'm not going anywhere, wife of mine."

Wife of mine. I closed my eyes and basked in those words.

"You do try so hard to take care of everyone, Cass, but it's time you let me take care of you. I'm not as ill-equipped as you may think." He quirked a brow, his tone lightening. "I don't know anyone named Olivia, either. You are the only woman for me. I knew it the first time we met, and you quizzed me about the meat I was slicing at your friend's wedding." His voice grew husky with emotion. "I'm sorry you had that terrible dream. I take responsibility for that. I never should have pressured you to have kids."

"I see someone is awake." A woman wearing light-blue scrubs poked her head through the hospital room door. "How are you feeling?"

"Okay, I guess. It's a little hard to breathe, and I'm sore all over, but I'm fine."

"That's to be expected. Your seat belt had caused some pretty severe bruising to your ribs and sternum. And your forehead required a few stitches."

Becoming aware of the bandage, I reached up and touched it.

"But no broken bones. You were lucky." She remained at the door. "My name is Andrea, and I'll be right back in to check your vitals and look you over. I'll also inform Dr. Meachem that you're awake. He'll want to give you a proper examination." She stepped back and let the door swing closed.

Daniel brushed my hair away from my face for the tenth time. "Yeah, that seat belt may have bruised your ribs, but it also kept you from being thrown from the car." His eyes teared some more. "Considering how badly I chastised you about getting that beamer, it handled the crash like a tank."

My lower lip trembled. "Are you sure this is real, and you haven't left me for someone else to start your own family?" I wept as the gravity of this moment seeped into my heart. Would I ever get past those memories that weren't real?

Daniel rested his head against mine and cried with me. Both of us blubbered for several minutes. "It's real, hon. I will always be yours."

Finally, Daniel wiped his eyes. He stood and grabbed an overnight bag from a bench that stretched out under the hospital room window. My husband opened the cloth bag and pulled out a small item. "Tell you what, if you ever decide you want to have kids with me, you let *me* know. You're not going to hear a peep out of me on that subject. *You* are my family, Cass, and you make me happier than I deserve." He held up a small container. "And to prove it. Here are your birth control pills. I didn't want you to miss a day while you were in here." He handed me a light-pink sleeve containing a blister package of pills.

That's right. I hadn't missed taking those pills. That was all part of the delusion. Daniel and I had just made love. We'd argued about kids, and he'd left for work. I was right back there. Isabella had never offered me senior partner either. And she probably never would.

I sat up straighter and looked to my right, where a small trash can sat. "You aren't the only one who has to prove something." I threw the pills into the trash can without hesitation. *Two points.*

"What are you doing? Cassie, you don't need to do that for me. I mean it. I'm okay with it being just us."

I pursed my lips. "I didn't do it for you. I did it for us. I saw what my future *could* be as a successful lawyer and a senior partner. And I witnessed all of what it took to get there. Professionally, I had everything, Daniel. Money, influence, prestige, respect, all of it. Except for you. I watched a lifetime of mistakes and bad decisions happen right before my eyes. That life is not for me. What I want is here. I can be a lawyer anywhere. But I can't find a Daniel anywhere, now, can I?" I gathered my thoughts. "I do want kids . . . very much. And when I'd thought I'd lost that option, I was empty inside. I wasn't just upset because you had moved on. I was upset because I'd lost my chance to experience one of the greatest joys in life with the man I loved. And I know that I will love you even more as the father of our children. I am so *all in* on this!"

And I was. Deep down, I wasn't ready before. But when the parental door closed for me and Daniel, it changed my perspective. I didn't just get to have kids with someone I adored, I'd get to do it with someone who would make every

A Collision with Love

day an adventure. All of a sudden, I didn't just want kids, I longed for them.

A smile creeping up the corners of his mouth, Daniel perched himself on the edge of my bed again, taking my hand in his. "Are you sure?" His eyes shined with untold memories yet to come.

I firmed up my chin. "I'm not only sure. I've never wanted anything more in my life."

Chapter Twenty-Three

Four *actual* years later ...

"We better hurry!" I wedged my oversized stomach into the front passenger seat of my beamer SUV, feeling like a ten-pound sausage inside of a five-pound bag. My mom used to say that when she felt fat. And I certainly felt fat these days. I was so ready for this little girl to come out. Olivia would be her name, inspired by my doppelgänger who showed me a life I was missing. Olivia Cassandra Griffin would grace our lives in four weeks, God willing.

My feet were swollen, my back ached, and I couldn't tell which was worse, how horny I was or my constant cravings, which would take months to exercise from my thighs. It was May, and I was also hotter than hell. What was I thinking going for two? I giggled to myself, realizing I had never been happier. I also had to remind myself how much Daniel enjoyed the horny part. Yup, we'd been having some naughty fun.

A Collision with Love

"Careful, hon. Don't bump your tummy." Daniel slid into the driver's seat, watching me with care.

"Be cawful, Mommy," Little Joey, short for Joseph, Daniel's middle name, said from the backseat. He wiggled his feet over the edge of his car seat, his eyes drawn to his wooden Thomas the Tank Engine that he couldn't live without. Our house had a room devoted to nothing but the wooden tracks, where Daniel and I—when I wasn't the size of a house—played trains with our son for hours.

"Don't worry, little man. Mommy's good." Before he started the car, my husband leaned over and kissed my protrusion. "You all good in there, Olivia?" He started the car. "Noah is pumped about culinary school. I wasn't sure he was going to actually go through with it, but I can't deny it anymore." Daniel peered over his shoulder; his right arm braced against my headrest as he backed us out of the driveway. When he was done, he reached out and ruffled Joey's auburn hair. "How's my boy doing?"

"Good, Daddy. Wanna play twains later?"

"You know it, little man." Daniel shifted the car into drive. "I think Sir Topham Hatt has some adventures planned."

Joey made train noises (which sounded more like raspberries) as he moved his wooden toy back and forth along a set of invisible tracks.

My heart swelled. My son was the cutest thing I had ever seen—next to my husband. And then I thought about Daniel's comment. "I'm so proud of Noah. He's such a nice young man." For a moment, I sounded just like my mom. "And I bet he'll be leaps and bounds ahead of most of the incoming chefs-to-be." I reached my hand out and touched my husband's cheek, then let my fingers run through his now shorter hair before I returned them to my baby bump. "Not everyone has a master chef for an uncle to teach them everything they need to know." I smiled with pride.

Daniel's cheeks flushed like they always did when someone paid him a compliment. Honestly, the man had no idea how incredible he was. "Well, I don't know about that. He did all the work on his own. I'm actually gonna miss having him around the restaurant. He's been a huge help, and my customers love his cooking."

We came upon a stoplight.

"Oh, I almost forgot. Kendra told me to tell you that she was able to reschedule the dress fitting for after the baby is born. She said she's going to call you later and fill you in."

Expelling a relieved breath, I lifted my hands and then let them fall gently to my belly. "Thank God! I wasn't sure how I was going to pull off a fitting with this huge belly." I ran my hands over the basketball that was my Olivia.

One other enhancement to my life, influenced by that strange delusion from four years ago, was having friends again. I missed that female kinship I had enjoyed back in college. I didn't have a chef named Kate, or an assistant named Maddie, or even an energetic colleague named Brenda. They all existed in my *imaginary* England.

But I did have Kendra. She became my first step toward that goal as it were. I'd always liked Kendra, but I'd never taken the time to get to know her. That all changed when I invited her to lunch, then dinner, then a movie and drinks. Before long, we were best friends, calling or texting each other regularly. She was an amazing woman and far more insecure than I had ever realized. Yes, she was gorgeous, but like her boss (my husband), she never seemed to realize that fact. She was also gay and single for way too long. Any men I had seen her with were friends (although I was sure they had hoped for more).

Happy to take on the role of matchmaker, I convinced Kendra to go on a blind double-date with Daniel and me. Her companion was Emily, the local artist who had beautified our restaurant as well as my new law office in downtown Richmond. My partners, Andy and Jim of the law firm Livingston, Tucker & Griffin, were more than happy to warm up the waiting room with a mural of Richmond's skyline, giving it a welcoming ambiance that most law firms didn't appreciate in town. Every one of our clients, including potentials, had commented on it.

That's right. I left Wilson & Bates the week after my accident, and I'd never been more eager to say goodbye to anything in my life. I called Andy and asked if his offer to hire me still stood. He quickly informed me that it did.

In Virginia, clients decided whether or not they chose to stay with their existing firm or leave with departing counsel, once they had been notified in proper fashion by the firm. Mrs. Dunbar didn't hesitate. She came with me. Into the Open - Equipment Inc. hadn't signed with Wilson & Bates, which also made them fair game, not that they couldn't have come with me regardless. It just made the transition less edgy. The rest followed. My entire roster. It brought tears to my eyes. Andy and Jim practically jumped for joy.

"I knew you were gonna be a force, Cassie," Andy had said as he immediately scouted out office space in the city.

So now, I worked until five, took my weekends off—plus major holidays—and even brought Joey to work when the need required. Daniel and I purchased our first house four months later when we realized our family was about to grow and prosper.

Kendra and Emily planned to be married this November. Kendra had asked me to be her maid of honor, and for the second time in my life, I had accepted. Where were they going to be married? Daniel's Garden Patch, of course. What could be more fitting?

When I wasn't working these days, I spent my time dancing around the house to songs like "Wheels on the Bus" with my family. We played trains, we laughed, and we celebrated life, ready to include little Olivia in the cheerful fray.

I never felt hollow inside anymore, and I never felt conflicted about my life. I was living the dream with my *dreamy* husband by my side.

Sometimes, in the middle of the night, when the house was quiet and sleep remained an elusive stranger, I thought about the accident and the dream (or hallucination) that took me on a journey of discovery. *Another life.* Yes, it was painful to walk through those fires, but it was also a miracle because it showed me another path, the only path that would allow me to achieve everything I wanted to be truly happy.

To the man driving the Bubba truck, I whispered *Thank you*, as I so often did. Unbeknownst, he had changed my life forever.

Tell me what you think ...

I'd love to know how you felt about this book. And I would be grateful for an honest review on Amazon and Goodreads. A few words are plenty and can make all the difference in how I plan my next novel.

Acknowledgments

When I first started publishing books, I leaned heavily on my team of editors, proofreaders, ARC readers, book bloggers, fans, plus friends and family for input and support. Now, all these years later, I still value those same people as much if not more than ever.

Melissa Shelton Harrison has been with me since the beginning of this crazy dream of mine. I have grown to appreciate our long-standing relationship immensely. Melissa knows my characters almost as much as I do. She understands them and sees their potential, striking just the right balance as she edits every story. She's also a sweetheart of a person, who never wavers in her generosity or kindness. Thank you, Melissa, for all you do.

My street team consists of two incredible people: Ryan LaRochelle and Hattie LaRochelle. Where Ryan offers expert advice on developmental issues, he also brings a mans's perspective, which helps authenticate my male characters. (Hattie does the same with the younger female generation.)

Hattie and Ryan proof like pros (I call Ryan Eagle Eyes), which also comes in very handy. Hattie does something else that has fast become a tradition on launch day. She shows up with a written note of inspiring words and a bottle of wine to celebrate. She does this out of the kindness of her very generous heart. To say I'd be lost without Hattie and Ryan, would be an understatement. Love you both. And thanks to Mary Tousignant who also does a stellar job finding those needles in my haystack of words.

There are so many aspects to publishing that have little to do with editing. Maddee and Riley at Xuni.com for website work as well as Amy and Lauren from Indie Penn PR present my books to the world in a thorough and professional manner. They make me look good, and I am grateful to them for the many hours involved to make it so.

I could never forget those incredible book bloggers who read books at a rate that would make most of our heads spin. Laura from Reading in the Red Room has been a huge supporter of my work—a pillar for me. You rock in my world.

A big thank you to my wonderful hubby, Bob, who has been there since this idea of publishing spawned. He celebrates the wins and consoles the losses. And I am truly grateful that he is with me on this exciting journey.

And no acknowledgement page would be complete without thanking my readers, subscribers, and friends who have stuck with me. Terry M, Anna P, Cheri G, Dawn M, Robyn X, Mary and Jess T, Marta M, Michael B, and Craig H (Craig writes the best book reviews on the planet), thank you all for being on my team. And to everyone else who I haven't mentioned here, but I keep warm in my heart. You all honor me with your presence in my life.

About the Author

Since she was a little girl, award-winning author Tricia T. LaRochelle has been obsessed with tragic love stories. No beach reads for her. In a true love story, it's the struggles and the sacrifices that two people endure *and* overcome to be together that make a romance interesting and compelling.

Growing up in central Vermont, she has seen her share of tragedy but remains a hopeful romantic. She now lives in central Virginia, where she continues to foster the possibilities of how love can conquer all.

Sign up for her newsletter at TriciaLaRochelle.com for updates, announcements, and giveaways, or follow her on Facebook, Twitter, Instagram, Threads, or Pinterest.

Also by Tricia T. LaRochelle

Sara Browne Series Romantic Suspense:
Flickering Heart - Book 1
Revive - Book 2
Handfast - Book 3
Bleeding Heart - A Holiday Romance - Book 4

Stand alone Contemporary Romances:
Sun in My Heart
A Collision with Love
Coming soon … Let Me Go

Made in the USA
Columbia, SC
11 April 2025